THE

Jean Hanff Korelitz is the author of eight novels, including *The Latecomer* and *The Plot* (both in development for limited series), *You Should Have Known* (adapted as HBO's 2020 limited series, *The Undoing*, by David E. Kelley and starring Nicole Kidman and Hugh Grant) and *Admission* (basis for the 2013 film starring Tina Fey). *The Plot* was featured on *The Tonight Show* as the Fallon Summer Reads 2021 pick. Korelitz lives in New York City.

ALSO BY JEAN HANFF KORELITZ

The Latecomer
The Plot
The Devil and Webster
You Should Have Known
Admission
The White Rose
The Sabbathday River
A Jury of Her Peers

MIDDLE GRADE FICTION
Interference Powder

DRAMA
The Dead, 1904 (with Paul Muldoon)

POETRY
The Properties of Breath

JEAN HANFF KORELITZ

THE SEQUEL

faber

First published in the UK in 2024
by Faber & Faber Ltd
The Bindery, 51 Hatton Garden,
London ECIN 8HN

First published in the USA in 2024
by Celadon Books, a division of Macmillan Publishers
120 Broadway, New York
NY 10271

Typeset by Typo•glyphix, Burton-on-Trent DE14 3HE
Printed in England by CPI Group (UK) Ltd, Croydon CRO 4YY

All rights reserved
© Jean Hanff Korelitz, 2024

The right of Jean Hanff Korelitz to be identified as author of this work
has been asserted in accordance with Section 77 of the Copyright
Designs and Patents Act 1988

*This is a work of fiction. Names, characters, places, and incidents are products
of the author's imagination or are used fictitiously and are not to be construed as
real. Any resemblance to actual events, locales, organizations, or persons, living
or dead, is entirely coincidental.*

*This book is sold subject to the condition that it shall not, by way of trade
or otherwise, be lent, resold, hired out or otherwise circulated without
the publisher's prior consent in any form of binding or cover other than
that in which it is published and without a similar condition including
this condition being imposed on the subsequent purchaser*

A CIP record for this book
is available from the British Library

ISBN 978-0-571-39122-6

MIX
Paper | Supporting
responsible forestry
FSC® C171272

Printed and bound in the UK on FSC® certified paper in line with our continuing
commitment to ethical business practices, sustainability and the environment.
For further information see faber.co.uk/environmental-policy

2 4 6 8 10 9 7 5 3 1

For Burton I. Korelitz

All novels are sequels.

—Michael Chabon

PART ONE

1

It Starts with Us

First of all, it wasn't even that hard. The way they went on, all those writers, so incessantly, so dramatically, they might have been going down the mines on all fours with a plastic spoon clenched between their teeth to loosen the diamonds, or wading in raw sewage to find the leak in the septic line, or running into burning buildings with forty-five pounds of equipment on their backs. But this degree of whining over the mere act of sitting down at a desk, or even reclining on a sofa, and . . . typing?

Not so hard. Not hard at all, actually.

Of course, she'd had a ringside seat for the writing of her late husband's final novel, composed—or at least completed—during the months of their all-too-brief marriage. She'd also had the master-class-for-one of his previous novel, the wildly successful *Crib*. True, the actual *writing* of that novel had pre-dated their meeting, but she'd still come away from it with a highly nuanced understanding of how that extraordinary book had been made, its specific synthesis of fiction (his) and fact (her own). So that helped.

Another thing that helped? It was a truth universally acknowledged that finding an agent and then a publisher were hoops of fire that anyone else who wrote a novel had to face, but she, herself, was to be exempt from that particular ordeal. She, because of who she already was—the executor of her late husband's estate, with sole control of his wildly valuable liter-ary properties—would never need to supplicate herself at the

3

altar of the *Literary Market Place*! She could simply step through those hoops, to effective, prestigious representation and the Rolls-Royce of publishing experiences, thanks to Matilda (her late husband's agent) and Wendy (his editor), two women who happened to be at the apex of their respective professions. (She knew this not just from her own impressions but empirically; a certain disgruntled writer had taken revenge on the publishing *monde* by ranking every editor and agent from apex to nadir on his website—and making public their email addresses!—and even people who thought him otherwise demented admitted that his judgment, in these matters, was accurate). Having Matilda and Wendy was an incalculable advantage; the two women knew everything there was to know about books, not only how to make them better but how to make them sell, and she, personally, had zero interest in writing a novel if it wasn't going to sell like that other novel, the one nominally written by her late husband, Jake Bonner. (Though with certain unacknowledged assistance.)

Initially, she'd had no more intention of writing a novel than she had, say, of starting a fashion line or a career as a DJ. She did read books, of course. She always had. But she read them in the same way she shopped for groceries, with the same practicalities and (until recently!) eye on the budget. For years she had read three or four books a week for her job producing the local radio show of a Seattle misogynist, dutifully making notes and pulling the most sensational quotes, preparing Randy, her boss, to sound like he'd done the bare minimum to prepare for his interviews: political memoirs, sports memoirs, celebrity memoirs, true crime, local-chef cookbooks, and yes, the rare novel, but only if there was some kind of a TV tie-in or a Seattle connection. Hers had been a constant enforced diet of reading, digesting, and selectively

4

regurgitating the relentless buffet of books Randy had no intention of reading himself.

Jacob Finch Bonner had been the author of one of those rare novels, passing through Seattle with his gargantuan bestseller, the aptly named *Crib*, to appear at the city's most prestigious literary series. She had lobbied hard to have him on the show, and she had prepared Randy as carefully as ever for their interview—not that it mattered, Randy being Randy—or perhaps even more carefully. She'd left the radio station and the West Coast a couple of months later, to ascend to the role of literary spouse and widow.

Matilda and Wendy weren't just gatekeepers to the kind of success writers everywhere fantasized about; they were capable of actually transforming a person's writing into a better version of itself, which was a real skill, she acknowledged, and something she personally respected. But it had nothing to do with her. She, herself, had never aspired to write so much as a Hallmark card. She, herself, had no intention of *ever* following Jake down that garden path of literary seduction, with its faint whispers of acclaim. She lacked, thank goodness, any wish for the kind of slavish worship people like her late husband had so obviously craved, and which he had managed, finally, to attract. Those were the people clutching his book as they approached Jake at the signing table after his events with a quaver in their voices, declaring: "You're . . . my . . . favorite . . . novelist . . ." She couldn't even think of a novelist she would travel across town to listen to. She couldn't think of a novelist whose next work she was actively waiting for, or whose novel she even cared enough about to keep forever, or whose signature she wanted in her copy of their novel.

Well, possibly Marilynne Robinson's in a copy of *Housekeeping*. But only as a private joke with herself.

Even deeply ungifted novelists had to have a vocation, she supposed. They had to believe they'd be good enough at writing to even *try* writing, didn't they? Because it wasn't the kind of thing you did on a whim, like making the recipe on the bag of chocolate chips or putting a streak of color in your hair. She was the first to say that she lacked that vocation. She might even admit that she had never had a vocation of any kind, since the only thing she had consistently longed for, since childhood, was to simply be left alone, and she was only now, on the cusp of forty (give or take) and cushioned by her late husband's literary estate, within striking distance of doing just that. At last.

Frankly she'd never have done the thing at all if not for something she had said without thinking, in an interview for that very same literary series in Seattle, her adoptive home-town, when a pushy bitch named Candy asked, in front of a thousand or so people, what she was thinking of doing next.

Next as in: once you are finished with this public mourning of your husband.

Next as in: once you've returned to your own essential pursuit of happiness.

And she had heard herself say that she was thinking about writing a novel of her own.

Immediate approbation. Thunderous applause, with a chorus of *You go, girl!* and *I love it!* There was nothing wrong with that, and she didn't hate it, so—not unreasonably—she'd made a habit of reprising the statement in subsequent interviews as she traveled around the country and abroad, representing her no longer available husband and in support of his final novel.

"What are your own plans?" said a professionally sympathetic book blogger at the Miami Book Fair.

"Have you given any thought to what you'll do next?" said an editorial director at Amazon.

"I know it's hard to see beyond the grief you're going through right now," said a frozen-faced woman on morning TV in Cleveland, "but I also know we're all wondering what's next for you."

Actually, I'm thinking about writing a novel . . .

Everywhere she went it was the same powerful icebreaker: wet eyes, vivid smiles, universal support. How brave she was, to turn her heartbreak into art! To set her own path, unafraid, up that same Parnassus her late husband had scaled! Good for her!

Well, she had nothing against free and free-flowing good-will. It was much easier to be admired than to be reviled, so why not? And also it helped that no one ever once referenced an earlier mention of this great revelation. *I hear you're writing a novel! How is that coming along? When can we expect to see it?* Not even: *What's it about?*

Just as well, because it wasn't about anything, and it wasn't coming along at all, and they shouldn't expect to see it ever . . . because it didn't exist. There was, as Gertrude Stein had once so famously said, no *there* there, and yet the mere notion of this mythical novel had carried her out of a grueling and drawn-out year of literary appearances on waves of applause. And not—it was worth noting—applause for *Jake* and his tragic mental health struggles or rumored persecution (probably at the hands of some jealous failed writer!), and not applause for his sad post-humous novel, either. Applause for *her.*

It was not in her nature to be troubled by an instance of such mild subterfuge, and she was not troubled by it, but she did wonder if there might be a horizon for all of this warm and fuzzy positivity. Was there some ticking clock out there, already set to expire when she mentioned her fictional(!) novel for the twentieth time, or the fiftieth, or the hundredth? Would some future interviewer, revisiting the tragic story of Jacob Finch Bonner and the success he barely got to enjoy after so much hard work, finally ask his widow whatever happened to the novel she herself was supposedly writing?

No one would, she suspected. Even if her vague ideation lingered in someone's memory or newspaper profile, wouldn't everyone just assume that the nonappearance of said aspirational fiction must mean that she, like so many others, had fallen short when it came to actually getting the thing onto the page? Yes, even she, the widow of such a talented writer, with all she must have learned from him, and with her very public fiction-inspiring personal tragedy—the spouse of a suicidal writer!—had simply failed to produce a good enough novel, or any novel at all. That was precisely what happened to so many people who tried to do so many things, wasn't it? A person says they're going to lose ten pounds or quit smoking or write that novel, and yet you spy them sneaking a cigarette out by the dumpster, or—if anything—bigger than they were before! And you simply think: *Uh-huh.* And that's the end of it. No one ever actually confronts that person who fails to do that thing they were almost certainly never going to get done. No one actually ever says: *So, what happened to that plan of yours?*

Besides, who really needed her to write a novel? The world was jammed full of people supposedly writing their novels. Jake was assailed at every appearance by people who were writing them, or said they were writing them, or wanted to one day be writing them, or *would* be writing them if only they had the time or the childcare or the supportive parents or the spouse who believed in them or the room-of-one's-own, or if some awful relative or ex-spouse or former colleague were dead already and no longer alive to disapprove of a book that would *sorta kinda* be based on them and might even sue its author! And those were just the people who weren't even getting the words onto the pages; what about the ones who were? How many, at this very moment, were in fact *actually writing* their novels, and talking (annoyingly) about writing their novels, and complaining (even more annoyingly) about writing their novels? So many! But how many of those novels would actually get to the finish line? How many of the ones that did would be any good? How many of the ones that were any good would find agents, and how many of the ones with agents would get publishers? Then, how many of the ones that got published would ever even come to the attention of that precious slice of the human population who actually *read* novels? Sometimes, when she was in bookstores, tending to the business of being Jake's widow and executor (and heir), she would stop in front of the New Fiction section and just gape at all of them, that week's new publications enjoying their brief moment in the limelight. Each of them was a work that had been completed, revised, submitted, sold, edited, designed, produced as a finished book, and brought to the reading public. Some of them, she suspected, were better than others. A few might actually be good enough to have earned the grudging approval (perhaps even envy) of her late husband, who knew a well-written and well-crafted work of fiction when he encountered one. But which among these many were those few? She certainly didn't have the time to find out. Or, to be frank, the inclination.

Anyway, in a week or two, all of those books would be gone—the not-good ones, the competent but undistinguished ones, even the few that might actually be exceptional—and the New Fiction section would be full of other new novels. Newer new novels. So who even cared?

It was the agent, Matilda, who waded into all of this uncertainty, referencing directly the supposedly-being-written novel (*News to her! But she was delighted!*) and suggesting she apply to one of the artists' colonies—or not actually, technically *apply*, since Matilda had an author who was on the admissions committee and could prioritize the special circumstances of a celebrated literary widow attempting to write a novel of her own. She herself hadn't heard about these colonies, not even from her late husband, and she did find that interesting. Had Jake never talked about them because he'd never been admitted to one, either as a young writer (not promising enough?) or later, as a blindingly successful one (too successful to deserve a residency, not when there were so many struggling writers out there!). She was surprised to learn that a dozen or more of these places were tucked into rural spots all over the country, from New England to—astonishingly—Whidbey Island, Washington, where she had spent a number of illicit weekends with her boss during her Seattle years. And apparently, according to Matilda at any rate, every one of these would be ecstatic to host her in support of the theoretical novel she was theoretically writing.

The colony to which she (or, more accurately, Matilda) had submitted her request for a residency was located in a New England town not so different from the one she'd grown up in, and comprised the home and expansive grounds of a nineteenth-century composer. She had a room in the main house, where the writers (and artists and composers) gathered for breakfast and dinner, and a little cabin down a path carpeted with pine needles, where she took herself each morning, like Little Red Riding Hood, except in this case the basket of food was delivered to her at lunchtime, set carefully on the back porch by a man who then drove away. The basket contained wax paper-wrapped sandwiches, an apple, and a cookie. Inside, the cabin was rustic and spare, with a book of testimonials from writers who'd worked there, a rocking chair, a fireplace, and a narrow cot on which she lay, staring at the cobwebs hanging from the rafters: empty, untroubled, mildly curious as to what she was supposed to be doing with herself.

The cardinal rule of the place was that no one should interrupt an artist at work (any one of them might be grappling with "Kubla Khan"!), so she was entirely alone for hours at a time. That was a powerful luxury. She'd been on the road for months by then, chatting away about Jake's posthumous novel (and even more frequently: his tragic, premature death), and she was thoroughly sick of other people. All of that concern, all of the personal offerings of tantamount mourning (*my mother, my father, my brother, my sister, my husband also!*) which was somehow meant to bind these strangers to her. After the first day or two at the colony, when she understood that no one would bother her for glorious hours at a time, she relaxed.

She was, of course, not writing "Kubla Khan." She was not writing anything, not for her first week in that little cabin, anyway. She spent the days moving from the cot to the rocking chair, lighting her fire (it was spring, but still very cold) and keeping it going, napping in the afternoons. She absolutely appreciated the stillness and warmth and the fact that her cell phone got terrible reception here. She spent a day reading a biography of the American composer whose home she was living in, and went for a few afternoon drives around southern New Hampshire. When evening came, she returned to the dining room in the main house and listened to the faux self-effacement of her fellow colonists, who preferred not to say outright how important they felt themselves to be. After dinner there was the occasional artist-talk about the sculpture or composition or performance art commission in progress elsewhere on the colony grounds. Two of the men—an aggressively atonal composer and a writer of metafiction—were having an obvious liaison, but this was abruptly ended by a surprise visit from one of their spouses, after which a toxic bitterness settled between them and emanated throughout the larger group. A silent elderly woman, apparently famous for her poetry, departed, and a ferocious young person replaced her, making each dinner a combative scene of barely suppressed hostility.

One night a novelist in residence gave an after-dinner reading in a separate building where the works of former colonists joined the surviving library of the estate's original owners. She sat in an armchair while he read a pained description of a farmhouse creaking through an Iowa winter. It was deadly, and she was too bored to do anything but concentrate on her own facial expression, keeping it as near as she could to engaged interest. This person had a newly minted MFA and a newly signed contract with Knopf for his first novel, of which this inert prose comprised the opening chapter. When he finished, there were polite questions: *How did a novelist incorporate visual impressions into written description? What was the influence of place on his work? How engaged should a writer be with the idea of gendered perspective?*

She wasn't paying much attention to this, either, so it was a rude interruption when the novelist tossed one of these questions in her own direction.

"What is it like for the rest of us writers? I don't want to speak for you."

He was looking at her.

What was *what* like?

"Oh," she said, rousing herself. "I'm not sure I can answer. It's very new for me, all of this. Writing, I mean."

Now they were all looking at her. Every one of them.

"You mean," said the combative young person, "you've never written before?"

"I haven't published yet," she amended, and hoped that would be that.

The person stared at her.

"How'd you get in here? I have friends who get turned down year after year. They have *books*."

Nobody spoke.

"Well," said someone, after a very uncomfortable moment, "it's not just about publications. It's talent."

A performance artist with three long skinny plaits now elbowed the offended person and began speaking into that person's ear.

"Oh, okay," the no-longer-quite-so-offended person said. "I get that."

Get what? Anna thought, but of course she knew. She knew that, to them, these *real* artists, she was no more and no less than the special case, the literary widow who was being indulged, by someone who ought to have known better. She was not to be admired for this, obviously. Neither was she to be pitied or given special consideration, let alone offered the undeserved leg up of an impossible-to-get residency at this temple to art, just because what she was attempting, in writing her nonexistent novel, was apparently very noble and redemptive! And also: so feminist!

Well, fine. She got that, but then again, why shouldn't she be as fine a writer as her dead husband, who had left literature so prematurely, so long before his many theoretically great works could be written? So what if she, the widow, had shoved unnumbered "real" writers out of the way in her noble pursuit of fiction! Perhaps this particular enraged writer, or their deserving friends, had been passed over for a cabin in the woods and a picnic basket on the doorstep, but did any of them have any idea what she had had to endure, just to get here? Which of these poseurs was remotely qualified to pass judgment on her?

None of them, obviously. This Iowa auteur with his creaking house on the snowy prairie? The other auteur writing his navel-gazing "metafiction"? The new person, who was apparently writing a thousand-page dissection of a dying Rust Belt town, the subject of a recent bidding war?

She might not know much about fiction, but she knew she had no interest in reading any of those books.

There was applause. This literary event, mercifully, was over. Across the room, somebody opened a bottle and eased the plastic cups out of the plastic sleeve. The performance artist slipped out into the night, to return to her studio. One of the composers began flirting aggressively with a wan young poet from Brooklyn. Every one of the writers gave her a wide berth, either because she had embarrassed them or because they were embarrassed on her behalf. She didn't know and she didn't care. She considered them absurd people who prioritized absurd things, like whether a review had a box around it or a star next to it, or who'd been invited to some festival to read their pages to the empty seats in the tent, or whether they'd been deemed a twenty-under-twenty or a thirty-under-thirty, or, for all she knew, a ninety-under-ninety. What did it matter? More to the point, what difference did any of it make to how good the books they wrote actually were, or whether a normal person—herself, for example— would even want to read them?

Anna Williams-Bonner watched them, the writers, as they drifted across the library to the opened wine and the plastic cups and offered up laughably shallow praise to the man who'd just read to them. Then, before her eyes, the group defaulted to their eternal topics: the shortcomings of their former teachers, the inadequacies of the publishing world, and inevitably the writers they knew who happened not to be present tonight, in the library of this old New Hampshire mansion that art had built, long ago in a less complicated time. And she thought: *If these idiots can do it, how fucking hard can it be?*

2

Ready Player Two

"You wrote all of it at the colony?" Matilda Salter was shaking her head. "I have a few National Book Award winners on my list I'd like to send to you for instruction."

"Well, no," Anna admitted. "Not all of it. But a lot. Once I got started, it just kind of came pouring out. I'd be racing out to my little cabin at sunup and going back at the last possible minute, for dinner. Sometimes I even went back after dinner. I mean, it helped that there wasn't anyone there I liked. So no temptation to socialize, if you know what I mean."

They were having lunch together at the Union Square Cafe, which was no longer in Union Square. It was the restaurant where they'd first met to have dinner with Jake, and where they'd continued to meet, to discuss Jake's posthumous life as a writer: agent and executor, in perfect accord.

"Oh, I've heard that, over the years." Matilda smiled. "I've never seen any of these places in person, but I feel like I could find my way around blindfolded, after all the stories. I've had clients tell me it's either a penal colony and everyone's hammering away in their cell, or they're ignoring their work and running around in the woods together like it's summer camp. Only with real sex."

"Well, someone was having a big affair, actually. Two people, I mean. And then they stopped speaking. One of them accused the other of going through his garbage."

"Oh, don't tell me!" Matilda grinned, showing her flawless teeth. "I don't want to know if one of them's my author. Or both!" She looked down at her plate. She had barely touched her paillard. "Okay, tell me." She laughed.

Anna told her. Matilda hadn't heard of the composer, and she considered the writer highly overrated.

"Anyway," Anna said, "I appreciate the vote of confidence, but I don't think we're talking about the National Book Award here."

Though even as she said this, she thought: *And why wouldn't we be?*

"Well, maybe not, though stranger things have happened. In general, the level of literary approbation tends to decline with the presence of an actual plot. And this enthralling manuscript of yours has both substance *and* story. I know it's a cliché, but I couldn't put it down, Anna. And the writing. Well, I won't say I'm surprised, but I'm delighted. Where have you been hiding yourself?"

But they both knew the answer to this: in somebody else's story. In literary widowhood: another tale entirely.

"I'm sorry, that was crass."

It was, indeed, Anna thought. She picked up her glass. She had wanted her wits about her for this conversation, but Matilda had gone ahead and ordered a bottle.

"Not at all. Neither of us saw this coming, that's the truth. Honestly, I don't know why I ever told anyone I wanted to write something. It just kind of popped out during an interview, and then people kept bringing it up. Suddenly I was in it, you know? And then I started to think, well, maybe it's true. Maybe I said it because it was true. But I'd never been conscious of wanting to write, I promise you. If I had, I wouldn't be winging it like this. You don't have to pretend you're not surprised, you know."

Matilda, to her credit, looked abashed. "Maybe a tiny bit surprised. Look, I'm surprised when *any* of my clients turns in an actual manuscript."

"Oh!" Anna said modestly. "Then . . . are you saying I am your client?"

Matilda smiled again. Those teeth, so white against her very red lipstick, were like something in a Lichtenstein. "Did I bury the lede? I apologize. How formal would you like this to be?"

She felt herself relax. Perhaps that was the moment when she understood how much she'd actually wanted this.

"Well, we're already in a nice restaurant, and we've got wine. So maybe if you just kneel, that would be enough."

"No ring?" Matilda said.

"No, I don't think so. I mean, we already have contracts."

It was true. They had many contracts between them, already. Contracts for the thirty-eight foreign editions of Jake's novels *Crib* and *Lapse*. Contracts for the television adaptation of *Lapse* and the nearly-in-production film adaptation of *Crib*, "helmed" (a verb she found ridiculous) by Steven Spielberg. Not to mention the contract for the reissue of Jake's first novel, *The Invention of Wonder*, and his collection of "linked" short stories, *Reverberations*, which Matilda had worked for a year to extract from their previous publishers, and which Wendy had published in tasteful editions, emphasizing their more "literary" nature. Beyond these, they had a contract formalizing their relationship as agent and executor for the estate of Jacob Finch Bonner. Still, this was new territory.

"Anna, you are a gifted writer. This is a matter entirely separate from the person you married, who was also a gifted writer. That you have arrived here by means of an atypical path, and not in the first flush of youth, matters not at all. Many people do all of the supposedly right things, in the supposedly right order, and never write a thing, or never a thing as good as this novel is. Let us not delay any part of our gratification—yours or mine—by questioning this. I am thrilled. And I would be proud to be the agent who represents this book, and any other books you might write." She paused. "Is that formal enough?"

Anna gave her a happy smile. "Oh, I think so."

"Good. Because I have old knees. I'm not sure I could kneel, if I wanted to. And by the way, do you realize how old-fashioned this already is? You sent me a printed manuscript, Anna! Through the mail! I can't remember the last time I accepted a new client who sent me a printed manuscript. Even the wannabes out in Podunk are using that newfangled *electronic mail* these days. I would have sent someone to pick it up, at the very least, if I'd known you had something you wanted me to read."

Anna tried to look embarrassed. "I don't know. It felt more . . . proper. You write something, you hope someone will read it. It's the least you can do to print it out and send it to them."

"Sure. In the last century. I mean, I still get a few printed manuscripts from little old ladies and people working off old copies of *Writer's Digest* or some 1986 edition of *Literary Market Place* they picked up at a garage sale. But today, my friend, most writers query by email and wait for me to send an invite. Or they don't wait. But there it was, your first novel, in all its glory, sitting on my desk. Not even a heads-up! I'm lucky I have such a great assistant. Someone else might have just consigned it to the slush pile, and I shudder to think how long it would have stayed there. We haven't been the most expeditious with our slush, historically speaking. You know, they used to call my office 'The Black Hole of Salter.'"

She looked oddly proud of the insult.

"Black Hole as in . . . Calcutta?"

"Well, so I imagine, only I don't think I'm Mother Teresa in this scenario. More like the murderer of dreams, letting untold numbers of Great American Novels rot away, unseen and unread, while I try to persuade Kourtney Kardashian to write a novel, or put her name on a ghostwritten novel. End-of-civilization stuff."

"Well, that *is* a serious indictment," Anna observed.

A waiter came to remove their lunch plates, and Matilda asked for coffee. "Want dessert?" she asked Anna.

"I'll finish the wine."

Briefly, they were interrupted by a visit from an editor from one of the old houses: Nobelists and Pulitzers, most of the living and recently dead poets of the American canon. He reached out a slightly damp hand to shake Anna's, then genially accused Matilda of withholding her wares. "I haven't had a thing from you in months. Maybe a year," he complained.

"Oh now, Sam, I know you remember David's book. We offered you an exclusive. You spurned us."

"I spurned that book. I'd be glad to see something else from him. I told you that."

"So, Pablo, not such a fan of the color blue. Can you get back to me when you have a green period?"

"Oh, c'mon." The editor named Sam grinned. "You know I love his other stuff. We had a lot of conversations about it, in-house, but we just couldn't go to the mat for it. Were you able to place it anywhere?"

"Oh, yes," Matilda said, mildly. "Viking offered a two-book contract, and David is well into the next book, much closer to his earlier work. So he'll have a good home at Viking from here on in."

"I see," the editor said. "Well, that's how it goes sometimes. I congratulate you, and David, of course."

"I'll pass that along," Matilda said, and by the subtlest adjustment of her shoulders, she dismissed him.

Anna felt as if she'd just been given a private lesson in management. Once he was far enough away, her new agent uttered a single word.

"Dickwad."

She couldn't stop herself laughing.

"No, really. He thinks he's on some Iron Throne of dead white guys in the *Norton Anthology*, so he doesn't have to think about the future. But he does. We all do. If we don't, we get swallowed up by somebody who's doing the thinking instead of us. It's like David Mamet says: Always. Be. Swallowing."

Anna drank her wine. "Well, I can't say I like the sound of that. But since you brought up the future, what do you have in mind for this . . ." She couldn't quite yet bring herself to call it . . . a novel. Maybe that was Jake, and the long reach of his writerly pretentions. "I mean, what I sent you."

"So glad you asked," Matilda said. She had sprinkled half a packet of stevia into her coffee and was stirring it in. "I do think it needs another go-round. Nothing major. I want a bit more of a middle act, something to suspend us between all that setup and the last eighty pages, which are perfect. And I want to go a bit deeper with Jerry. We need to really feel the sense of persecution he's experiencing. Also, I want to set up a sensitivity read—that's not personal, it's standard now. Our cross to bear. But before any of that happens, I'm going to take Wendy out for a drink and tell her to hold on to her hat, because she's about to get an exclusive on a very surprising new writer, and she can start thanking me right away, because this is beyond kismet. It's *beshert*. It's like, automatic Arts section

21

profile. Literary widow becomes literary phenomenon, and unlike her husband, the horizon's unlimited."

Anna frowned, and not just because Matilda's take bordered on tasteless. In fact, she had had no problem at all with being Jake's widow. She'd gone to a good deal of trouble in *order* to be Jake's widow. But when it came to what she was already thinking of as *her own work*, she was not sure she wished to be known *professionally* as Jake's widow.

"And you're not thinking this is just a one-off? I mean, doing it once wasn't a small thing, I realize that. But I get the feeling you're already thinking of me as a person who'll be able to do it again. Horizon unlimited? That's a bit daunting."

"Oh?" said Matilda. "And why is that? Why shouldn't the book world see you as a major talent, just because the person you married was also talented and had a Y chromosome? We've had centuries of that already, thanks very much. I'm as distraught as you are that Jake Bonner will never write another novel, but you can, and you will. It's a glorious discovery! And exciting! Who knows which direction you'll go. You could even continue with this character. She's captivating, you know."

Anna frowned. "You mean, like . . . a sequel? Is that really a good idea?"

"Sequels can be very enticing when the initial book has done well. Readers want to know what happens to a character they've connected with."

"But they're never as good as the first book, are they?"

Matilda seemed to give this real consideration. "I'm sure some are. Or at least . . . *as* good."

There was a pause as each of them tried to come up with an example of this.

"Harper Lee?" Anna said, finally.

Matilda seemed to shudder. "Quite the opposite. Harper Lee had a flawless literary career. One novel! A perfect novel! Utterly beyond reproach, both artistically and in its principles. It was on every middle school curriculum. It sustained her financially, all through her life. And not only that, it made her a national treasure. I can't think of another novel, a single novel, that's done that for a writer. Generations of parents named their kids Atticus."

Not to speak of the aspiring writers who took "Finch" for a middle name, Anna thought.

"Then, at the last possible moment: a sequel! Only now we've all been devastated by what we found out in that sequel, that later-in-life Atticus Finch joins the KKK! I mean, way to kill our dreams, Harper. I can only imagine what Truman Capote would have said."

"Something about . . . answered prayers?" Anna suggested.

"And all those kids who went to bed at night wondering what Jem and Scout were like when they grew up? Myself included! We got more than we bargained for. Unfortunately."

"So," said Anna, "you're saying: not a good thing, that sequel of hers."

"Well, not a good example, no. But I'm sure there are others!"

Anna wasn't sure.

"Anyway, it's just an idea. Take it or leave it, I just want you to have a long and invigorating career as a novelist. Because you know what the real story here is? It's not the tragic tale of a writer who dies before he can write more great books of his own. Or not only that. It's also the tragic tale of a writer who dies before he can discover how great a writer his *wife* would turn out to be! I mean, the two of you might have become a powerful literary couple. Like . . . Plath and Hughes."

Another not great example, Anna thought.

"Or, um, Hemingway and Gellhorn, except they got divorced," Matilda said. "Well . . . Fitzgerald was married to a writer, but she ended up in an asylum." She thought for another moment, then she named somebody else, married to somebody else, both supposedly famous novelists, but Anna hadn't heard of either of them.

"Anyway, the point is that you each had individual greatness, but life prevented you from having it at the same time. It's poignant. It's beautiful. It's . . . as I said, it's a great story. And the best part of it is how good the work itself is. His work was, and yours is. Do me a favor and don't start doubting yourself, Anna."

And Anna nodded with solemnity, because the moment seemed to call for that. But in fact, she'd never been a doubter, not when it came to herself, anyway. She wasn't about to start now.

Chapter 3

More Tales of the City

Not many first-time novelists get a profile in the *New York Times*. Then again, few first-time novelists come with the backstory of an Anna Williams-Bonner: recent bride of a wildly successful novelist who took his own life even as his fame seemed on the ascent. There were, too, the lingering rumors of some form of harassment—much speculated upon, but never fully detailed—that had driven the writer, Jacob Finch Bonner, to his terrible act. How easy it was to say anything about anyone, in public but anonymously, and end someone's career (in this case, someone's life!) without ever actually facing your victim, let alone proving your accusation! What a sad indictment of our culture that was!

Anna wasn't surprised that the *New York Times* wanted to write about her, though she let Wendy and Matilda know how excited she was, which was exactly as excited as they were. She had been readying herself for this, familiarizing herself with the contents of other author profiles, trying to judge what made the profile subjects seem sympathetic (if they did) or not (if they did not). The element of struggle, for one thing, was a clear advantage, but only if the author's new book and its associated success had been a long time in coming, following many unpublished or published but unread predecessors. If the author was young, or if their work and opportunities seemed to come too easily, humility was the active ingredient. In all cases, whether it was a miraculous first novel pole-vaulting onto the bestseller list, or a sudden, blinding success after a dozen thwarted attempts, the subject of the *New York Times* profile must offer up the purest, most self-flagellating gratitude.

Anna, at forty (give or take), did not fall into the new-young-author category, but she didn't fall into the anonymous midlist author category either. She had found, it seemed, a side door into her imminent literary success: a life entirely outside of literature and its striving discontents, a marriage of love to a complex and brilliant man, apparently also a tormented man, and the long veil of tragedy that followed them from the altar; then, abruptly, this flowering of words and narrative into an unexpected but wholly mature work of art. Here was Anna Williams-Bonner with her first novel, *The Afterword*, which, like her hyphenated name, was a tribute to Jake: her lover, her partner, and, as it turned out, her teacher.

Sometimes, she noticed, the profiles revolved around an activity: walking a dog, or making a meal, or shopping for a new outfit to wear to a book party or the premier of a film, based on the author's novel. Anna didn't have a dog. She'd had a cat, two years earlier, but she'd ended up giving it away to a neighbor in her building. She tended to cook only on special occasions, and she loathed shopping, always had. The idea of doing any of that, or anything else in a performative way, felt like too much of a burden on top of hitting that moving target of pride and self-effacement. So when the Arts section writer emailed to set up their conversation for a Wednesday morning in September, Anna was relieved to learn that a simple meeting over coffee was the proposal, and on the appointed day she walked from her apartment up to Café Grumpy in West Chelsea, preparing herself for the task at hand.

Rene was a solid person, thick waisted and powerful across the shoulders. She wore black leggings and a long white men's shirt, nearly to her knees, and she rose with a smile when Anna came into the back room.

"Oh, thank you," Anna said. "I didn't know if I would recognize you."

"I take responsibility for the recognizing," said Rene, amiably enough. "It's part of the service. Can I just say, before we start, that I loved your book?"

It might have been served as an ice breaker, and with another writer it might have been received that way, but the words only made her more cautious. "That's . . ." Anna said, visibly flustered, "you know, it's still so new, the idea of another person actually *reading* it. I suppose I'd better figure out how not to freak out anytime someone says that to me."

"Yes," Rene said. "I think you'd better. I think a lot of people are going to read this book. And love it."

Rene already had coffee, but Anna went to the front and ordered a drink for herself. She used those minutes to recalibrate, and remind herself, yet again, of what she needed to do here. A *New York Times* profile would set the tone for much that followed. She hadn't needed to be told that, but Wendy had felt the need to say as much, in an email a few days earlier: "People are unsure of their own critical standards. There's always a tiny doubt—*Yeah, I thought that book was awful, but what if I'm too dense to see the genius?* So when someone they respect tells them that a book is good, they're predisposed to agree." What happened in the next hour would determine much, in other words, and not all of it related to the book's critical reception.

When she returned with her coffee, Rene's iPhone was already recording.

"This okay? It means I won't have to scribble through our chat, and then not be able to read my notes."

"Oh, of course," Anna said, taking her seat.

"That looks good. What is it?"

"You know, I'm not sure," said Anna. "I just pointed at something the barista had made for the person in front of me in line. Coffee has become so complicated, hasn't it?"

And in that instant she imagined this as the opening sentence:

"Coffee has become so complicated," said Anna Williams-Bonner, whose first novel, The Afterword, *comes in the wake of her novelist husband's suicide."*

"I know!" Rene said, with enthusiastic—likely professional—camaraderie. "I'm one of those people who refuses to say anything but *small*, *medium*, or *large* at Starbucks. My little protest. But I like this place. It's quiet. All the Chelsea novelists out here in the afternoons, writing the next big thing."

"I thought that was Williamsburg."

"In Williamsburg's dreams!" said Rene. She smiled. "Did you write any of *The Afterword* in a coffee shop?"

"Actually, no. I was so private about it, I just hid away. Well, I was at an artists' colony when I started it. In New Hampshire. Then back in our—*my*—apartment. Sorry, I still have trouble not saying 'our.' But the fact is, I didn't want anyone to know I was doing it."

"Oh? Why is that?"

"I just . . ." Anna hesitated. "It felt a little bit unseemly, trying to do something my husband had done so well. I mean, who did I think I was? Jake had really prepared to be a writer. Studying it in college, and then going to the best writing program in the country. And he worked so hard, for years,

28

before he had any real success. So what's this former radio producer from Seattle who studied communications in college doing, thinking she can write a novel? I wasn't even sure I would show it to anyone until I'd finished it. I left it in a drawer for a month." She paused. "That's something Jake taught me. I mean, he didn't teach me, explicitly, because he didn't know I was going to write a novel any more than I did. But it's something he did and something he told his students to do. So I learned from that."

"Putting a manuscript in a drawer?"

"Yes. There's this rush you get when you finish a novel. I'm sorry, I don't mean to sound like a veteran. I'm obviously very much a newcomer, but Jake talked about that, too, as a thing writers feel, and from my obviously meager experience it was absolutely true. When you finish your first draft, you think: *This is amazing! And I'm amazing because I wrote it! And I won't need to change a word!* Every sentence is perfection, every character is chiseled in stone, the whole thing dictated by the gods, or the Muse, or whatever. And then when you pull it out a month later and start turning the pages, it's . . . 'Oh wow, okay, *this part* needs work, and what was I thinking *there*? And this whole chapter makes absolutely no sense. And these sentences are terrible. And why would the character do *that*?' It's a real exercise in humility. Well, humiliation," she amended, worried that "humility" had been a bit too on the nose.

"I've heard this before, from other writers," said Rene. "Though not so colorfully described. Let me ask you something. Do you think you always were a writer? Or did you become a writer because of your experiences over the past couple of years?"

Anna nodded solemnly. She had prepared for this question.

"You know," she said, truthfully enough, "I've spent a lot of time asking myself that. I was always a reader. I loved novels, and I read kind of indiscriminately for many years, which means that I read bad books and I read good books and gradually I was able to tell the difference. I wasn't paying attention to the literary world at all. I had no idea of anyone's reputation, or who'd been declared the most important novelists of my generation, or who wasn't supposed to be worth my time, so I got to make up my own mind about writers I loved and didn't love. I barely knew publishing, as an industry, even existed, so I had no conception of books that were new versus books that had been published years ago. I just went to the library and went along the shelves and took out what looked good. Later, of course, I got a big dose of publishing, because I was producing a radio show in Seattle, and I had to read the authors who were coming on the show. But they were mainly actors and sports people, some political people. I actually can't remember a novelist before Jake came on. And that was only because I begged my boss and guilted him into saying yes."

"Sounds like you went to a lot of effort. And this was before you'd even met."

"Yes. I couldn't stop thinking about his novel."

This happened to be an entirely truthful statement.

"But you weren't doing any writing of your own."

"Oh no, far from it. Well, not writing fiction."

She had ghostwritten a book for Randy, once, about his favorite Seattle places, but he'd paid her pretty well, and it had been a straightforward project.

"So what changed?"

Anna sighed. "I wish I had a really erudite answer for you. On the other hand, I don't want to imply that I was in the grip of some magical creative power, either. I just woke up one

30

morning with this idea that I could take some things that had happened in my life and make them into somebody else's story, and then see what happened to that person. It wasn't therapy, either. I mean, I was really grieving, but it never occurred to me that if I did this, if I wrote fiction that shared some content with my lived experience, that I would feel better about losing Jake, or I would understand why he'd done what he did."

Rene nodded solemnly. "And did any of those things happen?"

"Did I feel better?" Anna looked down at her untouched coffee concoction. "Actually, I did feel better, but it was gradual. And I don't think it had anything to do with the fact that I was attempting to write fiction. I think time was just passing, and as it did, I was giving myself permission to let him go."

"That's so . . . melancholy."

Rene looked appropriately embarrassed to say this.

"Well, everything was melancholy at the time. This was no exception."

"And what about . . . I hate that I have to ask this, but I'm sincerely curious, and I know others will be, too. Did you come to understand more about why your husband took his own life?"

Anna flinched.

"Is it something you feel you can't discuss?" Rene said carefully. Clearly, she was hoping this wasn't the case.

"I really haven't discussed it. Certainly never"—she nodded at Rene's iPhone—"for posterity. But I think one of the things people who commit suicide take with them is the possibility of resolution for their loved ones. We can howl into the wind for the rest of our lives, and there's never going to be anyone there to answer us. But maybe that's where the impulse to make fiction can come from. Where there's a void of information, we can always form a narrative and make that the information, the truth. Or at least . . . *our* truth. Does that make sense?"

It did, Rene said. But Rene *would* say that, wouldn't she?

"In your novel, a woman falls in love with a writer who has struggled for years. Then, just as he is on the cusp of great success with a new book, he becomes the target of anonymous attacks online. At first, he hides them from his wife, but eventually, she is so concerned about his deteriorating state of mind that she begs him to tell her what he's dealing with. Now," said Rene, "nothing has ever been written about this, but you have mentioned in interviews that your husband was the target of some type of anonymous campaign."

Anna took a sip of her now tepid coffee/drink. It was heavy on the chicory.

"I'm sorry to say that's true. We never discovered who was behind it. Someone accused Jake of being a thief, of having stolen his novel *Crib*. But even that was vague. We never knew if this accusation was attached to the entire manuscript of *Crib* or some part of it, or for that matter whether Jake was being accused of appropriating someone's work in its entirety or part of it." She saw that Rene was frowning. She saved her the trouble of asking. "I mean, what exactly was his crime supposed to be? To say nothing of the evidence, of course. Plagiarism isn't that hard to prove; you just show the similarity of texts and establish that one was published before the other. But we never even got a real indictment from this person, or maybe persons, never mind anything resembling proof. They just hid behind social media and anonymous letters." She looked disconsolately at a spot between her hands. "Anyway," Anna said, with a certain uncertainty, "there couldn't have been proof, because it never happened."

Rene waited for a moment, then, helpfully, she said: "But?"

"Well, but Jake was still deeply upset by it. The accusation didn't have to be factual in order for it to be harmful. The harm was *in* the accusation. After all, just being associated with the idea of appropriation is enough to compromise a writing career. Don't you agree?"

Rene nodded. Her hair, which Anna had thought to be blond on entering Café Grumpy, now had a reddish tint. Its cut followed the line of Rene's wide jaw.

"Unfortunately, that's true. I did a story last year about a novelist accused of a different kind of appropriation. I felt it was a very ominous development. We used to celebrate an author's imagination when they wrote about characters very unlike themselves. Now we get upset because they're somehow not supposed to. It does not bode well for fiction."

"I don't suppose it does," Anna agreed.

"So, Leo Tolstoy doesn't get to imagine himself into the mind of an adulterous married woman, and the rest of us don't get to read *Anna Karenina*. No *Madame Bovary*, either. Or *Tess of the d'Urbervilles*. Or Isabel Archer."

"Not to speak of the girl with the dragon tattoo," Anna said. They had wandered off track, but they were bonding. That was worth the diversion.

"Jonathan Swift was never marooned on an island. Mary Shelley never brought anyone back from the dead. No *Robinson Crusoe*. No *Frankenstein*."

"Michael Chabon wasn't a comic book artist in the 1940s. Jeffrey Eugenides isn't intersex. Shame on them! For that matter, what right did Jane Austen have to imagine life as a soldier or a sea captain? Donna Tartt's first novel had a male protagonist. Outrageous!"

Rene shook her head ruefully. "Well, I'm sorry that you've had to become a fiction writer at such a contentious moment. But I don't think this was the kind of appropriation your husband was being accused of. Or am I mistaken?"

"No, you're not. Whoever was hounding Jake wasn't suggesting he didn't have the right, as a male author, to write about a mother and daughter. They had something more concrete in mind—an actual theft of material. He knew nothing could be proven against him, but he also knew that no one waits for proof before making up their mind, not with everyone schadenfreude-ing away online. Of course, someone can be upset, even devastated, and not do what Jake did, and I still don't understand how he got from very understandable anxiety about this harassment to a feeling that he couldn't get out from under it. But he got there. I think it must have tormented him, that anyone could think of him as a plagiarist. No self-respecting writer would do that, and Jake held himself to a high standard. He held writing *itself* to a high standard. Stealing somebody's work . . . it's the last thing he would ever have done."

She emitted a brief, ragged sigh.

"You know," Rene said, "this isn't right. We're here to talk about your wonderful novel. *Your* wonderful novel. We can't allow this to become about your husband's work, remarkable and successful as it was. Can I declare the subject officially closed?"

"Oh," said Anna, smiling. "I don't have all that much to say about myself. I'm still amazed that I wrote a novel. And stunned that anyone thought it was worth publishing."

Rene didn't respond. She seemed to be considering something, then considering it again. Finally, she reached one fleshy hand out toward Anna, but not, thankfully, all the way. The hand stopped a modest hand's length before Anna's own hand began, and remained there, slightly poised but still. "You know," its owner said again, and this time Anna knew by its precedent that a statement of some weight would follow. "I'm going to say something to you that my favorite teacher at Columbia journalism would not approve of, but I'm going to do it anyway. I'm sure your feelings about this are very complex, and I wouldn't presume to know what it must be like for you, publishing this novel after losing your husband the way you did. But I do want you to know one thing, because I can tell it's part of your difficulty here."

"Okay," said Anna. "That's okay."

"I've been covering publishing for the *Times* for nearly ten years, and I know, from the outside, it can still look like a gentleman's club out of some Edith Wharton novel. But it's still a business, and it's fueled by business decisions. If your agent took this novel out to sell it, that was because she thought it was good enough for her to stand behind. And if your editor bought it, she felt the same. End of story. They might turn out to be right and they might turn out to be wrong, though in your case I strongly suspect the former. But whatever way it goes, you can be absolutely sure you're not being given, I don't know . . . some widows' courtesy. People don't stay afloat by making decisions like that. They stay afloat by publishing books readers will connect with."

Anna looked down into her drink. She was thinking of a nice bottle of Clos Pegasse that she had back at home in her fridge, and how much better that was going to taste.

"So whatever else is on your list of things you're worrying about, you can take that one off. This isn't some kind of a favor, because of Jake."

One thing she'd grown accustomed to, but no less annoyed by, was the sound of her husband's name in a stranger's mouth.

"Well . . . that's good to hear. I appreciate that."

"So, let's talk about you, Anna. I want to hear all about your writing process."

It was all Anna could do not to roll her eyes, but at least she had known to expect this one as well. And she was ready. She gave Rene a brave smile and offered up her carefully curated pastiche of a writing process: pine incense (to remind her of her childhood in the Pacific Northwest), a mug of Constant Comment tea (her favorite since freshman year at the University of Washington), and always the same chair—Jake's own favorite writing chair—at the very table by the window in her Greenwich Village apartment where her late husband had written his final novel. (And where he had eaten his final meal, though she saw no reason to include that particular detail.)

4

The Promise

"This will sell some books!" Wendy crowed. They were on a three-way call—author, agent, editor—on a Tuesday morning in October. It was her novel's publication day, and Anna had already been summoned to the lobby to collect an effusive arrangement of white roses from the doorman. Its note, when she extracted it, read: "From your proud publishers at Macmillan."

Wendy, of course, was talking about the *New York Times* profile, the online edition of which they all had on their computer screens. It would appear in the actual paper on Friday, but of course everyone who subscribed to the *Times*—in other words, everyone who mattered to Wendy and Matilda—could read it now. And was probably doing just that.

"I can think of a few novelists who are gnashing their teeth over this one," Matilda said.

"Oh, I'm sure not," Anna said. All three of them were probably picturing the same novelists.

"Honey, she compared you to Kate Chopin!" Matilda yelped. "I mean . . . Kate Chopin! This is amazing!"

"Face it, Anna," Wendy said. "You're an important arrival. And I hope I don't have to say this, but it's not about your biography. Or not just about your biography. Or, let's put it this way: all doubts dispelled as soon as they read the first page of the book. I hate to think how you've been hiding your light under a barrel."

A barrel named Jake? Anna thought. She knew that was what the two of them assumed, what everyone would likely assume: genius-in-her-own-right overshadowed by the male of the species, who'd convinced herself that she had nothing to say and no voice to say it with.

"This writer obviously *loved* you," said Matilda.

Rene obviously had, Anna agreed silently. The profile she'd produced was appropriately sober, befitting the fact of her widowhood, but it was also a celebration, a lifting of Anna's veil to anoint the newcomer with whatever the writerly equivalent of coronation might be. Her eye skimmed over the adjectives, snatching them up, marveling at them: *brave, astonishing, stunning, searing, unflinching*, and the one that would have sounded above all of these, were her late husband to read it: *literary*.

Literary. What a joke it was, Anna thought, listening to Wendy and Matilda in their jubilant duet. The two of them had done many books together, but there had also been books Wendy had declined to buy or Matilda had declined to offer, and authors who had opted for other editors despite Wendy's best efforts to reel them in. It was a dance of personal friendship and mutual professionalism, but when the stars aligned this was the kind of harmonic glee they apparently indulged in.

"Do you know how beyond unheard of this is?" said Wendy. "Nobody gets a profile in the *Times* anymore. Or if they do, they've already come out of nowhere to make the list, and the paper's playing catch-up. Like that woman a couple of years ago. From TikTok."

"Or that kid I turned down. Remember that kid?"

Then they were off on another frolic through the meadow of their shared professional history.

Anna, half listening, went back to the beginning of the profile and read it through again, forcing herself not to jump ahead this time.

Anna Williams-Bonner gazes into the surface of her coffee at a West Chelsea café and seems to ask herself a perfectly reasonable question: Why is her first novel, The Afterword, *about to explode in the consciousness of every reader of literary fiction?*

This café, like so many others, seems to be full of writers, more than a few of them likely novelists, toiling away on their laptops. Many will have spent years honing their craft in MFA programs or publishing short fiction in respected literary magazines. With one foot in middle age, however, Williams-Bonner is a complete neophyte as a writer and a stranger to publication of any kind (except, she informs a reporter, for a poem her adoptive mother once insisted she publish in a high school literary magazine). Yet The Afterword, *if the buzz in the publishing world is any indication, will soon be one of the most read and appreciated novels of this or any recent year.*

No one in the café seems to recognize this woman with the slender frame and the long silver hair as the widow of Jacob Finch Bonner, the immensely gifted writer whose second novel, Crib, *was an international bestseller with a Spielberg-helmed adaptation in the works, but who tragically took his own life only a few months before his final novel,* Lapse, *was published. But then, why would they? Williams-Bonner hasn't courted personal recognition either before or since the loss of her husband. Last year she spent a few months dutifully representing Bonner's* Lapse *on the book tour he himself would have undertaken, had he lived, but she has mainly been keeping a low profile in the New*

York apartment the couple shared. That's because she was writing a little something of her own.

"Believe me, I'm pretty surprised, myself," Williams-Bonner tells a reporter now.

A former radio producer in Seattle (she and her husband met when he was a guest on the talk show she produced), Williams-Bonner insists that she never aspired to write fiction, and she never attended a single creative writing class at the University of Washington, where she studied communications, or since. "There were novels I loved, of course. Jane Austen and Charlotte Brontë, Margaret Atwood, Toni Morrison. And living in Seattle I always read Maria Semple and Nancy Pearl, with great pleasure. But it just never occurred to me that I could write a novel, myself. It never once came up between me and Jake, that this was something I could do."

She seems to react to this as soon as she says it, and she looks furtively at the reporter across the table to see if this comment might have been interpreted as a criticism of her late husband.

"I mean, naturally he would have supported me if I'd ever said 'You know, I think I might like to have a go,'" she says quickly.

Also, she reminds the reporter, her late husband was no stranger to struggle, or even to failure, himself.

"He had a real problem writing a follow-up to his first book, and then he couldn't get it published. There were some awful years before he wrote Crib. He was teaching at an MFA program in Vermont."

She declines to name the program, saying only that it was "not exactly Iowa or Columbia." (Bonner's author page at Macmillan identifies the novelist as having taught in the *low-residency program at Ripley College, which closed in 2015.)*

Still, in a marriage with a certifiable literary star, the possibility of a second exceptionally talented writer of fiction seems to have occurred to neither of them.

In true first-novel tradition, The Afterword, *which publishes on October 8, seems to hew to the facts of her own biography: an off-the-grid childhood in the Northwest (the narrator's father is so distrustful of the outside world that he hides his money and valuables in the peg holes of a hundred-year-old rope bed) followed by a world-expanding university scholarship, a brief but loving marriage, a husband's devastating suicide, and finally a slow and painful return to purpose and life.*

Another unavoidable parallel: the husband's growing distress over a campaign of harassment from an anonymous tormentor, which Bonner and his publisher never made public but which was sporadically mentioned by literary insiders on Twitter and other platforms. Williams-Bonner makes a clear connection between that harassment and Jacob Finch Bonner's deepening anxiety and depression. In the spring of 2019, she returned to Seattle for a short visit in order to deal with a rental property and a storage unit, and it was during this absence that her husband took his own life. The antagonist, who has never been identified in Bonner's case, nevertheless became a character in The Afterword, *an opportunity that must have been very satisfying to its author.*

"It was cathartic to deal with whoever did that to Jake," Williams-Bonner confirms, taking a desultory sip of her coffee, which must surely be cold by now. "He never told me how satisfying it was to get revenge, if only on the page."

Catharsis aside, the honesty and the unflinching quality of the author's prose are enough to dissipate any sense of unfiltered

41

confession, let alone literary nepotism. Williams-Bonner writes with the lyrical honesty of a modern-day Kate Chopin, exploring the inner life of a brave yet vulnerable protagonist. Indeed, The Afterword's narrator, Celeste, opens her entire, astonishing self to the reader, courageously allowing us to experience the brutal aftermath of a beloved husband's shocking act, including a searing self-exploration of her own culpability.

How difficult was that stunning openness?

"I imagine anyone who loses a loved one to suicide must ask themself these same questions. Why did it happen? Could I have stopped it? What did I miss? It's a constant interrogation for us as survivors. In fact, I can't tell you how many readers I've heard from already, just from the galleys that have been circulating over the past few months. The letters are heartbreaking. I dread the ones I'm about to get, now that publication is imminent. But you know, there's no escape from that. Maybe there shouldn't be. This is our shared journey as survivors, and we have to do our best to offer one another comfort. No one else possibly can."

What Williams-Bonner seems not to have considered is that she may be every bit as gifted as her late husband, and with a disarmingly accessible quality to her prose that, for all his abilities, Jacob Finch Bonner arguably lacked. The Afterword is that rare novel that throws open the door to the reader and invites us inside to partake of the human condition in all its appalling realities.

How does she explain the sudden emergence of such an important literary voice?

"Oh, I can't explain it." She smiles ruefully. "I won't even acknowledge it."

One thing she does definitely acknowledge is that her late husband did not instruct her, at least not in the fine points of *writing fiction. "Jake and I didn't sit around talking about writerly things. He worked very hard at his craft. He sat in one special chair at the table by the window in our living room. I went to my job as a podcast producer. When I came home, we were like any other couple, going to dinner or to the theater, or out with friends. He'd ask after my day, I'd ask if his work had gone well. But there was no:* Here's how it's done. Why would there be?"

And yet, one day she herself would take that same seat at that same table and write one of the most poignant and affecting first novels in recent memory.

"I actually don't know which was harder," Williams-Bonner says now. "Starting a novel or sitting at that table. I'd avoided it for months, after he died."

Her novel, already a Read With Jenna selection for November, has appeared in Instagram Stories by Taylor Swift (who called it "relentless and ravishing") and Sarah Jessica Parker (who wrote that it was "the best novel I've read since A Little Life*"). There's a rumored film deal, too, but the new author is circumspect. Can the kind of fame her late husband experienced be far behind?*

"I don't care about that," she says, shrugging. "I care about having written a good novel. I care that readers connect to it. And I care . . ." She stops, reconsiders, reconstructs. "I just hope he'd have been proud."

"Maybe not worth the effort," Anna heard her agent say.

"Well, it seems like an easy call to me. What do you say, Anna? You're the one who'd have to go."

She was gobbling up that last line, remembering the precise moment in the coffee shop: that pause, that deliberate "reconstruction" masquerading as spontaneous speech. She did not *just hope Jake would have been proud.* She did not believe for one moment that Jake would have been proud. Besides, she did not remotely care whether he'd have been proud or not.

"Do you want to go?" Matilda said. "The place is a scene, but they throw a great author party."

"It's still Florida," said Wendy. "I wouldn't go under any circumstances."

Someone was inviting her to Florida?

"If you want, it's completely fine with us," said Wendy. "We're putting together a substantial tour for you already, as you know. But we can move something around if you want to go."

She'd missed the part about what was in Florida.

"Should I?" she asked them.

"Well, some people love it. It's kind of the mother of all book festivals. Tons of people running around, an event in every room. It's not sedate, like Charleston or Nantucket, where there's one thing at a time and big crowds. It's more like the Texas Book Fest, or the *L.A. Times* on the USC campus, just a madhouse. But that can be fun, too. And you meet up with people. And, as I said, there's a nice party, usually at The Standard."

"I've been to that party," Matilda said. "I went with Judy Blume, once. We were outside on the water, and all the women came up to her in tears, babbling about how she'd changed their lives."

"Sweet," said Wendy. "Well, it's the truth, I suppose."

"For all of us."

Anna said nothing. Judy Blume had not changed her own life, she was pretty sure.

"I'd like to go," she said, because she still had no opinion, and she had to say something, and her chances of being right were, she figured, 50 percent.

"Cool," Wendy said. "We'll make it happen. Maybe move that author lunch in Atlanta. They didn't invite you till last week. It'd serve them right."

Atlanta? She didn't particularly want to go to Atlanta. Atlanta was a bit too close to Athens, where she had spent a year a long time ago. Not that she resembled the person who'd lived in Athens anymore, not physically and not by name. Still. The entire state of Georgia was a place she'd rather not return to, all things being equal.

"Or we could just say no to Atlanta," she heard herself say.

After a minute, Wendy said, "We could do that."

"I'm so excited," Anna said. She didn't mean it, exactly, but she'd noticed how people tended to say they were excited when they meant a broad range of things. *Thanks for inviting me.* Or *How are you today?* Or *I'm encountering this product or service for the very first time.* She hadn't meant any of those things either, but later, after the call had ended, and after she'd leisurely read through the *New York Times* profile a few more times, and after she'd clicked over to the Google doc her Macmillan publicists had shared with her and seen just how long and crowded her maiden book tour had become, she found that she actually was, genuinely, excited. A little, anyway.

5

Dance for the Dead

Her first event was the Brooklyn Book Festival, where she'd been placed on a panel for debut novelists alongside a gruff trans man, a Dutch woman who wore her hair in a blunt, unflattering pageboy, and—of all people—the guy from the artists' colony, the one whose poetically creaking Iowa farmhouse had inadvertently set her own novel in motion. He did not appear to recognize her, and she did not renew the acquaintance.

The moderator, drafted from Shelf Awareness, introduced the four of them with scrupulous evenhandedness: one laudatory quote from a recent review, two sentences of biography, and a brief explanation of why the newly birthed novel represented an Important New Voice. Anna sat primly, her book, at last a solid object in the world, propped before her, as if to intercede between herself and all others. *I have accomplished this,* it seemed to declare to the room of upturned faces. Or, as she suspected was the case for her fellow panelists, *I am this.*

She herself was not this, she knew. She had been many things before this new thing, a writer. She had been a victim and a victimizer, a student, a striver, a planner, and a woman attempting to live an unfettered life, which meant, as it always had, that she had been a survivor, and she would never feel sorry for any of it. But now she was also this other thing: a debut novelist.

Debut.

It sounded like something out of the Gilded Age.

Novelist.

Like some form of a wrangler. A typist was a wrangler of the keyboard. A contortionist was a wrangler of the human body. A novelist was a wrangler of that exotic beast, the novel, presumably into submission. She imagined this person in a singlet, revealing undistinguished musculature, skinny arms braced to hold a wriggling volume against a filthy surface, until no one could be in doubt as to who had bested whom.

You. Are. At. My. Mercy.

That she had actually *made* the object before her was also not in dispute, not by herself and not, she certainly hoped, by anyone else. Unlike her late husband, she had never seen the need to appropriate even the smallest element of *The Afterword*, not a word or an idea or any other part of it, large or small. Even the jacket she had helped to finalize, taking part in a three-way back and forth with Wendy and Matilda, in which the variety of white rose was chosen and the angle by which it was to be observed, and to what degree it would be wilting, and whether the shade of lavender for the background should be darker (moody!) or lighter (too suggestive of romance?). She had modestly asked for the size of her own name to be made smaller and overseen the relative enlargement of the title: *The Afterword*.

And now here it all was: her words, her many words, all bound together in the just right shade of lavender, its vivid rose (White O'Hara, they'd finally settled on) facing out, full frontally, to greet each and every potential reader with its vague admission of being past its prime: two days out from the funeral, perhaps, or carted home from the hospital after the end had come, because somebody had gone to the trouble of sending flowers. Why not make use of them?

It was a beautiful jacket. Unquestionably beautiful.

She glanced at each of the other books, representing each of her fellow panelists, noting briefly that she was apparently feeling more competitive about their jackets than she was about what might be between their covers. *And why was that?* Anna wondered. Was she really so confident in her newfound abilities: to make sentences, string narratives, construct characters, and pin the wriggling novel to that filthy mat?

Apparently so.

The moderator began with the Dutch girl, asking what it was like to emerge as a new novelist in her home country. She asked the Iowa novelist what the famed MFA program had contributed to his work. She gave the trans writer a softball about the special challenges for unorthodox stories, and they all stood back to give space to his reply. And then she came to Anna.

"Your novel has had a very unusual path, and is having a very unusual reception. For those who may not know your personal story, would you share how this novel came about?"

She smiled through her irritation. Not only was she, apparently, the only one up here to have a "personal story" rather than, simply, a novel, but it seemed she was also under some obligation to share it with all of these strangers. Anna fought the temptation to explain that the novel had come about in the usual way, beginning with a first sentence, continuing to the last one. This was a test. It was just a very stupid test.

"Thank you, Jennifer," she said. "And can I just say, it's such an incredible honor to be at the Brooklyn Book Festival. I came with my husband a few years ago, when he did a talk about one of his books."

One of his books. As if there were any doubt which one. Brooklyn would hardly have glanced in his direction for the first two, and by the time the fourth one came out, he was dead.

"We both felt this was just a pantheon for writers. I want to congratulate everyone on the panel for their first books. We all know—probably many of us in the audience know—just how hard it is to write a novel, and how hard it is to get it published. I know we writers are famously self-critical, but I hope we can take a moment to just feel pride in the fact that we're here."

She was relieved that she didn't have to start the applause.

"So, for me," she began, when they stopped clapping, "as Jennifer points out, it wasn't a common path. I didn't know that I wanted to write. Or, perhaps it's more accurate to say that it never occurred to me that I *could* write. I was a reader, and then I was married to a writer, and maybe that was the first time I actually looked behind the curtain. I'd always been satisfied with the experience of a book as a book, something that just existed. I didn't spend any time thinking about who had written it, or what had gone into the writing. I either enjoyed a novel or I didn't, then I just went on to the next reading experience and hoped for the best."

This distinctly *outside* baseball approach seemed to land well. Many of the women—at least the women her own age, and older—were nodding their approval.

"After I met my husband, I was suddenly in this new world of writers. I was meeting them and hearing them talk about their work, and from that I learned—I know this probably sounds naive—I learned that the words didn't just magically appear on the page of a book I took out from the library or bought in the store. I learned that every single sentence had been like an Olympic contest to the person who wrote it. Total commitment required. Total effort. At the same time, I couldn't fail to see the variety in that process. I met people who seemed to write every day, and people who never seemed to write. But they both produced books. I met people who

49

talked about it all the time and people who never talked about it, and they were terrific writers. I was just amazed by the fact that there were so many ways to do this thing. And maybe that meant I could do it, too. But . . . let me put this delicately . . . when you want to do something that your loved one is already doing, and doing very successfully, it's complicated."

There was a vein of nervous laughter around the room.

"So I never told Jake. My husband. And when he died suddenly it was, I can promise you, the last thing on my mind. But when I came out of that first wave of just debilitating grief, I started to ask myself: What might make me feel better? I honestly didn't know what the answer was going to be. I was ready for *Leave New York* or *Get a Dog*. But when I really let the answer come, it was: *Write Fiction*. You could have knocked me over. But then, you know, I kind of felt I had an obligation to try."

The Iowa guy leaned forward and turned his head toward her. "An obligation? To whom?"

She decided to ignore the snark.

"I'm not sure I've figured that out yet."

Now the audience not only loved her, they also hated Iowa guy.

The formal portion of the panel wrapped up with a second round of questions from Jennifer, and then members of the audience lined up behind the microphone in the center aisle. Which was where the pieces of her new reality began to fall into place.

All of the questions were for her.

If, that is, you could call them "questions."

"Hi, this is for Anna? I just wanted to say, I've read a lot of books about suicide since my father took his own life. And

50

yours . . . well, I think because it was so fresh, and you are such a good writer, moved me more than any other."

"Um . . . Anna? I just don't understand how you managed this. And I have to ask myself, is it because you didn't go out and study how to do it? I mean, I know someone who's wanted to be a writer her whole life, and she studied it in school and got a graduate degree, but she's never even finished a novel. I want to share your book with her because it's so beautiful, but I'm honestly worried about how she'll react."

"I loved your husband's book, Anna. I mean, it was the best book I read that year it came out. And I was actually here at the Festival that day you mentioned before, and he was just amazing. I was just so devastated about what happened. I'm sorry to take up the time with someone who isn't on the panel, but I just wanted to say that."

By the fourth or fifth "question," she actually felt sorry for the other writers.

"Anna, when you actually sat down to write your novel, did you ever think: I'm not the real writer here, I can't do it?"

"Oh, we all think some version of that," Anna said, leaning forward. "I mean, every writer has this hostile voice in their head with a highly personal script, right? Mine might be saying, you're absolutely right, 'I'm not the real writer here.' But let's just go down the line. What's everyone else's?"

The trans guy's was: *I can't be a writer until I'm my authentic self, and when will that be?*

The Dutch girl's was: *No one wants to hear what I have to say.*

The Iowa guy seemed to think harder than the question warranted. What he finally came up with was: *I know writers who are more talented than I am. Can I work hard enough to compensate for that?*

And there you had it. Debut novelists exactly living down to expectations.

When it was over, the panelists were led to a long signing table in the lobby, and the lines for the four of them took on the form of an attendance graph for a suburban multiplex on a weekend when a new Marvel movie was released. Beside her, the Iowa guy chatted nervously to his pair of aspiring MFA students for as long as he could, painfully aware that no one was behind them. On her other side, the trans writer was doing a bit better, with a single file of four or five waiting readers. The Dutch girl had her publicist and a woman from the embassy who had brought her daughters straight from their soccer game. The girls were on their phones.

Anna's line coiled past the Books Are Magic table and doubled back, almost to the door of the auditorium. And every person on it was clutching a lavender-covered novel. Or more than one.

"Do you have a preference of Sharpie?" said Alex, sent by Macmillan to make sure this maiden voyage was smooth.

"I love the purple one. That's such a sweet touch, with the jacket design."

"Yes, we thought so. I hope you won't get sick of lavender."

She started to sign. She started to learn: how to look up, what to say, where to write her name, when to thank. She had seen Jake do this very well, having waited too long for readers to treat them with anything but gratitude. People who had come out in good weather, in bad weather, at personal cost, to hear him read or speak about a book they could just as easily have borrowed from the library or had delivered to their door, without troubling themselves to meet the author. People who had spent their money to buy a thing he had written, who cared enough to connect. People who, inexplicably, wanted his signature on the half title page, or a picture of him that they could put on Facebook, or who more understandably wanted to ask him how they could do what he did, or how not to get discouraged when the agent said no or the editor said no or the critics said no or the readers said no, and he had taken time with all of these people, which had been one of the very few things about him that she hadn't despised. But that didn't mean doing it was easy.

Besides, Jake never had to deal with the kinds of things these readers were bringing to her.

"My wife died."

"My sister took her own life."

"My daughter's friend."

"My coworker, suddenly. We had no idea. I was just shocked. She seemed so upbeat all the time."

"I found him. It was terrible."

"I will never understand."

And they cried. And then the people behind them, who were likely waiting to say something similar to what the people in front of them had said, and were already emotional, cried, too, in sympathy or in anticipation.

"I wish I could be a writer. I'd love to be able to get my feelings on paper."

Anna nodded grimly. If she had ever had those feelings, the last place she would have put them was *on paper*.

Most of the books had yellow Post-its on the covers, with the name or names to be written. "For Sarah," "To Rory's Dad," "Jillian," "Peter—I hope this will help." When there wasn't a Post-it she asked: "Is there anything special you'd like me to write?"

"No, just your name, thanks."

"I knew your husband," a woman said.

Anna froze. "Oh. Yes?"

"We met in Vermont."

She hesitated, then looked up. The woman wore an enormous parka, limp with age and wear. Even so, it was clear how painfully thin she was. She had an old face, but her long braid was a deeply insincere shade of red.

"Yes," Anna said. "He spent a lot of time there. Teaching."

"Yuh. He was supposed to send me a copy of his book," the woman said flatly. "I guess he forgot."

I guess he did, Anna thought. And I guess you could have gone to the bookstore, yourself, and bought one. Or taken one out of the library. That's usually how it worked. Was she supposed to apologize because Jake had fallen down on the job of sending free copies to random people who thought they deserved them?

The woman had a copy of *The Afterword* in her hands, and handed it over, but by the time Anna had opened to the half title page and looked up for instructions, the woman had backed away from the table and was making her way through the crowd to the doorway.

Lovely.

At the end of the line, a man came bearing no copy of *The Afterword*. He wanted her to sign Jake's novel *Crib*. She gaped at him.

"I can't sign this," Anna said.

"Oh no?" He was a portly man in a lumberjack shirt and heavy brown work pants. "Why's that?"

"Well, because I didn't write it."

"Yeah, but you were married to him." He paused. "And I would appreciate it."

So she did it, but only because he frightened her, and it seemed the quickest way to get him to leave. She even thanked him, but he was already finished with her and carefully placing the book into his shopping bag. He, too, left without saying goodbye.

6

From Time to Time

And so her travels began. After Brooklyn she made short trips to festivals in Brattleboro and Boston, stopped in Middletown, Connecticut, to give a reading at Wesleyan, Jake's alma mater (the head of the writing program definitely implied that he would be open to a writing award in Jake's name, provided she endowed it), and did a private event for mental health professionals at the New York Hilton, for which she signed five hundred copies in advance.

By November, she was on the road full-time, working her way around the country from the Louisiana Book Festival in Baton Rouge to the Charleston Book Festival (where she stayed in a glorious hotel on The Battery) to the Texas Book Fest in Austin, and out to Portland, Oregon, for Literary Arts, with a necessary side trip to Seattle. There she endured an enthusiastic homecoming at Elliot Bay, and a "profoundly meaningful" (in the words of the publicity material) visit to City Arts and Lectures, where she had first set eyes on her husband and where she had later returned to represent his posthumous novel, *Lapse*. She even stopped by her old stomping ground at KBIK's *Sunrise Seattle*, to sit in Randy Johnson's visitor's chair.

Naturally, Randy had not read her book.

"I probably don't have to tell you that," said the bright young thing who had replaced the bright young thing who had replaced Anna herself.

"No." Anna smiled. "You don't."

"But it'll be fine."

"Sure. It'll be fine."

"He's such a pro."

He was that, Anna thought. But this wasn't your typical host/guest situation.

She had slept with Randy Johnson for years, a period covering the gap between his second and third marriages, with overflow on both ends. She'd started at KBIK as his intern while still a student (albeit a mature student) at the University of Washington, and ended up as his producer, and along the way she'd learned everything she needed to know about the kind of male human specimen Randy Johnson represented so well. If she'd ever once thought to utter the words "sexual" and "harassment" to him, he'd have laughed in her face, shown her the door, and strongly implied that her *own personal history* could hardly withstand the scrutiny that any official report might bring to bear on her. Which was true, though it was also true that Randy Johnson was not in possession of the most salient aspects of her *own personal history*, because the only people who were weren't people anymore. Because they were dead. And Randy Johnson was very much alive.

But all of that was moot, because she never *would* have accused Randy Johnson of anything. She had no interest in sexual harassment, not even as a pressure point or a negotiating tactic. She had always been able to walk away from him, and that's exactly what she would have done if he had not served her purposes every bit as much as she had served his.

Randy's world—and Anna's, while she worked for him—was like a review platform at a parade: stationary and nonparticipatory but an undisputed front-row seat as the world came marching past. The tech people, the food people, the music people, the book people, the theater people, and of course any politician who had anything to say about the Pacific Northwest . . . everyone marched past, and a lot of those people ended up in Randy's malodorous studio, talking about everything under the sun. Until Nora Ephron set up her camera on Lake Union, the city of Seattle had been chiefly identified with *Here Come the Brides* (about the lonely lumberjacks of a hundred years earlier), but when Tom Hanks and his adorable son moved to a houseboat, all of that changed. By 2005, when Dr. McDreamy told the viewers of *Grey's Anatomy* that he liked ferryboats, the pioneers of the information superhighway were in full possession of the city, and everyone had generally accepted that cool, accomplished people who could choose to live anywhere were choosing to live in Seattle. Anna herself, who might have lived anywhere—or, at least, anywhere except Vermont and maybe Georgia—had chosen to live in Seattle.

She walked down the familiar corridor at her old workplace, the walls lined with the many framed photographs of Randy with the great and good, and entered the studio as he was finishing up a remote interview. That the unseen interviewee was somehow sports-related was obvious to her by her former boss's physical position: hunched forward, elbows braced on the table, hands at his temples, pushing back what remained of his scraggly hair. Randy only got genuinely hot and bothered when the subject was sports. Everything else was just a joke.

He didn't look up. That was probably on purpose, but she took his guest seat, the very seat Jacob Finch-Bonner had occupied on a fateful day three years earlier, and very deliberately made some notes with her now familiar signing pen on a small pad she carried. These were meant to be both accessible and distressing to the man across from her, should he attempt to read them, which of course he would.

LOCKSPOT (Randy's favorite restaurant, where he was routinely treated as a god, and where he had taken her too many times to count)

COUPEVILLE (Where she'd enjoyed, or at least spent, a number of not very restful weekends with him during her tenure at KBIK)

CIALIS (That would certainly get his attention, and not in a good way)

Under these, she drew a smiley face. Then she smiled at him for real.

He was still half listening to his guest. But he raised an eyebrow at her.

"Well, you and I are going to have to agree to disagree about that," Randy said.

The absent guest chuckled. "Won't be the first time. But in this case, I can tell you right now that you're wrong. They're dead in the water. Which is a sad thing to have to say about a team called 'Mariners.' But you know, defeat is also good for the soul."

"I wouldn't know," said Randy Johnson. "I've never experienced it."

The two men parted friends.

Then there were ads, playing at a lower volume, and Randy got up and left without another glance at either Anna or his own poor producer. He was headed for the bathroom outside his office, a nasty place she had once had to clean. She wondered who cleaned it now.

"Hello there," he said, her former boss and former something else, when he returned. "You're looking good."

"You too," Anna said, though he wasn't. He was looking terrible: puffy and sweaty, with that inner tube of flesh around his waist newly inflated. Whoever he was with now either had little control of his habits or actively wanted him to exit the stage as soon as possible. Well, she could understand that sentiment.

"How long's it been?"

"I left town three years ago. I came back once, but it was a quick trip. And cut short—I had an emergency back in New York."

"I heard. I guess I should offer my condolences."

Only if you were human, she thought.

"Thank you," she said. "It was a terrible shock."

"Ten seconds to air," said his engineer.

Randy took his seat and put his headphones on.

"So we'll just chew the fat," he said, glancing at the publicity material for her book, and the book itself, which was pristine, of course. Randy Johnson had given his ex's first novel the same degree of attentiveness he'd given the blockbuster *Crib*, by Jacob Finch Bonner.

"Can't wait," she said brightly. His theme music was beginning.

"Have fun," his producer whispered from two feet away. Anna wondered which of her own multiple roles the young woman was currently occupying, but she declined to feel concern. This girl looked like a realist. Probably, she could handle herself just fine.

"Well now," Randy said brightly, "from the ridiculous to the sublime, or is it supposed to be the other way around? I've got an old friend here in the studio. Back when she was my producer at the show her name was Anna Williams, but now she's Anna Williams-Bonner. How'd you manage that, Anna?"

"Oh, the usual," Anna said with extravagant sarcasm. "Fell in love and got married."

"Fell in love with a guy you met here on the show, if I'm right."

"Right as usual, Randy. My late husband was a novelist, and you interviewed him in this very studio."

"Things didn't work out so well, I gather?"

Anna paused to let the stunning insensitivity of this reverberate along the airwaves.

"Well, actually, I really loved my husband, so it kind of did. But I guess I can understand what you mean. We didn't have much time together, sadly. Jake was a wonderful person and an incredible writer. I'll never regret the time I was able to spend with him."

"Still, you wrote about all of that in your own first novel. It's called *Afterwards*."

Did he expect her to confirm this? Apparently, he did.

"*The Afterword*. Yes. When I worked here at KBIK I had no idea that I would ever try to write a novel, let alone get one published."

"Maybe your ex showed you how to do it."

"Oh, I wish it were that easy. There are some things you just have to try. Try and fail. Try and fail better."

It was a good line. She hadn't written it, but she doubted there were many Beckett fans in Randy Johnson's listening audience.

"So you thought, 'Hey, if my husband can do it, how hard can it be?'"

This was both surprising to hear and surprisingly accurate.

"As with most things worth doing well, writing a novel is harder than it looks. I certainly found that out. But I also discovered that there was something I wanted to say, and I wanted to use written language to say it. And . . . I'm not sure if you remember this, Randy, but I always loved to read."

She might as well have added: *I read all those books you were supposed to read before interviewing their authors. Remember?*

She did not add that.

"So tell us all about"—and now he glanced down at the lavender jacket—"*The Afterword.*"

And she did. She had it down now, after a solid month on the road, and before that a couple of meetings with the publicists at Macmillan, including one with the media trainer they brought in to consult, but in fact she hadn't needed much guidance. Years of exposure to authors—good and bad—parading through these very rooms in Seattle, and watching Jake recalibrate himself for interviewers—good and bad—and then her own attempt to represent her absent husband when his final book appeared posthumously, before a single word of *The Afterword* was written . . . all that had prepared her well. She half listened to herself as she described this entity, the novel, leaning hard on the words she knew to be most effective: *journey, grief, shock, horror, pity, compassion, rage, acceptance.* She might have written the whole monologue by way of Elisabeth Kübler-Ross, without ever having met Jake at all. But it was probably better this way.

"Okay, that's a lot," said Randy, with admirable understatement.

"Yes. But writing *The Afterword* really helped me get through it. And you know, we should be able to talk about these things. Even people who love to talk—I'm not naming any names here—who can talk about anything and every-thing, something prevents them from discussing death. And death by suicide has an extra stigma all its own. But so many people know someone who has taken their own life, and they need to feel the comfort of a community, too."

He was, she noticed, staring at her, but it was less of a you're-here-and-I'm-just-remembering-you're-hot stare than a when-did-you-get-so-pretentious stare. She decided to head it off at the pass.

"I know you're probably thinking, what happened to my tough-as-nails producer, who ran interference for me with every hard-ass publicist on the West Coast?"

Randy emitted a gruff laugh, clearly against his will.

"I'm still that person. Believe me, I've had to be, to get through the last couple of years. But I'm also a widow, and that's about the last thing I ever thought I'd be. Well, second to last. I never thought I'd be on Randy Johnson's show telling the world about a novel I'd written. But I'm so lucky. I found a way to take all the pain I was dealing with and actually make something from it. And I have to tell you, Randy, that the response I've had from readers is so powerful. You know, when somebody comes up to you with their copy of your book, and it's all messed up because they've folded down the pages and maybe dropped it in the bath or broken the spine so it opens to a page they've read again and again, and there are notes in the margins and underlinings, or maybe Post-it notes sticking out of it where they've wanted to go back to a page . . . it's just such a connection between you and them. I'm humbled by it, I really am."

But Randy wasn't buying it. Randy was, of course, still Randy.

"I never once heard you say you wanted to write a novel."

"No. Because I didn't know I wanted to. I was happy to just be a reader, but my husband changed me. Like I said, we didn't have much time together. But the time we had—"

She stopped herself. She'd been about to do something along the lines of "we loved a lifetime's worth," but Randy would totally have called bullshit on that. He might not have been familiar with Samuel Beckett's later works, but he certainly knew his Terminator movies.

"So the book is autobiographical?" he suggested.

Duh, Anna thought.

"Well, many first novels are, and I guess I'm not the exception. And they say: *write what you know*. Unfortunately, what I know is what it's like to lose a brilliant and loving husband to suicide, with no idea that it was about to happen."

"Caught you by surprise, I take it?"

He still overflowed with the milk of human kindness, Randy did.

"What people tell me is that it's always a surprise. Even if the person has been talking about it, warning their loved ones. Even if they've attempted before. Even so. It still feels like it's coming out of nowhere. It takes a lot to actually wrench yourself out of life, the sheer effort required to make the plan and then carry it out is just overwhelming. In Jake's case, I was absolutely stunned. I knew he was upset. Someone had been harassing him online. But I had no idea he was as desperate as he obviously must have been."

Randy seemed to perk up. Harassment was a concept he enjoyed.

"What do you mean, harassing him?"

She gave what she hoped was an audible sigh.

"Accusing him of plagiarism. Without a shred of proof. Just the insinuation. Jake was horrified. There's nothing worse for a writer to hear, and Jake was the consummate writer. He was principled about it. And, of course, the person was completely anonymous. Nothing could be done to stop it."

"You sure it wasn't true?" Randy said. "You met him after he wrote that book, didn't you? You can't be sure he didn't lift it off somebody else."

"Never. It's the last thing he would have done."

"Well, if you say so. I mean, you were together with him for all of a year, if that long."

Exactly that long, she observed. He'd been paying attention. "I wish I'd had longer."

Beside her, the young producer was holding up a note, just the way she herself once had. The exposed page said: CALL.

Randy glanced down, as if he wouldn't believe it without proof. "Yeah, okay," he said. "We've got a couple callers. Laurie? In Bellevue? What's up?"

"Oh . . . hi!" said Laurie from Bellevue. "Um, Anna? I just wanted to say that your book was so . . . just . . . amazing. I can't believe it's your first book."

"Thank you so much," said Anna, with warmth.

"Can I just ask you, did your husband's family have any feelings about you writing this? I mean, did you ask them, or what happened?"

Anna hadn't asked, exactly. But Jake's parents still clung to her. The three of them had continued to have monthly brunches in the city. It was a trial, but necessary.

"Yes, they were very understanding of what I was trying to do, and, of course, as the parents of a writer they understood what fiction is, and how making it carries its own set of responsibilities. They respect art, and I'm so grateful for that."

"Okay," said Randy, cutting off Laurie from Bellevue. "Esteban, my man."

Esteban, apparently, was a known entity.

"Yeah, dude. Good show, but I gotta tell you, you're wrong about the Mariners."

"Oh, I do not think so, man. Not that I doubt your sources. I know where you drink, after all."

Beside Anna, the producer held up a sign. ONE MORE.

Randy nodded, but with irritation. "You can tell me all about it next time I see you." He went to the next call. "Hi, you're on with Randy."

"Hi, Randy. Is the writer still there?" It was a man, but not with an especially manly voice. Reedy, creaky.

"You still here, Anna?" said Randy.

"Still here! Hello."

"Yeah, hello. You know, I knew your husband."

And how would I know that? Anna thought.

"I studied with him once, a long time ago."

"Oh," she said. "I'm happy to hear from you. Was that in Vermont?"

"In Vermont, yeah."

And he seemed to leave it there, like it was her job to draw him out.

"So you're a writer, too?"

"No, not really. I thought maybe I could be, but it wasn't for me. Anyway, congrats on the book. Take care, Randy."

"Bye, dude," said her former boss. "Thanks for coming by, Anna Williams-Bonner, the author of the fiction novel *Other Words*. But I knew her when she was just Anna Williams."

That's where you're wrong, Anna thought.

7

Bad News

"I knew your husband."

She looked up. It was a woman who might have been about Anna's own age but seemed determined to look older. She had short, thick hair dyed suspiciously dark, and wore makeup so heavy it had visibly caked into her deep nasolabial folds.

They were perhaps two-thirds of the way through the signing line, following her reading at the Tattered Cover. The Macmillan rep was somewhere nearby, loitering with the store's event coordinator and waiting to take her out for dinner, though Anna was planning to claim exhaustion at the last minute. (Denver's burgeoning restaurant scene held about as much appeal to her as the opening of a new vacuum repair shop in her own neighborhood.)

She looked down. The Post-it on her book's cover said: REBECCA.

"Oh," Anna said, with warmth. "Tell me more."

"When he came out here, on his tour for *Crib*. I interviewed him. My temple has a paper. Any Jewish writers who come through, we try to write about them."

"That's so nice. What do you remember about him?"

She was, after all, still a grieving widow, and still gathering memories where she could, however they might present themselves.

"Super nice. I remember thinking, you know, what a humble guy. Even though he was so successful."

"Yes. I loved that about him. Do you want me to write anything in particular, Rebecca?"

"Rebecca's my sister-in-law. I'm giving this to her for Hanukkah."

"Oh, okay." Anna started to write the name in her lavender Sharpie.

"Yeah. Her brother killed himself."

It was said so nonchalantly, Anna actually flinched. "Oh no," she finally managed. The tone was so flat, the woman might have been describing a missed tennis lesson, or an ingrown toenail. Even the choice of term was alarming. Today, people with an ounce of sensitivity didn't say "killed himself." They said "took his own life." This still-nameless woman apparently hadn't gotten that memo.

"Oh, I'm so sorry."

"Yeah, it was a while ago. But, you know, I think she'll read it. My sister-in-law."

Not: *appreciate it.* Not: *get something out of it.* At least she hadn't said: *enjoy it.*

"It's kind of you to think about her."

"She's hard to pick a present for, that's for sure. The worst taste. Never again would I buy her clothing, or even something for the house. I learned that lesson."

Anna glanced furtively at the next person in line. Words could not express how little she was enjoying this exchange. And she was good with words.

"But anyway, I don't think he was married to you yet. I asked him how long he'd been out on the road with his book, and when he told me, I was, like, that's a long time to be away from home. He said he was single and he enjoyed traveling around, and it was his first book that he'd done any traveling for."

That was true enough. Not many people had read *The Invention of Wonder* and no one at all had read *Reverberations*. There hadn't been anything like a book tour for either of them. Poor Jake had never gotten over the fact that he finally had readers, never mind what he'd had to do to get them.

"Actually, we met while he was on the same book tour. In Seattle."

"Yeah, I read that somewhere. He signed your book?"

She shook her head. "I was producing a radio show, and he came on."

"Oh." The woman laughed. "Signing your book would've been more of a meet-cute."

Anna summoned a rueful smile. "I suppose so. Well, it was nice talking with you. I hope your sister-in-law likes her present."

"I remember he said he came up with the idea when he saw this mom and her teenage daughter having a fight. Pardon me for saying so, but I never believed that."

Now Anna stopped furtively looking past this annoying person to the next person in line, who was also likely—given her very impatient body language—to be an annoying person.

"I mean, who sees a mom and a teenage daughter having a fight and comes up with *that*?"

I don't know, thought Anna. *A writer?*

"Must have been an interesting guy to be married to." The woman actually grinned.

"Oh, he was." And she turned her entire body to that next person, who held three copies of *The Afterword* in her arms, each festooned with a Post-it. They were for members of her book group, and she wouldn't leave until Anna had agreed to phone or Zoom in when the group met the following month.

"You'll make me the biggest hero," she insisted, before finally departing.

The next few were briefly complimentary and happy to move, efficiently, past. Then came a father in fresh bereavement, piteously decompensating in real time, until the crowd behind him became alarmed and they all looked around for someone to save them. That person, eventually, was the store's security guard, but the situation was fraught enough that Anna had to come out from behind her table and place a hand on his forearm. "I understand," she said, looking deep into his eyes. "Believe me, I know exactly what you're going through. I can't even tell you it gets better, because I'm not there yet. But I can tell you you're not alone. Unfortunately, there are too many of us for that."

The man nodded, wordless and shaking. There was nothing to fear from him, she was pretty sure.

"I want to thank you for coming, and I hope my book helps you."

They took him away.

A surge of women, overcompensating for that destroyed man with kindness and beautiful manners, happy to have their books signed and say something complimentary but blessedly impersonal ("That was a beautiful reading." "I do admire what you've accomplished." "Look forward to reading it!") before a pair, two cousins who had just lost their grandmother, though not to suicide. "It was a long goodbye, the kind that makes you wish it would actually go faster. Gruesome." There was a man who had written a book about his partner's death from cancer and published it on Amazon. He didn't have a copy of *The Afterword* for her to sign, but he pressed his own book into her hands, making her watch—making them all watch—as he signed it. At length. She thanked him extravagantly. And then she could see the end.

She began, even as she went about signing, and signing, and chatting and signing, to select the excuse she would offer the

Macmillan rep, who wanted so badly to sample Denver's hottest restaurant. Well, he still could once she claimed exhaustion, or rebound distress from that poor, bereaved man who'd had to be escorted out, or possibly that old standby, a migraine coming on.

"Thank you so much."

"I hope you enjoy it."

"Thanks, I appreciate that."

She was entitled to exhaustion. This, her third event in as many days, in her third city in as many days, in her third state in as many days, had been pretty typical for the size of the audience and the offering up of personal trauma, all varieties of loss but plenty of suicides. The constituency, it was clear, had claimed her, and word was spreading fast. Well, they bought books. They bought lots of books.

"Oh no, I'm so sorry. There's no way to prepare."

"Thank you so much for saying so."

"I wrote it to help myself, to be honest. I had no idea I could help anyone else."

There were so many names to sign, and so many varieties. The sheer variations on "Catherine" alone drove her to distraction. The "Caitlins," the "Christines," the "Micaelas." Thank goodness for the Post-it notes, because she had to sign as she listened to them speak to her, and as she tried to respond:

"Dear"—*K-I-R-S-T-Y-N*—"thank you so much. I hope it helps. All my best wishes for you in your journey, Anna Williams-Bonner"

"For"—*M-E-A-G-A-N*—"with very best wishes. Anna Williams-Bonner"

She looked up. The Macmillan rep was alone now, arms folded. He looked, if this was possible, actually impatient, as if she were holding him up. Well, she was, she supposed. Only two people were left, but they each had several books to sign. At least they seemed to be together.

They were sisters, and their story was terrible. Almost immediately, both were in tears. The books were for their children. Their surviving children. It was a phenomenon Anna recognized, this end-of-the-line attack, something akin to waiting until the doctor had their hand on the doorknob before asking about a suspicious lump in the breast. They knew they'd need a lot of time with the author. They hung back. They let people go in front of them. It was a necessary evil.

She spent nearly fifteen minutes with them. They were inconsolable, not that she tried very hard. What was the point? The suicide of a loved one left an unfillable hole in a family and in every person the lost person had been close to. Or so she had been told, repeatedly. She had no personal experience of it, herself.

And then, at last, they left, clutching their books, and the Macmillan rep edged nearer, and Anna recognized that she was genuinely as incapable of experiencing Denver's burgeoning culinary scene as she'd been prepared to pretend she was. She wanted an ordinary room-service burger and a whiskey sour and a slice of chocolate cake. She wanted to take a shower and get into a hotel robe to watch CNN until she fell asleep with the television on. But before she could get away, the booksellers brought her a stack of books to sign, stock for the Tattered Cover to continue selling and books that had been ordered online or over the phone, or even in the store, by people who weren't able to attend the reading in person.

She did the stock first: simple signature, nothing personal. Then she turned to the preorders, carefully reading the Post-it before writing on the half title page, grateful not to have anyone standing over her.

"For Chloe"

"For Joanne"

"For Susan"

"Happy Birthday, to Mikayla"

The final copy had no Post-it. She opened the cover to the title page, where people sometimes placed it, erroneously, wasting her time, but there was nothing there. She turned to the next page, the half title page, and there it was, its usual square, its usual yellow. She picked up her Sharpie, but she couldn't get her eyes to read the words, or rather her brain to process them. Something wasn't working, or the words themselves were not working, or weren't getting through. Anna read them again. Then again, but it made no difference. They still made no sense. *For Evan Parker, not forgotten*, they said.

8

Find Me

She kept the Post-it, of course. She had to. She didn't want anyone else to see it, or ask about it. She managed to write, with a barely controlled hand, "Best wishes, Anna Williams-Bonner," and give the defiled book back to one of the booksellers, then she gathered her things and asked the Macmillan rep to drive her back to her hotel.

"Thought we were going for dinner," he said. He looked terribly disappointed. She nearly hit him.

"I'm so sorry. I'm not feeling well."

Even he must have been able to see she wasn't lying about it.

"Oh no! Let me get you to the Hilton."

She held it crumpled up in her hand. Her hand was in her coat pocket. It was a radioactive scrap of yellow paper. It really was making her feel unwell.

The rep dropped her at the hotel. She apologized again, and again let him tell her how much he had admired her book. Then she made her escape.

Upstairs, she flung the Post-it onto the floor and sat down on her bed, glaring at it. It was an unlovely thing, moist from her hand, bits of dirt from her coat pocket sticking to the invisible stripe of glue on one edge. She fought an urge to grind it into the carpet or open the sliding glass door to the interior courtyard and drop it onto the walkway below, but inevitably she began to conjure a scenario in which someone picked it up, unfurled it, and read its radioactive message: *For Evan Parker, not forgotten.*

74

It was possible that she was overreacting, that she was being ridiculous. Both the name Evan and the surname Parker were far from uncommon, and it was certainly plausible that some innocent book buyer in Denver wanted a copy of *The Afterword* for a friend or a relative with that name. Though if this particular—*other*—Evan Parker was still alive to read her novel, what, exactly, was *not forgotten*? No, not one thing about this was ridiculous; ergo, the fact that she was here in her hotel room, hands clutching her knees, arms braced, breathing too quickly and still, somehow, short of breath, was in no way an overreaction.

In fact, unless the Post-it was some random act of coincidental nothingness, it was, in fact, the exact opposite of ridiculous: the first indication since Jake's death that someone had *not forgotten* the name Evan Parker, and that this same someone was aware of Evan's connection to Jacob Finch Bonner, her late husband and the obvious "inspiration" for the book that Post-it note had been affixed to. Perhaps similarly known and *not forgotten* were the clear similarities between Evan's amateurish attempt at a novel and the very assured novel Jake had so famously composed, only a few short years after her brother's death. And if this someone knew those things, how much danger might they one day pose to herself?

It had been years since a living person on the planet had been fully aware of who she was, and that she was not a childless woman in her late thirties, brought up in Idaho, named Anna Williams-Bonner, and before that, Anna Williams.

She had worked for so long to separate the two circles of the Venn diagram that was her actual life.

One of those circles held the few souls who had known or might remember the person called Dianna Parker—a person who had lived her entire, blasted, and resentful life in central

Vermont before dying abruptly (and unnaturally) in the north Georgia mountains.

The other circle, much more crowded, held the many colleagues and professional acquaintances in New York and Seattle, and the bereaved family and friends of her late husband, not to speak of those millions of readers around the world who had purchased and enjoyed Jacob Finch Bonner's novel *Crib,* and the much smaller (but already quite respectable) number who had read *The Afterword,* that first novel by the literary widow who suddenly seemed to be everywhere.

Only two people had ever occupied the tiny overlap between those circles, and she had gotten rid of both of them.

Fucking Evan, Anna thought; all of these difficulties had begun with him. He was her only sibling, already in situ when their parents brought her home to that ridiculous yellow house down the road from the old quarry, and yet she did not possess a single memory of her brother as a compatriot in the snake pit that was their family, and certainly no memory of sibling love. Evan, a rambunctious boy from toddlerhood, lacked the wit to be a true prodigal and actually *leave* home; why bother to leave when home was a place of such endless comfort for him? He had progressed from football glory (or what passed for that in Vermont) to the community college in Rutland, where he majored in light drug dealing and general impregnation (a discipline he had shown a real affinity for as early as tenth grade), and acts of predatory disdain for his younger sister, all without ever decamping from his childhood bedroom. Then, suddenly, he was the owner of an old Rutland bar (purchased with what money she never knew).

By then he was out of the yellow house, at least, and she had a baby of her own, then a toddler, then a relentlessly punishing girl named Rose. Their parents had also decamped, though less voluntarily—taken out by a carbon monoxide leak that somehow spared herself and Rose—and the yellow house was no longer such a haven for her faultless older brother. There were no warm meals perpetually at the ready for him in their mother's avocado-colored oven, no spontaneous infusions of cash from dad, and those raucous parties he had so enjoyed hosting whenever their parents were away overnight (the house full of his teammates and whatever girls were currently in pursuit of them) promised fewer Dionysian pleasures with a kid waking up to scream every couple of hours. He moved to the flat over his bar, and for nearly a decade she and Rose hardly saw him. He might turn up occasionally, looking for money (as if she had any) and, more often than not, taking away some object—an old chair or picture off the wall—to sell, which was only fair, as he liked to remind her. She would not understand, for years, that he was addicted to something: a substance, or substances. He would hardly have shared such a detail with her, and she lacked the understanding to see it for herself.

Still, she had considered the occasional visitation and appropriation to be . . . not unreasonable burdens. She would have had no reason not to leave Evan alone. If only he had left her alone.

It was not ridiculous, and she was not—Anna knew at her core—overreacting.

She had a terrible night, waking and sleeping in a broken cycle, surfacing to the same stories on CNN until she shut it down. She had to be at the airport by eleven, and she was up for the final time before six, lying like a starfish on top of her bed's quilted maroon cover, still in her robe. When she dragged herself up and through the shower and into her clothes, she had to wait hours for the Tattered Cover to open so she could go to the store.

Naturally she didn't remember the names of those smiling booksellers. Naturally she didn't want to call the Macmillan rep, who was probably still sleeping off his mile-high meal. But she couldn't do nothing, either. She checked out and took a cab to the branch of the bookstore where she'd read and signed the night before, and found a coffee shop across the street. There, she ordered a latte and sat outside, wrapped in her coat and drumming her fingers on the metal tabletop for nearly an hour before someone unlocked the bookstore's door and flipped over the OPEN sign.

Inside, no one looked familiar. She skulked around for a bit, waiting for more employees to appear, pretending to examine the table of quilting books just inside the front door. (WELCOME QUILTCON 2019 ATTENDEES! a sign said.) There wasn't much more in the way of disposable time; her flight to Minneapolis wasn't going to wait for her (given the mess the airlines were in, it was far likelier to be the other way around). The books she'd signed at the end of last night, in her posttraumatic daze, had been evenly distributed to the checkout clerks' stations, the most prime real estate in any bookstore, perfect for impulse purchases and hand selling, or impulse purchases as a result of hand selling. She went for the clerk who looked the least unfamiliar.

"Oh hi, I'm Anna?" she told the young woman, who had the ruddy complexion of a young person who had chosen to live in Denver, because: mountains.

"Anna! From last night!"

"Anna from last night." Anna smiled. "I recognized you."

"You were fantastic. We sold a ton of books!"

"I know, it was great. But I lost my favorite pen. I'm a bit superstitious about it, so I decided to come by on my way to the airport."

"Oh no!" said the nice young woman. "What kind of a pen?"

"A Sharpie. Nothing exotic, only it's the pen I used to sign my very first copy, and I put a mark on it so I'd remember. I kind of decided I'd keep using it till it ran out. So far it hasn't."

She nodded in sympathetic pain. "I absolutely believe in that kind of thing."

Anna was not surprised to hear it.

"Black Sharpie?"

"Purple. Like the book cover. I know there were a few of them last night. I can't believe I lost it."

The young woman was already rooting around behind the counter. "We are going to check every Sharpie in the store. We will leave no Sharpie unturned."

She sent Anna to the café, told the barista to get her whatever she wanted, and disappeared on her mission. Anna hoped it wouldn't take long. She didn't really want to go to Minneapolis, but even more than that she didn't want to miss her flight. It would wreak havoc on everything else: Chicago, Cleveland, Louisville, St. Louis. Beyond these, a week at home beckoned like an undulating maiden in a mirage.

Finally, the bookseller returned with the store's supply box for author events, full of autograph stickers, pens, and stands to prop the books against.

"I had a quick look. I didn't see any purple."

Anna made a sad face. "Oh dear. Let me go through it myself, just to be sure."

She began, not too quickly.

"You do a lot of events in this branch?"

"More and more," the young woman said. "They're catching on. Were you pleased?"

"Oh yes. Well, it's all very new for me. First book."

"I know! It's hard to believe!"

You're not alone, Anna thought.

"And all the people. Some of them are great, but some of them are . . . a little odd, aren't they?"

The woman grinned. "Bookstores have always attracted odd people."

"Yes. But they say such strange things. Somebody said something really upsetting to me last night. I was so scared, all I wanted to do was go back to my hotel. It's probably why I left my pen behind."

"But that's awful. I can't stand that you had a bad experience. We want writers to feel safe here. Who was it, do you remember?"

Anna shook her head. "They didn't say it in person. They left it in a note, inside the book. I didn't see the person at all. Was there anyone, you know, weird or kind of off, that you noticed last night? Especially at the end of the line?"

The young woman frowned. "There was one guy who didn't want to buy the book. He just wanted to give you *his* book. Self-published, I'm pretty sure."

"I remember him." Anna nodded. She had dropped it in the trash bin in her hotel room. "Anyone else?"

"There were some people who'd been crying. I noticed that."

"Yes," Anna said. "That does happen. It's a hard topic."

"Of course, of course. You said it was in a note? Sometimes people come in before the event and pay for the book and leave a note inside for the author. How to sign it. You know, their name, or the name of the person they're giving it to. That kind of thing. Then we hold it for them to pick up. Or sometimes we send it to them."

"Yes." Anna nodded again. She was growing impatient. "That's probably exactly what it was. Can we figure out who

80

might have bought it, and if they were planning to pick it up, or getting it sent to them? I'm sorry, it's probably against all kinds of rules, but . . . I don't know how much you know about my husband . . ."

It was a far more desperate move than she wanted to make, but maybe the woman just needed the right fire lit under her.

"Oh! God, I loved that book. He was such a good writer. I'm so sorry for your loss."

"Did you know that he was being harassed, for months? Before he died?"

The woman looked blank for a moment, and then the synapses started firing. "Right. Wow. Yeah, I did read that. It's so awful. People can be so horrible. I had a bully in high school."

Anna didn't have time for this.

"So you can understand. I mean, that person was never identified. And now I've written this book, and . . . the idea that the person is still out there? I'm sorry, I'm just, really afraid." She waited a beat. Then: "I shouldn't be burdening you with this."

"Wait here," the woman said again, and she left again. Anna picked up her phone. She really did need to leave for the airport soon. The event tonight in Minneapolis was a big one, at the Hopkins Center for the Arts. She couldn't skip it. She opened up Uber and set the destination for the airport. A ten-minute wait. That meant fifteen minutes, probably.

Then the woman was back, trailing a printout. She didn't extend it right away.

"It's possible I could get in trouble for sharing this," she said.

"I will absolutely keep it to myself."

There were six books purchased in advance of the reading, for her to sign. Five were purchased with credit cards, to be held for pickup by the purchaser. The sixth had been paid for in cash, and was to be sent out by UPS once it had been signed.

"Can you tell me where?" Anna said. The woman ran her finger down the page. The recipient was a person named Evan Parker. The address was a long-defunct college in Ripley, Vermont.

Anna got, unsteadily, to her feet.

"I'm really sorry about your pen," the woman said. "And . . . everything."

"I found my pen," Anna managed to say as she left.

9

No Longer at Ease

Evan Parker was dead: to begin with. There was no doubt whatever about that.

She had been present for the event itself, and the aftermath, because of what she'd needed to do in that house after Evan was past threatening her. When she left it, many hours after the fact, he was still dead, and even after that, according to what she had managed to glean from public sources, the body had not been discovered for a further five days. By that time the possibility of resuscitation would have been far, far beyond the skills of even the finest Vermont physician.

No. Whoever had purchased that copy of her book, it wasn't Evan Parker of Ripley College or anywhere else.

She got herself to the airport in Denver. She got herself onto her plane and to the Hopkins Center for the Arts in the Twin Cities, and thence to the Library Association Conference in Chicago and the Healthy Mind Conference in Cleveland and the One Book event in Louisville and the Festival of Women Writers in St. Louis. But she never stopped looking back over her shoulder, back to the end of the signing line.

More often than not, there was some nasty surprise back there, though never the exact nasty surprise that had begun to dominate her thoughts. A bereaved mom who wanted to show her photographs, an angry man who felt Anna was trivializing suicide and wanted to make sure she knew how offended he was by that, an entire book group who were eager to talk about her *process*. It was a fallacy to look back and think: *just three more people waiting, just two more, just one more,* because that final *one more* might take as much time as half a dozen swift signings-and-pleasantries. Sometimes, out of the corner of her eye, she saw these back-of-the-liners step back to allow someone to go before them, an action that did not, to her newly educated eye, convey goodness or politeness; rather, it suggested a specific intentionality—to be the final person, to linger with the author after everyone else had gone.

Somehow, she got through it all: the travel and the transfers, the events and their aftermaths. She did not explore the cities she visited, taking her photo underneath The Bean or touring the Rock & Roll Hall of Fame. She did not sample the local cuisines—St. Louis barbecue or Hot Brown sandwiches in Louisville. But she kept herself on schedule and she kept herself fed; every hotel had a turkey club, and it was pretty hard to screw those up. Macmillan hadn't sent her out with a minder, like that guy who'd accompanied Jake when they met back in Seattle. She knew she wasn't that important, not yet, and while *The Afterword* was exceeding everyone's expectations (including her own), she was still far from *Crib* territory. Occasionally, as in the Denver stop, one of the publisher's representatives would appear to collect her at the airport and drive her to her events, but mainly she was on her own to make the flights and greet the booksellers and the long lines of her readers. And Jake's, who were hers, now, as well.

And then, a reprieve: after nearly three weeks of constant motion, ten days without a travel event, and a chance to go home to New York and catch her breath, with only local readings and something on Long Island that they were sending her out to in a limo. She arrived at LaGuardia late on a Thursday and somehow found her Uber in the labyrinth that was the eternally unfinished airport. Traffic was predictably bad, and they crawled back to the Village. She paused in the lobby long enough to accept a box of mail from her doorman. Many of the items inside were still addressed to Jake.

She went up in the elevator with the only neighbor she knew, a woman who had once agreed to look in on their cat when they went away on their honeymoon, and who later took in the cat for good. She hadn't liked owning a cat nearly as much as she'd imagined she would, and after Jake was gone, Anna just couldn't seem to settle with him. He—his name had been Whidbey, but she suspected that her neighbor had changed it—was always bolting from her when she entered the room, and Anna sometimes imagined that it weirdly grasped that whole final drama in the apartment. Sole witness, pathetically unable to tell anyone about it: the stuff of Greek mythology.

"You know, I'm not sure I've seen you since that fantastic story about you. In the paper."

New Yorkers of a certain ilk did not need to qualify which paper, although the city still had four healthy dailies.

"I know. I still can't believe it."

"I'm so happy for you," the woman said. She was a real Village type, with long hair that had never been dyed, an African top, and red feather earrings. "After everything you went through, for you to have this success."

"I'm trying to appreciate it," Anna said with all the humility she could muster. "I'm trying to feel it, not put it aside."

"So hard for women," her neighbor said. "To feel pride in our work. To own our success."

This neighbor had marched down these streets, back in the 1970s, demanding something—various things—along those lines. Anna had heard all about it, any number of times.

"How's my feline friend?" she asked as the door opened on their floor.

"He loves a cuddle," her neighbor said.

"Well, give him a cuddle for me."

They parted good neighbors, to their doors at the opposite ends of the corridor.

Inside, the air was stale, and a film of dust lay over the dining table. She could have afforded a cleaner, but not the presence of a stranger in her home while she was far away; the irritation of returning to disorder was simply the lesser of two evils. She knew she wouldn't be comfortable until at least a rudimentary effort was made, so she wet a paper towel and wiped off all the surfaces, then cracked open a window to clear the place out. She put her much-worn clothing into the washer and went gratefully into a hot shower, shampooing her hair and letting the water pound her shoulders. She wouldn't leave home at all for a day, not if she could help it. She would order in and deal with all the nonurgent emails and texts she'd been stockpiling. There was also an update with the team developing *Crib* as a feature film, and a few Zoom meetings with the West Coast attorneys affiliated with Matilda's agency. But she could stay home for all of it in a stupor of ease.

In her robe, she ordered from RedFarm and made herself a Sea Breeze, a drink that had struck her as the height of sophistication when she was a teenager and somehow retained its charms. She put on the news and sat on the sofa. Then, after a moment, she went and got the box the doorman had given her and began to lift out handfuls of mail.

Marine Layer and Company Store, both addressed to "Resident." *Poets & Writers* and the *New York Review of Books* (Jake's) and *Seattle* magazine (hers). There were many examples of the kind of stuff you got sent if someone connected your name to the word "writer": brochures for MFA programs, notices of classes that might take her writing "to the next level." There were at least a dozen galleys of upcoming books from editors, each accompanied by a letter of lavish praise for *The Afterword* and an embarrassing supplication for a blurb—she stacked those separately—and a manila envelope from Macmillan full of what she presumed was fan mail. Most of these had handwritten addresses and were clearly sent by real people rather than the institutions that tended to get in touch via email to her agent or publisher, or occasionally through the website she'd set up at Wendy's request. A few, though, were from libraries or colleges, or—increasingly—mental health organizations, and probably contained invitations to speak or read. Those would have to be dealt with case by case, as she had little interest in traveling far afield for a paltry "honorarium," as if the honor of being asked was adequate compensation for the time and travel. But there were outlets considered, by Wendy and her PR team, to be so important that they did warrant acceptance; the Cleveland conference, for example, Healthy Mind something something, with its thousands of caregivers and doctors in attendance, had been a good call on the part of the Macmillan publicists. The signing line had been interminable and very arduous, but she had sold hundreds of copies of *The Afterword* through a local independent bookstore that reported to the *New York Times* bestseller list.

There was also one dubious letter from a person mercifully far away in Micronesia that began with gentle appreciation for her novel but quickly descended into a mad dissertation on something called the "blood-brain barrier." (Which she had apparently crossed? Or was threatening to cross? It was beyond her limited attempt to understand.) There was a letter whose envelope was addressed to her, via the publisher, but actually written to her late husband, including a long and strident appraisal of *Crib* (negative) and a directive to do better in his future novels. Did the letter writer think she had Jacob Finch Bonner somehow in her possession? Was this the last American reader to learn that the author of *Crib* had died tragically by his own hand, leaving a distraught yet gifted widow to carry on both his and her own literary legacy?

Apparently so.

At the bottom of the box were flyers for local restaurants, a free community circular, and a reminder from the co-op that the Halloween party would take place in the lobby on the Saturday before Halloween, which made no sense to Anna. And a few larger envelopes that she suspected contained pages of prose, sent to her for her opinion, advice, guidance, or championship, none of which they would be receiving. But writers—Jake had taught her this—were delicate creatures, and to be handled with great care. A writer rejected is a writer eternally offended, and unlikely to ever forget who'd done the offending. Some of these people would eventually become published writers, even successful ones. Some of them would become critics. Some of them would become reviewers on TikTok or Goodreads. None of these were people you wanted out there hating you.

Wendy had once told her that Macmillan, like other publishers, now had an official policy of not even looking at material that hadn't been sent by an agent. True, they were giving up that slight chance of finding a great project by a new writer no one had yet discovered, but the steady stream of lawsuits by writers who'd submitted their manuscripts or story ideas and later seen some element of its plot or characters in Jodi Picoult's new novel or Tom Hanks's latest film made it impossible to keep that door open. It was a necessary policy, and perhaps even an improvement to keeping unsolicited manuscripts in some dusty corner for months or even years, as Matilda had apparently done during her previous assistants' tenure. *The Black Hole of Salter*, indeed.

Anna, for her part, had adapted the language on her publisher's website, and so far it had kept the influx to a trickle: "Thank you for taking the time to send me your work. Unfortunately, I cannot read or review any unsolicited material. If you have provided a return envelope and postage (S.A.S.E.) I will send it back to you without delay. If not, it will be disposed of. I very much regret that I am obligated to return your work unread, and sincerely wish you the best for your writing. Anna Williams-Bonner."

Though she usually took a peek first. Of course she did. Life did not offer so many diversions that you could dismiss the available ones, and the entertainment value of truly execrable writing and the endless range of human weirdness, coupled with the kind of delusional self-confidence one associated with twice-impeached ex-presidents, was simply too tempting to decline out of hand. And sometimes the material in those envelopes was actually good! A fierce little prose excerpt set in a truck stop on an unnamed highway. A short story about a summer colony in Maine, populated by the kind of summer people Anna had grown up observing: visitors to Vermont from the cities who brought their dogs and even horses along to their summer homes, and then, incomprehensibly, sent their children to sleepaway camp.

She had finished her meal of chicken and sugar snap peas and was about to make herself a cup of tea when she slid the pages out of the final manila envelope.

*Ruby could hear her mother, all the way upstairs in her
bedroom and on the phone. She couldn't hear the actual
words, but she knew when Diandra was on one of her
Psychic Hotline calls because the voice went up and got
billowy, as if Diandra (or at least her psychic alias, Sister
Dee Dee) were floating overhead, looking down at
everything in the poor caller's life and seeing all. When her
mother's voice was midrange and her tone flat, Ruby could
tell that Diandra was working for one of the off-site
customer service lines she logged in to. And when it got low
and breathy, it was the porn chat line that had been the
soundtrack of most of the last couple of years of Ruby's life.*

She was up before she realized anything was wrong, on her feet
and lurching for the bathroom, where she vomited up fifty
dollars' worth of chicken and sugar snaps, as well as one of
RedFarm's signature pastrami egg rolls, a dish she had been
craving all through the American Midwest. Now she watched
the sad aftermath swirl away in the flushing toilet, too stunned
to understand what had just happened.

I must be very upset, she thought, absurdly.

Yes, she was very upset. But why?

Ruby. Diandra. Sister Dee Dee of the Psychic Hotline.

God, Evan. It was Evan, alive again in those horrible sentences. They had torn their way through her once before, years
earlier, and now they were suddenly with her again, here in
this apartment: her own home. These exact sentences from the
pages of that foul book Evan had been writing. About *her*.
About *her life*. Jake had read these exact words, she knew,
because she'd found a photocopy of her brother's application to
Ripley's low-residency MFA program among the drafts of the
"work" in their old house in West Rutland: two pages of prose

he'd evidently judged to be his best writing. Perhaps he'd been right. These pages had won Evan a spot in Ripley's not very exalted roster. Whatever that was worth.

Except that the pages, like the horrendous manuscript they belonged to, no longer existed. She had eradicated all of it, along with the laptop that generated it, and all the items she had extracted from their childhood home at the time of her brother's tragic death had been disposed of as she zigzagged her way south from Vermont. Not one page of Evan's novel was still with her when she arrived in Athens with her sordid series of tasks at last behind her. Evan was gone. His "work" was gone. His all-too-consequential interference in her life: finally, blessedly, irreversibly gone.

Except, obviously, none of that was true. The pages flung to the floor of her living room as she bolted for the bathroom had unquestionably been composed by her older brother, Evan Parker, and they were as real in the world as she, herself, was.

10

Little Men

In the morning, she made herself examine the manila envelope. It had—she was not surprised to see—no return address. It also had, and she was equally unsurprised to see this, a postmark from St. Johnsbury, Vermont, from three weeks earlier. (Where had she been, three weeks earlier? Seattle? Los Angeles?) She read the whole thing standing in the middle of her living room, holding the pages between thumb and forefinger, as if they might contaminate her. As if they had not already contaminated her, the first time she'd read them years earlier. It was all appallingly familiar.

The house was so old. It had belonged to her grandparents, and her grandfather's parents even further back, and though there'd been changes, wallpaper and paint and a wall-to-wall carpet in the living room that was supposed to be beige, there was still a faint old line of stenciling along the ceilings in some of the rooms. Around the inside of the front door, for example: a row of misshapen pineapples. Those pineapples had never made sense to Ruby, at least until her class had gone on a day trip to some early American museum and she'd seen the exact same thing in one of the buildings there. Apparently, the pineapple symbolized hospitality, which made it about the last thing that belonged on the wall of their home, because Diandra's entire life was the opposite of hospitality. She couldn't even remember the last time somebody had stopped by with a misdelivered piece of mail, let alone for a cup of her mother's terrible coffee.

Ruby returned to her test. The tabletop was sticky from that morning's breakfast syrup, or maybe the mac and cheese of last night's dinner, or maybe something her mother had eaten or done at the table while she'd been at school. The two of them never ate at the table together. Ruby declined, as much as was possible, to place her nutritional well-being in the hands of her mother, who evidently maintained her girlish physique—literally girlish: from the back, mother and daughter looked absurdly alike—through an apparent diet of celery sticks and Diet Dr Pepper. Diandra had stopped feeding her daughter around the time Ruby turned nine, which was around the time Ruby had learned how to open a can of spaghetti for her own damn self.

Ironically, as the two of them grew ever more physically similar they had less and less to say to each other. Not that they'd ever enjoyed what you might call a loving mother-and-daughter relationship; Ruby could remember no bedtime cuddles or pretend tea parties, no indulgent birthdays or tinsel-strewn Christmas mornings, and never anything in the way of maternal advice or unsolicited affection, the kind she sometimes encountered in novels or Disney movies (usually right before the mother died or disappeared). Diandra seemed to skate by with the barest minimum of maternal duties, mainly those related to keeping Ruby alive and vaccinated, sheltered (if you could call this freezing house a source of shelter), and educated (if you could call her unambitious rural school a source of education). She seemed to want it all to be over every bit as fervently as Ruby herself did.

But she couldn't want it as fervently as Ruby herself did. She couldn't even come close.

The previous summer Ruby had gone to work for the bakery in town, off the books, of course. And then, that fall, she picked up a Sunday job for a neighbor, watching a couple of the younger kids while the rest of the family went to church. Half of whatever she made went into the house account for food and the occasional repair, but the other half Ruby wedged into an AP Chemistry textbook, which had to be the last place her mother would ever think to look for it. The chemistry had been a necessary slog the year before, a deal she'd made with her advisor to let her move ahead in her school's bare-bones science track, and it hadn't been easy to manage alongside her humanities classes at the community college, the independent French project, and of course her two jobs, but it was all part of the plan she had formed around the time she'd opened that first can of spaghetti. That plan was called Get-the-Fuck-Away-from-Here, and she'd never deviated from it for a single second. She was fifteen now and an eleventh grader, having already skipped her kindergarten year. In a couple of months she'd be able to apply to college. A year from now, she'd be away from here, for good.

She hadn't always been this way. She could recall, without too much mental heavy lifting, a time when she felt at least neutral about living in this house and in the orbit of her mother, who was pretty much her only extant family member (and certainly the only family member she ever saw). She could recall doing the things she supposed most other children did—playing in dirt, looking at pictures—without any accompanying grief or anger, and she knew enough by now to recognize that as unpleasant as her home life and "family" might be, there were endless versions of worse out there in what she had come to understand as the wider world. So what had brought her to this bitter precipice? What had made her normal

*child-self into the Ruby huddled over her at-home history test
on which so much—in her mind, at least—depended, who
(literally) counted the days until her departure? The answer was
inaccessible. The answer had never been shared with her. The
answer was no longer of any concern, only its attendant truth,
which she'd figured out years ago and had never once
questioned: her mother loathed her, and probably always had.*

*What was she supposed to do with such information?
Exactly.*

*Pass her test. Ask Mr. Brown to write a teacher
recommendation (for which, with luck, he'd regurgitate this
very anecdote about the girl who insisted on being assigned
extra work). And then, take her clearly superior brain out
from under that canopy of old pineapples and into a world
that would at least appreciate her. She had learned not to
expect love, and wasn't even sure she wanted it. This was the
most profound wisdom she'd managed to glean from the
fifteen years she had spent in her mother's presence. Fifteen
down. One—please, God, only one—to go.*

And then, something else, something she hadn't noticed the
previous evening as she'd hurled the page away and raced to the
bathroom to divest herself of her expensive dinner: at the bottom
of the final page someone had written two words, chicken
scratch in black ballpoint pen: *"Seem familiar?"* Unlike the text
itself, there was nothing remotely familiar about the handwriting. She stared at it, forcing herself not to tear or crumple
the pages, so intense was the impulse to eviscerate them.

Seem familiar?

It certainly did. In fact, she'd read this particular sample of
her late brother's writing too many times already to be shocked
by a single word of it.

She recalled the first time, in the Vermont house, in the room she had once slept in, seated in her own chair, at her own desk, the insult of the content doing battle with the insult of—and yes, it still pained her to acknowledge this!—her brother's *wholly unexpected* accomplishment. Nearly three hundred pages of this . . . thing, neatly stacked on the oak desktop where she had once done her own high school homework, this vicious fiction an affront to her very factual suffering. On that particular August night, seven years ago, as she'd made her way through the stack, turning those repellent pages in that chair, in that dark house, her brother was miles away in Rutland, working in his tavern. That was a vile but necessary night, preceding another vile but necessary night, one which Evan Parker—not to put too fine a point on it—had not survived.

No, these pages were not meant to exist. Not today. Not in any format, let alone this one—an apparent photocopy of the original manuscript. She had personally extracted that manuscript, eradicated it, expunged it, eliminated it, or so she'd had every right to believe; and yet these pages in her hands were undeniable. Unkillable. Unlike their author, who had been—in corporal terms, at least—eminently killable.

Here was the thing about Evan Parker: he believed he knew all about her life, despite having been so notably absent for most of it. Even when he was physically there in the house with her and their parents, or (briefly) with her and her daughter, he hadn't *really* been there, not in any way that counted. From conception, and through a childhood bathed in the eternal sun of their parents' obvious worship, Evan had lived a singular life, mindlessly strolling along on the red carpet in his head as it perpetually unfurled before him, anticipating his precious footfalls. Because, as far as he was concerned, none of the other members of his family had anything at all to do with *him*.

If only she, too, had had that option, of having had nothing to do with *them*, so much unpleasantness might have been avoided. All four of them, in fact—her entire family of origin—might now be alive and well, contentedly pursuing their individual interests, perhaps exchanging Christmas cards or enduring an annual Thanksgiving meal in their ancestral house in central Vermont.

But no. A very different life had been presented to her, and she had not been given the option of deviating from it. Well, that was a shame for all involved, and Anna was the first to acknowledge it.

She'd always understood that her older brother was the maypole around which the rest of their small family danced. It was not enough to say, merely, that her own existence was an afterthought; even from a young age it was plain to her that she was at best unplanned, at worst unwanted, an actual inconvenience to the mother and father who lived to attend Evan's sports events and bask in the approval he seemed to generate wherever he went. In short, a bare minimum of attention had been paid to this second child from the get-go, and certainly her own interests, talents, and aspirations failed utterly to attract the focus of her mother and father. Until puberty, at least, she wore her brother's outgrown clothing as a matter of course, cinching his old pants with one of his old belts, stuffing his castoff sneakers with his castoff socks. She slept on sheets bearing his former enthusiasms, Teenage Mutant Ninja Turtles and animated Transformers, and inherited the toys he'd lost interest in and the books he'd never read. A brief experiment in which she announced that she would no longer eat meat yielded no deviation from the family menus, which leaned heavily on (an admittedly tasty) meat loaf and pork chops. Weekends were devoted to her brother's sports. Later, a resolutely blind parental eye would be turned toward the many young ladies who spent many nights in her brother's bedroom *across the hall* from their own. Because he was the wonder and the glory of their lives: Evan Parker, their firstborn, their son.

Meanwhile, downstairs, down the hall from the kitchen, as far as she could have been lodged from this family nucleus and remain under the same roof, she got on with the business of her own life. Already, even as she slept on those Transformers sheets and read those handed-down books and pulled up her brother's corduroy pants and stuffed his too-big sneakers, the idea of eventual escape was lodged in her thoughts, a constantly clarifying notion of what needed doing in order for her to leave. One weekend morning when she was seven or eight and on her second day of a fever, they'd brought her to the Rutland Sports Complex to watch Evan's youth soccer team in its regional tournament. It was early November and already bitterly cold, and she'd been given a thin blanket to hold around her shoulders. She could remember, even today, so many years later, the cold and the yelling, the discomfort, and certainly the outrage of being so thoroughly ignored when she obviously needed attention. Within a few days she was in the pediatric ward of Rutland General with pneumonia, and even then—she had no specific memory of this, but later she would see the photographs of their parents with her hero brother and reconcile the dates with her own hospital records—they had both gone up to Barre for the state championships. That's right: leaving their daughter in the hospital with a plastic tent over her head.

She certainly did have a specific memory of the hospital, and of that plastic tent, so claustrophobic, and of the sharp stick of the IV in her arm, all of it combining to bring her out of the fog of childhood and into a brutal awareness that still defined her, today. It was a feeling of being not *sorry* for herself, exactly, but highly *irritated* by her apparent lot: that of a small, uncomfortable, left-alone, and put-upon girl who was not remotely as important as her brother, and never would be.

From middle school soccer triumphs Evan had sallied forth into high school, where he handily seized the banner of most valuable human male imaginable, unleashing social mayhem according to his whims, which were many. He mouthed off at teachers, openly derided the poor woman who was then the principal (she later left the education sector), and of course tormented any female classmate who wandered into his range of awareness, punishing the pretty ones for being pretty and the unpretty ones for failing to live up to his personal standards. This pastime continued alongside his official gamesmanship in soccer, then baseball and football—even he knew that he wasn't tall enough to excel at basketball—until there was hardly a girl who hadn't been favored with his attentions. Still, girls being girls—as she herself was all too aware—some of them came back for more, again and again: supplicating, self-flagellating, pathetically in search of his approval.

Evan was a heartbreaker, all right. She might have been too young to witness the scorched earth he left behind him in middle school, but she would come to recognize the emotional devastation that trailed him through the halls of West Rutland High. Girls in tears. Girls blaming themselves for his many changes of heart. (What heart?) There were even suicide attempts—two that she was aware of—and one girl left school, for that reason, anyway. Another left school for a different reason.

Evan Parker. Satyr at large. A regular Apollo.

None of it made a dent in their parents' regard. Evan was the light that shone from their little family. Evan was the reason they walked proud in West Rutland, and in Rutland (though there weren't many places you could walk in Rutland; the genius who'd allowed Route 7 to run up the main street had seen to that). Not even the parents of one of those departed girls, family friends for as long as she could remember, succeeded in puncturing the great balloon of their pride, not even when they came to the house one night to confront her then sixteen-year-old brother about his callousness toward their daughter. Their daughter, who had become homebound with depression. Their daughter, who had wanted to go to college, who'd intended to become a nurse, but would now fail to complete her junior year of high school. That evening, they put Evan on the spot, but he quickly rose to the occasion, and she—listening from the top of the stairs, eager for some faint strain of justice at last—heard him denounce the girl as a popular—even at eleven she understood what he meant by "popular"—girl-about-school, and if it was going to become a question of his moral worth, these parents (family friends, remember) had better be ready for *her* moral worth to become a matter of debate.

Their parents showed the bewildered couple out, and Evan went back to his room, stepping over his sister at the top of the stairs as if he were barely aware of her as an object, let alone a person.

Having to be related to him was its own special kind of misery.

What did Evan even want out of life? She had been asking herself this question long before that evening at the top of the stairs. High school was all well and good (if the actual experience of it was well and good and not, say, miserable and debilitating), but high school did not last forever, and then what? You had to go out in the world, make your way, make your living, make some version of connection with others. What did her older brother intend for himself? What, even, did he wish for? What, in the absence of intentions and wishes, did he expect to default to in terms of daily existence, sustenance, diversions? From what she could tell, he had no meaningful relationships at all, not with their parents, whom he openly despised, and not with his social companions, whom he ordered around like a high-stepping backup group. Certainly not for any of those supplicating girls, who were only briefly of interest to him, she believed, when he was on the point of inserting a part of his physical body into a part of theirs. The notion of responsibility troubled him not at all. The notion of purpose never seemed to enter his ken. The notion of a plan or a goal from which to chart a course through his earthly sojourn . . . utterly alien.

And when it came to anything of a literary nature? *Please.*

Never once, never at any point in the time they shared a home, did she see her brother pick up, let alone read, an actual book. *Sports Illustrated*? Perhaps. The *Rutland Herald*? Possibly, at least if there was a write-up of one of his games (or a court report concerning a teammate or acquaintance). But the written word? The written word was for getting through an unavoidable high school test or plagiarizing a paper from some eager female. The written word was for the operating instructions when the new appliance didn't work the way his own superior instincts would seem to indicate it should. She had no idea how he passed most of his classes; probably a combination of charm and appropriation, and it was just possible that he had some small aptitude with numbers. But when had he ever indicated even a grudging respect for the language he spoke? When had he expressed a wish to write that language down, into sentences on a page, for total strangers to one day read, for the purpose of conveying to those total strangers an actual story to elucidate and entertain, or an insight to instruct or inspire? Well, that would be . . . never. As she had once told her late husband—though he might not have taken in the full implications of her narrative, given his sensory and cognitive limitations at the time—she had learned of Evan's alarming literary pretensions on his Facebook page, and a very uncomfortable surprise they had been, too. On Facebook, Evan had smugly announced his acceptance to a program at a Vermont college she herself had never heard of, from which he expected, ultimately, to receive a dubious-sounding degree ("Master of Fine Arts") in . . . if you could believe this . . . *writing*. Her brother, who had certainly declined to write his own assignments in high school and at the community college in Rutland he'd subsequently—if briefly—attended. Her brother, who had never, to her knowledge, made up a story of his own to be conveyed in words of his own, had decided to pursue, in his own words, "*an advanced degree in 'fiction.'*" As in: *fiction that he intended to write.* That certainly did seem out of character. In fact, it sent alarm bells ringing all the way down in Athens, Georgia, where she herself had recently completed a deeply fulfilling year as a college student, a thousand miles from everyone who'd ever claimed to know her.

Now, in her New York apartment, Anna placed the repellent pages facedown on the table, but that did nothing to stall the panic or stop her from reeling backward through the intervening years. Back and back along roads she had no wish to travel, to a destination she'd never stopped leaving, and into that dark house where so many dark things had taken place.

Her year in Athens had been exhilarating but fraught. Never, not for one day of that time, had she stopped expecting someone to come looking for her: a police officer, an administrator of the university (finally wondering why she did not look like every other freshman, or at least, every other homegrown freshman: an effusive and feminine seventeen-year-old readymade for the U. Georgia sororities). She had appealed the freshman year mandate to live on campus and chosen the decidedly down-market Athena Gardens for its general shoddiness and its distance from campus, a far cry from the more expensive complexes with their landscaped pools and tennis courts and clubhouses. Unlike those others, Athena Gardens hadn't featured much interaction among residents; there were no pool parties or barbecue gatherings or regular groups heading over to one of Athens's eighty-odd bars on a Saturday night, or any other night. After a full school year in her little apartment, the only person in the entire complex who called her by name was Bailey, the woman who cleaned the common areas and some of the apartments. And that wasn't really her name.

But she'd been worrying about the wrong people, as it turned out. The Vermont State Police, wondering why Rose Parker had never come home after her mom's tragic accident, or the Georgia state troopers, or one of those helpful people she'd crossed paths with up in Rabun Gap, belatedly suspicious about a tent fire in the middle of the night—not one of those people she'd been keeping an eye out for had ever come looking for her. Instead, it was the only other living member of her immediate family who materialized one winter day on the street outside Athena Gardens. When her eyes met Evan's he was sitting in his old Subaru, and it was hard to say which of them was more stunned. She had been the one to run first, doubling back toward downtown, darting through lots, finally taking refuge in a motel near the veterinary college. She stayed there for days, sneaking back in the middle of the night to see if his car was still there, and trying to figure out if he'd managed to get into her apartment. As far as she could tell, it wasn't and he hadn't, and she knew he couldn't afford to stay in Georgia indefinitely, not with his tavern back in Rutland. But he had seen her. That was undeniable. He knew she was alive. That meant he must know, or at least suspect, that her daughter was not, and that the Rose Parker enrolled at the University of Georgia was not the same Rose Parker who had left Vermont.

From that day on, she began to keep a very close (yet necessarily remote) watch on Evan Parker, and soon enough, an alarming new persona began to appear in his social media: aspiring writer, joiner of fiction-related Facebook groups, attendee of literary events in central Vermont, and ultimately accepted student at Ripley College. She observed him in the photographs of his fellow Ripley students, a smirking figure on a picnic table bench with a thick arm slung across the shoulders of a pretty woman, or seated with others at a long table, trying to look interested in someone else's pages. The whole thing mystified her. In fact, the only thing she understood about Evan's sudden desire to become a writer was that it wasn't benign.

After the in-person portion of his Ripley course was over, his new persona didn't end; it only deepened. Somebody formed the public Facebook group (Writers of Ripley), and her brother joined right away, though on the whole he kept pretty quiet in the forum, giving no indication that Ripley had inspired or encouraged him, or done anything at all to confirm his dubious "calling." Occasionally he would like some other student's announcement of a completed story or an agent submission that didn't result in outright rejection, but he never posted any news of his own.

Then, only weeks before her own fall term at the University of Georgia, something did succeed in making her alarmed. Very alarmed.

"Does anybody have any advice for me about writer's block?" Some pathetic whiner had written that to the rest of the group. "Some days I sit down and absolutely nothing comes. All suggestions welcome, but no aromatherapy please! I'm sensitive to smells."

And there, mixed in with the usual folderol about meditation and morning runs and timed writing and green tea, was this priceless nugget from that apparent creative sage, Evan Parker:

"I haven't really had that much of a problem. My novel is really coming along. In fact, I kind of wonder if writer's block even exists, if you want to know the truth. Do we need to invent some disease to cover for the fact that the work isn't going well? Just my opinion."

Just my opinion. Like his opinion counted for anything at all.

But it was "my novel" that left the worst taste in her mouth. It implied that Evan himself—this nonbeliever in writer's block, let alone its various cures—was blithely filling page after page up there in West Rutland, Vermont, somehow finding time between that tavern he ran and those NA meetings he presumably still went to, if his annual declarations of continued sobriety were to be believed. Was her brother, in fact, actively fulfilling that bullshit credo on the Ripley MFA website, about how *every single person had a unique voice and a story nobody else could tell*? Had he really drunk that particular Kool-Aid? Meaning . . . that he actually was doing the bona fide work of writing? And if so, just what had so inspired him to sit his ass down and get those actual words onto that actual page? Was it possible that his new-found work ethic, and his ability to transcend writer's block, might somehow result in a completed and indeed publishable . . . *book*? And more disturbing even than that, was there any chance, any chance at all, that the life-changing inspiration that had sent him to Ripley and was keeping him productive and inspired up there in West Rutland, Vermont, had something, had anything at all, to do with *her*?

Surely not. Surely, for all that was righteous, not. And yet. She couldn't take the chance of it. She needed to see—or better still, *not* see—for herself.

She bought a car and drove north, retracing her steps of a year before (though giving Rabun Gap, in the north of the state, a wide berth), her destination that home she'd hoped never to see again. Her purpose was to discover once and for all what her brother knew, or what he believed he knew, and what he still did not know about her life. It took her two and a half days, because she kept off 95 and the Thruway, where there were so many cameras. Maybe that was overly cautious, but you never got into trouble by being *overly* cautious.

This time, she had been the one waiting outside his—or, more accurately, *their*—home in West Rutland, the car tucked into a little grove of maples off an old logging road not far away. When he left for the bar that first evening, she let herself in by the always open back door, and it took no time at all to get the full impact of what he'd been up to. There, on that desk in her own bedroom (had he chosen it for "inspiration"?) was the first (but not the last!) act of literary thievery to be committed against her: eighteen chapters printed in standard twelve point Times New Roman, in responsibly double-spaced lines on good-quality paper, stacked neatly beside his (unfortunately password protected) laptop. Earlier drafts were sorted into files of different colors, their dates of completion written on the front. Notes were in an accordion file, with sections labeled DIANNA MEMORIES, ROSE MEMORIES, and—alarmingly—PSYCH NOTES.

It was quite a story, Evan's story. Her story, more accurately, since it was her own life, but reduced, sliced up, and then mutilated into a shlock-horror B movie starring herself as the vixen man-eater, destroyer of promising young lives, and psychopathic teen mom of that angelic—yet spunky!—and certainly tragic heroine, Rose Parker: her own victim and sacrificial lamb.

She sat reading it for hours, using a small flashlight so no one driving past would notice a light on in the house, alternately amazed at what Evan had done and vibrating in outrage that he had done it.

It was unforgivable. There was no mitigation. Also, there was no possible way back from this, or forward with this. There was only the indestructible wall of his transgression, and he knew it was a transgression, because he knew her—better than he deserved to know her, certainly, and better than she would have wished him to know her, and, unfortunately, more accurately than any other person on the planet. He knew what she had endured, because he was the one who'd forced her to endure it. Now, and entirely because of his actions, they had come to this, and if he suffered because of it . . . well, as with so many other unpleasant things that might have been avoided, that was a shame. This time, however, it wouldn't be her doing the suffering. This time, the punishment for his bad acts would fall where it belonged.

Obliteration—that was the only option.

Later, in her makeshift camp in the woods behind the house, she seethed. She knew better than to act on impulse.

This was too important, and too dangerous, for her not to be deliberate, careful, and thorough. The spot she'd chosen was one she'd known all her life on the far side of the brook, and from there she had a clear view of her brother's after-work routine. First, Evan went to the kitchen and used the electric kettle to make coffee in a French press. Then he sat at the kitchen table, drinking a first mug, and looking at his phone. After half an hour or so, he took the mug and the rest of the French press down the hall to her own former bedroom and sat working at her former desk, in the very chair she had recently vacated, in that very room where she had once responsibly done her homework and dreamed of escaping them all. He worked with admirable tenacity, for hours, until nearly five in the morning, before turning out her old desk light and going upstairs. There, to her surprise, he did not even enter his own childhood bedroom, which faced the back, and that could only mean he had moved into the room across the hall, the one that had once belonged to their parents. She imagined him climbing into the big rope bed their great-great-grandparents—family legend—had hauled to Vermont when they migrated up the country from New Bedford in the 1850s, and in that awful bed he slept (presumably) untroubled, even virtuous sleep. The bastard.

The next day, after he'd left for work, she had returned to the house and begun an exhaustive examination of every fetid corner, excavating each mold-infested box in the basement, reading every scrap of paper that might contain even a single highly self-indulgent sentence of his great magnum opus. She carefully noted the presence of every trace of this "novel," each scrap and draft and Post-it note containing some not-to-be-forgotten plot point or character description, making a room-by-room inventory. Upstairs, she confirmed that he had taken their parents' bedroom for his own, and she looked care-fully through his mounds of discarded clothing and stacks of books (books! It was still a shock to see them): *Bird by Bird, Writing Down the Bones, On Writing, Still Writing, On Moral Fiction* (ha!), and the inevitable *Literary Market Place*. He had a habit, apparently, of bringing his most recent pages upstairs with him at the end of his writing nights and correcting them in bed when he woke up the next day. A dozen of them were on the floor, next to a pair of his discarded boxers. Vile. She didn't touch them. She didn't touch anything.

In the bathroom, she found his drugs. Of course she did. Of course Evan Parker was still using drugs, despite the epic virtue signaling on his Facebook page, the humble brag on each sup-posed sobriety anniversary, the gratitude he expressed to his anonymous fellow travelers. Evan proved to be in possession of a robust pharmacopeia, including a white plastic jar of a hundred 5 milligram diazepam tablets and numerous prescrip-tion bottles containing a hundred 10 milligram OxyContin tablets. Enough to induce opioid addiction in an entire Sackler-sponsored football team. More than enough for her own far less ambitious purposes.

She took a handful of the yellow diazepam tablets and removed one white OxyContin tablet from each of the pre-scription bottles, twelve in all.

Before she left on that second day she also went through her own left-behind belongings from the year before, any-thing that might include her likeness, medical records, official documents, random photographs. Also anything connected to Rose. She was reassured to find nothing. She had known what she was doing, back then, despite the stress she'd been under. She had known that neither mother nor daughter would be coming back—one because she was going to be dead, the other because she was going to be careful. She was still being careful.

Again, that night, she watched him perform his routine, from the kitchen to his "work room" to their parents' bedroom upstairs. Those were unpleasant hours in the woods on the other side of the brook, spent in near-constant rain. In the morning, while he was still sleeping his oblivious sleep, she returned to her car and drove west, across the state line to a Tractor Supply in Glens Falls, where she bought a box of the 35 cc livestock syringes and large-gauge needles. (She also bought, in case anyone asked about the needles at checkout, a bottle of injectable B12 for "sheep, swine and cattle," a designation that was absolutely one-third accurate, but in fact the teenager at the counter could not have been less interested.)

At a dollar store, she picked up a couple of small mason jars and a box of latex gloves, some rubber tubing, a fine-mesh kitchen strainer, and a few granola bars that promised High Energy. She was going to need High Energy for what lay ahead.

Then she went north to Lake George and found a motel, where she passed out on the lumpy bed for hours. When she woke up, she used a smooth stone from the motel parking lot to crush Evan's diazepam tablets on the bathroom countertop, sweeping the powder into one of the mason jars with some water from the tap and giving it a good shake. She repeated the process with all twelve of her brother's Oxy tablets, taking the extra step of running the cloudy liquid through the kitchen strainer to remove anything big enough to obstruct the needle. Then she drew the liquid into one of the syringes, filling it up. She didn't know how much of the drug her brother was taking on a normal day, but if one 35 cc syringe of dissolved drug turned out not to be enough, she'd have at least a second syringe worth of liquid in the mason jar for a second shot. She only hoped it would be fast, too, because she'd have a long drive ahead of her when it was over.

Then she'd taken a long and much needed bath, staying in until the water was cold. She was running through it, again and again. She was trying to think of everything she still needed to know and prepare for.

It served her, she supposed, that brother was, like so many writers, a creature of habits, rituals, repeated soundtracks and favorite aromas: in a word, *process*. On both the nights she'd watched him, he had entered by the kitchen door, made his pot of coffee, and drunk a first mug as he looked at his phone. This, apparently, was his transitional time, the liminal space between her brother's life as a social bar owner and that other version of himself, one that had somehow produced hundreds of manuscript pages. The act of disabling him leaned heavily on that assumption of routine, because her brother, for all his moral dissipation, was still far stronger than her, physically, and possibly very motivated to cause her harm. (It was lucky for her that his ongoing drug use had seeded his own incapacity. In fact, it might have been the first time in either of their lives that she felt actual gratitude toward Evan Parker.)

Late in the afternoon, she drove back, hid her car, and did a sweep of the campsite to make sure she hadn't left anything behind, then she donned some latex gloves, entered the house, and added the dissolved diazepam to the water in the electric kettle. After that, there wasn't anything more she could do; though it was highly tempting to make a start on the many tasks she faced before she'd be leaving this place, she couldn't take the chance of alerting him to the fact that someone had been, and possibly still was, in the house. With hours to go, she waited for him in her daughter's bedroom across the hall from the "writing room," passing the evening in an ongoing effort to still her mind. At last, through the crack of the door, she heard the sounds she'd been expecting: his car's arrival, the kitchen door, the click of the electric kettle's on switch. Their mother's avocado-colored refrigerator door made its familiar creak as it was opened. A mug hit the counter-top. Then came the distinctive rumble of boiling water, and the sound of pouring. There was an accompanying smell of coffee, too—something she'd missed from her perch in the woods, and the radio was turned on—another part of the ritual she'd missed. Nineties rock. Of course. Then nothing: he might have taken his coffee to the kitchen table, or not. He might be drinking that first cup, or not. He might be slipping into darkness, but perhaps not. Perhaps he was wide awake, thoroughly unaffected by that extra ingredient in his coffee. Perhaps he was drinking it at the kitchen table, just as he did every night, looking at his phone, preparing to distort Dianna and Rose Parker into fictional immortality for the ultimate glory of himself. What did the absence of unexpected sounds signify? That she had misjudged the amount of diazepam a chronic consumer of opiates required to become docile if not unconscious? That the drug had altered the taste of his coffee, alerting him to the fact that all was not normal—let alone well—in his world, and preventing him from consuming enough? Could Evan know, in fact, that his sister, his *literary inspiration*, was actually here in the house, committing or attempting to commit some outrage against him? She couldn't hear. She couldn't tell. She didn't know.

Then, from the kitchen: a groan. Deep and animal, a sound she had never heard him make, not once in her life. Evan, the star of their family. Evan, the football hero. Evan, the thief of the only thing she felt entitled to, which was her own story . . . had made a sound from a horror movie soundtrack, loud enough to penetrate the walls.

She stepped out into the hall and walked toward the fluorescent light of the kitchen.

Her brother was slumped over the table, reaching for his phone. He had knocked over the mug, spilling coffee, making a mess. She put the phone in her coat pocket.

"Hello, Evan," she said, taking the seat opposite.

He managed to pick up his head, but she wasn't sure he was registering who she was. He needed a shave. That was good. It made him look more like the drug addict he was.

Another groan, but thinner, softer.

"I thought I'd come find out what you were up to. And wow: you've been productive. Three hundred pages, nearly!"

He tried to say something. His mouth was moving, anyway.

"So not cool," she told him. "And can I just point out how selfish you are? I mean, I gave you the house. I walked out and left it all to you. Some people are never satisfied. But you had to come looking for me. Well, looking for Rose. Same thing, isn't it?"

He was trying to speak. She could see that. She had never in her entire life been less interested in what someone had to say.

"What did you want to see her about, anyway? I'm assuming it wasn't personal concern for her well-being. You were never much in the family love department, were you? Was it money? Maybe the bar was tanking and there wasn't anything of Mom and Dad's left for you to sell? Were you thinking of putting the house on the market? Splitting the proceeds with Rose? You'd need her signature for that. Even you must have known that. She wouldn't have put up with your bullshit. The way I did."

This time he could barely manage to open his eyes.

"Anyway, I have a better idea. Much simpler. Also, much more just."

He did not favor her with a response, but it seemed advisable to get him moving. Watching him, these past days, she had seen the beginnings of his middle age, the flash of scalp through that legendary hair as he made his coffee, the hint of a jowl, even far away and through a window. More relevant to the present circumstances, however, was a certain thickening to Evan's trunk. He was a good thirty pounds heavier than his football weight. Her irresistible brother had become a nearing-forty bar owner who lived alone in his parents' house, pretending to be sober as he mined the only vein of real worth available to him, which was herself. How he must be raging against the loss of his looks, she thought. Maybe that had been another thing attracting him to the literary life: nobody cared what a writer looked like.

"Let's get you upstairs," she told him. "I'll be honest, you look like you've put on some weight. I'm not sure I'm up to hauling you around."

But she was motivated. She wedged herself into his fetid armpit and hoisted him up, lurching them both across the kitchen. It was uncomfortable as well as malodorous.

At the foot of the staircase, he took a swing at her, but it came with such a loud grunt that she had plenty of time to duck. Unfortunately, it also took him down, meaning that she had the additional task of getting him up. That was a pain in her neck, literally.

"Don't do that again, asshole," she said. Then, fueled by rage, she hauled him up to the second floor and down the hall to their parents' bedroom: the source of all her misfortune and the place where, in clear-eyed retrospect, she had truly become her authentic self. It hardly surprised her that Evan, when he returned to live in the house, had taken this bedroom for his own. It was, by far, the biggest in the house, just as large as the long parlor on the floor beneath it: the obvious place for a returning heir. And this was not even to speak of its massive ancestral bed or the adjacent bathroom outfitted with marble from the family quarry! Still, when she'd been the one living here as an adult, she had never once considered exchanging her own small bedroom downstairs for this one. (Nor, for that matter, had Rose, though she must have been tempted. The size and private bathroom? The distance from Mom? It was almost as if she sensed the wrongness of this place and its direct significance to herself.) In fact, she had never come into her parents' room at all, not unless she had to. Tonight, she had to.

With the end of her strength, she pushed her brother onto the bed. He made a risible effort to kick her away, but she hooked her arm under his helpfully extended leg and hoisted him up. She had the syringe ready in a coat pocket along with the rubber tubing, but when she took them out he came alive again, swinging his meaty fists at her head. They were easily parried, and the accompanying curses similarly failed to land, but she decided to wait until he was a bit further gone. This next part, after all, was the critical bit, and she wasn't exactly at home with a syringe. She had neither the wish nor the physical ability to fight a two-hundred-pound former athlete, even if he had gone to seed. He was going to have to hold still for her.

"Do you even know why I'm here?" she asked him, as much to pass the time as to have her entirely reasonable question answered. Her voice, to her own great surprise, sounded perfectly normal.

Evan, of course, did not respond, and in that vacuum a truly eloquent summation, worthy of Daniel Webster, began to assemble itself inside her. She was here because Evan was a terrible person. She was here because he had always been a terrible person, though she'd done him the great favor of never having said so, at least not to his face. Every shitty thing, from the ordinary childhood snubs to the violent derailment of her life when she was in tenth grade to this current bullshit with the "novel"—she'd never understood why any of it was necessary. All she had ever wanted was to leave, to never see him again, to never ask a thing of him, but he just couldn't let her alone. The prospect of his own sick fun at the expense of his weird little sister had been too compelling to resist. And had it really been that satisfying to him? Apparently, it had. And did that make him, truly, far more of a monster than anyone could justly call *her*? The answer, to her at least, was clear.

The two of them, she wanted to say, were hardly unique; the world was full of siblings who loathed one another, but they did none of the things Evan had felt it necessary to do. They simply left one another alone to get on with things, to live fruitful, autonomous, *separate* lives, perhaps offering a stiff embrace at the family reunion or a highly impersonal card at Christmas. She'd have been up for that. She had offered Evan that very exit ramp. But he? He'd just kept coming back. He'd just kept taking, insinuating himself, inflicting harm. Worst of all, the more harm he caused, the more his resentment seemed to actually grow, until here they were, with the proof of his utter and comprehensive appropriation neatly stacked in her own bedroom downstairs. No, it hadn't been enough to deprive her of her dignity, to cause her physical pain while he smirked and laughed. It hadn't been enough to brutally upend her life, to strip her of that same self-command he'd claimed so greedily for himself. He wanted nothing less, apparently, than the complete and appalling appropriation of the life she was entitled to. *Her own life.* For *his* glorification and enrichment.

And if he thought she was going to simply let him do it, he didn't know her at all. Obviously.

But alas, she never managed to get any of that out. It died in her throat as she glared down at him in utter disgust, and there it remained, roiling and sputtering. The gaze he returned was hazy at best.

In the end, and at the last possible moment, she asked him only one question. It was the only question she truly did want an answer to.

Leaning over his pillow, her mouth very close to his once handsome face, she asked it:

"Just for the record, and just because we're here, was it all your idea? Or something the two of you cooked up together? And also, I've always wondered. Did you watch?"

He failed to respond in any meaningful way. Of course he did. Maybe he was giving up, the thought of which was profoundly satisfying. His eyes were closing and staying closed. She had waited too long. Then again, maybe she had waited too long on purpose. Maybe she didn't want to know, after all.

"Well, never mind," she said, almost soothingly.

She took the rubber tubing from her pocket, rolled up the left sleeve of his flannel shirt, and tied off his arm above the elbow. Everyone knew how to do that, and the vein, obligingly, popped out. Then she took the syringe from her pocket. His eyes were barely open, but he tried, halfheartedly, to move away from her. That didn't work, of course. He flinched when the needle went into the vein, which was admirably healthy, and even for a first-timer like herself, easy to navigate. Immediately his breathing slowed, and he stayed that way, deeply underground and undeservedly at peace. She sat watching him for nearly half an hour, but nothing changed. She wasn't going to leave him like that, not after all she'd put herself through, so she withdrew the syringe and filled it again from the mason jar, then slid the needle back into his vein. Then, immediately, there was a change, each new breath both fractured and shallow. Even so, it took another twenty-five minutes for him to stop breathing entirely.

This was a fitting place for him to go: on this bed of horrors, in this detestable room. It was a righteous place. It satisfied her.

She left his phone on the bedside table with a few of the pill bottles from his bathroom stash, the needle in his arm, a hastily loosened tourniquet just above it. In all: a perfect over-dose tableau.

Then she got out the inventory she had made and tried not to rush as she went from room to room, filling a heavy-duty contractor trash bag with the items she'd earmarked. Most important of these, of course, was every trace of the manu-script: his laptop, those color-coded drafts (including the neat stack of pages he'd so professionally—and optimistically—marked "working"). Also the thumb drives, old floppy disks (she had no idea what was on them, but she wasn't taking any chances), the inspirational books on writing and the *Literary Market Place* and the legal pads filled with his slanted scrawl. And the laptop itself. She doubted she'd ever be able to get into it without help, and that was help she wouldn't be asking for. She'd find another way to dispose of it.

In the end, she would remove every last speck of written language that even suggested her brother was a writer, or was working toward being a writer, or maintained some vague fantasy about one day becoming a writer. She left behind only one pathetic effort she'd found deep in a drawer, about a hero defensive tackle who scores a winning touchdown at the big homecoming game. Right. So even if someone ever wanted to make the point that Evan Parker entertained a pipe dream about his glamorous life as a published author, this little sample remained to demonstrate how delusional that dream actually was, and how far he himself was from anything you might call . . . *talented.*

In the kitchen, she cleaned up the spilled coffee from the kitchen table and added the French press and the electric kettle to her contractor bag, along with Evan's final mug and the two mason jars. Then, after some hesitation, she took down her mother's book of recipes from a shelf beside the avocado-colored stove. She wasn't much of a cook, really, but there were a few things in there she'd always enjoyed. A meat loaf covered in mashed potatoes, and a casserole with lentils and chicken. Also a bright green soup her mother liked to make to use up the winter kale. That was tasty. (It froze well, too, if she remembered correctly.)

And then she left that house for what she fervently hoped would be the last time in her life, driving west, then south-west, then south, following, unwittingly, a part of the route Jacob Finch Bonner would one day assign to "her" character in *Crib.* All along the way she got rid of the contents of that bulging trash bag: the books on writing, the French press and kettle. The manuscript pages she burned in the fireplace of a cabin she rented in western Pennsylvania. Vividly, she remembered dispatching it, page by noxious and offensive page: one working copy of the opus on heavy white bond— so pretentious—and two photocopies of the same, as well as a separate file containing various excerpts and outtakes. And, in an act of appropriately foul finality, her brother's laptop went into an especially filthy Porta Potty near a buffet restaurant in Virginia, not far from the convergence of two major highways.

And that was the end of Evan Parker's never-to-be-seen debut novel, three hundred pages of lies and libel in the grand tradition of literary thievery. Done!

It was also the official termination of her family of origin, well past its time and not a moment too soon, in her honest opinion. She was, at long last and without question: alone in the world, which was all she had ever wanted to be. Some things were worth waiting for, not that she'd had much of a choice.

Of course, there'd always been a chance that Evan had shared an excerpt of his novel-in-progress with classmates while at Ripley—she knew that usually happened in workshops, she wasn't an idiot—but none of the drafts she'd examined in West Rutland showed evidence of a reader's suggestions or edits, nor were there any letters about the book from someone who'd read it, creative pep talks from fellow aspiring writers he'd met at Ripley, let alone one of their teachers, and nothing at all from an editor or agent he'd gone so far as to submit his opus to. Even so, she had continued to watch the Writers of Ripley Facebook group carefully, and not one of the others had mentioned Evan's novel with any hint of familiarity, not even in that period just after his death became known, when there was the expected jockeying for the position of most-intimate-friend among his fellow writers. Then, a few years later, when a novel with a plot so strikingly similar to her brother's was published and became a massive international bestseller, not one of those Ripley colleagues had made so much as a peep. That was her final reassurance that Evan had been going it alone, declining the groupthink and the camaraderie that Ripley and the rest of the writing world seemed to adhere to. He hadn't shared the novel he was writing. She'd been sure of it.

Now she was far less sure.

This morning, here in Anna's own home, these actual pages were in her actual hands—they could not be argued with. They were tactile. They were inscribed with language. They were also potentially limitless, in that whoever had sent them might already have copied them, any number of times, and sent them to any number of people: a horrifying notion. She could not and would not do what her late husband had done when faced with a similar threat, namely shove her head into the sand and hope that it would all, somehow, cease to exist. It would not cease to exist. This person or persons, whoever they were, meant business, and it was Anna's burden, now, to discover the nature of that business and shut it down: decisively, permanently, and, if necessary, with the kind of extreme prejudice she had become pretty well known for, if only to herself.

11

Son

Once a month, she met her former in-laws, Jake's parents, for brunch somewhere in Manhattan. She let Jake's mother, Louise, pick the place because Louise was a self-proclaimed foodie, and the city made a nice change for her when it came to dining out. Of the two of them Louise wore her grief more obviously, but she was strong; her husband, Frank, on the other hand, never mentioned Jake, but it was clear to Anna that he was destroyed.

She liked them both, or at least there was no reason not to like them, apart from the fact that they had created Jake in the first place. Given the delicacy of their circumstances, it just made sense to keep them close, or at least as close as she could bear.

Their appointed Sunday rolled around less than a week after the arrival of the manuscript pages, and Anna wasn't in much of a mood to see anyone, let alone the two of them. But she couldn't cancel. She wanted no scrutiny, or no more than she typically got from them. This appointment would be managed as efficiently as the ones before it. There was no alternative.

Louise's choice that month was a new place down in the South Street Seaport she had read about in some newsletter for people like herself, and it had taken a few weeks to get a Sunday reservation.

Anna came up from the subway at Fulton Street and looked around, disoriented by the asymmetrical intersections. Eventually she took out her phone and let Google Maps guide her east, into an earlier Manhattan. As she caught sight of the East River a gust of wind came hurtling past the tall ship anchored there and into her face; when it passed, and she opened her eyes again, Anna was mildly surprised to see that the cobblestoned streets were full of people who did not look like the tourists she'd been expecting. They were walking dogs and holding children by the hand. They looked like they might actually live here.

She found the restaurant on a narrow lane, tucked between a wine store and an ice cream place with an unpronounceable Nordic name. Her in-laws were at a prime table in front of one of the windows. Anna put on a big smile for them.

"Hello!" She shed her coat as she went in and gave Frank a squeeze around his meaty shoulders. She gave Louise a kiss on the cheek offered to her.

"You look a little pale," her mother-in-law observed.

"I've just walked through a wind tunnel."

"Oh, I know. Bracing, isn't it? I haven't been down here since the '80s. I think the old fish market was still open. We came with Jake once, to the seaport museum."

It was hard-won, this nonchalant mention of her son, Anna knew.

"There was a shopping mall. Just tourist stuff. It's changed so much."

"We went into that Tin Building," said Frank. "A hundred dollars for a little cup of olive oil! They must have read poetry to each individual olive. And dogs everywhere!"

"Obviously they want us all to think we're in Europe," his wife said. "Sure, bring your dog into a restaurant. We're too hip to worry about hygiene."

Anna liked them best this way: focused on others, casting derision around. It kept the three of them away from more dangerous topics.

They ordered from a menu suggestive of nineteenth-century New England: cod and herring, potatoes and swedes, dark brown bread with salted butter. "Just like a meal in Historic Deerfield," said Frank when the waiter left.

"I think it's adventurous," said Anna. "When I was growing up in Idaho, I used to read about this kind of food."

"Well, good," said Louise. She herself had grown up on Long Island, just a few towns from where she'd raised Jake and where she still lived and worked as a high school guidance counselor. "The article I read said this whole neighborhood is now a food Mecca. I wish they'd stop calling things a this-Mecca or a that-Mecca. I'm sure that's offensive to Muslims."

Anna and her father-in-law exchanged a glance.

"I suppose you're right," said Anna. "What have you two been up to?"

They had been up to missing their son, she knew perfectly well, but each of them found things to talk about instead. Frank, who had finally retired as a tax attorney, had enrolled in some American history classes at Hofstra and taken up, of all things, upholstery. He seemed stable enough. Louise was still in the trenches at her large public high school, where things were getting crazier every year. Four hundred in each class, nearly half of them applying to Ivy League colleges.

"My nights are completely taken up by the parents," she complained as the waiter poured wine into her glass. "They have no problem phoning me, even after ten. Why did I tell Madison she couldn't get into Cornell? Why am I not calling my personal contacts at the Penn admissions office to tell them Jimmy's a National Merit semifinalist?"

"Do you have personal contacts at Penn?" Anna asked. "I mean, is that how it works?"

"No, that is emphatically *not* how it works. But the parents aren't thinking about how it works. They're thinking about their own kid. And the people reading their kid's application don't need me to tell them he's a National Merit semifinalist. It gets reported to them. It's right there on the application. In fact, it's right there on the applications of most of their applicant pool." She sighed. "Let's not talk about it. How are you doing?"

Anna took a breath. It was hard, sometimes, to hit exactly the right note with these two. She knew when Louise asked her something open-ended like this that what they actually wanted to know was something else: Was she moving on from Jake? Specifically, was she seeing anyone who might, one day, occupy the role in her life that Jake had occupied? She had it fully in her power to set their minds at rest on this score (the truth being that no one would ever, for very good reason, occupy the place in her life that Jake had occupied), but it was all so much more complex than that. They wanted her to live her life, but of course they had only the most remote grasp of what her life actually was. They wanted her to be "happy," but they also feared the prospect of her "happiness," because of how it would put their own eternally lost happiness in such bold relief.

"Fine," she said, relieving them. "I mean, you know, the same. I'm getting through. Not too much travel this month, but I'm back on the road soon, and then there's a lot around the paperback. Also, I might go to Europe. I mean, Germany wants me to come for the publication there, and the UK."

"It's so fantastic," Louise said. "We're so thrilled for you, Anna."

"I think Jake went to London when his book came out there," said Frank.

"Yes," Anna confirmed. "He did. There was some epic mix-up with the hotel." She had made up this part, a fictional flourish.

"Right," said Louise. "I remember that."

"They want me to come over for some festival in the west, near Wales. It's all in tents in the middle of a field or something, but thousands of people come to it."

"That's so exciting," said her father-in-law. "You worked hard for this."

Had she? She knew a few writers who might disagree with him.

Their food came on earthenware plates. Anna picked up her fork, a dull metal, like pewter, and regarded her slab of cod and three ancient-looking root vegetables of indeterminate species. It was only once a month, this ordeal. It might all be worse.

"Listen," said Louise, "there's something we need to talk to you about."

Suddenly they were looking at her grimly from across the table, as if she were about to be fired.

"What's happened?" she said. "Has something happened?"

"We didn't want to upset you," said Louise, infuriatingly.

And yet here you are upsetting me, right now, Anna thought.

"I don't think it's anything to worry about," Frank said, with an emphasis on the "I."

"Oh, no," said Louise. "I mean, not *worry*."

"Some weirdo sent us a manuscript," said Frank. "I mean, it was sent to Jake, but at our address. No return address, of course. What's he going to write? 'I'm a creep from Vermont and I just felt like tormenting you about your famous novelist son'? I thought . . . well, I assumed at first that this person didn't know Jake had passed. You know, they got hold of our address somewhere and wanted to send him their fan fiction. I

126

thought I should look at it before I wrote back, and that's when I got a bit weirded out."

She was concentrating on her own tone of voice now, trying to get the shake out of it.

"Okay," she said carefully. "Fan fiction?"

They looked at each other.

"Well . . . maybe," Louise said. "Maybe that's all it is," she told her husband.

"No," he said shortly. "More than that."

More than what? Anna thought, wishing he'd get to the point.

"I don't understand," she said, running out of patience. "Is it similar to *Crib*? Or what?"

"Yes and no," her mother-in-law said, maddeningly. "This excerpt doesn't have a mother murdering her daughter, but these characters . . . you know that's where they're going. They're the same people, in the same old house. It was like he, or . . . I guess maybe she, appropriated the people Jake wrote about and tweaked them a little bit. Here the mom's named Diandra, and her little girl is Ruby."

Ruby and Diandra. The names sent the deepest chill through her. So like Evan to pick those taunting names. Samantha and Maria, Jake's character names for *Crib,* had been comfortingly random, because Jake had had no conception that there was a "real" Samantha and a "real" Maria out there. Ruby and Diandra, though, were just close enough to their real-life counterparts that they might as well have had a *fuck you* attached, just for her, just for the day the author's sister might catch wind of his great creative project and—presumably—race for the nearest book-store to contribute to his sales figures and net worth. As if!

"But it's her parents she murders, not her daughter. In this version," Louise explained, unnecessarily.

"A variation on a theme," said Frank, trying for levity.

"First I just thought: here's somebody trying to write like Jake," Louise said. She was moving something around on her own plate as she said it. Something that looked like succotash. Watching her, Anna lost whatever small appetite she'd had. "Not so much the style. I'd say the style was kind of . . . not very ornamented. Just the plain prose, just sentences doing what they needed to do, to convey the information. Not like Jake's. Jake's was so . . ." She petered out. Maybe she was waiting for Anna to fill in the adjective. So what? So beautiful? So uplifting? So superior in every way? She couldn't bring herself to do it.

"In our opinion," said Frank, "this isn't plagiarism. But it feels related. Of course, we're not writers. We wouldn't know where the line is. But it made us uncomfortable."

I can certainly understand that, Anna thought, staring down at her plate.

"It made me wonder," said Frank. "You know, what is this? Is it some kind of a tribute? Is this person trying to say that Jake inspired them to write? Because there's nothing wrong with that."

"Wishful thinking," said Louise, morosely. "There's a message on the last page, from whoever sent this. Or a comment. But it doesn't feel laudatory."

"What do you mean, 'a message'?"

"Something about how it's a little too close for comfort."

It hit her like a truck. "Oh my God."

Someone said it, and Anna was surprised to discover that the someone was herself. None of them were eating now, Anna noticed. Not even Louise, the foodie.

"Like I said: not laudatory. But maybe I'm too sensitive on this topic, after that awful business with Jake."

Anna wouldn't have said she was too sensitive. Louise was appropriately sensitive. Jake's parents knew all about their son's anonymous correspondent. At least, they knew what she had chosen to tell them.

"It's horrible," she told them now. "Putting you through something like this."

Frank sighed. "It's not pleasant. I agree. Just a nasty tone. Not much in the way of details, though."

"But why send this to you?" Anna said. "I mean, if he—if the writer—has something to—if there's some kind of accusation here—"

"*What kind of accusation?*" Louise cried, and Anna saw that she was suddenly, alarmingly, at her breaking point. Or past that point. "Jake was an artist. He wrote a work of fiction. I'm sure it had similarities to other books. I'm sure there've been books published since *Crib* with similarities to his work. So what? It's called a literary tradition."

She'd been listening to her son for far too long.

"Well, yes," she said, "but if there was some kind of grievance, no matter how misguided, why complain to you? Why not . . . his agent or his publisher? Or his executor?"

But perhaps because they'd already been in touch with the executor, it occurred to her. Weeks ago. Because the executor was herself, and the executor had failed to respond. This was an escalation.

Frank shrugged. "I don't know, but also, I don't really think this is about us. I'm not even sure it's about Jake. Basically, I'm mystified."

"And upset," his wife added, unnecessarily.

"I'm so sorry," Anna told them, though "sorry" was far from the top of her list just now.

"So . . . what do you want me to do? Read this? And . . . what?"

"Honestly," said her mother-in-law, "I'm not sure. It's not as if I had something specific in mind. I just knew that however bad it was going to be to tell you, it was going to be worse not to tell you."

After a minute, Frank spoke. "You know, Anna, the world is full of people who are nasty enough to do something like this, even to the point of writing pages of prose just to send them to a couple of bereaved parents, but they're not quite nasty enough to take it further than that. I don't think there's any actual danger here."

Oh, don't you, Anna thought. *I wish I agreed with you.*

"I just think, you know, 'attention should be paid.'"

It's attention must *be paid*, she nearly said. Luckily, a waiter interrupted.

"Everything okay here?" he said, looking unhappily down at their full plates.

"Oh, it's delicious," Louise said.

"We're just in the middle of something," Frank said.

Anna merely looked at the guy and thought: *go away.*

He went away.

"Okay," she said. "So . . . not something for a lawyer, then. Or, I don't know, a police officer?"

"Oh, I wouldn't think so," said Frank.

"Perhaps Jake's agent?" said her mother-in-law.

My agent, Anna thought.

"Maybe," she said. "But I should read it first."

"Yes, if you want to. But, honestly, you might spare yourself." He gave a forced laugh. "In addition to anything else, as I said, it isn't very strong."

You sound like your son, Anna thought, unkindly.

"Like something one of his students might write," Louise added, and that was truer than she knew.

Which reminded her.

"You said Vermont before. What made you think the writer was from Vermont?" She paused before asking, because it was too much to hope for: "Was there a return address?"

"No." Frank was making, at last, an effort to eat one of his potatoes. "But a postmark. From St. Johnsbury. I know that isn't far from the place Jake taught. What was it?" He turned to his wife, not to his son's wife.

"Ripley College."

Fucking Ripley College, Anna amended, but silently.

"Just give it to her," said Louise to her husband. "I hate the idea of burdening Anna, but I don't hate having it out of our house, and that's the truth. It's like a monkey's paw. It gives me the creeps."

Frank sighed. He removed one side of his winter coat from the back of his chair. The pages, folded in half, were in an inside pocket. About six or eight of them, fastened with a staple in the upper left corner.

"No envelope?"

He shrugged. "I must have misplaced it. But as I said, no return address. I happened to remember the postmark. There wasn't any cover letter or anything like that."

"Did you ever go up there with him?" Louise said. She was losing the thread, evidently. Certainly, she had lost the chronology.

"I met him after," Anna said shortly. "A few years after."

"Right. But I mean, did he ever take you up there, to show you where he'd taught?"

"No. I don't think he was sentimental about the place. It was a survival job, and the students were . . . I mean, they weren't all that gifted, you know?"

"Is that so?" said Frank. He had stopped even trying to eat his food. "He never said."

He wouldn't have, Anna thought. What's worse than explaining you've failed at the only thing you ever tried to be, and now you have to teach other people how to become that thing you couldn't become, only to realize that your students are talentless shits like Evan Parker?

"But *he* was gifted," said Louise. "I mean, as a teacher. So he helped them, even if they weren't . . . if they didn't have all that much in the way of talent. I think of him as talented that way, too."

And you're certainly welcome to that fantasy, Anna thought.

She said: "Yes, of course he was gifted as a teacher. But it didn't hold a candle to how gifted he was as a writer." She was irritated now. She was finding, as always, that it was more than a little annoying to talk about Jake. Still, talking about Jake was what she was here to do, and what this monthly ritual had always been about: to keep them close, to learn right away if they were changing toward her, if they had learned some surprising thing that might have altered their view of their cherished son's cherished wife. Anna was more than ready to stop lamenting about Jake now; she also wanted to stop talking about Ripley, and thinking about Ripley, but it was already too late for that. Even as she sat here on this uncomfortable chair with these dreary and lachrymose people, picking at her unappetizing food and looking out the window at this ridiculous street—like something from a *Gangs of New York* theme park—her thoughts about Ripley had slipped past her control and were racing northward. Whatever this present bullshit was, ignoring it had not de-activated it, and it was somehow enmeshed with that place. She hadn't found the link to her brother, and that was beyond annoying, but Anna felt more certain than ever that this— and whoever it came from—wound back to Evan's time at that absurd place. Obviously, she would have to haul herself to Vermont, land of her childhood, and people, and the home she had left years before, never—she fervently hoped—to return. Which was yet another item on the extremely long list of things for which she blamed Jacob Finch Bonner.

12

War and Remembrance

That night, when she got home, and after fortifying herself with a strong Napa merlot, she read the pages Louise and Frank had given her. They were as familiar as the earlier excerpt, but that did not blunt their brutal impact.

Their parents considered Diandra's pregnancy a good thing, or at least not totally a bad one. Certainly, they were humiliated by the prospect of everyone in their town and church communities knowing their fifteen-year-old daughter had managed to get herself pregnant, but at least they expected their Christian values to direct what happened from then on. They also viewed Diandra's pregnancy as a possible reset for her character, a shock to the system of a girl who had always been stubborn and selfish, because from now on her life would have to revolve around someone else, not just herself.

The baby was named Ruby, and after she was born everyone hoped Diandra would at least find some kind of new purpose in her life. After all, the needs of an infant are immediate and constant. Everyone except, apparently, Diandra understood that it was a part of a mother's calling to meet her child's requirements. Diandra, though, seemed to cling to the idea that she could somehow decline the responsibilities of motherhood. She acted as if some person around her would change their mind, breaking the logjam and affording her an exception, one that allowed her to go back to the singular way she had always lived. It was no secret to anyone in the family that Diandra was smart and that she'd wanted to leave home just as soon as she could, which is one reason it shocked everyone that this had happened in the first place. At various points during the pregnancy, she had announced her intention to procure an abortion, but she was too young to make that decision for herself, and their parents would not consider providing the necessary approvals. In the later months, she tried to suggest that she intended to give the child up for adoption, but here again their parents stepped in. It was a horror beyond words for them that their daughter was pregnant, but almost worse than that was her intention to abandon her responsibilities. She would have that baby and she would raise that baby, so long as their parents were the heads of the household.

None of this was really new behavior, not where Diandra was concerned. She had been one of those babies who announced her character in the cradle and never changed it. As a little kid she was always either too warm or too cold, always uncomfortably dressed in clothes that were either too snug or too loose, always dissatisfied with the food their mother made, wrinkling her nose over the soup or the stew, and pouring herself a bowl of cereal instead. By the age of eight she was a confirmed vegetarian. A year or two later, she wanted chicken at least once a day, though that didn't last more than a few months. There was a period when she wouldn't eat "anything with a bar code" or "anything processed," and that included the apples and bananas their mother brought home in an effort to please her. She had little time for either parent, and as for Ethan, she barely acknowledged her older brother's presence at all. When she did it was to observe that he was no more than a football-playing moron.

Ethan was doing a lot more than playing football. He was excelling at football. Even as a freshman, he started most games on the field, and dominated play. By sophomore year he was the team's high scorer and captain, and it's not an exaggeration to say that every student, teacher, and administrator in the high school knew who he was and the position he occupied in the community. He had friends. He had, as he got older, a great deal of attention from girls. He had the respect of his teachers, who wanted him to succeed and gave him the necessary support. All of which irritated Diandra considerably.

At home, Ethan sometimes witnessed his mother try to connect with his younger sister, but it was always a losing proposition. Diandra showed no recognition of their mother's efforts, or the fact that their father's job paid for her expenses, let alone any more meaningful tie between them. What Diandra wanted from her family was the bare minimum, but what she wanted to give back was even less, and as close to nothing as she could get away with. A cursory "thanks" after a meal, a gruff nod when their mother brought her clean and folded clothes to her bedroom, which was down the hall from the kitchen. These were the least she could muster, and all she managed. It was no wonder their parents considered Ethan their favorite.

All through his childhood, Ethan had been able to hear their parents talking in their bedroom at night, which was across the hall from his own. It was too far to hear what they were saying, but he could recognize the intense droning sound of their bitterness and disappointment, and there was only one thing in their lives capable of causing that much bitterness and disappointment: Diandra. He felt so sorry for them, and he tried even harder to make his parents proud of his own accomplishments, but it was like hitting away at a hurricane with a tennis racket. Or that's how it felt.

Their parents' bedroom was the biggest one in the house, and the bed where their parents slept was even older than the house. He'd never known anyone who had a bed like that, and the only time he'd ever even seen one was on a school trip to the Shelburne Museum, where there were a few of them in the various buildings. Still, none were as massive and solid-looking as the one in his own home. It was so old that there had once been ropes held up by pegs on the bed frame that supported the mattress, though this had been updated, at some point, to a wooden platform. Their father had always said that an ancestor brought it on a horse cart when the town of West Rugby was still woodland west of the Green Mountains, and the quarry their family would one day own was still a decade from being opened. After the platform for the mattress was added and those pegs became unnecessary, someone made a few of them into secret compartments, where their father sometimes hid cash and their mother put her wedding ring when it got too tight. After the baby, Ruby, was born, the master bedroom was even offered to Diandra, a generous suggestion that acknowledged the extra room she and her child would need. But she refused. She kept the baby in her own little room downstairs, at least while she was still a baby. Later, Ruby moved to a bedroom across the hall from her mother. By then, the two of them had the whole house to themselves.

Ethan was never clear on exactly what happened the night their parents died. The firefighter who explained things to him didn't seem very sure of the details himself, and all he could say was that it was a miracle all four of the people in the house that night hadn't died. He himself hadn't been home that night. He'd slept at a girlfriend's house in Rugby where he was attending the community college and working part-time at a local tavern, but his parents, in their bedroom upstairs, both

went to sleep and never woke up again, and his sister Diandra
and niece, Ruby, then less than a year old, were taken to the
hospital in Rugby and treated for several days. While they were
away, the fire marshal and a home inspector went through the
house and took apart the oil furnace, which was where the
carbon monoxide leak had come from. That part was
straightforward enough. What didn't make sense, either to the
marshal or to Ethan, and never would make sense, was why
none of the carbon monoxide alarms had worked. He couldn't
get it out of his mind that this had happened because of
something his sister had done. How she'd done it, and how
she'd survived it herself, and her daughter, too, he had no idea,
and obviously there was no proof of anything. If there had
been, the fire marshal would have mentioned it, or the police
would have come to see him, and neither of those things
happened. Even so, it troubled him.

Still, he supposed there were more awful ways to die, and
as much as he missed his parents, he was kind of grateful that
neither of them had had to mourn the other one. At first, he
intended to move back into the house, but just a few nights
there before and after their parents' funeral were enough to
make him reconsider. The baby cried all the time, making it
impossible for him to rest, and Diandra made it as obvious as
she could that he wasn't welcome. He took a few things that
had belonged to their parents, for sentimental reasons, and
left. And it would be many years before he returned to live
there again.

There it ended, except for the snide commentary: *Too close for comfort?*

Same chicken scratch. Same black ballpoint. Same snark. And a serious uptick from *"Seem familiar?"*

Anna put down the pages. It was only moderately comforting to be reminded, yet again, of what an unexceptional writer Evan actually was. The clunkiness of his prose, its obvious self-service—"Ethan," the athlete-hero and star of his family!—not to speak of the glaring absence of facts (facts well known to himself!) that explained how "Diandra" had "managed to get herself pregnant" at fifteen. It all added up to a boy's own story of myopic self-pity.

As tempting as it was to go down that rabbit hole of loathing, the many flaws of her dead brother were not, at this particular moment, her most pressing concern. Far more serious, from where she sat, was the recurring problem of who had sent the pages, and how those pages had been procured, and what the intention had been in delivering them to her in-laws. Still more compelling than any of those: What did she need to do to make this stop?

It took some serious effort to pull back from all of this, to separate what she actually knew from what she merely feared, and to decide which unknown things she needed to prioritize. Was there a possibility that she had missed some version of her brother's novel in their Vermont house, despite what had seemed such a thorough search at the time? Of course there was. But she didn't think so. Much more likely was that a person outside of that house had seen and been in possession of Evan's novel, someone her brother had shared his writing with, someone he'd even entrusted with a precious copy of the entire manuscript. Who might this person be, and how had they crossed paths with Evan? Also, if the point was redress for her late husband's presumed theft (an impulse she was personally very much in sympathy with), then why wait till now?

But they weren't particularly useful, those questions, because those questions represented the *benign* end of the spectrum when it came to her present situation. At the other end was the reality she had already accepted, back in Denver when that cryptic message—*For Evan Parker, not forgotten*—materialized on a Post-it note in a copy of her own novel. The building wave set in motion by that Post-it was cresting now with terrifying certainty, and she didn't know how to stop it.

For Evan Parker became *I know what he was to you.*

And that became: *I know what you did to him.*

And all of it meant: *I can expose you, whenever I choose.*

None of this was really about Jake, despite the special malevolence of involving his parents. The pages in her hands had been sent to Frank and Louise in order to make a special point, that no one in her life was beyond the reach and the intention and the malevolence of this person. The words they'd written—*"Too close for comfort?"*—had not been addressed to her dead husband, nor to his parents; they'd been addressed to a person she had tried just as hard to render just as dead as Evan Parker and Jacob Finch Bonner. That person was the artist formerly known as Dianna Parker. In other words: herself.

13

Everybody's Fool

One clear contender for that position of Evan's most intimate Ripley friend was a person named Martin Purcell. He was a teacher in South Burlington, and in the Writers of Ripley Facebook group he had alluded to emails from Evan, visits with Evan, and even rock concerts with Evan in his mournful recitation of post-Ripley activities the two aspiring writers had shared. Despite so much evidence of intimacy, Purcell had never claimed to have seen so much as a page of Evan's novel in progress, let alone that he still had pages of the great work in his possession, but in the deepest hours of a sleepless night, his was the name she continued to circle back to.

Her brother would not have chosen to share his novel-in-progress with some random person from Rutland, someone he might have known in his everyday life. He was too much a narcissist to value the empty praise of a mere civilian, some high school crony who hadn't read a novel since being forced to choke down *Catcher in the Rye* for tenth-grade English; Evan, like so many other writers she'd met these last years, both with Jake and after, would only have wanted the approval of other writers, from the community of strivers who under-stood his aspirations and respected his toil. Nor could she conceive of a literary encounter at his tavern or, conversely, at the twelve-step program, that might lead to such an editorially satisfying relationship. People like that were in short supply in most places beyond Manhattan, Brooklyn, Boston, Iowa City,

Seattle, Portland (both Portlands), and just possibly any college town from sea to shining sea where you might find . . . an MFA program.

It was Ripley, in other words. It had to be Ripley. It was time to look—at last, and very carefully—at Ripley.

For some reason she couldn't yet understand, Martin Purcell was the person Evan had chosen to form some version of a friendship with when the course was through. Purcell, as she knew perfectly well, had also been a stop on her late husband's little Vermont tour of discovery; in fact, meeting with him had been the primary purpose of Jake's trip to Rutland just before he'd traveled south to Athens and Rabun Gap. Anna knew where Jake had met with Martin Purcell—the Birdseye Diner, a local landmark from her own childhood—and she even knew what the two men had eaten, thanks to the credit card receipt still in Jake's wallet when he died—a bowl of soup and one of the diner's massive hamburgers, though she couldn't have said which of them had eaten which. But she did not know what they'd discussed. And for obvious reasons, she hadn't pressed Jake too hard to find out.

It had taken only a few hours to come up with a plan, something open-ended enough to adapt to a number of possible scenarios but laser focused on Evan's life at Ripley, affording her the best possible aperture into who might have sent the excerpt. Purcell might never have mentioned Evan's novel to his fellow mourners in the Facebook group, but he was still a viable source for the pages she'd received—not to mention that vile Post-it in Denver. Anna would not, of course, be initiating contact as the sister of dead Evan Parker but as the widow of dead Jacob Finch Bonner. Even so, she'd need to be vigilant.

As it happened, she was good at being vigilant.

Dear Mr. Purcell,

We don't know each other, but I believe you knew my late husband, Jacob Finch Bonner, during the time he was teaching at the Ripley College MFA program. I don't know whether you are aware of this, but you were actually one of the last people to spend time with Jake before his sudden death. He told me about your dinner together when he returned from seeing you in Vermont, and said that he'd had a chance to discuss your work with you. He also said, and I remember this exactly, as one remembers conversations with someone who is shortly to pass away, that he found your work to be very exciting. In the same conversation he told me that he wanted to help you find an agent, and eventually a publisher.

I have been thinking about that, and about Jake's teaching in general, over these past two years, which have been a very sad time for me. So much attention has been paid to Jake as a writer, and rightfully so, but Jake loved teaching, and he loved watching his students grow as writers. Nothing gave him more joy than seeing one of his students succeed in publishing a book. And so it occurred to me that one way to memorialize Jake would be to help some of those students to publish their work. I have been discussing with a publisher friend the idea of an anthology of fiction by Jake's students, perhaps with an introductory essay about Jake's work with writers at the beginning of their careers. Is this something I could reach out to you to discuss? Or perhaps you have stayed in touch with other Ripley students Jake knew or worked with, and there is someone else I should be speaking with.

I hope this is not an intrusive request. I wish you all the best, and hope to speak with you soon.

> *Very best wishes,*
> *Anna Williams-Bonner*
> *AWB@AnnaWilliamsBonner.com*

There are carrots and there are sticks, and then there is the outright offer of publication to an unpublished writer. He was in her in-box inside of ten minutes.

Dear Mrs. Bonner,

I am so pleased to hear from you, and may I say how very sorry I was to hear about the tragic loss of your husband. As you noted, I did see Jake very shortly before his passing, and I was shocked at what took place less than a week later. Of course, one can never know the kinds of pain people may be in, but to me he seemed distinctly upbeat and full of interesting things to say.

I am just bowled over by your comments about my own work. Jake was enormously encouraging, but he did not convey to me that level of commitment to assisting me, and I am so very moved to hear about his intentions. Even the intention alone puts him among the most generous of teachers and mentors. The actual project you propose is even more astonishing. Yes, of course I would love to discuss it further.

Our particular Ripley group did remain very close. One student died tragically soon after our course ended, and others drifted away from writing, but there are about ten of us (about half were Jake's students, the other half assigned to the other Ripley instructors) who are in regular contact. We have a Facebook group called "Writers of Ripley" and it's a rare day that someone doesn't post on it. I am sure that every one of these people would relish the possibility of contributing to the kind of tribute volume you describe, and speaking for myself, I would be proud to write an introduction.

Please let me know how you would like to proceed. I am generally unavailable during school hours (I am a high school history teacher in South Burlington, Vermont) but I will do my best to accommodate your schedule.

Yours Truly, Martin Purcell

Well, this was both good and deeply unsurprising. She had never really understood this hunger of writers to be *seen* between the covers of a book. Obviously, a crucial part of making art was presenting it, somehow, to the world, but she herself had never experienced such extravagant hunger for publication. Even during the months when she was writing her own novel, first at the artists' colony in New England and later in this very apartment, she hadn't obsessed about what would become of it; she'd simply tried to focus on the actual making of the book, which seemed to her the only part of the endeavor that she could control. Thinking about publishing something before you'd written it was like the classic Aesop fable of the milkmaid who imagines spending all the money she'll earn from selling her milk, even as she carries that milk to market, the distraction of which causes her to trip and spill it, thereby ending all of her visions of acclaim, praise, and self-worth. Such people, Anna thought, did not deserve to cry over their spilt milk, but they cried anyway. They cried a lot. Through Jake she had met so many unpublished writers, and they were bitter people, but the irony was that they remained bitter even if they did manage to publish. Now they were just bitter about other things: reviews and marketing attention from their publishers, invitations to festivals, places at colonies like the one she'd visited a year and a half earlier, all of the magic fairy dust that a few books and authors received, and most books and authors did not.

Publication, though, was everything to these people. It was slathered across the covers of their magazines, flung about in their conferences, and omnipresent in their conversations. Self-publication had let some of the air out of the outrage balloon but created new areas of defensiveness, since what had once been unironically termed "vanity publishing" was now a hydra of undulating designations: Indie-Publishing, Hybrid-Publishing, and the at least simple-to-understand "Self-Publishing." Half the time, when people asked her about these matters, she had no idea what iteration of publishing she was supposed to be having an opinion about, but the truth was that she had no opinion, or no strongly held opinion. Jake would have preferred death to vanity publication, she was sure. Writers of Jake's ilk had a horror of anything that did not originate in one of American publishing's seven . . . no, six . . . no, five . . . but in any case, ever-diminishing number of traditional publishers, the Penguin Random Houses, Simon & Schusters, HarperCollinses, and Hachettes and Macmillans. Keeping up with who had merged or split was, in her opinion, a highly unnecessary drain on her time and energy, which was why she tended to deflect the questions about publishing she had been asked while on the road. Besides, whatever the question was, its subtext was always the same and always quite clear: *You cheated, because your husband paved the way for you, and that's not fair.*

Okay.

In your opinion, fine.

Well, here was her news alert: life wasn't fair, and never had been.

Seriously, these people. It's like they sealed themselves into a bubble and never even tried to get out.

Would Jake have ended up like that if he'd never crossed paths with Evan Parker and his (that was, *her*) incredible, irresistible plot? Would Evan himself have become like that if his gold-plated debut novel had failed to impress an agent or

146

a publisher? How closely the two of them resembled each other, when you came down to it! She could imagine either of them becoming *that guy* at the end of the signing line, lurking in order to say some witty, caustic thing to the twenty-four-year-old who'd just published her first novel with Knopf, solely because she was pretty or had a powerful mentor or was the child of a celebrity or had graduated from Harvard or was known to have had an affair with a famous author and written a novel about it, or any of the reasons some writer who wasn't *that guy* got to leapfrog over the rest of them. It was behavior unbecoming a person, and to be frank, both Evan and Jake had been living lives that looked pretty golden from her own perspective. Parents who were blind to their flaws? Good health and roofs over their heads? In Jake's case there'd been a gold-plated MFA. In her brother's case there'd been unrelenting teenage success. Her husband had even been one of those young, or at least youngish, first novelists with a big-five publisher, no less. So what was there to complain about? And despite her brother's postcollege slide into drug use, which would have killed many a man in the same circumstances, he'd managed not to lose all his money or kill himself (or anyone else) on the Vermont roads. His tavern hadn't gone under, and after she and Rose went south to Georgia he'd even had their childhood home to live in, free of charge. He'd managed to claim sobriety without actually having to give up his drugs. He'd managed to proclaim his virtue from the back of the bar in his very own tavern, before going home to his generous stash of opioids in a bathroom of West Rutland marble from the family quarry, and to the writing room where, without an ounce of guilt, he'd trashed his sister in deadly prose before slipping into narcotic slumber on their parents' horror show of a bed. No accounting.

Certainly no "rock bottom." Just continual and escalating offense, crying out for justice.

They ought to have been grateful, both of them. They ought to have tended their own gardens and left her alone. But they hadn't, and here the three of them were. Again.

Anna, of course, hadn't needed Martin Purcell to tell her about the Writers of Ripley Facebook group, and she had no doubt that Purcell would soon be on it, trumpeting to his gang—or at least to Jake's actual students in the group—that they might soon be published in a major anthology. She hoped no one would jump the gun and contact Matilda or even Wendy directly, but if either of them called to ask about this book she was supposedly publishing, she would say that it was something she intended to do privately, for Jake, and for these nice former students. It was a reasonable risk for an important reward; this rock in the pond of Jake's Ripley associates was bound to bring something helpful to the surface. Hard though it might be, she would wait and see what rose.

14

One Good Turn

Anna didn't respond to him right away. She wanted the power dynamic to be clear from the beginning. A few days later he emailed her again. Apologizing. As was only correct.

Dear Mrs. Williams-Bonner,

I'm sorry that we haven't been able to connect regarding your project in honor of Professor Bonner. Is there a good time for me to phone you to discuss?

With very best wishes,
Martin Purcell

She let another few days slide by. She went out to Long Island in that limousine, to do the event on the North Shore. She received a last-minute invitation to a Young Lions evening at the New York Public Library, obviously in place of someone who'd canceled, but she decided to go, because Matilda came as her date. She kept a vigilant eye on her mail, but nothing new arrived. Not yet.

After another week, she emailed him back.

Dear Mr. Purcell,

I am so sorry. I missed this and your earlier email, which have been buried beneath a few hundred work emails! Yes, we should speak about the project. Would you phone me this Saturday morning at 10:00 A.M.?

(She had chosen Saturday at ten because she knew from his Facebook page that he coached the Robotics Club at his high school, and there was an important statewide event at exactly that time.)

Then she gave him, magnanimously, her cell phone number, and wrote: "I look forward to speaking with you! Anna."

He phoned that Saturday, promptly at ten.

"Can I just say," said Martin Purcell, "before anything else, that I thought your book was fantastic."

"Oh, thank you so much!"

"So powerful. So honest."

She had heard this before, of course.

"That means so much to me. Thank you."

For a moment he was silent. She heard what she imagined were the sounds of a statewide robotics event in the background.

"So, about this anthology . . ."

"Yes! It's an idea I had. You know, there was a memorial here in New York, with all of his publishing friends, and family, but it was barely mentioned that he was a teacher. And that was so important to him."

"I understand," said Martin Purcell. "It was important to us, I can assure you."

"And so I thought I would approach Ripley to see if they wanted to do anything. I guess I hadn't realized the college is completely gone now. I think they went online for a while, but even that seems to be over."

"Yes. It's a great shame. That place was so important to us."

"I can only imagine. I never pursued a writing degree. To be honest, it came as something of a surprise to me that I would be a writer at all."

Anna let this hang between them, giving oxygen to all of the resentment she imagined Martin Purcell might hold toward her: how effortlessly she had come out of nowhere, with an agent and editor already in place to usher her toward publication. Surprised to find herself a writer, indeed!

"Well, you had something important to write about. And you did a superb job."

It sounded as if it hurt him to say it. Good.

"So, how would you like to organize this?"

"I'm sorry?"

"The anthology," he said, with deliberate patience. "Shall I tell Jake's other students? Or were you planning to make an announcement somewhere?"

She paused, as if she were considering these matters. "You know, I think, first, I'd like to just hear from the writers he taught. Then perhaps I can talk with them individually about what they might contribute. I'd like to keep it personal, and private. For now. Besides," she said, "if we go out with some big public announcement, I'm going to get submissions from people who didn't actually know Jake, or weren't his students. I don't want this to become something out of *Writer's Digest*."

"Oh, I completely understand."

"I am so grateful to you for helping me with this, Mr. Purcell."

"Please call me Martin," he said.

"Martin."

He was quiet for a moment. Then he apologized. "I'm afraid I can't stay on the phone right now, I'm actually at a school event."

"Oh, I'm sorry! I know you're a teacher, but I thought it was safe to call on a weekend."

"Normally it would be. But I coach a team and we have something today. May I phone again?"

She told him he could. She wanted to hear more about Ripley, she told her new friend Martin Purcell. It was embarrassing how little she knew about something that had been so important to Jake: the students, the faculty members, any administrators or hangers-on from that brief summer session years earlier. She wanted to hear *every single thing* he could remember, and as soon as possible. He would be doing her such a favor if he could help her with this.

Truer words she might never have spoken.

Then she let him go, and gratifyingly, he wasted no time in delivering the very important message she'd entrusted him with.

Over the next few days, "queries" about the anthology began to arrive via the contact form on her website. First, they were a trickle; soon, a relative flood.

Dear Mrs. Williams-Bonner, Martin has shared with us your marvelous plan to publish the work of your late husband's devoted students . . .

Hi, I was in Jacob's class at Ripley and it CHANGED MY LIFE!

I considered Professor Bonner my mentor . . .

All of them were fulsome in their praise, of Jake, of his guidance, of herself for her generosity. They wanted more information. What kind of work was she looking for? Did it have to be fiction, because they had started writing poetry, and even though Professor Bonner hadn't actually seen any of the poetry, they thought they had always been a poet, really, and that the years of writing fiction had led them here, to this ultimate distillation of language and concept, so could they submit their poetry, please? Should they send options or only the work they considered to be their best? Would she accept flash fiction? Metafiction? Could it be an excerpt of a novel? Did she have any genre specifications, because for the past fourteen years they had been working on a cycle of novels set on a planetary system at the far end of the Milky Way galaxy, and they knew sci-fi wasn't for everyone. Was it okay if Professor Bonner hadn't been their technically assigned teacher because they had been hoping to get him and had even written to Ripley requesting him, but they'd been assigned, instead, to somebody else, somebody not as good, though they had taken every opportunity to speak with Professor Bonner at Ripley events like the opening night barbecue, and he had been so kind, so encouraging, that they remembered his words of support even now . . .

As the "submissions" began to appear in her in-box she scrutinized them, though not for talent, of course. She was reading the seminar room through their emails, searching between the lines of their condolences and their praise for the personalities who'd inhabited Jake's Ripley seminar room. Virtually every one of these people was exaggerating their relationship to Jake, falling over themselves to declare him the greatest teacher, cheerleader, inspiration, and critic (in the best possible way) they had personally encountered since beginning their writing journeys, exploring their creativity, wrestling with their muses. His loss had been shocking, devastating, and—although not in the same category as her own, they assured her—deeply personal. And yet, in this generous and caring offer of publication, Jake's great spirit was being so appropriately honored! And if their own humble submission to such a book were to be accepted, they would feel they were able to acknowledge, in some tiny way, their own great debt to this amazing lost man.

Blah, blah, blah.

She raced through their praise of her husband only slightly less rapidly than she raced through their submissions: grandmother's house, father's rages, disembodied dialogues in the club (Still? Really?), bad breakups, the woe that was in marriage, the woe that was in parenthood . . . the pieces were all, she imagined, somewhat autobiographical, but no one had written about any specific "lived experience" that had touched the lived experiences of either her late husband or her late brother. The submissions themselves were a wash.

It was disappointing, but not really a surprise. She'd felt it very unlikely that any of these eager writers would turn out to be the person she was looking for—the one who'd left their calling card in Denver or sent the excerpts of Evan's novel to her New York City home and to Jake's parents on Long Island. Such a person would hardly go charging through the door she was so obviously flinging open for them. But it had been worth doing, nonetheless; Ripley's MFA was a small and insular world, in a remote and rather depressed part of Vermont, and any one of these people might inadvertently lead her in the direction she needed to go.

Anna wrote back to every single one of them. She thanked them profusely and said nice things about their work. Then she asked them for more: not more pages, but more stories, more impressions, more recollections of Jake and also of anyone—students, teachers, locals—who might have been a part of their Ripley experience. She told them how badly she wanted to know everything she could, to reconstitute that time and that community that had been so meaningful to her late husband. Their memories were the price of the ticket, she implied, and she hoped the carrot of publication would be enough to get it done.

If not, she had a stick in reserve.

Well, not precisely a stick, but a supplication that would be difficult for these great admirers of Jake to ignore: a plea to assist her in another purpose of her project, which was the exposure of that terrible person, that never identified tormenter whose accusation had undermined Jake's mental health, driven him to suicide, and robbed them all of this extraordinary person, her husband.

She had spent the past eighteen months pouring her grief into her own novel, she would tell them, but now she wanted this person brought to justice, or if not justice in the technical sense of the word, then in the public shame sense of the word. What use was a cancel culture if those most deserving of cancellation were unjustly spared?

She would explain to these writers that they were in a unique position to help her, because for some time she'd had the strongest suspicion that this person had first crossed paths with him at Ripley, and therefore wasn't it possible that they, too, had shared a room, a table in the dining room, or a seminar with this person? And could they please, please assist her in this final work of her husband's too-brief life and help identify his antagonist?

But again: not unless this first and less direct approach proved unsuccessful, because conjuring Jake's nameless tormenter would necessarily bring her far closer than she wanted to her own "lived experience." She certainly hoped it wouldn't come to that.

15

Beggarman, Thief

In all, there were thirty-two submissions to Jake's tribute anthology, each requiring its own email correspondence (and, in a few cases, excruciating phone conversations) with the Writers of Ripley, an experience that brought her closer to sympathy for her late husband than she had ever come before. What could even the best teacher have done with these people? One of them was writing a series of mystery novels somehow based on "numerological principles." Another was endlessly revising a "fictionalized memoir." A man from Montana named Richard Rosen, who'd given off a strong odor of crazy on the phone, said he was—and she wasn't entirely sure she understood this—somehow rewriting *Les Misérables* but with Victor Hugo's "mistakes corrected."

Mixed in with the emails from Jake's students were several from her late husband's teaching colleagues: a poet named Alice from Baltimore and a fiction writer named Bruce, who told her that his annual beer with Jake at the Ripley Inn had been a highlight of his summers. There was also a Frank Ricardo, who described himself as a "multigenric" writer and who definitely implied that Anna ought to have heard of him. (Both of the men made a point of asking whether the anthology was for Jake's students only.) But again: there was nothing specifically alarming about any of them. No one mentioned a student who'd taken up all the oxygen in the workshop, or whose work in progress might well have become a massive international bestseller on the order of *Crib* (and featuring a similarly unlikely storyline). No one who'd thrown their fatal charm around, hinting at greatness to come. It was as if Evan Parker had never bothered to enroll at Ripley, never entered the seminar room or gone for an after-class drink at the Ripley Inn to continue discussing a classmate's short story. Her brother's name was not spoken. He wasn't even a shadow of a presence in the glancing and nonspecific way Martin Purcell had conjured him during their phone call: some talented but unlucky novelist who'd passed away not long after their course had ended. Not one of her husband's students suggested, for example, that perhaps the anthology could include a brief tribute to this other lost writer? Or even an excerpt of the work that writer had left behind, which they'd discussed in class or passed to someone from a different seminar because it was so very worthy. Not a single person gave a single indication that Evan Parker had even existed, let alone that he'd once walked among the Writers of Ripley, physically or virtually. Had her brother made such a negligible impression on his peers, for once in his life? Or were these students of writing simply too intent on their imminent publication to recall the second loss in their little circle, and the special tragedy of a young writer who—unlike Jake Bonner, awarded all the glittering prizes publishing had to offer!—had never even finished his novel, let alone had a chance to gift it to the world.

They weren't too self-focused to notice the other writers in the room; not at all! Several of the writers Anna spoke to mentioned the Victor Hugo guy, the "fictionalized memoir" woman, and someone who had apparently added the adjective "honeymelon" to the English language (to describe a dead body's breasts, no less). But the magnetic man-child writing a novel about a mother who murders and thereafter assumes the identity of her own daughter? Which ought to have been, to state the obvious, memorable? And which would in fact closely resemble the plot of a famous author's global bestseller only a few short years after his passing?

Nothing.

Not a wisp of a memory, not even a vague but lingering impression. Her brother, it now seemed clear, had declined to share his astonishing book in progress with his Ripley peers. He had kept his cards uncharacteristically close to the chest. How frustrating that was. For her.

Then, nearly a month after the submissions had tapered off, another manila envelope arrived. It had no return address, no letter or note, but it did have a Burlington, Vermont, postmark, and it contained the most loathed chapter of that loathed novel, the one she had hoped never to see or think about again. Now, however, she steeled herself to read it one more time, in case there was something she might see from where she was currently sitting, that she hadn't seen before. As if she hadn't been there for the nonfiction version, otherwise known as the truth.

What happened that night happened because Diandra had made up her mind. Who knows how long she'd had her eye on Perry Donovan, one of Ethan's football teammates and his best friend since the two boys were in first or second grade, and Cub Scouts in the summer. Perry was a quiet guy from a big family in Rugby, and he'd grown up in a loud house full of kids, almost all of them older. His dad had a dairy farm just north of town, and Perry had that farm kid hardiness from early mornings in Vermont weather, something that came in handy on the football field.

Mostly when the two teammates got together it was at the Donovan house, which had a basement with a pool table and a big TV on one of the walls. (Ethan, who had dated one of Perry's older sisters on and off through school, was very familiar with the couches down there.) Perry was an undemanding friend, who mainly let Ethan take the lead, whether it was something to do with football, with academics, or with their social life. Admittedly, this had led to a few close scrapes, including a time when the two of them "borrowed" some test answers for a chemistry midterm from a girl Perry was seeing (she was a year older and had taken the class the previous year) or the time the two boys lifted some beer from a store in town, just for fun, and were seen by the wife of a Vermont State Trooper. Luckily, Ethan's father got them out of that one.

Ethan's parents didn't go away very often, but when they did, it was an occasion the two friends definitely took advantage of. In the spring of his senior year, his father took his mother down to Boston for some tests at one of the special hospitals there, and it seemed like an excellent time to invite some friends over. Technically, he was in charge of Diandra at this time, but in a practical sense that didn't mean much. Diandra pretty much took care of herself in terms of food and getting herself up and ready for school. At home, she spent all of her time in her own bedroom down the hall from the kitchen, doing homework at her little desk and almost never coming out. The only thing the two of them had to do together was drive between home and school, because Diandra was fifteen and didn't have her license, let alone a car to drive. These drives took about ten minutes each way and were completely silent. It's hard to say which of them preferred that more.

Until the night of the party Ethan had no idea Diandra had any special feelings about his friend. With Perry's broad back and curly red hair, he was a good-looking guy, and while he wasn't much of an intellectual it was generally held that he was a sweet boy who wouldn't say a bad thing about anyone. As a result, Perry was very popular with girls. Half their own grade of girls would have dated him, or had dated him, and girls all through the school smiled at him when he went by. He could have had his pick of them, and for a long time he did.

Ethan had invited about six people over that night, but this being high school, about twenty ended up coming over. Most were good friends and teammates, and everyone brought something to share. It was a mellow vibe, which also softened the blow of having so many people in the house, and most of those people ended up in the living room sharing some weed or beer. It wasn't on its way to being a rowdy night either because there was school the next day, and even if that didn't matter to most of Ethan's friends, there was also a football game at the weekend, a big one against their main rival school, so even the guys who felt indestructible knew they needed to be rested.

Diandra had been in her room most of the evening, but Ethan started to notice that she had a way of walking past the living room, standing in the doorway with a hand on one hip and glaring at the group. She glared harder as the number of people went down but the volume of the music didn't go down with it. At first she was still in her school clothes, a pair of jeans and a loose white shirt, but eventually he realized she had changed into a nightgown, one of those flowered cotton ones their mother also wore. Even though the living room wasn't on the way from his sister's bedroom to the kitchen or the bathroom, even though there was no reason for Diandra to be continuously standing at the doorway of the room he and his friends were in, Ethan gradually realized that his sister was making it her business to watch them.

"What do you want?" he said at one point. Diandra said what she wanted was for everyone to go home. She was trying to study.

"Stop trying so hard," one of his teammates suggested, and everyone laughed.

She also wanted the couple who'd gone into the room across the hall from her to stop making noise.

"Good for your education," one of the guys said.

"Education is important," said somebody else.

The couple was another football player named Jonah and his girlfriend.

"If it's rocking don't come knocking," someone laughed.

"I'm trying to study," said his sister.

This continued over the next hour or so. "She's such a brat," Jonah said when he came back to the living room. "She banged on the door."

"I hope you all feel sorry for me," Ethan told them. "You're just visiting. I have to live with her all the time."

People started leaving the house at around nine that night. By ten, only a core group remained with Ethan. By midnight it was only Perry who was left, and he'd already told his parents he was staying over. When it was just the two of them still in the living room, Ethan took out the bottle of Jack Daniel's he'd been holding back and got glasses from the kitchen. Within minutes Diandra was back.

"Are you going to clean up?" she said. She usually had a nasty edge when she talked to him. But this time she was obviously furious.

"I'll get to it," Ethan said. "Don't worry your pretty head."

After she stomped off, Perry said: "Why doesn't she just go to bed and stop worrying about it?"

He looked at his friend, and that's when he realized what was really going on.

"Dude," he said. "She likes you. That's why."

Perry grinned. "Right," he said.

"No, seriously. It's obvious. She even changed into her nightgown, just for you."

They each had a second glass of Jack.

They had problems to discuss. Ethan had a class he was worried he might actually fail. It was French, and the teacher wasn't exactly a football fan. Perry wanted to break up with the girl he was seeing, but she cried all the time, even when things were going well.

"Just tell her. You know, 'We've run our course.'"

"I tried that once. She was so upset. I had all her friends sending me notes. And, you know, she won't do anything. She's religious."

Ethan tried to sympathize. He hadn't been in that particular situation himself.

"You deserve better. You deserve a girl who likes you enough."

Diandra came back then, and this time she stood there in the opening to the front hall, her legs planted apart, and both of her hands on her hips. With her standing that way, the hallway light was right behind her and made her nightgown almost see-through. That was obviously on purpose.

"Will you guys at least turn the music down? I'm trying to sleep."

Perry was looking at those legs, Ethan noticed.

"Hey, Diandra, come join us," he said.

To Ethan's great amusement, she hesitated. Then, as he watched, she turned her attention to Perry, and there it stayed. Something came over her. Before Ethan's eyes, that hip shifted, bending toward his sister's hand. He was used to seeing a girl in that posture, but not his sister. She was just like any of them, he realized.

"Sure," she said, and into the room she came, that white nightgown swishing around her legs. She had let her hair down, too. Usually she wore it up on top of her head in a kind of twirl. Now it was down.

"I'm sorry we kept you up," Perry said, but Diandra looked almost surprised to hear him say it, as if she hadn't been complaining about the noise all night.

"Oh, it's all right. I wasn't doing anything important."

"Your education is *very* important," Perry said. "You're a smart girl. Everyone says so."

Diandra looked past him to her brother. She gave Ethan one of her customary glares. She didn't say it, but the meaning was clear: My brother *doesn't say so.*

"I would like to be smart," Perry added. "I wouldn't mind going to college."

"Of course you should go to college!" Diandra said, as if she had suddenly become their age, or even older. She was actually talking down to him. "Why wouldn't you?"

Perry shrugged. He was two Jacks down, and maybe half a joint earlier in the evening, but he was all there. He was blushing, actually. "Not a good fit, I don't think. Besides, my dad is counting on me."

One of his older brothers was in the army, another was determined not to stay on the farm. The rest were sisters.

"Well, you should do what you want to do. It's your life."

Perry shook his head. For a minute, Ethan thought he might do some crying, himself. But it passed.

"You're how old now, Diandra?"

She was fifteen. But she was an old fifteen.

163

*All of a sudden it occurred to him that he didn't want to
see any more of this. Maybe it was his own two Jacks catching
up to him, maybe just the thought of what his little sister was
obviously determined to do made him sick. He knew he
should say something to his friend, warn him that Diandra
was not this person fawning over him, pretending to care
about his troubles. Always, with her, there was a scheme of
some kind going on. Always she was thinking ahead to some
objective. Anything between her and that thing was going to
get at least ignored, and at worst badly hurt.*

*"Dude," he said, but Diandra was shooting him one of her
looks.*

"Dude," he tried again, "we should turn in."

*"I'm good," said Perry. "Maybe I'll hang out here a bit.
Get the tenth-grade perspective on life."*

*"I wouldn't," Ethan tried. He was already giving up. He
knew how useless it was when she wanted something.
Diandra's nightgown had an opening in front with buttons
to close it up. He was sure he'd never seen it unbuttoned this
far down. Then again, he'd never really thought about it
before. She had gathered up the nightgown and tucked her
legs underneath her on the couch.*

*"Could I have a glass of that?" his sister said. She meant
the Jack.*

Perry glanced over at him. "I don't know."

Ethan got to his feet. "I'm going to bed. Be careful."

*"You be careful," Diandra snapped. She picked up his own
empty glass and held it forward to Perry. Ethan didn't want
to see another thing.*

*He went upstairs to his room and collapsed onto the bed
without changing out of his clothes. He decided that if he
couldn't hear anything over the music it was as if nothing*

unpleasant could possibly be happening downstairs, and that was good. That meant he could sleep, and he did sleep, even though at some point the music went off and then he actually could hear, but the sounds weren't downstairs anymore, they were across the hall in his parents' room. Too loud. Too close. And totally on purpose. Of course she would bring him there when she had a room of her own, far away downstairs. What was the point of doing it if he didn't know about it?

If it's rocking don't come knocking.

And it was, and he didn't, because it made him sick. He never once said anything to Perry about it, though it changed their friendship, which was a big part of the reason his sister had done it in the first place. And he didn't once bring it up with Diandra either, not even after Perry was dead. But they both knew exactly what happened that night, and who her baby's father was.

At the bottom of that last page, there was another note in black ballpoint:

"At least your husband didn't rip off this chapter."

For a moment, she couldn't breathe.

Then, when the first wave of that passed, she began to persuade herself that the message, for all its venom, was actually, surprisingly reassuring, at least when it came to the deepest core of her concerns. For all the vitriol of the scribbled note, and in spite of the fact that it formed a far more pointed accusation than even *"Seem familiar?"* or *"Too close for comfort?,"* the sender's focus remained clearly on the crimes of the author, Jacob Finch Bonner, rather than anything she herself might have done in some former version of herself.

It had been a small comfort to her that *Crib*, at least, presented a version of her impregnation that bore so little resemblance to the truth. Jake had given his character Samantha a local Humbert Humbert, a lecherous innkeeper in a nearby town. Evan, however, had been in possession of many more relevant facts, and though this vile excerpt represented a gross distortion of actual events, it was accurate in its basic personae, timing, and settings.

Later in the manuscript, when it came to the matter of "Perry's" death, her brother would provide yet another approximation of the truth, but there, and unlike the night of the party, he hadn't actually been present. In fact, he would deal with the event quickly and in a general way, without anything that elevated it beyond an ordinary, even common accumulation of Vermont circumstances: teen driver, icy road. He would not even add the relevant fact that the car had belonged to "Perry" but that "Diandra" had been the one driving, or that "Perry," in the passenger seat, had been riding without a seat belt. That had been interesting to her. Had Evan been thinking like an author after all? Had he decided an accidentally-on-purpose accident would make for one too many nefarious crimes in a single novel, even a novel with such an abundantly evil anti-hero as . . . herself? Perhaps he'd been uncharacteristically unsure about this one, or uncharacteristically hesitant to accuse.

That was the thing about a private experience. You could speculate all you wanted. You could fictionalize. You could assume. And Evan had done every one of those things, repeatedly. But you couldn't know for sure.

The fire marshal, for example, hadn't known for sure how she and her baby managed to survive the same carbon monoxide poisoning that took out her parents. The parents were older, of course, and less healthy. (Her mother, who had been diagnosed with breast cancer two years earlier, and had already undergone one round of chemo, was decidedly unhealthy. And her father was a smoker.) Also, there had been an open window in the room she shared with the baby, so that was obviously fortunate. But really, it might easily have been four people going to sleep in the house that night and never waking up, and instead it was only two. Who could say why?

When it came to the person Evan had based "Perry" on, there had been even fewer people present for the event in question: herself and Patrick Bessette in Patrick's car on a dark Vermont road at the tail end of winter—after a rain, after a freeze. It was a situation he had tricked her into by arriving to pick her up at school, after a nighttime student government meeting. She'd been waiting for her brother, whose responsibility it was to drive her, and she would not agree to get in the car with Patrick without a concession. He had to let her drive. Because—as she told him, seizing her opportunity—she was a new driver and needed the practice, but already what she told him and what she intended had diverged. Yes, she was that miserable, and that enraged with the people around her who had rendered her so helpless. And Patrick had agreed to the request, because he'd been so very motivated to speak to her, and because he believed that her rumored and now very visible pregnancy was something they needed to *discuss*, and that he was *entitled to discuss it with her*. But she did not want to have any discussion with Patrick. It made her sick to be alone with him, and she was trying to concentrate on the road, and it was dark and she was looking hard for black ice, because she might be an inexperienced driver but she was also a Vermonter. And also because she was a sixteen-year-old under-going a forced pregnancy that had itself resulted from a forced act, otherwise known as rape, and she had recently been informed by her parents that there would be no mitigation for either of those things, not even after the baby was born. Involuntary act. Involuntary pregnancy. Involuntary motherhood.

As with that open window in her bedroom a year later, she truly did not care, at that moment, whether she would herself survive the drive home along those treacherous Vermont roads.

But she had lived, and the involuntary pregnancy that would in due course become a baby—her daughter, Rose— had also lived. And Patrick Bessette, the father of that unwanted child, had died. Who could say why?

"At least your husband didn't rip off this chapter."

It was nasty and it was personal, but its focus was, mercifully, on Jake's literary transgressions. And so there remained in place that final partition between her identity as Jake's widow and her identity as Evan Parker's sister: the actual and actually harmed person in all of this. Whoever had sent these pages couldn't yet know her connection to Evan Parker, the wronged writer, but it was still, as they themselves had written: *"Too close for comfort."* And it had to stop now.

After weeks of wakeful, restless nights, the only person she could imagine this hate-filled and hateful correspondent to be, the only one she could settle on, was Martin Purcell. So far, Purcell had been obsequious in his communications, helpful and eager, but beneath all that there might be a reservoir of anger, informed by conversations with her brother, both at Ripley and after, when they met in Rutland or in Burlington. Perhaps there had been phone calls between them, or emails, because the two of them were fellow writers, or thought of themselves as such, and they might have been literary correspondents as well, baring their souls to each other. At any point—in an email, over a beer, after a concert—Evan Parker might have passed along a copy of his great work, his sordid and offensive *fictionalization* of her life.

She didn't know for sure. It was time she knew, for sure.

PART TWO

16

Eventide

For the next few days, Anna made herself do nothing. After that, as if she were being rewarded for her care and restraint, the planning began to come easily.

First, she emailed Purcell and asked if he would be willing to meet with her. Predictably, he apologized for not being able to travel to New York.

"I would absolutely love that. Unfortunately, however, I am in the middle of the school term, and it just isn't possible to come down."

"Oh no," Anna emailed back. *"I was thinking I would come up. You know, there are places that were important to Jake that I've never even visited. One of them is Ripley. I was actually hoping you might meet me there. We could look through the submissions together and make our final decision about which to include."*

She could almost feel, herself, the surge of power that reading those words must have sent through him. Mastery over his comrades! The final decision about who would get published, and who wouldn't!

"I am going to make a reservation at the inn up there, next Saturday? And I wondered . . . perhaps you could drive up from Burlington?"

That would take less than two hours, she knew. Even a self-important high school robotics coach could tear himself away for an afternoon. Or, if absolutely necessary, an overnight.

"*Yes, certainly!*" he agreed. He said something about a morning event but promised to join her in Ripley by midafternoon. *All the better*, Anna thought. The closer their agenda got pushed toward evening, the easier her own task would be. They agreed to meet at the inn at three and take a walk through the campus while it was still light. Their editorial work would follow.

She began to tell everyone what she was doing. Jake's parents were delighted, and Matilda praised her selflessness. Wendy, however, seemed a little worried.

"So . . ." her editor said carefully, "this isn't something we'd be a part of, I don't think. I mean, we have such reverence for Jake, as you know, but something like this would have to go through our editorial board, and I'm not sure . . ."

"Oh, Wendy, no," Anna told her, and she could hear her editor's relief through the phone. "I know an anthology of work by his students is hardly a commercial endeavor. This is just a private thing. I'm going to underwrite it myself. A limited edition, for them. And his friends."

Jake hadn't had that many friends, in fact.

"I just thought it would be a nice thing to do."

"It *is*," Wendy said, passionately. "Maybe we could help arrange a reading for you, here in the city."

"Well, that would be *lovely*. I'm just going up to Vermont next weekend, to meet with this one friend, a former Ripley student. We're going to go through the submissions and decide which will go in."

"That's a long way to go," Wendy observed. "You could just do it over Zoom, couldn't you?"

"I suppose so. To tell you the truth, I was a little bit surprised that he felt so strongly about my going up there. But then I thought, I never saw the place, and it was important to Jake. So I don't mind."

There was a moment of silence. Then: "You know, Anna, sometimes I worry about people taking advantage of you. I hear from the reps and the booksellers how generous you are at the events, with all these people. It can't be easy, knowing the stuff they're bringing you—their own problems and all that. This kind of a book . . . it comes with a certain extra freight, as I'm sure you've discovered. I won't say it isn't good for sales, because of course it is, but I can only imagine how much it takes out of you, personally. You need to prioritize yourself, you know. Do you know?"

Yes, she knew.

"I try," said Anna. "But . . . it's not always possible. And then, I just had this idea of something nice I could do for these students of Jake's. And for Jake, obviously. Or . . . well, at least for his parents . . ."

"Oh God," said Wendy. "I can't stand thinking about his parents. How are they?"

Anna sighed. "Not the best," she admitted. "And you know, Jake was a teacher in addition to everything else. And nobody has really addressed that part of his legacy. So I thought . . . you know. I would."

"Well, it's extraordinarily kind of you. I just hope it doesn't take up too much of your time. You have your own work to do."

This was Wendy's first and very oblique nod to the notion of a second book. Anna had to admire her subtlety.

"Oh, I know," she said. "Not that I've started anything."

"Take your time," her editor said. Meaning: *When can I expect it?*

After they hung up, she sat for a long while in the fading light of her apartment. She had never been a person who cared much for her surroundings. When she came to New York she had joined Jake already in situ, and made only a few practical improvements—getting rid of an awful reclining chair, for example, and some old posters he'd held on to for far too long—but she hadn't changed anything since his death. Still here, for example, was the kilim-covered couch she'd chosen to replace some monstrosity he might have picked up off the street in Iowa City or Brooklyn, and the old oak table where her husband had written his final novel. (It was also the table at which she'd finished her own novel, after bringing home most of a first draft of *The Afterword* from the artists' colony.) It was a solid and square thing, that shade of Victorian beige so popular in quaint bed-and-breakfasts, with a few never-used leaves they kept in the hall closet. She and Jake had had their coffee here in the mornings, sharing the *New York Times*. They'd unpacked many bags of delivered Thai and Chinese food from their favorite restaurants onto this table. And she had also served Jake his final meal right here, before helping him up from his chair to stumble across the living room and into their bedroom. She had no feelings about the table one way or the other, and it had not occurred to her to replace it, or its matching chairs. Why would she?

Still, sitting here in this place she hadn't chosen, looking at the view across Abingdon Square, it did occur to her that she had no reason not to move on to a place of her own choosing and her own design. The apartment, in an older and well-run co-op, in a desirable Manhattan neighborhood, had real value, and selling it would allow her to buy just about anywhere. She had enjoyed New York, but it wasn't exactly anonymous for her, not now, not in the version of the city she inhabited, with people who might think they knew her from her noted fiction or her noted life. She might be better off in some small city where people didn't obsess about books and the writers who wrote them, somewhere not entirely devoid of culture, with pretty neighborhoods full of people who understood the importance of not intruding. Maybe somewhere in a flyover state that people like her late husband hadn't yet colonized. Eureka Springs, Arkansas. Lawrence, Kansas. Red Wing, Minnesota. They were out there, towns or small cities she might live in comfortably, and perhaps even—if she felt like it—continue the "work" her editor was evidently hoping for. But also: be left alone.

First, though, this matter would have to be dealt with, this unanticipated connection to her actual history: identified, and then severed, and then cauterized.

At Ripley she would have her best chance to walk Martin Purcell through the group of people who had known her brother, using their literary submissions to elicit whatever memories or impressions he might have. Perhaps visiting the campus itself would help bring other information to light. Perhaps there would be some stray reference to a lurking character, a hostile presence, someone her brother might have felt competitive enough with to confide in, or, more likely, brag to.

Most of all, though, she needed to make up her mind about Purcell, himself. Nothing he had actually said so far had placed him nearer to Evan than any one of those fans her brother had always managed to gather around himself, the kind of acolyte he'd drawn as a high school star or a charismatic bar owner, perhaps even as a (self-proclaimed) exemplar of sobriety in his final years. Evan had been made for praise, spoiled with it as a little child, cushioned by it as an athlete, kept afloat by it as a business owner, and Anna could only imagine how he'd have flourished as a writer of "fiction." Whatever fate his book might have met among the kind of New York literati Jacob Finch Bonner longed to impress,

Anna knew that the state of Vermont would instantly have covered Evan Parker in glory. *Vermont Magazine* and *Yankee* would have hailed the homegrown prodigy, and Vermont Public Radio would have given him his own show, just to talk about himself. "Vermont Native's First Novel Makes the *New York Times*' Bestseller List," the *Burlington Free Press* would have declared. Bennington and Middlebury Colleges would have pissed themselves, hurling their laurels at him. Of course, the state boasted more than its share of novelist-imports, but Evan Parker was something different—a "native"—and that would have made all the difference. Born in Vermont? Educated in Vermont? A lifelong Vermont resident, and with bona fide working-class credentials to boot? Because this debut novelist was no child of a Brahmin family who'd opted to live year-round at their Stowe retreat, sending their kids to Green Mountain Valley or Putney (when they weren't all out on the slopes). This was a real Green Mountain family; descended, perhaps, from successful quarry owners, but now, after a century and a half of classic Yankee downward mobility, just as hardscrabble as almost everyone else in the state. And did it get any more authentic than an author whose day job was running a bar in Rutland? Every *New Yorker*-reading liberal from Brattleboro to Thompson's Point would have risen to their feet in praise of Evan Parker's homegrown success.

Thank goodness some karmic justice had prevented *that* from happening.

She called the Ripley Inn and booked a room for herself. She asked about a dinner reservation, too, and the woman on the other end of the phone actually laughed.

"Oh, you don't need one. Just, you know, walk in. It's pretty relaxed."

Frozen hamburgers and lowest-common-denominator pizza, in other words. Maybe with parsley sprinkled around the rim of the plates, for that fine dining touch. God, she hated Vermont.

17

Ripley Under Ground

Martin Purcell, in a red down vest over a white shirt and a green linen tie, was waiting for her in the lobby of the Ripley Inn. She had driven up the day before, and, upon arrival, purposely overshared with the innkeeper who checked her in, the waitress in the restaurant (which had absolutely lived down to expectations), and, earlier that morning, the owner of the coffee shop next door, where she'd had her breakfast. The town of Ripley—already dying and now with an actually crumbling college campus across the road from the inn—might barely be clinging to the map, but by her second day most of its population knew who she was: a widow whose husband had once taught at the college, here to see the place that had meant so much to him and meet one of his former students. Everyone she'd spoken with was also up to speed on her project, a collection of work by her late husband's Ripley students, a labor of love if ever there was one! Still, she made sure to introduce Purcell to the innkeeper when he passed through the lobby.

"Oh, yes," he said. "Up from Burlington."

"South Burlington. I'm a teacher."

"Good to have you," the innkeeper said, and went about his business.

They walked out shortly afterward, crossing the road to what had been the main entrance to the campus, and passing the college sign, sadly diminished by the loss of its *L* and *Y*.

"What a shame," Anna said.

"Oh, it's a sad story. This whole part of the state is a bit, you know, down on its heels."

"Somebody told me they call it the Northeast Kingdom," she said. "Do you know why?"

He shifted smoothly into his teacher persona, which was predictably tiresome, and delivered a treatise on the region. From there he turned to the college's own history: Depression-era foundation, experimental and progressive philosophy, the desperate shift to low-residency programming in the 1990s, and the death spiral that ensued.

"Who owns it now?" she asked, looking at the dilapidated buildings, the neglected pathways.

"I'm not sure. Possibly the State of Vermont."

They had stopped in the middle of what might once have been a quadrangle, or at least there were older buildings on three sides, and a patch of woods on the fourth.

"I remember we had a barbecue here on the first night. There were some picnic tables. Well, one's still here."

And it was, alongside an outdoor grill entombed in a cement platform.

"I probably met Jake here. But I don't have any special memory. Everybody was here, faculty and students."

"Oh, tell me what you do remember," she said, trying not to sound too eager.

He talked about his own assigned professor, a guy who taught at Colby the rest of the year, and the other members of Ripley's lauded MFA faculty: that poet named Alice (though he, himself, hadn't had much interaction with the poets, either students or faculty), and the "multigenric" guy called Ricardo, he couldn't remember the first name.

Anna didn't press him on any of it. Later, when they went through the submissions, she could drill down on each and every one of the names. Now was not the time to seem too interested.

"That's where our classes were held," Purcell said, pointing at a sorry specimen of academic cinder block. It looked designed to eradicate even the possibility of hope or joy from any soul unfortunate enough to enter here.

"Ugh," she couldn't help saying.

"What?"

"Oh, it's just . . . so ugly."

He looked at her. "Is it? I never thought about it, one way or the other. A room full of writers, that's all I cared about. I'd never been in a room full of writers before. I think you mentioned, you didn't get an MFA?" Bizarrely, he spoke it as if it were a question.

"Me? No. I never even thought about being a writer, let alone getting a degree. It just kind of happened."

"Oh, is that right?" And there it was, that unmistakable edge. He might as well have added: *Until your husband paved the way for you and his agent and publisher felt sorry for you and got you a first-rate contract for your maiden effort?*

"I worked in podcasting and radio," she said, feigning cluelessness. "Do you think we can go inside?"

She followed him up to the main door, and it swung open, emitting a creak. Inside, a plaque read: NAMED IN HONOR OF RICHARD PENG, RIPLEY CLASS OF 1958, WHOSE GENEROS-ITY TO THE COLLEGE WILL INSPIRE THE GRATITUDE OF ALL FUTURE STUDENTS.

"Did it, though?" she said out loud.

"Did what?"

"Did Richard Peng's generosity inspire the gratitude of all future students?"

"I couldn't say. Never even noticed it before."

So much for that, thought Anna. "Do you know where Jake's classroom was?"

It had been upstairs, across the hall from his own seminar with the Colby professor. They climbed a flight of stairs and went down the hallway. There was a vague smell of mold, and the overhead light Purcell had turned on outside the men's room flickered dispiritedly. At least it worked.

"This one, I'm pretty sure," he said, and he opened a door into an equally soul-crushing space: dingy cinder block and institutional furniture—a desk, a seminar table, and chairs.

"Like I said, my group was across the hall. I never came in here."

"But this is the table where he held his workshops?" she asked. She sounded pitiful, but that was how she meant to sound.

"I would say so. Probably had ten or so students."

"Do you think we've been able to reach all of them? I'd love for them all to submit work for the anthology."

"Well, I think I mentioned one student passed away, not long after our course ended."

"Oh." She nodded. "Right."

She stood for a long moment. Then, carefully, she asked: "An older person? The one who died?"

"Unfortunately, no. I don't think he was more than forty, actually. A terrible tragedy."

Debatable, Anna thought, but she didn't respond. Later, they would get to this. Right now she was trying to imagine Jake here in this ugly room, sitting in the chair at the head of the seminar table surrounded by his students, or at the chair behind the desk, in conference with them individually, trying to come up with something decent and encouraging and not wholly dishonest to say. She attempted to conjure her late husband and her late brother here, staring at each other across the gray and cold desk, jockeying for control of the conversation. She knew who had won that contest, because of what must have taken place within these walls: the story Evan had ultimately told his teacher. The irresistible story. *Her* story, making its passage from its first thief to its second. Where else could that have happened but right here? It made her feel sick.

"Could we leave?" she asked Purcell.

"Of course. I don't think there's much else to see. Maybe the dining hall? Or the dormitories?"

But those buildings were, in fact, no longer there. The dining hall had been replaced by a prefab building that looked like temporary administrative quarters, now, abandoned. The dormitory had been cleared away. Possibly it had fallen down before that.

So they walked back to the inn and asked for coffee, and Anna went upstairs to retrieve the manuscripts from her room. She had gone through them only that morning, at the coffee shop next door, and had sorted them from least to most interesting. According to her own metric, at least.

18

Either/Or

All through the afternoon, they sat together in a corner of the lobby, at one of the oak tables. There seemed to be no other guests in residence, though a few people began to turn up as afternoon shifted to evening, stamping their feet in the entryway to dislodge a light dusting of snow, then moving into the bar, ready for their first drink of the day. She could hear a genial hum from that room, and the indistinct drone of a sportscaster from the television over the bar.

Purcell was taking his editorial responsibilities seriously. He frowned down at the manuscripts of his fellow Ripley students, assessing them as he might his own students' essays on the Green Mountain Boys or the French and Indian Wars, tempering encouragement with real-world criticism, though the encouragement—alone as the two of them were—was obviously unnecessary.

"I think I can tell where she's trying to go with this," he said of some woman's lame opening chapter, which she had submitted for the anthology on pages clearly reused from their last submission (there was a notation in ballpoint pen on the final page: "Thanks for sending!"). It involved the discovery of a corpse on a beach and actually featured the now infamous word—if it was, indeed, a word—"honeymelons."

"Okay," said Anna. "But is it any good?"

"Well," he said, diplomatically, "we don't know where it's going."

Oh, I think we do, thought Anna.

"It's not the kind of work I imagined we'd be including," she said. "I imagined, you know, literary work."

"But Ripley welcomed writers in all genres. Some people were doing work we might think of as literary. Myself, for example. But it was more of a big-tent approach, institutionally. There were people writing genre fiction alongside literary fiction and literary nonfiction."

"It's so confusing." She shook her head. "I never gave a thought to any of these terms."

She looked up to meet his eyes. Purcell was, she was certain, refraining from some commentary here, something along the lines of: *Of course you didn't. Why would a person with a side door to publication trouble herself with such things?* It was a second strike against him.

"Do you remember this writer?" she asked.

"Yes. Vaguely. She came from the Midwest somewhere. This was from a novel she'd been writing for years, already. About a group of sorority sisters meeting at a resort, and one of them washes up on the beach. I wonder if she ever finished it."

"Nice woman?"

"I thought so. Not a huge impression. She turns up in the Facebook group a lot but doesn't post about her own work at all. It's possible she never got past this excerpt," he said, a bit sadly. "You know, once you go back to the real world, it's hard to get your groove back. For some people."

Not for Evan, thought Anna. *More's the pity.*

"Well, we'll publish this part, anyway. She sent such a nice note about Jake with it. How he praised her inventiveness with language. I hope he wasn't talking about 'honeymelons.'"

"He was very diplomatic," Purcell agreed. "As a teacher, I recognize the impulse to find something to praise."

Or the desperation, she thought.

The next submission was an excerpt from a memoir in which a DNA test revealed the author to be "part African."

"He seems deeply affected," Anna commented.

"He was obsessed," said Purcell. "Talked about this constantly. Breakfast, lunch, dinner, it was the only thing on his mind. We all got tired of hearing about it."

"Sounds like a charming guy."

"He'd had a shock, obviously. I remember, he was from Cape Cod, real New England guy all the way back, he said. And then his daughter gave him a DNA test for Christmas and he didn't even send it in, at first. Because he thought he knew everything."

"Maybe he had a suspicion. Maybe that's why he didn't do it."

"Well, at any rate, when the results came back he had a total crisis. Repeated the test twice. Went into therapy. I think his therapist suggested he write about what he was going through, and he started doing this memoir."

"Nice guy?"

Purcell took a slug of his coffee.

"Frankly, it's hard to say. He had, literally, only the one thing he could talk about. That can wear on even the most patient person. And he was totally uninterested in anyone else. After a while he kind of went off by himself. He doesn't take part in the Facebook group, though he's enrolled. Otherwise he wouldn't have heard about this project, or submitted work."

"He told me Jake changed his life," Anna said, exaggerating a bit. "Sensitive teacher, took the time to discuss the real-life experiences that powered his memoir."

"Well," said Purcell, "I'm glad to hear he got something out of the class. And that he took the time to express his appreciation."

185

She let it go at that. She didn't think the "part African" from Cape Cod was her man.

Next was a novel set in a beaver dam "deep in the forest."

"Like *Watership Down*," she said brightly. "But without the rabbits."

Purcell was reading. "I haven't seen this one before," he said. "I don't recall any conversations about woodland creatures."

The author's letter said that she had found Jacob Finch Bonner's class to be "deeply enriching, inspirational, and profoundly spirit-giving." *Jake would have rolled his eyes at that*, Anna thought, but she took care not to do the same.

"What a nice woman," she said. "Do you remember her?"

"Not really." He shook his head. "I remember what she looked like. Short, with short white hair. She lived off campus because she'd brought her cat with her, I remember that. She couldn't bring the cat into the dorms. She must have rented something."

"Animal lover, obviously."

"Yeah. But not around all that much outside of class, and obviously we were in different seminars. I don't think it was ever published."

She looked at the cover letter again. "An excerpt in an online journal."

"Okay. Well, we'll include this first chapter. Why not?"

But he was already looking at the next manuscript. "Oh wow, I remember this. The guy had a whole series of mysteries organized around numerology."

"Another loon?" she asked, not unreasonably, but Purcell shook his head.

"Actually, no. Or at least, you'd never have been able to tell what he was writing. He looked like a completely average guy. Had a very boring job. Maybe insurance? But he'd been a math major. I think writing about this was like his road not taken, as far as math was concerned. He'd written two or three of these already, but he couldn't get an agent."

Forcing her way through a few of his sentences, Anna was hardly surprised to hear this. And every page featured some impenetrable equation.

"What should we do with this?" she asked.

"Oh, I'll look at it, if you want. I can find a readable excerpt. I mean, if there is one, I'll find it. And if there isn't—"

"I guess I'm just surprised," she interrupted him. "You know, so far these have been the same things, more or less, that Jake's students were working on when they were at Ripley. You remember them, and here they are, eight years later. Didn't anyone write anything new?"

He shrugged. "It's hard to write something new, especially when you feel you haven't finished what you were already working on. Or even if you feel it's finished, if there's no resolution, no completion through something like publication, you keep getting thrown back on the same project, trying to resolve it. Maybe it's hard to imagine that, since you were able to write your book and move directly to publication."

Strike three, Anna thought. She sat with this in silence. He could not have made himself more obvious. Well, that wasn't true. *Maybe it's hard to imagine because you cheated* might have been more obvious. But he was making himself increasingly obvious, as far as she was concerned. Whether he knew it or not, he was revealing himself to her.

"I'm sure you're right," she said, finally. "It must be terribly unsettling to work on a project for years and not be able to say it's completed, or move it off your desk, so to speak."

"It is," said Martin Purcell.

187

After a moment she said: "This man from Montana. I don't know what to think about him."

"Oh, that guy." Purcell laughed. "Richard Rosen? That guy *was* a loon, plain and simple. What did he send you? His Victor Hugo thing?"

"Yes indeed," she said, spreading out the pages on the oak tabletop. They both beheld a passage from *Les Misérables*, photocopied from a large-print edition of the novel. Each page had been speckled with notations in red pen, modernizing words that might have been considered archaic. In a passage about an old man trapped and dying beneath a fallen cart, for example, the sentence "It was impossible to disengage him otherwise than by lifting the vehicle off of him" had been corrected as "The only way to save him was by lifting the vehicle up off of him." Which Anna wasn't sure was much of an improvement.

"I don't understand this," she finally said to Purcell.

"Nobody did. I mean, of everybody there, this was the only guy I had serious concerns about. Like, sanity-wise."

"Because he was copyediting Victor Hugo instead of writing something of his own?"

"Not just copyediting. He was 'correcting Hugo's mistakes.' That's what he called it. I remember this part," he said, pointing at the manuscript. "We actually had a conversation about this. Next page."

Anna turned over the page, and there was a "correction" that went further than mere contemporary clarification.

"This is where Inspector Javert recognizes Jean Valjean, who's been living under an assumed name." He pointed: "Madeleine. Because only Valjean, the escaped prisoner, could possibly be strong enough to lift this cart off of the old man."

Anna could still read the original text, though Jake's student had run a red pen through the several lines:

Madeleine raised his head, met Javert's falcon eye still fixed upon him, looked at the motionless peasants, and smiled sadly. Then, without saying a word, he fell on his knees, and before the crowd had even had time to utter a cry, he was underneath the vehicle.

A terrible moment of expectation and silence ensued . . .

All the spectators were panting. The wheels had continued to sink, and it had become almost impossible for Madeleine to make his way from under the vehicle.

Suddenly the enormous mass was seen to quiver, the cart rose slowly, the wheels half emerged from the ruts. They heard a stifled voice crying, "Make haste! Help!" It was Madeleine, who had just made a final effort.

The reconstituted passage, with, apparently, Victor Hugo's mistakes *corrected*, read as follows:

Madeleine raised his head, met Javert's falcon eye still fixed upon him, looked at the motionless peasants, and smiled sadly. Then, without saying a word, he dashed into the woods and came back with a strong branch, which he inserted beneath one of the cart wheels and braced against a boulder.

A terrible moment of expectation and silence ensued . . .

All the spectators were panting. Then Madeleine pushed down upon the branch with all his might, and *suddenly the enormous mass was seen to quiver, the cart rose slowly, the wheels half emerged from the ruts. They heard a stifled voice crying, "Make haste! Help!" It was Madeleine,* pressing down hard against the lever he had employed.

"Okay, I still don't understand this," she said, shaking her head.

"It's probably better you don't," said Purcell. "Frankly, the fact that he submitted this for the anthology gives me the creeps. I never saw his name listed in our Facebook group, so either he's in communication with someone who participates or he's joined under a pseudonym. Either way, I wouldn't touch this. I know you want to honor your husband, but . . ."

"It's good advice," Anna said, deliberately removing the excerpt from the pile and placing it back in her folder, even as she flagged it for additional scrutiny. "Besides, I don't want Jake associated with plagiarism of any kind. Especially since . . ."

"Of course," he said. "It's the last thing any of us would want."

19

Doctor Sleep

Just after 8:00 P.M. they picked up their work and moved into the dining room, sitting in a booth as far from the bar and the big screen as they could get. Purcell ordered a cheeseburger. She ordered a salad and a bottle of Malbec she'd chosen from the abbreviated list. When it was brought to the table by their waitress, Anna noticed the vintage wasn't the one she'd requested.

"Wait," she told the waitress, just as the woman was about to stick the corkscrew in. "I asked for the 2005?"

"Oh, I know," the woman said. "But I found a fresher one."

Purcell didn't react. Anna simply nodded.

"What else?" she said, when the waitress had left.

The "fictionalized" memoir about growing up in Cleveland, by a woman Purcell had kept up with and liked. She had self-published the first part of her book and strong-armed every member of their group into buying a copy.

"It wasn't bad, actually," he said, taking a sip of his wine. "But I'm surprised she submitted it for this. Did you specify unpublished work?"

No, Anna had not. She hadn't wanted to limit submissions in any way. She'd wanted every one of Jake's former students to check in.

"I probably should have."

"Well, it might be up to whoever publishes this. Do you have a publisher yet?"

"Well . . . no. I mean, I've spoken with my editor . . . Jake's editor. Wendy Marder? At Macmillan?"

His eyes widened. "Macmillan is going to publish this?"

"It's a possibility," said Anna, because anything was, if you got right down to it. "We also talked about doing an event for it. In the city."

It might have been her imagination, but Martin Purcell appeared to sit up straighter. "This is such a wonderful thing you're doing," he said. "What a gift."

"It's a gift to me," she said, with warmth. "This is the first thing, since Jake died, that I've felt . . . you know, passionate about. The memorial service, I was so numb I barely registered what was happening, and anyway I let his mom and dad make the decisions. But this, I feel like, maybe because I'm a writer now, too, but I can really honor him this way, through the writers he impacted."

Purcell sighed. "I wish he'd impacted a few of these people a bit more. Some of these folks, I don't think they got the benefit from the experience. You know? I also wish I'd been his student, myself. I know he could have helped me."

"He wanted to help you. I told you how he talked about finding you an agent."

"Yes," Purcell said. "I'm still, just, stunned."

"I want to help. If I can. Not just for Jake but for you. I'm grateful to you for doing this with me. I meant to say, before. If there's something you'd like me to show my agent. Her name is Matilda Salter? She—"

"Oh, I know," he said. "I know who she is. She's only the best literary agent."

Yes, Anna knew. Only the best literary agent for Jake.

"Well, whatever I can do for you."

He was nodding. Then he sat back in the booth as his cheeseburger arrived, his eyes upon it, already devouring it, and for a moment he was reduced to his bodily hunger, his human greed, and Anna could see what an uncomplicated creature he was: simply a high school teacher who wanted— like so many others, like countless others—to be a writer like Jake was, and like she herself was, a guy who drove to work past a Barnes & Noble every single day wondering why his own theoretical volume wasn't in there, on the front tables, on the Staff Favorite shelves or the Discover Picks of the Month shelves, alongside those books by people who weren't any smarter or more deserving than he was. That's all. Just another wannabe writer, no different from the multitudes of people who had never, for all their posturing, put the words onto the page in front of them, or who had but whose words were the wrong words or in the wrong order, or inelegantly chosen, or correctly arranged but still lacking that elusive element—the distinctive voice. Or the writing was fine but the story was ordinary and unremarkable, or it had been told too many times before, or it just wasn't all that interesting, and the writer had been turned away at the agent's office or the editor's office, or at the bookstore itself by that final gatekeeper: the reader. There were so very many ways to fail at this, and so very many people who had done precisely that. Martin Purcell was obviously one of those people, and hardly the mastermind of torment she had somehow, in her private fear and worry, anointed him to be, appointed him to be. It pained her to admit this, but she now believed, on balance, that she had been wrong about him, that the small fact of wishing it were Purcell, the troll, the accuser, did not make it so. Martin Purcell, it appeared, had taken his personal writerly disappointments and tucked them away alongside his uncompleted writing projects and gone on with his life. He wasn't angry at Jake and he wasn't angry at her. Whoever the person was—the one who'd left a calling card in that Denver bookstore, the one who'd sent hateful messages to her home and the Bonners' home—it wasn't this guy in the green tie and the down vest, it wasn't this robotics coach whose cheeseburger was already half gone down his fleshy throat. This had been a waste: to have come all this way, to have taken this risk of returning to her home state. All she wanted, now, was to get rid of him so she could leave the restaurant, the inn, the stinking pit of despair that was and always would be: Vermont.

Her own salad was by now before her, though untouched. It looked especially dreary—iceberg lettuce with dried cranberries and, bizarrely, pine nuts sprinkled on top, overdressed with something beige that had the consistency of tapioca pudding. She picked up her fork.

"So," said Purcell, "there's something else I wanted to talk to you about. Or somebody else."

Anna looked at him. "Oh?"

"It's just . . . of course I'm grateful for myself, but I'm thinking about another writer who could be helped by this. Well . . . *helped.*" He sighed. "Arguably, he's past being helped. But he was a writer."

"Martin," Anna said, "I'm a little confused here. Are you talking about someone who hasn't submitted work for the anthology?"

"I'm talking about the student who died," said Martin. He had lifted his half-empty wineglass and was rubbing it nervously between his palms. Damp palms, Anna saw. The moisture, imprinting and smearing on the glass, made her stomach turn. Or perhaps that was simply Evan, finally entering the conversation. He was certainly present.

"Okay," she said.

"So. His name was Evan Parker. Has anyone else spoken about Evan?"

She shook her head. "You're the only person I've been working with."

"Yes, but I wondered if anyone had mentioned him, maybe in their communications with you."

Why would they? she thought. Every one of the Ripley writers had been concerned, first and last, with the imminent publication of their own work.

"No. No one has. Why?" she asked. "Was this person the most talented writer in the room or something?"

Purcell shrugged. With most of his cheeseburger obliterated, he had paused before the next assault. Anna took the opportunity to refill his wineglass.

"It's possible. Again, I wasn't in the classroom, but judging by these submissions I think it's very possible. It's more because he died so soon after the program. Just a couple of months. And you know, when that happens, it leaves a strong impression."

"Well, maybe for you," Anna said evenly. "But not one of the others has mentioned a . . . did you say Evan?"

"Evan. Parker. He was writing a novel."

Anna leaned back against the booth. She wanted to seem interested, but not too interested.

"And you read this novel?" she asked, and she was surprised to see that he actually shrugged.

"No, he never let me see it. It was more the way he talked about writing, and his process. He was just really serious about what he was doing. He was definitely doing the work, you know? I think he might have been the real thing."

The real thing? Anna didn't say it, but she hoped she was conveying her skepticism.

195

"I mean, the best writer Ripley produced. Would have produced."

That's not saying much. Another thing she didn't say out loud.

"Which is why it was so tragic, him dying so soon after the course ended."

"You're being very modest, of course," Anna said carefully. "You know how highly Jake thought of your own work."

"I'm very flattered by that, obviously. But yes. Quite possibly better than me."

"But what was his novel actually about? I mean, what was the plot of it?"

"Again, he never told me," said Purcell. "But I *can* tell you what it wasn't about. It wasn't about a body with 'honeymelon' breasts. It wasn't about adorable beavers deep in the forest. He wasn't fixing Victor Hugo or obsessing about his surprise African ancestry. He was doing serious work."

She picked up her wineglass and pretended to look contemplatively into its depths.

He said: "So, I wondered if you might consider, you know, including something by Evan. In the book. It would be very meaningful."

"To whom?" Anna said. "He's dead."

"To us as a group."

Even he must have known this to be untrue. Not one of the writers they'd discussed today would pause for one moment on their own roads to publication to think wistfully of that lost companion, Evan Parker.

"To me."

"You're a good person," she observed.

To his credit, he shrugged.

"Probably no better than anyone else. But I think Evan had talent. And I think Jake, who also had talent, might have recognized that. It feels right that Evan should be a part of this."

"But . . . even if I wanted to include the work, where would I get hold of it? You said you never read any of it, yourself."

"Unfortunately, no," Purcell said. He picked up the remaining piece of his cheeseburger. "I always felt bad about that. We were going to read each other's stuff after Ripley, but we never got around to that. He lived in Vermont, though, so we did manage to get together a couple of times, for concerts or a beer."

She sighed, heavily. "Well, that's a shame. But then there's nothing to publish, so it's kind of a moot issue."

"No, but I've been thinking about it, and I could ask the others. I guess it's possible Evan showed somebody else some pages, or they covered something in the workshop. Maybe someone still has a copy. It's possible. And also, he did have surviving family."

A chill went down her spine.

"Oh?" she managed.

"Or one person, anyway. I remember, there was a niece."

"A niece."

It was what she had been waiting for, until she'd stopped waiting. And here, in its own time, it was. About Martin Purcell, she had not, in the end, been wrong. Not that she was happy about it. She was not happy at all.

"I don't think they were close," he went on, oblivious. "There was no sign of her at the funeral, I noticed, and I introduced myself to everyone there. But she was the person who inherited everything after he died. The house, whatever was in it. For all I know, he'd finished the whole novel before he died, and it's still in a box somewhere, ready to be published."

A horrifying notion, Anna thought. But she managed a thoughtful nod.

"I mean, we don't know. She might have all of it stashed somewhere, everything he wrote, and not even know what it is. Even if she didn't know her uncle that well, she might agree it could be published. Should be published. Anyway, I could find her and ask. I would like to, with your permission."

His glass, when he set it down, hit the tabletop a tiny bit too hard, sending the remaining wine swirling around the inside.

So she poured him a little bit more. Then she asked the waitress for a fresh bottle, adding: "Whatever year you want."

"Worst that can happen is, she tells me no. She never saw it, or she threw it out, or whatever."

That was not the worst that could happen, Anna thought.

"And you know, it's the least you . . ."

She stared at him. Until that moment she hadn't been sure. Now, she was sure.

"I mean. *We* could do. For him."

Coming at her across the table: withheld speech, coated in accusation. Or maybe that was coming *from* her. At that particular moment, it hardly mattered.

"Martin," she finally said, "I think this is a beautiful idea. I think we should do it."

"I was hoping," he said, with evident relief. "I mean, I'm sorry, I didn't mean to imply—"

But she cut him off. She didn't want to hear what he hadn't meant to imply.

"Do you really think you can find her? The niece?"

He nodded. The rest of his burger had gone the way of the first half. "I think so. And if I can't, a couple of the kids on my

198

robotics team are super good at this stuff. I can put them to work."

Oh wonderful, Anna thought, nodding her assent. What could be worse than Martin Purcell rooting around the Parker family tree? A gang of computer hacks from South Burlington looking for Rose Parker. Way worse.

"Aha."

"Yes. So I think, probably, we could find her. Vermont's a small state, you know, and people tend to stay put. She's probably still here. She's probably here right now."

And there it was. All of this denial on her own part, all the benefit of the doubt she'd so kindly extended. She wondered at herself—she really did. Wendy had been right that she allowed others to take advantage of her! How long had this man in his ridiculous green tie been jerking her along? How much had he been enjoying himself at her expense? It really didn't bear thinking about, but it was hard to stop. She got to her feet and edged out of the booth. "Would you excuse me?" she said, looking down at him. "I have an awful headache. I need to get something from my room."

"I've got Tylenol," he offered. "Somewhere."

"No, it's prescription."

She walked out into the lobby, saw that the innkeeper was alone behind the desk, and promptly began to cry.

He looked up as she went past, heading for the stairs.

"Are you all right there?"

Observant, Anna thought. She leaned on the desk. "I'm sorry. It's just . . ."

"Can I do something?"

"No. I mean . . . remember I introduced you to my late husband's friend?"

"Sure," the man said. He was a classic Vermonter in red

flannel and gray sideburns, currently also fashionable in Brooklyn and possibly both Portlands, but nowhere else. "Working on the book together."

"Yes. But . . . oh, God, I should have been prepared for this, but I wasn't. He made a pass at me. He wants to spend the night here, in my room. I keep trying to make a joke out of it, and put him off, but he just keeps trying. I don't know what's worse, the stuff he's saying or the hands under the table."

"How awful for you," the man said, obviously uncomfortable.

"He's pretty drunk, though. I keep hoping he won't remember any of this tomorrow. So humiliating for him."

"Well, he won't be the first drunk to wake up blissfully unaware of how he made an ass of himself," the innkeeper said, sanctimoniously.

"But also," Anna said, taking a tissue he offered and wiping her eyes, "I can't let him drive, obviously. He's on his second bottle of wine. He can barely walk. And he lives, like, two hours away."

"It's not your responsibility," the man said, full of Yankee flint.

"I think it is. My husband would have wanted me to make sure his friend was all right."

"Would you like me to go and talk to him?" said the innkeeper, clearly not relishing the prospect.

"No! No." She emitted a ragged, post-tristesse sigh. "But . . . why don't you let me book him a room. Do you have a vacant room?"

He had many vacant rooms, she knew perfectly well.

"Something as far away from mine as possible."

She was on the second floor, down at the end of the corridor. He gave her something on the fourth floor, all the way at the other end.

"Thank you," she told him, accepting the key. "And also, I know you don't live here. I mean, on the premises. But would you mind giving me your number? Just in case," she said, trying to laugh. "You know, if he manages to come banging on my door in the middle of the night?"

"Of course," he said, and wrote it down for her. "Not to worry, though. Our doors may be old, but our locks are modern. He might make some noise, but he can't get in. You give me a shout and I'll come running over with my brother-in-law. Who happens to be the sheriff up in Guildhall."

"Oh, that's good to know," said Anna. "I'm just going upstairs to wash my face. Thank you for understanding."

When she returned to the restaurant a few minutes later, the waitress had cleared their plates and Purcell was sitting with the numerology manuscript, frowning as he read through it again. The level of liquid in his wineglass hadn't moved much, if at all.

"Are you feeling better?" he asked.

"Not yet. It takes a few minutes to kick in."

"What is it, a migraine?"

"Yes. All my life. Luckily, I have this magic pill now. I take it at the first sign. I'm almost normal in half an hour."

"How awful," he said. "Never had one, myself."

"You're a lucky man."

The waitress came, asking about dessert. "You know, I will," said Anna. She ordered an ice cream sundae. "What about you?"

"Oh. Coffee, please. I probably shouldn't have had so much wine."

"You did have a lot of wine," Anna agreed, mainly for the waitress's benefit.

After the waitress left, he said that he needed to get on the road soon. Then, conveniently, he excused himself and went to the bathroom, and by the time he returned, his coffee was waiting for him, with the crushed tablet she had brought from upstairs already stirred in. He added sugar and milk and drank a third of it right away.

"Martin," said Anna, "I was thinking about what you said before. I hope you don't mind if I bring it up again."

"Oh?" Already he seemed, though it was possibly just her imagination, not so fully *there* behind his vapid smile.

"About how it was the least I could do."

He was shaking his head, vigorously. "I shouldn't have. I didn't mean."

"What didn't you mean, Martin?"

"Because . . . what happened to you, was good. It's okay."

She nodded at him, as if this made perfect sense.

"What did happen to me?"

"I mean, your book."

"My book. The book I wrote about Jake. *The Afterword.* Is that the book you mean?"

He seemed to be losing his words. So he nodded.

"Um . . . your book."

Your book, your book. Anna sighed. It was all they thought about, these people.

"You wrote . . ."

"Yes. I wrote it. It didn't just *happen to me.* A person still needs to do the work, you know."

The waitress arrived with her sundae, and the sight of it, the smell of it, made her want to consume it right away. But first she picked up a spoonful of chocolate sauce and let it drip down, hypnotically, over the white whipped cream.

"And then . . . the agent."

Ah, the agent. "Matilda," she reminded him. "Matilda Salter. You said she was the best agent, and you were right. She was Jake's agent. Now she's mine. Don't I deserve the best agent?"

He was staring at her.

"Drink your coffee, Martin. You want to sober up, before you get on the road."

Obediently, he did.

"Don't I deserve the best agent?" she asked again. "Or did I not suffer enough first? Did I not work hard enough? Was there a step I missed?"

"Step," he repeated, as if he didn't understand the word.

"I was supposed to write books that didn't get published. I was supposed to get an MFA from some crappy place like Ripley, am I right? But I didn't. I just married a writer and when he died, I got his agent. And his publisher, too," she said, as if she'd just remembered this part. "That's the long and short of it, right? That's why you're so pissed at me."

It was moving pretty fast, she saw. She hated having to abandon her sundae, but she thought she'd better get him upstairs.

"Not. Pissed," he said, pathetically.

"Oh no? That's not what all this has been about?" She scooped up an enormous bite of her ice cream and brownie. The chocolate sauce was from a can, obviously, and the cream was definitely Reddi-wip, but it was all delicious.

"This," he said, with a baffling nod.

"This. Campaign of yours. The note you left for me in Denver. The pages from Evan's book you sent to me at home. The ones you sent to Jake's parents! Nasty, Martin. Don't you think those people have suffered enough?"

He was looking alarmed, but also ill. "No, no," he said.

"They haven't suffered enough?"

"No. No."

She sighed. She held up her credit card, and the waitress came over.

"Not going to finish that?" the waitress said, indicating the sundae. "You want me to pack it up for you?"

For a moment she actually considered it.

"No, I think I have to get this guy upstairs to his room while he can still stand up."

The woman didn't even look at Purcell, but she did give Anna a sympathetic nod when she came back with the check.

"Come on, then," Anna said. She stood by him at the edge of the booth and took him by the elbow. He looked ridiculous now, in his green linen tie and the down vest he had never removed, all through the afternoon and evening. She draped his arm over her shoulder, but that was mainly for show. He didn't need actual support. "I have a nice place for you to rest," she told him, and he nodded.

"Need help?" said the innkeeper as she passed his desk.

"No. He said he wanted to stay. He agreed not to drive, thank goodness. Wouldn't want that on my conscience."

"No indeed," the innkeeper said.

20

Closing Time

The bar stayed open till midnight, though the last guest left at
eleven. The innkeeper was long gone by then; she'd watched
him climb into a truck below her window and pull out onto
the road, disappearing behind the trees. By 1:00 A.M., as far as
she knew, she and Martin Purcell were alone in the building,
but she resolved to act as if they were not. She let another two
hours go by, listening for anything. Then, just after three, she
slipped out into the hall.

The floors, being old in an old house, were not silent. She
experimented with how she put her weight down—rolling
from heel to toe, landing on the outside edges of her feet—but
it didn't make much difference. She kept on the carpet runners
and moved swiftly. The stairs were better. They were compliant
with fire codes, and made of concrete, and her feet produced
only the mildest whooshing sound as she climbed. She opened
the door to the fourth-floor corridor and stood for another
moment, listening and looking. There was nothing.

She had kept the key from earlier, of course; now, after
using it to open Purcell's door, she placed it on his bedside
table. She'd put him to bed fully clothed, and he had turned
onto his side, the green linen tie thrown back over his shoulder.
He was deeply asleep. She looked around, trying to see the
room through a stranger's eyes: a drunk man who hadn't
expected to spend the night in a hotel, no change of clothes, no
toothbrush, only a phone still in his pocket. It was glowing

green through the fabric of his pants, its screen full of messages. Well, she wasn't going near that.

"Martin," Anna whispered, and to her surprise he sat up immediately, as if called from the dead. "Martin?"

"Yes?" said Martin Purcell.

"You need to come with me now."

"Okay." He stood up. It was an amazing drug, really. She'd carried it with her for a number of years, always at the ready, just in case some person in a restaurant or on a plane or at a book event let her know that she'd been recognized, noted, attached to her real name and even the tiniest part of her real history, because the tiniest part was too much as far as she was concerned.

Didn't we go to school together?
I remember you, from Rutland!
I knew your brother.
I knew your daughter.

No one could ever say those things to her, not for the rest of her life.

Or they could, but she would make them forget they ever had.

Because what they said about this drug was true, which was why people who wanted to do bad things—and not have those things be remembered by the people they did them to—used it all the time. But this was not a case like that. This was a special case, requiring a special outcome.

"Come with me," she told Martin Purcell again.

He walked before her down the hall, and she opened the door to the stairway for him. Then, standing behind him, she unbuttoned his belt and unzipped his brown corduroy pants, letting them fall to his ankles. He teetered for a moment; then, with her upper body, she nudged him forward into oblivion.

This time there was noise, unmistakable to anyone who might be nearby and listening, but no one apart from herself was doing either of those things. Something had cracked open inside Martin Purcell, and now blood was spreading across the gray cement. She thought she'd better move before getting past him without leaving a trace became an issue, so she pulled the ends of her shirtsleeves down over her hands and gripped the handrails through the fabric, vaulting over that broken body and landing several steps lower. Then she moved quickly down the second flight and back along the corridor to her own door.

A final interlude, listening to the silence and the motionlessness, and also for the sounds of a person calling out, a person who was possibly not as dead as she'd imagined him to be. But nothing like that could be heard because nothing like that was true. She was alone in the Ripley Inn, a failing establishment in a failing town beside an already failed college that once both employed and pretended to educate failed writers, and all was right with the world.

Then, finally, and for the first time in months, she slept without fear, because surely it was over now.

21

Paradise Regained

They came to wake her up at about eight the following morning, knocking at her door not loudly but with an intensity that came right through the wood. She took a moment to organize her thoughts before she answered.

It was the innkeeper, he of the unfashionable sideburns, and a police officer, short and bald and obviously upset.

"Good morning!" she told both of them, appropriately concerned.

They delivered the bad news, like a poorly rehearsed vaudeville team. The only words that came through were *sorry*, *terrible*, *stairs*, and *injury*.

"Wait, what?" She gaped at them. "I don't understand. Who did?"

"Your friend. Your husband's friend," said the cop.

"Late husband," said the innkeeper.

They were not capable of making sense, so she burst into tears, and her apparent womanly hysteria helped move things along. Thus was she given to understand that the chambermaid, entering the inn that morning through its back door, had found a small dollop of viscous black fluid on the second-floor landing, and soon discovered that said fluid had originated in the body of Martin Purcell, two floors above. A nasty thing. Nasty and, naturally, so very sad.

But Anna was still too shocked to take it all in. She asked if she could see Martin, but he had already been removed, so she got dressed and went with the innkeeper's brother-in-law to the coffee shop next door, in order to give her own version of the previous day's and night's events. Periodically through this conversation, she cried, and periodically she went silent, as if in shock. Once she said: "Oh my God, I think he has a wife. He might have kids!" Which was terrible, but really, her own interactions with him had been so brief and at such a distance. They'd never even met, face-to-face, before the previous day, and their communication had been entirely concerned with a book he was helping her organize, a kind of tribute to her late husband, Jacob Finch Bonner, whom Martin Purcell had briefly known at Ripley College. Even as she said all this she was on her phone, forwarding each and every one of their emails to the sheriff. The entirety of their online conversation, she explained, had been about the book: how it might be organized, who might submit their work to it, which day they each were available to meet at Ripley and go through the selections. They had spent that day walking through the campus and discussing submissions, right there in the lobby of the inn with who knew how many people walking past, and it had all been very friendly. Yes, he had had a lot to drink over dinner, the better part of two bottles of wine, and yes, she'd begun to worry that he might insist on driving home in that inebriated state. Luckily there was a vacant room for him, which she had paid for, herself.

Responsibly, because there had been a death involved, the sheriff reminded her that Mr. Purcell had also made unwanted advances toward her, or so she had reported to his brother-in-law, the innkeeper, which made Anna nearly weep again. But she got control of herself.

"It's true. He did. But I would feel terrible if that became something . . . his wife . . . I mean, I don't know her, but how awful. Besides, he was drunk and fell down the stairs. That's what you're saying, yes? So it had nothing to do with that."

"He was on his way down the stairs in the middle of the night," said the sheriff. "To the floor your room happened to be on. And it's also the case that he had unzipped his pants. In fact, they were what tripped him. Of course, it could be that he was too inebriated to have done that with any intention at all, but it's an unfortunate combination of facts, I would say."

"Oh my God."

There seemed to be nothing more to add.

By noon she had been told that she was free to leave, but she took another walk through the sad campus across the road, now saying what she hoped would be a final goodbye to the three of them: Evan, Jake, Martin, men who had harmed her, threatened her, and stolen from her. Really, she had never been a person who imposed herself on the lives of others. Anything she had ever felt, everything she had ever done, was in response to some unprompted aggression against herself, and how much better the world would be if everyone could show some fraction of her own restraint when it came to other people. Live your life, leave everyone else alone, and stick to your own story . . . that was the key to personal and communal happiness, wasn't it? It was just too bad that this succession of men had taken it upon themselves to violate her space, when all she had ever asked for was the peace that anyone deserved.

Well, she thought, taking a last look at that sad Richard Peng Hall, where so many of her troubles had begun, she would at least have peace now.

After that, she got in her car and drove south, through and away from this hated place, this tall and narrow state with its bony spine of mountains, escaping it, this time, for good. Or so she had every reason to expect.

22

Independence Day

When spring came, she did it: she put the apartment on the market, not that she was close to making a decision about where she might want to live. Sometimes she took her laptop to one of the neighborhood cafés, finding a table among the tables of hard-at-work writers, and browsed the lists of livable cities and up-and-coming towns in every state. New England, of course, was out (though she did linger over some of the lovely places on the Connecticut coast), and a single year down south had proved sufficient for a lifetime. Seattle, a place she'd absolutely enjoyed, still felt like going backward, and she was enough of a New Yorker now that most of the other major cities felt like poorer versions of that city. She'd now been several times to Los Angeles for meetings with the team developing Jake's novel *Crib,* and the one at Netflix which had optioned *The Afterword* as a limited series, and while it had been fun to be squired about and taken to nice restaurants with appropriately fawning film people, the city itself had left her cold: an industry town with a single metric of success and its far more plentiful counterpart—failure. That was a nice place to visit, but not a place for her to live.

In the end, she decided to move forward without a concrete plan. If the apartment sold by summer—and her new Realtors, Lori and Laurie of Village Properties, assured her it would—she would take a road trip and visit some of the places she was still considering: San Francisco; Santa Fe; Madison, Wisconsin, and—ironically, given the deeply unpleasant experience of her last visit—Denver.

She felt light, unburdened, and ready to move on.

The business of the tribute book had been wrapped up quickly. She wrote to everyone who had submitted work, accepting and praising their submissions, then had one hundred copies privately printed. Everyone seemed thrilled with this outcome, and if any of these former students had shared Martin Purcell's hopes of a Macmillan (or even a Macmillan-endorsed) publication, they were good enough not to mention it. Once the copies of *A Ripley Roundtable: New Work by the Students of Jacob Finch Bonner* arrived, she arranged a reading at the McNally Jackson on Prince Street and invited the writers to perform. Every one of them, apart from the Victor Hugo revisionist in Montana, said yes, and Anna—though she was hardly looking forward to the event itself—was relieved; she wanted a last look at them before she put this entire episode behind her.

"You're a bit of a saint to do this," was Matilda's response when Anna called to invite her. "Of course, I understand how meaningful it must have been, to honor Jake."

"Not only Jake," she said. "You heard what happened when I went up to Vermont last fall, to meet with that friend of his who was helping with the project."

"Oh yeah. Just awful."

"So now, it's like, I *had* to do it. I wrote a little introduction about both of them. And honestly, I think Jake would have wanted me to. It's been a nice distraction."

This, predictably, gave rise to a not-subtle suggestion that a new writing project might also prove a nice distraction.

"I know, I know. I just don't have a good idea yet."

"Sometimes it's better not to wait for one. Sometimes it comes when you start something else. I had a client, once, who described it as jumping off a diving board and landing in a different pool."

That sounded very unpleasant, Anna thought. She was the kind of person who wanted to know where they would land *before* they jumped.

"But you're happy, right?" she asked her agent. "With how things are going?"

"We're very happy, yes. You should be, too."

The Afterword, though it had not cracked the uppermost echelon of the *New York Times* Bestseller List, had nonetheless settled into a strong and sustaining groove just beneath it, making her novel a great favorite of booksellers and putting it in a strong position as the paperback publication drew closer. Already there was talk of a second tour for the new edition, but it was more accurate to say that the initial hardcover tour had never truly ended and would now flow seamlessly into what lay ahead.

In the meantime, *Crib* was finally—after some delays—set to begin filming in June with a theatrical release planned for the following summer. "Wendy is hoping you'll be willing to add some events for the tie-in edition to your own schedule."

"Of course," said Anna. She would do everything she could to continue promoting her late husband's work. She expected it to sustain her for the rest of her life.

She managed to persuade her agent to attend the McNally Jackson reading, a big ask, she knew, and so she was surprised when the not-much-looked-forward-to event rolled around, to see that Matilda had brought Wendy with her.

"This is so kind of you both," Anna said, finding them out on the sidewalk, probably reluctant to enter the bookstore until they absolutely had to.

"Not at all!" said Wendy, brightly.

"I told her, you never know, our next Jake might be in the basement at McNally Jackson tonight!"

Not likely, Anna thought, but she smiled.

"Or our next Anna!" Wendy corrected.

"But actually, we were both hoping we could take you out for dinner afterward. That is, if you're not committed to the group."

She was not committed. She had wanted very much to avoid the awkwardness of taking ten writers out for dinner, let alone in one of the city's most expensive neighborhoods, so she had asked the bookstore if she might bring champagne for a post-reading toast to Jake. After that, and whatever conversation proved necessary, she welcomed the excuse to depart.

The events coordinator greeted her just inside. Anna had done more than one reading here, first of Jake's work and later of her own. "We don't usually do events for a privately published work," she told Anna, who already knew this, and who likewise understood that "privately published," in this instance, was a euphemism for "self-published."

"I am really grateful," she said. "I hope it hasn't been too much trouble."

"We put it on the website. Most of the calls have been about whether you'd be here, and signing your own books. I ordered more copies of *The Afterword*, and *Crib*, too."

"That's great," Anna said.

"But I also heard from your authors about whether they could bring their own stuff to sell. I had to tell them no," she said, not very regretfully. "I hope that isn't a problem."

Not to me, thought Anna. "Oh, I'm sorry about that," she told the coordinator.

Downstairs in the basement, she unpacked the bottles of champagne she'd brought and tried not to make eye contact with the people already milling around, but they wasted no time in greeting her. In quick succession she met the creator of the beaver story, of the former sorority sister with the colorfully described breasts. She met the man who was "part African"—he looked every inch the New Englander Martin Purcell had described him to be—and the author of the "fictionalized memoir" about growing up in Cleveland. She had flown in from Cleveland that afternoon.

"It's so good to put the faces to the writing," Anna said.

Two of them gave her copies of their books, also "privately published." Anna slipped them into her purse. One of them brought an ornately tooled leather bookmark with the initials *AWB* carved into it, to thank her for this great occasion, and for the anthology itself. The numerology man was tall and thin and lived in New Jersey, closer to Philadelphia than New York. He was the only one to ask for her help in getting an agent for his series of thrillers, but she noticed how closely their conversation was attended to by the others. "Write to me after tonight," she told him.

She hoped that none of them would recognize Wendy or Matilda when the two of them, at the last possible moment, descended the stairs and joined the writers, their guests, and whoever else had, for whatever unimaginable reason, decided to spend an hour of their lives listening to these people—reading work in honor of a teacher none of them had cared enough about to remain in touch with, even after his own great success.

A month earlier, when the copies of *The Ripley Roundtable* arrived, she'd sent each contributor six copies and a personal note. The rest of the run was on a table beside the podium, available free to anyone who wanted a copy. She did not expect to walk out with a single book once the event was over; after tonight, she preferred to have none of these people in her home, even in their written manifestation. And besides, Lori and Laurie would soon be supervising the emptying, repainting, and staging of her apartment in preparation for an open house. It was a time to purge, not to accumulate, not to retain, even the desirable objects. This "privately printed" book was hardly a desirable object.

The events coordinator introduced her as the author of *The Afterword* and the creator of the very special anthology they had gathered to celebrate. The book had a very small print run, and tonight's event was made even more special by the fact that so many of its contributors had gathered to launch it. Most special of all, she finished, was the spirit of another great writer, gone too soon, whose presence was also with them, and while the world had known Jacob Finch Bonner as a gifted and successful novelist, it was deeply meaningful to know him as the committed teacher he also was.

With that, the podium was turned over to Anna.

First, she thanked the store for its generosity in hosting them, and the participants for traveling to be here, some from as far away as Cape Cod and Ohio. She thanked her husband's former students for indulging her wish to honor him, though she'd been unable to offer them what all writers deserved: appropriate payment for their work.

This went over well, with approving nods throughout the basement.

"I've said this to many of you, individually, but I want you all to know how important teaching was to Jake. He truly believed in it, and the fact that anyone who wants to be a writer has that potential to tell their own story. I also want to say how much I've appreciated hearing your memories of Jake, and your accounts of how he was able to help you in your writing practices. You can't imagine how healing these stories have been for me."

"Yes we can!" said a bright voice from the back.

"So when people asked me, why did I want to pursue this project, those are the reasons, and the fact that Jake loved his students. He always said, when he was in the classroom, he sometimes forgot who was the teacher and who was the student."

"Hear, hear," said the woman from Cleveland.

"And just one other thing before we get to the reason we're really here. I wanted to acknowledge the contribution of Martin Purcell, who died in an awful accident while we were working on this book. I can't believe he isn't here tonight to share in this celebration. He so believed in this, and he was so generous with his time, even though he, himself, wasn't one of Jake's students. I took the liberty of dedicating the anthology to him, as well as to my husband." She wiped a discreet tear from the corner of her eye. "Thank you, Martin," she said.

Then she sat down, trying to make herself comfortable in the folding chair for what promised to be a grueling test of her endurance. Eight readers had been asked, by email, to read for no more than ten minutes each, but the first one went to twenty and the rest, emboldened by that, did the same. The Cleveland memoirist read an excerpt about a high school dance at which she'd been elected queen. The numerologist read a chapter in which a math professor described a mind-numbing equation. The man from Cape Cod, to his credit, did not read anything about his surprising DNA discovery; instead, he delivered a turgid description of a pond near his home in Falmouth, and after he finished, Wendy slipped her a note and escaped up the stairs with Matilda. The note said that they'd wait for her at Balthazar. She could hardly blame them.

It lasted a good two hours, after which she insisted they all share in a toast to Jake. Not one of them had given her the slightest note of concern. Apart from the single request for help with an agent, none of them had even suggested remaining in touch with her after tonight. More significant still, the loss of Martin Purcell had not seemed to strike any of them in a personal way; no one had even paused to say the *generically* nice things about him that they'd said about Jake. The notion that Martin had confided in one of these people about the excerpts he'd mailed to her and to Jake's parents, let alone that he had done those things in coordination with one of them, seemed less and less likely with each of Jake's students she spoke to. The name Evan Parker was never mentioned; that long-ago classmate, she now felt sure, had left no trace at all. And when, at last, it felt safe to leave them behind in the basement of McNally Jackson, Anna climbed those stairs to street level with a sense of real relief. Then, newly invigorated, she texted Matilda that she was on her way.

23

Son of a Witch

She arrived at Balthazar as the two of them were being led from the bar to a table against the back wall, and they greeted her with obvious relief. "Oh my God," said Wendy, gripping Anna's arm as she pulled her along with them. "I can't believe you had another hour of that."

"I had to stay," Anna said. "I was the host."

Her editor and agent slid onto the banquette, and Anna took one of the chairs facing them. The famously faux-smoky mirrors above their heads were tipped slightly forward, reflecting a flawless rendition of a Parisian brasserie. Or at least she supposed it was. She had never been to Paris, herself.

"I know, but . . . after that first one went on for so long, I was looking at Wendy, like . . . really?"

Anna shrugged. "They were excited to be there."

"Anna! You're too nice. This whole thing was: *Just. Too. Nice.* Enough with the nice!"

"Okay!" She smiled. "No more nice. Only mean from now on."

"No, I get it," Wendy said, looking for their waiter. She wanted wine. "This is about Jake. It's . . . honestly, I'm moved by it. We should have done more."

It was easy to say that now, Anna thought. But she brushed it aside. "Not at all. This was always a very personal thing. Macmillan has done so much for Jake."

"It was mutual," said Matilda, merely stating the obvious.

Soon their wine was delivered. Anna, who had lost her taste for red wine since her trip to Ripley, asked for a Kir instead.

"Would anyone be up for one of those seafood towers?" Matilda said. "They're so good here. I'd be happy with sharing one of those and eating the bread."

"I'd be happy with just the bread," said Wendy. "But it goes straight to my upper arms."

"Real French women don't care about their upper arms," Matilda said.

"That's because real French women have glorious upper arms," said Wendy.

"That's because they smoke instead of eating."

"Not anymore, surely," said Anna.

"Oh yes. A bite of foie gras and a cigarette. That's lunch. Imagine not caring!"

Anna, for her part, did not need to imagine. She was profoundly bored by the conversation, already.

"So here's to you, Anna," her editor said once the waiter had left with their order. "A good writer, a good wife, a good person."

Anna lifted her cocktail and touched it to their wineglasses. "I'll tell you the truth, I'm more than happy to end the evening this way. In fact, thank you for saving me. I was afraid I'd have to take them all out for dinner, then help them all get agents. I still might have to," she said, remembering the numerology thriller writer. "But it's much nicer being here with you, too. Unless you've lured me here to talk business, that is."

She could not miss the glance the two of them exchanged. Her spirits sank a little. She was not in a mood to be encouraged to get back to work.

"Well, not business, exactly," said Matilda. Tonight she had her hair loose, and every rich brown lock looked as if it had been carefully placed. She wore a large and misshapen single pearl that fell perfectly into the notch at the stop of her sternum. She looked, quite suddenly, uncomfortable.

"You guys are worrying me," Anna said, but with a grin.

"Yeah, well, we don't want you to worry," said Wendy.

It was exactly what people said to you when they did, in fact, want you to worry.

"Wendy and I have been putting our heads together about something," Matilda said. "It's more of a pain in the ass than a thing we need to react to, but in light of our shared . . ."

"Experience," Wendy inserted.

"Yeah. It's better we take it seriously before it *is* serious."

"Well," Anna said, now very wary, "I hope you don't think I know what any of that means."

This was the moment their food arrived. The tower of shell-fish, which Matilda was about to have all to herself, thanks to Anna's rapidly diminishing appetite, glistened over three tiered platters of ice.

"Somebody sent me a manuscript excerpt," Wendy said. "Unsolicited, obviously. The cover letter said it was a chapter from a novel. Okay, fine. It said the novel was about a mother who kills her daughter and steals her identity. Not so fine, but not really something I'm inclined to worry about. After a book like *Crib* it's not unusual to see a whole surge of similar books, all by writers who couldn't come up with an original story of their own. Why they bother, that I don't really understand." She turned to Matilda. "Do they think we're dying to publish *another* series about a boy wizard who goes to wizarding school? Or *another* novel about a kid who survives a museum bombing, somehow in possession of a priceless painting? It's done! Somebody else did it, and it was brilliant and successful, but now all the writers are going to have to think of something else to write about."

Matilda just nodded.

"Who sent it?" Anna asked impatiently.

"No one who felt like sharing their name. Or address. If my assistant hadn't been on the ball enough to keep the envelope, we wouldn't even have the postmark, but where does that get you? Anyone can go anywhere to mail something, can't they? The cover letter, though, had plenty to say. It accused Jake of stealing the idea for *Crib* from the person who'd written this excerpt. Someone he'd taught up in Vermont, where those students tonight were from. As if he'd have lifted work from one of *them*! You know, no offense to these very earnest writers, but we're not talking Iowa here!"

"Ripley," Anna said. She'd been speaking the name all night, but now it seemed to carry a fresh assault.

"Right. You know, I don't understand the impulse to go to one of these places, I really don't. Okay, maybe if you get one of those Stegners at Stanford, or it's Columbia, but who goes to a place like this Ripley and expects to become a great writer? I once gave a talk up at the Bread Loaf Writers' Conference and someone asked me about getting an MFA. I said: just take the money you were going to spend on a program, rent a cheap place somewhere, and buy a paperback of Stephen King's *On Writing*. They were scandalized."

Matilda was laughing. "I hope you're not holding out for an invite to the AWP conference."

"I am not," Wendy said. She had yet to begin the Dover Sole she'd ordered.

"But . . . this is terrible," Anna said. She was beginning to feel distinctly unwell.

"Yeah. It said the person Jake stole it from was dead, but he finished most of his novel before he died."

"As opposed to after he died?" said Matilda with abundant sarcasm. "Well, at least we're not dealing with somebody

222

who's channeling a dead novelist. That is so not on my bucket list. And also: *Most* of a novel? This is one of the most elastic words I've ever encountered. You know how many times I've asked an author how much of their book is finished? 'Most of it!'"

"Well, that's what it said."

Matilda extracted an oyster from the uppermost tier, put it on her own plate, and seemed to lose interest in it.

"And the manuscript excerpt that came with the cover letter?" Anna asked. "It was part of this mostly finished book?"

"Well, so I assume. A section of the theoretical masterpiece that Jake supposedly stole *Crib* from." She rolled her eyes.

Anna was feeling it now, the dread. It had begun at the back of her throat and was pulsing its way through her, electric and dull.

"And . . . was it a masterpiece?" she heard herself ask.

The two of them looked at each other.

"It wasn't terrible," said Matilda, who had apparently seen it, too. "The writing was competent. But I think I speak for both of us when I say that we don't care about the writing. We care about the fact that it was sent to Macmillan with a cover letter accusing our late author of plagiarism. Well, maybe 'care' isn't the right word. I'm so completely pissed that we apparently have to deal with this again."

"Yes," said Wendy, passionately.

"Anyway, the last thing I was going to do was bother you about it. I shared it with Matilda, because, I don't have to tell you, we went through all that shit with Jake after *Crib* came out, and I don't think either of us had any idea how it impacted him. Until . . . well, the idea of having that happen again and not addressing it, forcefully, was just . . ."

"But with Jake, you know, it was just internet bullshit," Matilda said. "*He's a plagiarist, He's a thief.* I've probably had a dozen authors accused of the same thing. It's happening a lot more than you hear about. It's, like, a special kind of doxing, just for writers, and it's rare you get anything to actually back it up. So with Jake, big surprise, there was only an accusation, no details about this supposed thievery he'd committed, and we were never sent anything to support the accusation. Which really makes me think this has to be a totally different asshole, completely unrelated to the person who came after Jake. Just two separate people sharing the character trait of general shittiness, right?"

Anna nodded, but her head was spinning.

"So . . . when did you say that excerpt came to your office?" she asked.

Wendy shook her head. The arrival of any envelope through the US mail—let alone one containing an unsolicited manuscript excerpt with an anonymous cover note—did not rank highly in her pantheon of priorities. She was at or near the top of every agent's submission list, and the manuscripts they sent her arrived all day, every day, often with deadlines or scheduled auctions attached. Work sent without representation went straight to her already overtaxed assistant. Sometimes that work accumulated until it could be read by a temp, if it got read at all.

"No idea. I just know when my assistant brought it to me."

Anna was calculating, furiously. Purcell had been dead since November. Now it was March. Could he have put this excerpt in the mail just before his sudden and certainly unanticipated demise? Of course! It was a coda—that was all. A coda of Martin Purcell's harassment, of a piece with what had come before. *Okay,* she thought. *Final point to you, Martin. Well played!* And yet, Purcell remained precisely as dead as he had been before tonight. It was still just as over as it had been yesterday. Albeit with more mess.

"We're not always so quick off the mark when it comes to the mail," Wendy said. "Nearly all the submissions are electronic. I mean, gone are the days of the manuscript boxes, right?"

This was addressed to Matilda, who was cracking a lobster claw.

"Oh yeah. The stacks of them, like color blocks. And we had to lug them everywhere. My assistant told me she was on the subway once, reading a manuscript in a box, and there was a girl watching her from down the other end of the car. It was the author."

"Oh my God," said Wendy. "She said something to your assistant?"

"Well, she apologized for staring. She said she recognized the box. Her agency always used the same yellow, and she knew the book had been sent around that week. But: creepy, right?"

"Definitely. That's something I don't mind consigning to the past. Not to mention the weight of all those manuscripts, and all the wasted paper, but also the lack of privacy. Today, if I'm on a plane or in an Uber, I'm reading on my tablet. Anyway"—she turned to Anna—"the point is, the only people out there who are still mailing us printed manuscripts are the unrepresented writers. Things can sometimes sit for a bit. Obviously, we try our best, but . . ."

"Don't apologize," said Matilda, rolling her eyes. "I'm the one whose office used to get called the 'Black Hole of Salter.'"

She did seem to be inordinately proud of that, Anna thought.

"I remember," Wendy said. "After you promoted Jenny."

"Jenny was *legendary* as an assistant. I don't know how many I've gone through since her."

But Anna found that she was less than interested in hearing about Matilda's former assistant, who'd been legendary.

"I'd have kept her as an assistant forever if I didn't have a conscience."

"You mean if she hadn't threatened to leave." Wendy laughed. She refilled Matilda's glass and then her own with the last of the bottle.

"Well, possibly. The office never ran as efficiently after she was promoted, I can tell you that. The one after Jenny let years of slush accumulate. There was a corner of her office that was all envelopes and manuscript boxes. Every day she just piled more on top of the last, like her own personal episode of *Hoarders*. Even I felt terrible about it. And the next one after that one just began a new pile. When Claudia started last summer, she said, look, we really need to deal with this, it wasn't right to keep such a backlog. She showed me the chatter online, about what they were calling my office. We hired a temp, just to go through it—not even to read anything, just to apologize and send it all back. We had to buy extra postage for some of those self-addressed envelopes, they'd been there so many years the rates had gone up."

Anna watched this exchange, wondering if anyone at this table actually felt genuine sympathy for those people, the writers who had so optimistically sent their work to this best-of-all-possible agents . . . only to have it languish for years in the Black Hole of Salter.

"What are we going to do about this?" she asked.

Right away, the two of them got serious again.

Wendy said: "What I think is, if there was any truth to what this person wrote, or any real proof to back it up, there would be

226

some form of contact information, but there isn't. It's totally anonymous, which means it's bullshit. Some hoax or something, or some random nastiness. Obviously, we won't be dignifying it with any kind of a follow-up. If it weren't for what happened to Jake, it would have gone straight into the trash where it belongs. But Matilda and I talked it over, and really, this is one of those choices that comes down to bad versus worse. Having to tell you about it is bad, and I can't stand that I'm doing it, after what happened before. Because even though we had no idea how much it upset Jake at the time, we saw it through your eyes when we read *The Afterword*. I told you, I cried."

"Me, too!" Matilda chimed in. "I was bawling."

"So obviously we wanted to protect you," Wendy said. "To me, this is just infuriating. Taking a potshot at a wonderful writer who actually *did* write a fantastic book? This *person* should be ashamed."

Anna nodded into her untouched plate. Just at this precise moment, she was having difficulty locating her own fury.

"And also," Matilda said, "just to be clear, what we've got here are some pages of prose that could have been written anytime— before *Crib* was published or after *Crib* was published, we have no idea—sent by a person who has declined to identify themself, from an unknown address, and without any kind of a request. So, like, what are we even being *asked* to do? Acknowledge the similarities? Recall Jake's book? Or maybe publish the manuscript this came from? I agree with Wendy. I am feeling a low level of threat. But because of Jake, because we know, now, how affected he was by this exact kind of harassment, we just felt we needed to make you a part of the conversation, make sure we respond in a way that feels right to you."

Then, as if to punctuate this thought, she dunked her shrimp into a ramekin of cocktail sauce and ate it at last.

"Unfortunately," Wendy said, "we don't have the option of responding privately, because *this person* hasn't favored us with any means of contact, so even if we wanted to try what we tried last time, with a cease and desist from Macmillan, we can't. So really, the options are either do nothing or just the opposite. Go nuclear."

Anna looked at her editor in alarm.

"By which I mean, and I hope you'll consider this before you just say no, that you could choose to write about this. Yourself. I know you've mentioned the harassment in some interviews, but you never offered any details, so people may be aware of the rumor but they don't know exactly what happened to Jake. Maybe this is a way to get some closure on that, and shut down our latest creep at the same time. And I personally think—"

"We think," said Matilda.

"We think. It's a good idea. People seem to have a special hatred for anyone who accomplishes anything, and we have a culture now where it's just too easy to tear someone down. Readers should know about the kind of harassment creative people can be targeted with. The kind Jake experienced."

"I'm sure the *Times* would take an Op Ed from you," said Matilda. "I could call, or Wendy could call. You would have the undying gratitude of every writer out there. Everyone I know is hiding under the table because they're afraid of something like this. *We need a hero, girl!*"

It sounded so wrong. Anna just stared at her.

"Anyway," Wendy said finally, "why don't you sit with it awhile, and we can talk about it again when you're ready. And if it's what you want, I'm more than happy to bring in the attorneys. The laws haven't caught up to all of the fun new forms of harassment out there, but they can reassure you, at least."

Anna blinked. "Reassure me? Of what?"

"Of your safety. Of our support."

Oh, good, she thought, feeling confident of neither.

"I mean, these guys hole up in their basements, getting all riled up about the so-called elites up north, and they think they're safe, nobody's going to find them. I would love to see this redneck asshole dragged out into the light."

Wait. She'd just said . . . what?

"We should get another bottle of wine," Matilda said. "Should I?"

Elites up north? Redneck asshole?

That pounding from inside her own body. Like something out of Edgar Allan Poe.

"Glad we got that off our chest," said Wendy. "Chests."

"Honestly?" said Matilda. "Sometimes I think we could do our job so much more easily if it weren't for the writers. You know?"

"Oh, I know." Wendy shook her head. She seemed, at last, to be enjoying her Dover Sole. "Half my day spent on matters entirely unrelated to literature. Even to marketing. And my father said it was a mistake to major in psychology. How wrong he was!"

"Well," said Matilda, diplomatically, "your authors love you. You know that. Most of your colleagues . . . how shall I put this? You can't call them up to chat about your unresolved childhood trauma."

Wendy smiled. "That's me. Full service."

"Uh . . ." Anna said. They both looked at her, politely waiting.

"You said . . . there was a postmark on the envelope?"

"Athens, Georgia," Wendy said, as if it were the most unremarkable place on the planet, not a radioactive clarion call surging through every nerve of Anna's body.

"Never been there. Never want to go," said Matilda helpfully. "You guys aren't going to make me drink this alone, are you?"

"I won't," said Wendy.

"Anna?"

But Anna couldn't speak. She thought her heart might have stopped, and she actually put her hand to her chest. But it was still there, and clattering away, desperate to escape.

24

The Testaments

The following day, at her request, the excerpt of her brother's awful book was messengered to her apartment. It arrived with its infamous cover letter attached, and its original envelope, complete with radioactive postmark.

Athens, Georgia.

The postmark, handily shattering what little remained of her post-Martin Purcell tranquility, was also stamped January 14 of the current year, fully two months after the unfortunate teacher's unfortunate tumble down the very hard cement stairs of the Ripley Inn.

There was nothing left to do but read what that bastard had written.

Dear Wendy Marder,

I write to you with great concern about the actions of your late author, Jacob Finch Bonner. He may have presented himself to you as the sole author of the original work, Crib, *but this is far from the truth. In fact, Bonner appropriated the material from a novel about a mother who murders her daughter and assumes her identity, written by a student he'd encountered while teaching in the MFA program at Ripley College in Vermont. Bonner then presented that work to you as original. No acknowledgment of his student's work was ever made, either by Bonner or by you, his publisher, in any edition of* Crib. *The student had*

completed most of his own novel before his death and made
an attempt to have it published.

I am enclosing a sample from this novel. I'm sure you will
agree that the plot and subject matter are far too similar to
those of Crib *to be coincidental, especially given the*
relationship between the two writers. Quite frankly, your
author's actions were reprehensible.

I am prepared to expose this matter, and I encourage you
to address it with your author's "widow."

A concerned reader

Even without the postmark, its origin and date, she'd have known that this was not the work of Martin Purcell. It lacked Purcell's obsequiousness, or any emphasis on his own closeness to that poor, wronged author, Evan Parker, and was also—from what she had seen of Purcell's own writing—simply too well written.

That was the only good news, however. This was the letter of a person who was only too aware of the harm they could cause, financially and to her late husband's reputation, which was all too relevant to her own finances and reputation. This was a letter that opened a pathway to some specific action, likely involving the signing of agreements and the transfer of funds. This was, in other words, the letter of an attorney. Subcategory: a venal and corrupt attorney.

From Athens, Georgia.

Neither Wendy nor Matilda had mentioned the fact that the accompanying note had cited her directly, nor those obviously disparaging quotation marks around the word "widow." That new element did mystify her, and not in a good way. Because she was, whatever else she was, Jake's widow. What living person would question that?

She could think of a few who were not living, who might.

Unlike the other excerpts she'd seen, this one actually began in the middle of a sentence. And what a sentence it was.

but no matter how many times she went through it in her mind, she couldn't get it to stick. And it got later and later and the night got darker and finally quieter, when Ruby at last began to make the recognizable sounds of her nighttime routine: walk down the hall to the kitchen, take a glass from the cabinet, pour water, walk back, stop in the bathroom at the end of the hall, run water again, turn off the water, flush the toilet, then close her bedroom door with one final click of the latch. After that, the low music from her radio, that folky stuff she liked from a college radio station an hour to the south, as if they lived in Appalachia or something. It would play all night, as it had for years, now.

Years and years. But that was about to end.

Three days, she'd said. She was already packing, preparing to drop out of this: her life. Their life. The life Diandra had given up for herself in order to make and care for this ungrateful child.

She had not wanted to have a child, and if it wasn't going to be possible to not have a child, at least she had not wanted to raise a child. It was obvious to everyone who knew them both, most of all to Diandra herself, that she and Ruby were alike this way. They had both been clever, both been disappointed with the hand they'd been dealt: this family, this house, this town. What she herself had wanted was no different from what her daughter wanted. The difference was that Ruby was about to get everything, while she herself got nothing, and this epic act of cruelty was going to happen without even a gesture of understanding, let alone gratitude, on Ruby's part. How was that fair?

Here's how: it wasn't fair.

Three days. In three days Ruby was going to walk out of this house, probably with the bare minimum of her belongings, determined to travel light. And when did she expect to return? They both knew the answer to that: never. Ruby was never coming back. She would go from the university down south to some scrappy first job, and then begin to ascend and ascend, to innovate, to command, to expand, to achieve, to live a big life in the big world. Diandra's life. Or at least, the life Diandra was supposed to have led, deserved to have led, with travel and accomplishments.

Instead, Diandra was here in her midthirties, prospectless, without even a high school diploma. The only thing she'd accomplished, at least the only thing she could admit to accomplishing, was the making and the keeping alive of her remarkable daughter. And that would be irreparably over. In three days.

For hours, she raged. At some point she drifted off, only to wake with a start before dawn, and when she did she discovered that she knew one thing she had not known when she fell asleep, which was that she would not allow this to happen. Not the way Ruby had in mind, anyway.

After that, it wasn't hard to plan. The university was expecting a young person: she looked like a young person. She could be the young person. It was what she deserved. Everything her daughter had today and anything she might have tomorrow derived from her own great sacrifice, so by rights it already belonged to her: ethically, logically, pragmatically. And let's face it, Diandra would do far more with those opportunities than even her smart daughter would have done. Where did Ruby think she'd gotten her smarts in the first place? Not from that sweet and trusting boy she'd seduced, that was for sure. Ruby might as well have been a solo creation. Ruby had been a solo creation. And property of the creator. All Diandra had to do was what she had not been brave enough to do all those years earlier, and every day since: assert her own autonomy, reclaim her own life story. Be brave.

Ruby packed. She got everything she was taking into a single suitcase and a duffel. Diandra also packed, but privately. Unlike her daughter, she couldn't take more than she would need for a few days of travel. She made a point of showing herself in West Rugby, announcing to anyone who knew her even slightly that she was about to take her daughter very far from home and leave her in an alien southern state to begin college. She took her car to be serviced, making sure the mechanic was aware that they had a long cross-country journey ahead. She called Ruby's doctor—still a pediatrician—and asked about vaccines for college, because her daughter would be starting a full year earlier than expected.

She collected the approval everyone offered. Why not? It was late in the day for approval.

On the final morning, Ruby went into town to say goodbye to her friends on the town green. As soon as she was out of the house, Diandra went out, too: down the slope, up a hill belonging to their neighbor (a summer resident from outside of Boston), and down again to a creek bed on the neighbor's property. There was a good spot there, and well out of sight, but it was still an arduous day. She hoped the nearness of the water would speed up decomposition, but it wasn't something she was going to look up on the internet. From here on in, she would need to trust her instincts, and hope that no one would bother looking for a person who wasn't missing.

235

When evening came, she waited in her bedroom for her daughter to come home. It was late, nearly midnight, when that finally happened: the car pulling into the gravel drive, the back door's heavy hinge, the steps down the hallway between their rooms. She heard the random clicks and beeps of her daughter's phone, the closet opening, the drawers closing. Then: those familiar sounds of Ruby's ritual: kitchen faucet, clink of glass, running water, flushing toilet. And finally, the sound of banjo and fiddle from the college radio station, low into the night.

An hour, to be safe. Diandra tried to rest without falling asleep. It would be a long time, once she began, before she would be able to rest.

She got out of bed. She went to the garage and collected the plastic tarp she kept there. She went to the kitchen and took the knife she had decided on, and sharpened, earlier that day. Then she stood outside her daughter's room for a final moment, giving herself permission to change her mind, but she did not want to change her mind. She wanted to go, just as she'd wanted to go for so many years: before her parents' deaths, before Perry's death, before Ruby. Finally, she was on the point of departure. She felt deeply calm. Then she opened the door.

It was as if she had been preparing herself for this specific thing. Her arm knew how to rise and then how to fall: one wound, but the right one, and in the instant before the blood came she had the tarp on the floor and the body of her daughter down flat on it, and then rolled up in it and dragged out the back door. There wasn't even a moon. She got her belongings, and Ruby's suitcase and duffel bag, and her purse, and her phone, and Ruby's phone, because she knew she couldn't go back into the house after the woods, and those things she brought to the garage and put into her car. She took one final walk through the rooms she'd lived in her entire life, asking herself if there was anything she needed or wanted from this place, or that her daughter wouldn't have left behind for a year in college, or that she wouldn't have left behind for a six-day trip there and back, but she'd already made those decisions, and made them the right way. So she carried the rolled-up tarp into the woods. It had been a fifteen-minute walk without a body in a tarp. It took a little longer now. A few hours earlier, she had gotten the hole down to five feet. She had hidden the shovel out there, just in case anyone came hiking through. She had also hidden a change of clothes, a new pair of shoes for herself. Now she did what she'd been preparing herself to do. The moon came out from behind the clouds. She shoveled and shoveled, and then she rolled some stones down onto the place from where they had been, a little uphill, and moved some branches, until it looked like just another place in the woods. Finally, she went upstream, stripped off her filthy clothes, and washed herself. She changed into her new clothes, put on her new shoes, and walked out of the woods a new person.

By sunrise she was hours down the road, and already farther away from home than she had—

Well, Anna thought, setting the page down. That certainly was *fiction*. Evan, naturally, had had no idea how Rose actually died, and so he was starting from a clean slate, but it struck her as pathetic that this was the best he could come up with. *Really?* She knifes her kid in the heart, rolls her into a tarp, and buries her in the backyard? It was boilerplate, all right, and also unwise; people walked through those neighboring woods all the time, especially in the fall, no matter how many no trespassing signs an absentee landowner might

237

post. They hiked, they hunted, they ran their snowmobiles. You'd have to be an idiot to bury a body so close. And she wasn't an idiot.

Still, the very fact of these pages, the fact that an unknown person had possessed them, read them, sent them to Wendy, with a citation of herself as the "widow," no less, meant that there was something she had missed, some tendril growing out of her prior lives and coiling around this one, entangling her. Some imprint she had left behind for the right—or the wrong—person to find and interpret. Correctly or incorrectly.

This person was not Martin Purcell. Obviously.

She had maintained no contact with anyone in West Rutland, which was, in any case, a place where people tended not to think beyond central Vermont. There was no classmate, no teacher, no neighbor who had any idea that Dianna Parker wasn't dead in a long-ago accident, which was exactly the kind of thing bound to happen if you did something as crazy as driving your kid *across the country* to college. (If somebody had to go to college, there was always Rutland Community, where Evan had gone, or UVM, if you really wanted to get away. One kid in her own class—who'd taken her slot as valedictorian after she'd been forced to leave school—had gone all the way to RPI. But he was an engineer.) There was no doctor still trying to get Dianna Parker (or Rose Parker, for that matter) to come in for a checkup, no postmaster looking for the right place to forward a rebate check. The last business of her life in West Rutland had been the sale of their family home, and the attorney handling those transactions, a man named Gaylord, was dead, something she'd only discovered when she checked on his website and found herself redirected to the site of another Rutland attorney. Gaylord's obituary in the *Rutland Herald* said he had died after a brief illness.

Not that she'd even dealt with Gaylord, or at least not directly. She'd still been in Athens in those fall months of 2013, extracting herself from the University of Georgia, monitoring the online chatter of her brother's friends and acquaintances to make sure that, even amid the general hand-wringing about his fatal loss of sobriety, no one truly doubted that he had died by overdose, and disposing of the real estate her brother had been so kind as to bequeath her (though not—she assumed—by choice). She hadn't been Anna Williams-Bonner, then. She hadn't even been Anna Williams. She'd still been Rose Parker, or at least that was how the Athens-based attorney who'd handled the transaction had known her. But Arthur Pickens, Esq., hadn't really known her, that was the point. Was he under the impression that he knew her now? Had he sufficiently exerted himself, with his questionable intelligence and even more questionable work ethic, to put together some shards of information and actually find her? And if he had, what was his purpose in doing so? Pickens was hardly the literary type; he was about as likely to read a book review or attend a bookstore event as she was to attend a NASCAR race. But even if he'd woken up one morning and taken it into his head to come after Rose Parker, there was no scenario she could conjure that put him in possession of Evan Parker's novel. No matter how many times she tried to bring those two distinct parts of this story together, she could not do it—at least not with Arthur Pickens, Esq., as the point of contact.

And yet . . . that tendril, that imprint, it had to be there. It had to be. Because the letter in her hands spoke the voice of Arthur Pickens, Esq., as clearly as if she were with him right now, seated opposite him across his lawyerly desk and attempting not to inhale his cloying cologne. And even if it didn't, he was still the only person she knew in Athens, Georgia.

25

Through the Looking-Glass

Anna hadn't received all that much from her father—not in the material sense and certainly not in the more amorphous realms of affection or instruction—but that wasn't to imply she'd learned nothing from him. Her father had been a great mistruster of many things, and as far back as Anna could remember he had held an especially hard line on the matter of cash. Of course, he hadn't lived long enough to experience the ease and ubiquity of online credit payments, nor of websites like Venmo and PayPal, let alone the conceptual outrage that was cryptocurrency, but his life span had certainly overlapped with the credit card. He'd never owned one, naturally. Cash was his currency, and if he couldn't pay for something at the moment he wished to purchase it, well, that was a very strong indication that he did not need to acquire that thing. He kept his family's day-to-day money in a kitchen drawer, his own retirement fund in the Green Mountain Bank, West Rutland branch, and certain deposits of personal wealth in the old rope bed, beneath the now redundant pegs on its side rails, where they were nobody's business but his own—not the government's, not his wife's, not even his darling son's. That his darling son had even known about the stash had come as something of a surprise to Anna when she'd read his appalling fiction shortly before Evan's unfortunate demise. Perhaps he really had possessed a novelist's eye for detail.

By then, Anna herself had fully absorbed the wisdom of cash as a way of life. Cash, unless you had just robbed a bank to acquire it, carried no tracker. It did not follow you onto a flight or into a hotel room, or connect you to a car you needed to rent. It did not watch you buy an unusual new outfit or a wig, so nobody would recognize you from, say, an author photo on the back of a book you'd written. Even before she left Vermont, she had adopted her father's habit of setting aside extra cash, as if she were a housewife from an earlier time, slowly and stealthily planning for her own escape with leavings from the house-keeping allowance. It had been a personal challenge to extract, at the end of each week, a single bill in the highest denomination to be found in her wallet—sometimes a five, sometimes a fifty—and enter the new week without it as the cash accrued (in a plastic toiletry kit, in her suitcase, in her closet, only a few feet from the old desk where Evan would one day write his cock-roach of a novel). For years, that suitcase never went anywhere, because she never went anywhere, but by the time Evan sat down to spin his falsehoods into indifferent prose, both suitcase and toiletry kit had long since left the building, packed into the car she drove to Georgia alongside Rose's belongings and an old propane heater—they were planning to camp along the way, to save money. On the night of that tragic fire in the north Georgia woods not far from Rabun Gap, Anna hid the toiletry kit beneath a cairn of stones, just out of sight of the about-to-be incinerated tent. A few days later, after the hospital and the police interviews and the funeral, with its donated coffin and lachrymose, uninvited strangers in attendance, she returned to the campground "to say a private goodbye," and pushed those rocks aside. On that particular morning there were almost eight thousand dollars in the plastic toiletry kit. Eight thousand dollars with which to begin her long-awaited new life: a testa-ment to the virtue of cash, the value of ritual, and the importance of regular tithing to the notion of one's own worth.

That was already eight years ago. Since then, she'd become a person even better versed in the value of mastering one's own history, and naturally she'd maintained her good habits, though these days the fives and fifties were more likely to be of even higher denominations. And she had continued to learn, not just the old lessons but the new ones that came her way, like the value of establishing a trail, and the even greater value of eradicating one.

The last time she'd made use of her stash had been when she set out from Athens, Georgia, for her new life on the West Coast, and by the time she'd settled in Seattle with a newly adjusted name, a virgin credit history, an in-state scholarship to the University of Washington, and a part-time job at KBIK, she had gone through nearly all of it. Since then, it had been a priority to rebuild her reserves, something that became—ironically—much more difficult, as she had begun to make a living as a radio producer and then a fortune as a literary widow and a writer of fiction.

Still, over these years with and since Jake, Anna had managed to put away a comfortable sum, withdrawing a few hundred dollars each Monday and letting whatever bills were left at the end of the week migrate to an old Coach bucket bag she'd brought with her from Seattle. During her marriage, that bag had lived on a high shelf in the closet, in a suitcase full of flannel shirts and Birkenstocks, items even her late husband might have recognized as unsuitable for Manhattan living. After Jake's death, however, she moved the money to a drawer of her bedside table—so much more convenient—and the last time she'd checked it the amount was just under twelve thousand. More than enough for a cash-fueled excursion to a place she hadn't expected to visit again.

Lori and Laurie wanted to hold their open house on a Saturday in April, and they walked her through the apartment, pointing to pieces of furniture that needed to disappear before that time and requesting the eradication of personal items.

"It doesn't have to be a chore," said Lori, brightly. "It can be more of a catharsis! People love this part!"

"Some people," Laurie admitted.

Anna volunteered that she would be among those *some people*. "I think I've been looking for an excuse to do it since my husband died. Go through every drawer and every closet. Make some decisions about his stuff, finally."

"I'm sure," Lori said sympathetically. "But remember, you don't have to, right now. You can kick the can down the road a bit. Just move it all to storage and look at it on the other end, after you've moved into your beautiful new home."

Wherever that may be, thought Anna. In fact, she considered storage for her late husband's junk to be a terrible idea, so she packed up nearly everything—including that sad table by the living room window where Jake had written his novel, and the chairs in which they'd sat as he ate his final meal—and sent it all to Housing Works. A few other items, too far gone even for the thrift store, she put out on the sidewalk on her neighborhood's designated Large Item Day, and before she'd even finished getting it all downstairs somebody had posted it on one of those free-furniture Instagram accounts. By the time she took herself out for dinner it was all gone except for one especially battered floor lamp.

Afterward, the apartment was refreshingly spare.

The agents were itching to get her out and let the painters in, so she finished the last of her triage and let Jake's parents know that she was taking a vacation while the apartment was being shown. She told Wendy and Matilda that she was heading back to Seattle to see friends, and then to a private place she knew on Vashon Island, to work on an idea for a new book.

As expected, this excited them so much that neither mentioned the other thing on all of their minds.

She turned off her phone, and "forgot" it in the drawer of her bedside table.

And then she took her leave of her marital home with a black suitcase on wheels, an old Coach bucket bag full of fifty-dollar bills, and a mousy brown wig with bangs that she'd found at Lana Beauty Supply on Nostrand Avenue in Brooklyn. And paid for with cash.

PART THREE

26

The Burden of Proof

Her final official acts as Anna Williams-Bonner were the purchase, by credit card, of a round-trip ticket to Seattle and an Uber to Newark Liberty Airport. From there, she took New Jersey Transit to Trenton and a bus to Philadelphia, another to Washington, and another to Atlanta, paying cash for each leg of the journey. The trip was long and boring, and her scalp itched madly under the wig. She read magazines, local papers, and one terrible paperback that someone had left behind, trying to divert herself with athletes and actors she had never heard of, and in the case of the paperback, a romance between a feisty redheaded woman and the rough but handsome frontiersman leading her wagon train to California.

Clearly, she had acquired some of Jake's contempt for certain less-elevated corners of the literary landscape.

In Atlanta she found a not-too-disgusting motel near the bus station that didn't require a credit card, and there, after a long shower and some very sober consideration, she separated herself from about eight inches of her gray hair. It now fell to just below her jawline, allowing the wig to sit more comfortably on her scalp. She already hated the wig. In the afternoon, she hailed a cab and negotiated a price to Athens.

The town hadn't changed much. A few of the downtown restaurants now had different names, and lots of people were on electric scooters. More of the women had visible tattoos, and everyone stared into a cell phone at all times—while seated, while walking, even while crossing the street, secure in the notion that their bubble of privacy was more powerful than the laws of physics. By night, the students still thronged the bars on Washington Street and then stumbled back to their gated apartment complexes. By day, everyone wore red or black running shorts, or red and black sweatpants, as if exercise were a thing perpetually about to happen, but somehow never did. Years earlier, as a student, she'd aimed for a liminal space between not trying to fully merge with the mainstream and not trying to be notable in defiance of the mainstream, which had meant that year's version of official UGA T-shirts and athletic gear, items of clothing she had been more than happy to leave behind when she'd moved west. But now, after checking into a motel near the public library on Baxter Street, she walked downtown to the bookstore across from the stadium and bought herself a pair of bulldog sweatpants and a gray T-shirt with a red football front and center. In the check-out line she grabbed a hat as well, though it made the wig even more of an irritation. She was older, of course, than even the "mature" student she'd been the last time she was in Athens, but years in the rainy Northwest (and conscientious application of sunblock in general) had been kind to her face. Anywhere else, and without the contributing factor of her gray hair, she would have been a naturally aging woman in her thirties. But Athens wasn't anywhere else. Athens was home to a massive university, and thus a constantly regenerating population of pretty eighteen-year-old girls, most of them intent on staying eighteen just as long as dignity allowed. For the purpose of these necessary days, Anna had decided to comport herself as if she were a graduate student, faculty spouse, or possibly UGA grad who hadn't been able to tear herself away from the *most awesome place she'd ever lived*: not the norm, in other words, but not out of the zone of possibility, either. It would serve—she hoped—for as long as she needed to be here. Which wouldn't—she hoped—be long.

Years earlier, on her return from that unpleasant trip to Vermont, Anna had visited the public library every day to read the *Rutland Herald* online. Nothing seemed to be happening up there (which worried her, even as she knew delay worked to her advantage in the long term), and while she waited she kept to her routines, saying cheerful hellos to the few people who knew her (or thought they did) and reminding herself that what she'd done up there had been entirely necessary. The earlier incarnation of Dianna Parker, the one who would ignore her own needs, wishes, and rights, truly *was* buried in that graveyard in north Georgia; the later incarnation, the one who'd repossessed her own property from Evan's desk (her desk!) in Evan's writing room (her room!), then made sure he would never write another word about any of it . . . *that* person would calmly go about her business and wait for the world to find her brother's body.

It took five days, ultimately. (Concerned employee? Irritated girlfriend-of-the-moment? Bad smell from an open window? The paper never said.) Then the keening commenced in earnest, much of it, conveniently for herself, on Facebook. About a month after that, a court-appointed attorney named Gaylord made an effort to contact Rose Parker through the University of Georgia, and the message reached her at her off-campus address despite the fact that she'd recently unenrolled. Only then did Rose Parker select a local attorney of her own.

Arthur Pickens, Esq., was already in trouble with the Georgia Bar Association, mainly due to the complaints of some female clients but also regarding a DUI (his own) which he'd naturally tried to fix. She also had no trouble connecting him to a cheating scandal involving his college fraternity. These delightful attributes made him by far the most desirable man for the job of handling the sale of her family home in central Vermont, though naturally she hoped she wouldn't need to weaponize them. The transaction itself was breathtakingly straightforward; that same court-appointed Vermont attorney would be doing most of the heavy lifting, and really, even a lawyer of Pickens's narrow talents ought to be able to execute a simple house sale and uncontested probate process without getting all personal about it. Pickens, to his credit, hadn't screwed up the paperwork, and the only pass he'd made was downright genteel—"surprising" her with a catered lunch when she came to the office one afternoon, expecting to sign final paperwork that (shockingly!) had not actually arrived. All in all, she had looked forward to the bright prospect of never having to think about him, let alone be in contact with him, ever again.

And yet, here she was all these years later, back in Athens, back on College Avenue, back in an approximation of the sweatpants and T-shirts she had worn in her prior life in this town. She ascertained that Pickens's office was still where she had left it and still, apparently, open for business, which mainly meant that the Georgia Bar Association hadn't caught up to him and none of his female clients' fathers or brothers or partners had rendered him incapable of going about his business. For most of a day, she watched the street, blending into the sea of red, reading and rereading the UGA newspaper she'd picked up at the bookstore, then the *Atlanta Journal-Constitution* when her brain refused to process any more information about football.

Even now, she wasn't certain. She had traveled all this way, raided her own cash reserves, and actually *cut her hair* in order to be, finally, certain, because at the end of the day it wasn't enough that Arthur Pickens had *feasibly* been the one sending chapters of her brother's book—to herself, her in-laws, and her editor, when only a few months earlier it had seemed equally feasible, then likely, then convincing, that Martin Purcell had been the one doing all of those things. If she'd been mistaken in that conviction . . . well, that was obviously regrettable, especially when you considered the risks she herself had been forced to take up in Ripley. This time, she knew better than to persuade herself. This time she would need to discover something concrete, something irrefutable, before she put herself in harm's way.

Pickens had belonged to a brief and discreet time of her life, during which there'd been no connection at all between the UGA student Rose Parker and the novelist Jacob Finch Bonner, two people whose paths wouldn't even converge for another five years. Pickens had known her as the unfortunate (or fortunate) heir to the modest estate of a relative she wasn't at all close to, whose funeral she hadn't even traveled north to attend. (After she'd volunteered this information during their initial meeting, Pickens had unforgettably informed her that he, himself, had "never ventured north of the Mason-Dixon Line.") The attorney had done his job and received his payment. That ought to have been the end of it.

Instead, here he was again: smarmier, louder, and clearly angrier than even that rejected suitor trying to pour her a glass of chardonnay in his well-appointed law office. Because if it was true, if Pickens had indeed been responsible for the excerpts, the cryptic commentaries, even that long-ago Post-it back in Denver, then Arthur Pickens, Esq., had managed to wade into the most intimate, dangerous place in the deepest, most secret part of her life. Attention must be paid, indeed.

And what made it worse? If it was true, then she knew exactly who had planted the crucial connection in his head, who had enabled Pickens to know her far better than she wished to be known, and that person . . . was herself. This was her own fault, the fault of her weakness when she learned that Jake, despite her very strong objections, intended to travel to Athens, and that he would be looking there for traces of Rose Parker wherever he was able to find them. He had already made a visit to the Rutland attorney, Gaylord, and even Jake would probably manage to find the name of Rose Parker's attorney of record. And so, on the day Jake flew south, she had given in to that weakness, calling Arthur Pickens from a very rare working pay phone (she'd managed to find one at Penn Station, after a highly frustrating search) and warning him not to speak about her to anyone who might be asking. She mentioned the Bar Association, the DUI, and, for good measure, that business at Duke, and he, by way of response, had asked what she'd been up to for seven years, and where was she calling from?

Anna had hung up the phone.

Weakness.

He'd probably googled Jake the minute Jake left his office. And it was a matter of public record that Jacob Finch Bonner had married a Seattle woman named Anna Williams, whose staff photograph was on the website of the podcasting producers she worked for. And all that was bad, certainly, but it wasn't enough to explain why he'd sent those manuscripts to New York. That could only make sense if Pickens also knew—*somehow*—that she was connected to a second dead author, an *unpublished* dead author. If he had *somehow* discovered that, and *somehow* come into possession of Evan's manuscript pages, and *somehow* come to understand what they meant . . . well

252

then he would know more than enough to destroy the life she had made for herself. And that was unacceptable. That was not to be tolerated. And she would not leave Athens without putting a stop to all of it.

On the first day she watched him leave his office at four, alone. He was carrying a burgundy briefcase, and he crossed College Avenue, walking past the coffee shop where she hid her face behind a copy of *The Red and Black*. He went into the underground garage next door and emerged a few minutes later in a Mercedes SUV. Silver. And off he went, apparently without a care in the world. The next morning, she was back in the coffee shop at eight, but the silver Mercedes didn't turn up until nearly ten. He stayed inside all day, and only once did someone else open the street-level door and go upstairs. That was a pair of college boys in khaki shorts, one in a striped button-down, the other in a Georgia lacrosse T-shirt. (The one in the button-down, Anna guessed, was the client. Georgia lacrosse was there for moral support.) They stayed half an hour, and Pickens left again just before four.

Gentleman's hours.

Under ordinary circumstances she might have given it a few additional days, to be more sure of his schedule, but she was nearly a week out from that dinner at Balthazar, and already four days into her supposed writing sojourn on Vashon Island. She didn't have time.

Pickens lived exactly as she might have imagined: alone, in a house that was too big for any one person, in a gated community named Club Harmonie, just east of town. The complex encompassed one thousand acres of woodland, lakefront, and of course not one but two "award-winning" golf courses, plus the usual clubhouse with restaurants, exercise facilities, tennis courts, and pro shops. And a spa.

It took her just under an hour to power walk from down-town Athens, having swapped her UGA apparel for a logo-less white track suit and a sun visor. Her Coach bag would have looked wrong on a jogger, so she left it in her room and trans-ferred the money into a nylon belt bag and zipped it around her waist, where it chafed. At the turnoff to Club Harmonie, a large sign informed her that she was about to enter a *SOUTH-ERN LIVING* INSPIRED COMMUNITY. With her head down, she waved at the teenager in the guard house as she jogged past. He waved back.

Anna had studied the map of the complex at her library terminal, and she knew the number of Pickens's unit, nearly at the farthest point from the entrance. The path, on which she was far from the only jogger, hugged the edge of one of the golf courses and passed under white and red oaks and the occasional southern magnolia, and the houses were built in a uniform style, something akin to Neo-Craftsman with certain southern flourishes like wraparound porches. When she reached his street, Sycamore Lane, she ducked behind a mercifully empty playground and through a patch of woods to the bottom of the slope that was his backyard.

Pickens had to be doing well enough, financially. Either that or he'd gone out on quite a limb in order to live like the southern gentry he obviously felt entitled to be. According to the records she'd accessed at the library, this home had been purchased for $1.2 million five years earlier, with an 85 percent mortgage. The Benz SUV retailed for over sixty thousand dollars, and rent on the College Avenue office was another sixty thousand per year. Also, the annual membership and maintenance fees at Club Harmonie ran to forty thousand. (More, if he actually played golf. Did he play golf? He prob-ably did.) There was no way drunk UGA undergrads and out-of-state probates were putting that kind of money in his accounts. Then again, Pickens might just be the kind of guy who was comfortable living beyond his means, coasting for years as he waited for a landlord to lock him out, fighting his mortgage company every step of the way, hitting up his friends or family members with a nonexistent investment opportunity, or taking up extracurricular activities like blackmail and embezzlement. He looked the part of a southern lawyer; why shouldn't that make him one? Really, couldn't everything just be as simple as that?

Ten A.M., more or less, when he arrived at his office. Four P.M., more or less, when he left. It was nearly noon now, and the SUV was not in the drive. She thought she must have three or four hours here, but she wasn't going to test that. One hour. Two at the most, then the long walk back to downtown.

The wraparound porch wasn't even screened. She'd seen that in photos on the Club Harmonie website but she hadn't been expecting an unlocked door. There was no entitlement like that of a southern man who assumes nobody could conceivably invade his personal space. The back door swung inward when she turned the doorknob, using an accommodatingly large oak leaf that had drifted onto the porch. She went inside.

Every room was larger than it needed to be. The "gourmet" kitchen's four-burner Viking might never have been turned on, and the double-door Sub-Zero contained only beer, plus a gel eye mask. The trash bin under the sink was full of plastic clam containers, most still containing the residue of his meals. It smelled. In the vaulted living room there was a hearth of river stones that climbed to the second floor, but the only sofa was turned in the other direction, to the massive wall-mounted television.

In the dining room there was a baronial mahogany table that had likely never seen a single dinner guest, let alone the kind of formal gathering it was intended to evoke. It was covered with files and legal pads, and she raced for it, consuming its offerings as if they were, indeed, edible. Here was a smorgasbord of messy lives: UGA students who'd gotten behind the wheel after too long an evening on Washington Street, nasty divorces, vindictive custody battles, bankruptcies, and property disputes. Arthur Pickens, Esq., was far busier than he deserved to be; despite the many reasons to confer one's legal business on just about any other Athens attorney, a dizzying number of clients had unwisely entrusted their private affairs to him. One stack, at least two feet high, was devoted to something called *O'Reilly v. Phi Kappa Tau National Council*. Another involved a paternity suit (Pickens's client, naturally, was on the receiving end of this). There was a slip-and-fall involving a bit of wobbly cement outside Sanford Stadium, and a dispute involving a toy poodle whose alopecia made him ineligible to show.

Even with all of this, however, Anna had no trouble locating her own corner of Pickens's busy world. Down at the far end of the long table was a plastic Kroger bag, and in that bag she found, to her horror but no longer to her surprise, an intact copy of the "working" version of Evan Parker's uncompleted masterwork. It might as well have been labeled smoking gun, and yet she was more—not less—mystified at seeing it here, lifting it in her own hands from the surface of this never-dined-at dining table, in this brand-new sort-of-Craftsman house, at the edge of an award-winning golf course in a SOUTH-ERN LIVING INSPIRED COMMUNITY. The insanity of it all made her feel, suddenly and yet powerfully, dizzy, but maybe it wasn't only the insanity of it all. Maybe it was also the bee sting at the back of her right thigh, still flush from the jog and the adrenaline and not incidentally the powerful surprise of encountering a bee *inside a house*, which was not where you necessarily expected a bee to be. *Maybe southern bees are different*, she was thinking, but only the first half of that thought made it through all of the synapses it needed to get through in order to be officially received as "thought," because she still wasn't sure what she meant when she thought it, and anyway she was falling backward so it mattered less and less what she had or had not meant in formulating that thought, or that half-thought, or however much of a thought it had managed to become before it ended. Unseen hands caught her as she fell, but by then she was too far gone to know that, either.

27

How to Save Your Own Life

At first, the thing Anna was looking at, if not actually seeing, resembled a blurry ribbon of darkness, running against the sky. Only when the ribbon slowed now and then could she watch it break down into parts, successively smaller—tree parts, branch parts, leaf parts—before speeding up again, blurring again into that ribbon of before. Then the sky itself changed: blue to darker blue, to barely blue darkness. She could feel the places where her back pressed against something not exactly hard but not soft, either. It was cumulatively unsubstantial. It was vaguely disturbing. The strangest thing of all was that she wasn't actually—or at least physically —uncomfortable.

Sometimes there was music: rock anthems of the '80s, crossover country bands. Sometimes there were men on the radio complaining loudly about female people and ungrateful Black people and immigrants, all with their hidden agendas and traitorous intentions. But she was in and out, and the voices, interrupted by stadium anthems, came in a staccato of impressions:

". . . woke terrorism . . ."

". . . jackbooted thugs . . ."

". . . the abortion industrial complex . . ."

". . . our children . . ."

Never, not for one moment, was there silence. How she craved silence. She craved silence even more than the other things she craved, which were, in no particular order, to know where she was going, to know why she was going there, and to put a knife in the back of Arthur Pickens, who was apparently driving her to that destination.

She couldn't see him, and apart from the occasional belch, she couldn't hear him, but she knew it was him. Never, before the first time she entered his office in downtown Athens all those years ago, had she encountered a human male who leaned so heavily into cologne. He'd worn then—and he apparently wore still—a smell so cloying and obtrusive that it seemed to hover above her in the car, an olfactory version of Pig-Pen's dust cloud, a miasma of misguided courtliness.

Yes, this was a car. Yes, that was the only way this ribbon of trees rushing past the window made any sense, and the awful radio voices, and the intermittent music. This, she was willing to hazard a guess, was in fact Pickens's silver Mercedes SUV, the backseat of which had been folded down to accommodate her length. How he had gotten her here she hated to imagine, and how long ago that might have been—an hour? Twelve hours? Surely no more—she hated to speculate, but here she certainly was, being driven *somewhere* by Arthur Pickens, Esq., an officer of the court with an obligation to promote justice and uphold the law, certainly against her will and obviously without her permission.

And yet, she suspected that she was not in a position to object, either.

Now, at least, she was fully awake. She was lying with her head toward the front, her feet toward the back, one wrist— her left—and one ankle—her right—were fastened, by something that felt thin and pliable but hard, to something fixed inside the car. She couldn't make out the something fixed, which had to be some part of the car itself, or perhaps something itself attached to the car, but she could lift her arm enough to see what was on her wrist: it looked like a cross between a zip tie and a plastic ring for a six-pack of soda cans. It bit into her skin when she attempted to rotate her hand and then her ankle: a deeply unpleasant new reality. Obviously, wriggling out of it was not going to be a practical solution to her problem. Neither was breaking the thing itself. She was here until she was released, and that was that.

There was nothing to be gained by revealing that she was awake, so she set her mind to making an inventory of what she knew and what she still had at her disposal.

Left behind in her Athens hotel room: the Coach bucket bag, the black roller suitcase containing only extra clothing, and nothing at all that would have made a difference to her now. This was good, or at any rate not terrible, because nothing among her left-behind belongings could identify her, either as Anna Williams-Bonner or as anyone else, so she didn't have to worry about police being called to her abandoned room by concerned hotel staff. (If, that is, the hotel staff were even concerned. They were more likely to be angry about an unpaid bill than a disappeared guest.)

Not as good: the nylon belt bag was no longer around her waist, meaning that it, and all of her remaining cash, was now in the possession of Arthur Pickens, along with her wig, the tracksuit still on her physical body, and, most significant of all, her physical body, itself.

In the possession of.

It was getting dark. It had to be the same day. She hadn't spent more than half an hour at Pickens's house. Had it been plain bad luck? A fluctuation in his routine? Or had he somehow been alerted to the fact that she was here in Athens, and planning her own raid on his home and life? Had he, in fact, been waiting for her? Expecting her to turn up? And if so, how long had he been waiting? Since mailing his letter to Wendy at Macmillan? Or even longer, since the excerpts he'd sent to Jake's parents and to herself?

Those excerpts and those taunting messages had been, she now understood, less a warning than an invitation to discuss terms. Obviously he wanted her to come to him, and she'd obliged! She might as well have clicked "Will attend" on an Evite, in full view of the world! It was a bad mistake, and quite possibly a fatal one, but why the car ride? What could there be inside his SUV or wherever it was going that he didn't have back at Club Harmonie, in the privacy of his own home?

That was the part she couldn't understand, and it didn't help that the caustic male voices of conservative radio kept surging through her thoughts, disrupting them.

Her right leg, the one restrained at the ankle, was throbbing now, and the calf threatened to go into spasm. She worked, silently, to stretch her muscles, staving off the cramp but only just. She was trying to identify any and every item in the back of the SUV with her, but the tally only added to her concern: a flashlight, a half-full five-gallon jug of Poland Spring water, a tarp, and a long wooden handle that—when she slowly and very carefully moved her head—proved to belong to a shovel. These were objects that might, separately, distress anyone in her situation; in combination they were deeply upsetting.

And yet, of all the disturbing activities the lawyer might have had in mind, she couldn't persuade herself that killing her and burying her body made any sense. For one thing, if he was simply looking for a place to get rid of her, that ribbon of trees overhead signaled untold acreage of forest. Pickens was investigating none of these wooded places. He wasn't venturing down dirt tracks or driving onto abandoned properties, looking for some ideal spot. He had a destination in mind.

And besides. He didn't strike her as the murdering type, and that wasn't mere desperation, either. Pickens was a user. He did things as a means to an end, for the sole benefit of himself, and while those attributes made for a less-than-endearing human being, they also made for a motivational construct she personally understood—and even endorsed. Why undertake actions on behalf of other people when there were so many actions one might undertake for oneself? It was simply logical, and a great saver of effort. Pickens wanted something from her. If he didn't, she wouldn't still be here, and he wouldn't have gone to the trouble of luring her back to Athens. Whatever might happen to her eventually, it wasn't going to happen until she'd either given up that thing or persuaded him that she never would.

It was not the best of weapons to bring to a fight, obviously. But it was not nothing, either.

She brought her attention back to those treetops through the window, streaming away overhead, darkness flickering among branches: late afternoon. The sun had been setting around 7:00 P.M. when she'd left New York, so it might be approaching that time. Six? Six thirty? If he'd hustled her into this car right away, that could put them as far as a five-hour distance from Athens, at least if they'd driven at highway speed. But these roads they were driving weren't highways. They were neither straight nor fast, and they were far rougher under her back than even the worst-maintained highway would be. Not highways. On the contrary; these were the back roads of a state with plenty of back roads to choose from, and this car was undulating along them, moving slowly but intentionally toward some particular spot she could not begin to identify.

Another factor: he might have been expecting her, but had he been ready for her on this particular morning? Obviously, he'd kept whatever he'd injected her with near to hand for just this happy occasion, but preparing for their little road trip must also have taken some time—time to locate these very effective restraints, for example, and possibly more of the drug. Food so they wouldn't have to stop anywhere, attracting unwelcome attention. And, of course, any necessary supplies for whatever errand they were on, including that most disquieting shovel and the tarp, the flashlight. He certainly hadn't been driving around Athens with a full complement of grave-digging tools. Say he'd left her on the living room floor while he'd run around, gathering what he needed, locking the house up, wheeling the garbage down to the curb, perhaps canceling a golf date or a training session or even a professional appointment. That might set him back another half an hour before he could load up this car in the privacy of his own garage, and set out. So: four hours on the road since leaving Club Harmonie, assuming they'd been in motion ever since. But where to? Or, at the very least, in which direction? It infuriated her that she could not answer the most basic questions.

"I know you're awake."

For a moment she vaguely assumed that the radio voice had said it. The same voice, or one of the same voices, that only a moment ago had been railing about the liberal agenda and its various assaults on American decency. Her brain was trying to understand what this new outrage might signify, in right-wing radiospeak—*I know you're awake out there, I know you're listening, I know you feel what I feel, I know you won't stand for menstruating politicians or people who insist on voting even though they aren't white*—but it continued to elude her.

263

"Rose Parker. As was, I mean. I didn't give you that much. Just a touch of the good stuff. You were feeling no pain when I put you in the car," he said, like—she supposed—the gentleman he considered himself to be.

She found her own voice, or a version of her voice, one that sounded like a woman decades older than her age—either of her ages, fictional or real: "I'm assuming you know that kidnapping's a crime. Kind of a serious one."

"So is breaking and entering," he said from the front seat. "And fraud. And theft. And murder, last time I checked. Of course, I've never murdered anybody, myself, so I lack your expertise."

She took this to understand that he knew much more about her than the single fact of her being Rose Parker. As was.

"Where are you taking me?" she said, coming straight to the point.

"Oh, nowhere you haven't been before," said Arthur Pickens, Esq. "Just lie back and relax."

The words washed over her in a wave of disgust. Perhaps he did not understand how specifically offensive they were. Perhaps he did.

"Clearly, we're going to need to talk. You might as well take off the plastic ties. They hurt. And I could use a bathroom."

He actually laughed. "To go out a window or find someone to call the cops? No. But we don't have much farther to go. You'll be fine."

"I won't be," she said, introducing a note of panic. It wasn't much of a stretch. "And it's such a nice car."

From the front seat, she actually heard him laugh, drowning out the radio voices. Now he turned them off the rest of the way.

"This may come as a shock to you, Rose, but we're not all helpless idiots put on earth for you to play with. You walked into my office with your out-of-state property sale. I started investigating you before you were out of the building, not that I wouldn't do that for any new client. But you stood out from the get-go. My typical clients are people with what you might call roots in the community. Friends of friends, or referred by other clients. You were more of a come-out-of-nowhere, disappear-into-nowhere kind of a person. Not that there's anything wrong with that."

Something they could agree on, she thought.

"In your case, though, there were some unusual elements right from the start. First of all, you came all the way from Vermont to Georgia for college? Not exactly common. You said you were a 'mature student'—okay. Again, not the ordinary thing but not out of the question. So far, you're on the side of the angels. But you also came right up in the state database as a witness in a Rabun County case, where a woman said her sister burned up in a tent. Now that's a sad story, but it helps explain why you had a house to sell in Vermont. I noticed the accident file said Rose Parker, the witness, was twenty-six. Twenty-six? Well, okay. To me you looked older than twenty-six, but believe it or not, I am not an infallible judge of a woman's age, especially past what you might call the first bloom of youth. The ladies down here take good care of themselves. For all I know, this is what twenty-six looks like up north. I hope I have not offended you," Pickens said, his voice dripping with insincerity.

She was lying in the back of his SUV with plastic restraints around her ankle and wrist, being forced to feel every rock in the road in every muscle of her back and to listen to right-wing radio along with his unique and horrifying bullshit. Yes, he had offended her.

"Anyway, I was more than happy to handle your property transaction and let you go on your way. You're not such a nice person, I could see that, but I was fine with doing our business and getting paid. And that would have been the end of the story, except, a couple of years ago, there you were on my phone, giving me an actual warning about who I can and can't talk to. New York number. Public phone, apparently. Don't y'all have cell phones up there?"

He laughed at his own joke.

"And I'll tell you the truth, I found this very interesting, because from time to time I've thought of you and wondered how you were getting on, but every time I tried to look up Rose Parker, formerly of Athens, Georgia, and before that from up north, I came up with exactly nothing. Now there you were, warning me not to answer somebody's questions about you, and saying if I tell this person anything you don't like, you'll call the Bar Association and claim I assaulted you. So that, at least, gave me some information I hadn't had before. Thank you for getting in touch."

It was said mockingly, and Anna did feel thoroughly mocked. *If only she'd been able to leave it alone*, she thought as the SUV jolted forward, the dark trees now barely extractable from the general darkness overhead. If only she'd toughed it out, let Jake go down to Georgia without a fuss and certainly without intervention, and simply spent those days preparing for what she'd need to do on his return. But even as she berated herself, she also remembered the night he'd returned from Vermont, how he had unspooled his investigation for her and recounted each progressively horrifying step of what he'd been up to in Rutland: talking to Evan's friend, visiting his bar, even stopping at the house. Yes, it had spooked her, thinking about Jake in those places, having those conversations with those people. It was disorienting to know that even Jake, who had failed to recognize her highly fictional life story as the work of

Marilynne Robinson (one of the most important literary novelists of his time, which was shameful for him, but also kind of funny), had come disturbingly close to knowing a whole lot more about who he was married to. Of course she hadn't wanted him to go to Athens.

"So after your friend you don't want me talking to came to see me at my office, it took me all of a minute to learn that he wasn't lying about being a writer. He'd done pretty well for himself, making the bestseller list and hanging out in Hollywood with Steven Spielberg. Also, it surprised me not all that much to see he was married to my long-lost client Rose Parker, even if she's changed her whole look around since I handled her house sale in Vermont. And I'll be frank, it makes no sense to me that a woman with the potential to be attractive—no offense—would let herself go like that when she doesn't have to, but as I said, the girls down here take care of themselves. I'm just used to that."

He was charm itself, this one. But she was conserving her energy.

"I suppose you had your reasons. Maybe it's the style out there in the Northwest, or New York City, or wherever you went off to when you left here. Maybe you were through trying to pretend you were young enough to be attending college. Even as a 'mature' student. But even if I don't know any of that, at least I know where you are now: up there in New York, living high on the hog in the big city. If you were anybody else I'd be thinking: *Good for her! Little Rose Parker! Happy at last!* and wondering where I should send my very overdue wedding gift. But, of course, you're not anyone else, are you? You're not even Rose Parker."

He waited for her to react, but she wouldn't give him the satisfaction.

"Don't you want to hear how I found that out?"

She did not want to hear it, especially. But she needed to hear it. What she did next would depend on what Arthur Pickens knew and how much of it his ego would force him to share with her. The car was nearly rocking now, as if they had progressed from a road to a track. Was this even a place meant for cars?

"I went back to that news story from north Georgia. I phoned up the coroner in Rabun County. You remember him?"

He didn't wait for an answer.

"Trusting soul," Pickens said, with abundant sarcasm. "Gets called out in the middle of the night to examine a burned-up girl in a tent at a campground, chooses to believe every single word the sole survivor tells him. I wouldn't have. You probably wouldn't have, either."

He was right about that, Anna thought.

The car had slowed to a crawl. The trees overhead were no longer a streaming ribbon but a series of distinct dark shapes against a darkening sky. The road, if it was a road at all, was so rough she could feel every pebble they jolted over.

"He tells me a propane heater started the fire. He tells me how badly burned the body was. He gives me some line about hearing hoofbeats and thinking 'it's a horse,' not 'it's a zebra.' But what good is that when there really is a zebra running around?"

Pickens stopped to admire his own cleverness, or the coroner's hubris, Anna couldn't tell.

"He tells me the goodhearted people of Clayton donated a casket and a plot for that poor girl. He tells me all about the funeral. Small group. Him and a few ladies from the hospital and also the very sad surviving sister. Then he tells me I'm not even the first one to come asking about all this. It so happens, a fellow from up north, a writer, came to see him in Clayton. And when was that? By strange coincidence, just a day after I saw that same writer in Athens. And somehow this does not surprise me. And by the time we're off the phone I'm pretty sure I know where Rose Parker has been, all this time."

"But that isn't me," Anna said sharply. It was true that she had given nothing away, not yet. He'd been doing all the talking. She was still, to anyone else, at least, a victim of a kidnapping, being transported uncomfortably to some unrevealed destination. What she meant, she supposed, was: *You are mistaken. I am not this person. I am Anna, a widow, a writer, and I don't know who you're talking about, and if you don't want to spend the rest of your life in prison pull the car over right now and let me go.* But even as she said it, she was faltering, backtracking, capitulating. "I mean," she said, with far more supplication than she wanted to acknowledge, "I'm not Rose Parker."

And he laughed, which was when she finally understood. *He already knows I'm not.* That was his point. He'd been talking about someone else entirely.

"I didn't say you were. I said I knew where she was."

And then, horribly, she knew, too. Where Rose Parker was. Where all three of them were. The car had stopped. The forward motion had been so slow at the end that she hadn't even noticed, but now he turned off the engine, and there was sudden and total silence. They had reached their destination.

28

Bring Up the Bodies

A moment later, he opened the car door and came around to the back; then he cut the plastic at her wrist and her ankle and actually helped her out. He was so tall: she remembered the way those long legs had been concealed under his desk that first day she'd entered his office, and how he rose and rose to his full height. Unctuous in his manners, plainly duplicitous in his smile, and that cologne. She couldn't make out much more than his outline; then, as her eyes acclimated, she saw the graves, so many of them dating to the 1800s, and she remembered the fading names they bore: Pickett, Ramey, Shook, and Wellborn. Names of formerly living people who were probably related to many of the currently living people in the surrounding towns. No one was here and able to help her. The shovel she'd been riding with in the back of the car was now on the ground at her feet. Also, he was pointing a gun at her. She stared at it.

"Pick it up," he said. He meant the shovel. She didn't do it. She couldn't move. No one had ever pointed a gun at her before. It had a paralytic effect.

"Oh, come on," said Pickens. "Do I need to explain this to you? The rules are: You will do exactly what I tell you to do. You will listen to my questions and respond completely and honestly, though you don't have much of a track record with honesty, so I'm already giving you too much credit. And if you follow these rules, I might just let you scoot off again and get on with your life, or somebody else's life, whatever floats your boat. I am completely uninterested in retribution for anyone you may have harmed, at any point, under any name you might have called yourself at the time. I could not possibly care less. You understand?"

Anna nodded.

She picked up the shovel.

"That way," he said, pointing.

She turned to see where he was pointing, though it was hardly necessary.

"You've been here before," she observed.

"After I talked to the coroner, I came up to see it for myself. Poor Dianna Parker, buried so far from home. Tough on the family, I'd say. Wouldn't you?"

But it was obvious he wasn't looking for an answer.

"Let's go. I think you know the way."

She took a step. Already the shovel was heavy in her hands. Already one foot landed unsteadily, on uneven ground. He was behind her, also walking.

Her foot caught on a root or a branch, and she fell, bracing an arm against the ground. It didn't matter. She hurt her wrist and knee both. He didn't reach down to help. Why would he? She felt around for something she might use—a stone, or a bottle left behind by someone who inexplicably liked to drink in old graveyards—but there was only a handful of earth.

"Come on," said Arthur Pickens, with clear impatience. She got back onto her feet. They weren't far now.

He had brought her to a place at the edge of the woods, where the grave and the gravestone were not as old as the others, and the few words cut into the granite could be easily read. Her feet, in the running shoes she had laced on only that morning in Athens, were sinking into the moss and the soft dirt underneath.

"You know how they say you get a chill when a person walks over your grave?" Pickens said. She looked at him. His very white teeth flashed in the darkness. "You feeling that, right about now?"

"I don't know what you mean," she said, but even to herself she sounded inauthentic. "What is it you want, anyway?"

"I want to know what you did. And how you did it."

He was spreading out the tarp on the ground beside the grave. Her daughter's grave.

"But why? What does it matter?"

"Morally? Criminally? It doesn't matter to me. But financially, it matters a lot. Because you and I are going to make a private arrangement concerning your late husband's literary estate, and like any business partners we both need full access to the same information."

She stood, watching him adjust the corners of the tarp, daintily, as if he were making a bed.

"You're going to want to start digging," he said, as if she were thick. He was pointing the gun at the shovel she held.

"You're kidding," was all she managed to produce.

"Now, Rose." Pickens shook his dark head. "Already? So soon after we've established the rules? *I ask, you answer. I tell you what to do, you do it.* Seems pretty simple to me, and yet, there you go. It's almost as if you don't want to get on with your life at all. You'd rather stay here?"

"No, I . . . I'm confused, though. What is the point? I take it you know who's buried here."

"I take it you're correct," said Pickens, with merriment. He had seated himself at the edge of the tarp, his long legs crisscrossed. "But you know, in my profession I have always hewed to the notion that you can't have too much information. You are going to dig her up, and unappetizing as I personally find the prospect, I'm going to take some samples of the . . . biological material, let's call it. For the kind of reassurance only a DNA test can bring. I might take a few photographs, too. Don't you think I should? Wouldn't you?"

In his position, she supposed, she would.

"And just to keep us both entertained while you're digging, you can tell me the whole story of how the real Rose Parker ended up down there. You don't mind if I record, do you?"

And he pulled out his phone and placed it on the ground. A button on the screen was already glowing red.

"You have a gun pointed at me," Anna said, halfheartedly. "Anything I say is because of that."

"Oh, don't get yourself worked up. This is just to help us trust each other. You might save me the trouble of editing out any more statements like the one you just made. Not that I don't rejoice in the fact that you still think I'm stupid. Truly, I do. It's endlessly entertaining to me. But I'm better at the tech than you might imagine. Even an old-fashioned soul like myself! And you don't need to get all exercised about this gun. It's more of a 'Finders Keepers' situation. No chance it will ever get traced to me."

He was grinning. The moonlight glinted off his teeth.

"Besides," he added, "I'm hoping we're going to have a long and fruitful partnership, and I'll never need to use either the recording or the gun. You should know that I'm fully intending to leave you at a bus stop in Clayton or even drive you down to Atlanta, but it's entirely up to you. I just want the information, and after we're done here, off you go. Of course, I'll be sending this recording to my own attorney with some instructions in the event of my unexplained disappearance, but there's no reason you and I need to reunite in the future. You can go wherever you want, live your life, or somebody else's life. Doesn't matter to me, so long as we conclude our business here."

There was nothing to be gained by expressing her very real doubts about this. He wouldn't have driven her all this way for a conversation, not to speak of whatever he intended to do with that shovel, and you didn't point a gun at someone you intended to drive to the bus stop afterward. On the other hand, she was not in a position to demand better terms. The haze of whatever he'd injected her with had finally lifted, but the ongoing fear and the long car ride's various discomforts and a certain deepening uncertainty about her prospects had combined to hold her fully in his thrall. This was a tough place to be. If she yelled, no one would hear, and if she ran, she'd probably fall to the ground, and quickly. The wits and smarts and habit of prioritizing herself that had carried her so far through life were all she had to rely on, and unfortunately for herself, Pickens easily matched her in at least two of those qualities. The bald fact was this: no one else was here with them, and no one else was coming. She was alone with a profoundly untrustworthy man, who was armed, in the dark, at the edge of a cemetery deep in the north Georgia woods. She was, in other words, on her own. Which was all she had ever been.

He paused. "You're waiting for something?"

She wrapped her hands around the wooden shaft.

"I hurt my wrist when I fell back there."

"My heart breaks for you. Dig."

She pushed the cutting edge into the dirt. It sank like the soil was butter. Anna set her jaw. Her wrist did hurt, and her ankle, which was also the ankle that had recently worn a hard plastic zip tie. But there was nothing to be done about that, so she resigned herself and she began, moving in a grid, taking off the top layer of the soil in sections and setting them on the far side of the plot from where he sat. But even as she dug, she was thinking. At least she was thinking. And for all the horror of the blade and the shaft and the dirt, coming up in shovelfuls, rotated to the side and dropped onto the tarp beside him, the first inkling of a plan began to build. Whenever she looked over at him she could see that grin and the metal of that gun. He was taking his attentiveness seriously. Unfortunately, he wasn't stopping at mere attentiveness.

"I don't hear you talking, Rose."

She gritted her teeth. "What do you want to know?"

He wanted it all, and the questions he asked told her that he already knew far too much. He wanted mommy and daddy and the older brother, Evan: future MVP, bar owner, budding novelist, and tragic victim of an accidental overdose. He wanted the actual Rose Parker, that ungrateful girl, and the escape she'd nearly made, and the propane heater she herself might or might not have knocked over, purposely or otherwise, on her way out of the tent in the middle of that Georgia night not far from where they were at this moment. He wanted her statements to the EMTs and the fire marshal and then the coroner, and her description of the ill-attended ceremony at which the burned-up girl, whose name was not the name on this gravestone, was buried in a donated coffin. He wanted her dealings with the University of Georgia and the sale of the Vermont home after the death of Evan Parker, all of which she gave him. But when he pressed hard on the *why* of any of it, she stopped talking. It was the only thing she refused to tell him.

She had no idea if Pickens believed her to be telling the truth, but in fact every bit of it was true. For one thing, it was easier to say what had happened than to conjure, on the spot, some alternate version skewed to the current circumstances, and that cleared more space in her head to extend and refine the plan that had begun with that first square of moss from the surface of the grave site. Also, she had never heard herself tell her own story out loud, and it was weirdly calming, weirdly affirming; it entered the stillness of that forest clearing like something incantatory, as if the whole graveyard and its inhabitants had become her silent interlocutors. Here she was, for the first time revealed as the right girl born into the wrong family, her gifts negated, her wishes—clearly—disdained, her physical body all but imprisoned, made use of and discarded, the girl who nonetheless had made a long-term and good faith effort to do what was right. She marveled at herself as she was attending to her own narrative, inwardly praising the self-belief she had managed to extract from such a neglectful and oppressive childhood, the self-reliance that had come with her out of Rutland and remained with her every day since. She was self-reliant right now, as the heavy blade sank deeper and deeper into the dirt, her palms ragged with blisters, her ankle aching. She believed in herself, right now. She believed in her ability to do what she needed to do.

"My belated condolences on the death of your husband, by the way," Pickens said. "To go with my belated congrats on your marriage. Close together, weren't they? Still, you can't define a great love story with a stopwatch, can you? What an awful blow it must have been, to lose him like that. Very sudden and unexpected, from what I read in your own little fiction. And he seemed so vibrant and healthy when I met him, just a few days before he passed! Waltzing into my office looking for Rose Parker, full of beans. Zipping up here to a little town in the north Georgia mountains. Then, just a couple of days later, he's back in New York City, tragically taking his own life. What a terrible, terrible thing, leaving you all alone to inherit his money and safeguard his literary reputation. When you're the one who took him out. Correct me if I'm wrong."

She had to breathe through this, dismay replacing dismay.

"I didn't realize you care so much about literature."

He laughed again, loud and deep, the sound of it filling the graveyard, merging with the heavy smell of earth. "Your husband announced he was a writer like that was something I was supposed to be impressed by. I didn't know or care who he was, but you know what I did care about? The fact that I suddenly had Rose Parker on my line, years after she left Athens. Because I'll be frank with you, you're not a person I was expecting to hear from, ever again. So no, I didn't go rushing out to read the collected works of Jacob Bonner after that day in my office. I didn't even know he'd died until a few months ago, when those two up in Vermont called me and told me. They gave me an earful about Jacob Bonner."

Abruptly, she went numb: the absurdity of what he'd just said battling the sheer alarm of it.

"Those two?"

"The two women up there. The ones who bought your house."

Now she was scrambling to find and reinsert the long-ago set of facts she had happily expunged, once they were no longer needed. *Those two. Vermont. Bought. Your house.* She could not remember a single thing about them. Were *those two* friends? Were they a couple? Sisters? Who cared? They'd been buyers! They wanted the place and they wanted to pay money for it; that was all that had mattered at the time. For what possible reason should it matter now? Pickens in Athens and another attorney up in Rutland had stood between herself and *those two*: multiple degrees of separation, multiple years, multiple lives. That was how little she cared about the first non-Parkers who would ever own her family's ancestral house.

That house. That fucking house.

"You're a lot like your husband, aren't you?" Anna heard him say. "Waltzing right into harm's way."

Waltzing. She was forcing herself back to that last day in the house, before that last night with Evan, and her exhaustive inventory of every room and hiding place: the manuscript pages, legal pads, and floppy disks, the draft marked "working" and the laptop. She had left nothing—*nothing*—behind for those two women to find. So how?

"I don't understand," she finally admitted. It was all she could manage, and it happened to be true.

Nothing she might have said, she knew, could give him greater delight.

"Are you aware that your husband paid those women a visit a few days before he died?"

Of course she was aware. But the visit had been no more distressing than anything else Jake had done in Vermont. And besides, neither those home buyers nor Jake himself knew of any possible connection between Anna Williams-Bonner and Evan Parker's childhood home, so there was nothing Jake could have told them, and nothing the women might have told Jake, to connect the two.

"So?"

"He told them he had a student who'd grown up in that house. He sat at their kitchen table and talked about meeting Oprah and he drank a cup of coffee and ate a doughnut. I heard all about it. And he promised to send them a signed copy of his book, when he got home."

Yes, and? But Pickens was clearly waiting for her. He wanted to drag her down each individual step.

"All right. So what?"

"Well, he didn't do it. And that pissed them off. You know, big author, friend of Oprah, sits in their kitchen and drinks their coffee, promises them a signed book. Two signed books, in fact, because he was supposed to send another one, for somebody's sister. A fan."

He was getting more and more ridiculous. Was she really supposed to care how many books her dead husband hadn't mailed to Vermont?

"So, he forgot."

"He didn't forget, Rose. He died. Just a couple of days later. He never sent those ladies their books. You get it?"

Obviously, she did not get it. But at least she didn't have to ask again.

"So they're annoyed. And then, one day last summer, they open up their mailbox and there's an envelope there, a big fat envelope sent to your dead brother. And maybe there's been the occasional flyer or subscription coming to Evan Parker since they bought the house, but nothing like this. And here's the thing: same address to and from. There's a term for it, apparently. In the world of *literature*."

There was, but it belonged more accurately to the world of publishing, and it wasn't a name so much as an acronym: S.A.S.E., meaning self-addressed stamped envelope, a standard item in the lives of aspiring authors, at least in the days of yore before everything got sent via email. S.A.S.E. was what you mailed along with your printed-out manuscript when you submitted it to an agent, so the agent could send it back to you—after, perhaps, having given it a cursory glance—without undertaking any expense of their own. Evan, who had failed to acquire an agent by means of his low-residency Ripley course, was playing the traditional submission game, and apparently by the rules. Still, how many years must have gone by since he'd sent his novel out? Even if he'd done it at the last possible moment, in the days before she returned to Vermont and administered his tragic overdose, that was still . . .

"What kind of company sits on correspondence for six years?" Pickens said, as if he were truly offended on Evan Parker's behalf. "There was a note with it: *Sorry, sorry, blah, blah* . . . it was overlooked, on some shelf, along with others, and *We hope you have found a good home for it*. Like it's a puppy? Who puts up with that? You'd think the author would make a stink."

You'd think, and you'd be thinking correctly. But not if the author in question had been dead all that time.

"Which agency sent it back?"

He failed to answer, the question having failed to interest him, but Anna, listening to the nonresponse, found that she no longer required the name. Of course, her brother would have wanted the best agent for his wonderful, unmissable novel, the same agent that Jake, with all his knowledge of the industry, had chosen, and the same agent who had chosen Anna, herself. He'd wanted the one whose office had been nicknamed the Black Hole of Salter?

"Fine. So what?"

"So they're not like you, those two. They're good people. They don't feel right sitting on something so meaningful, that belonged to a person who died. They want to send it to his next of kin, and that's Rose Parker, the niece, who lives somewhere down south. Or at least she did when they bought their house from her. The lawyer up there had died, but they dig out the contract, and my address is on it, so they write to tell me about this manuscript and would I be willing to forward it to this theoretically loving and grateful next of kin? Now, I have no reason to believe an unpublished novel by a dead author I've never heard of is going to be of any interest to the Rose Parker I know and love, and who the last time I spoke to her threatened to lie about me to the Bar Association, so I told those two that Rose Parker left Athens shortly after the sale, back in 2013, and we're not in contact. As far as I'm concerned that's the end of it. But then they write to me again."

He stopped. He wanted her to beg, obviously.

"And?"

"And this time they're actually sending me the manuscript, and they're insisting I read it, too. Because they have detected . . . what should I call it? A certain *similarity in content* between this unpublished book by the dead author who once lived in their house and a bestselling book by another dead author who was, by his own admission, the dead guy's teacher at some writing program in Vermont, and who also happens to be that same asshole who promised them a signed copy and never sent it."

Two signed copies, she corrected him, but silently. Her arms were heavy now, and she could feel the dirt under her sweatpants and in her socks. Even with a certain intentional deceleration in her digging, there wasn't much farther to go.

"So now they're thinking this Jacob Finch Bonner isn't just a celebrity author who knows Oprah and drank their coffee and didn't send the books he promised. Now they're thinking he's some kind of a thief, and maybe even worse than that. They know Jake has passed on by this point, and maybe it's a shame he's dead, and maybe it lets him off the hook for not sending those signed copies like he promised, but there's still the matter of his big bestselling novel with the same story as poor Evan Parker's novel, and that's definitely something the poor niece Rose Parker needs to know about. But, no offense,

I can't adequately convey to you how little I care about these two dead authors who wrote the same book, neither of whom is my client. I'm not much of a reader at the best of times, as I've said."

She was down to her knees in the hole now. With every careful descent of the shovel blade, she feared the obstacle of the coffin lid.

"And as I said, I wasn't all that eager to have you back in my life again. I don't think I even wrote back to those two. Then one night, I was up at the clubhouse, getting a drink with a friend, and I saw a sign on one of the boards: Club Harmonie Book Group. And the selection for January was a book by Anna Williams-Bonner. Nice author photo. And it's my own Rose Parker again, so solemn, so grieving widow. And this does surprise me, that you have also become a writer of fiction! I lived my whole life before Jacob Bonner without ever meeting one, and suddenly I have three of you in my life! But the surprises don't stop there, because this book, her book, is all about a woman whose writer-husband kills himself, which is a real coincidence because the author's real-life husband was also a *famous* author who did exactly that. And I have to say, it strikes me as odd that so many people out there just tell the story of their own lives and call it fiction. It speaks to a certain poverty of imagination, if you don't mind my saying so."

She was nearly up to her waist in her daughter's grave. She was well past minding such a thing.

"So I decided, maybe it was time to read that book your husband wrote, seeing as I'd been fortunate enough to know him personally. I took myself out to Athens Promenade, to Barnes and Noble, and I got myself a copy of that book everybody but me had read a few years ago, and what a story it was! Some woman kills her daughter, takes her own kid's scholarship, and her name, and goes off and lives her daughter's life. I can absolutely see why that thing was such a bestseller. Then I go looking for the novel those women sent me, the one they say Bonner stole, which I still have down at the office, and you know what? That one was a pretty good read, too. The writing wasn't as fancy, but I'm not picky that way. And this is more fiction novels than I've read in a long while, and I wasn't skimming them, either. But even if I had, you couldn't miss the headline. Some of the details were different—character names, and how the murders happened, but those two books had the exact same plot. Evil mom who murders her own daughter and steals her life? Now that's a story you don't come across every day, and what a coincidence that the authors of both these books were in a classroom together, one as the student and one as the teacher! I could see the point those women in Vermont were making, about how that poor missing niece should be notified."

"But did you actually tell them any of this?" Anna said. She hoped it was her imagination, but it felt like there was now something solid under her feet. She began to pile less and less on the shovel. It was fully dark now, and he was fully in thrall to himself. She hoped he wouldn't notice.

"Why would I? Those two had no idea who the missing niece really was, what her connection to the story was. All they wanted was to find her so they could tattle on a dead writer who helped himself to another dead writer's novel. They wanted to take a big moral stand and right some horrible literary crime. But I'm not all that exercised about big moral stands or literary crimes. To tell the truth, I don't really care what your husband did. I'm a lot more interested in what you did, Rose."

She gripped the shaft of the shovel. Her palms were screaming, and she had all but stopped even pretending to move the soil.

"Because even a casual reader like myself can see how much you have in common with the main characters of both those novels, published and unpublished. You, a student from far away, maybe a little bit older than your typical college student? With a dead . . . sister, was it? Who'd passed unexpectedly, only a few days before you turned up in Athens? And now I'm thinking, maybe those two books aren't fiction after all. Maybe they're about you, and maybe you have a personal objection to people writing about your private business. Which is maybe why you were so worked up about somebody coming to ask questions about you that you took the trouble of getting in touch with me after all those years."

How Anna wished, now, that she hadn't. But it was too late. She was actively feeling beneath her feet for the dimensions of Rose Parker's coffin.

"Now, like I said, this isn't so much a moral issue for me. I don't personally need to see you strung up for something you might have done, at some point in the past, but at the same time, it's obvious to me that you and I have business to address. That's why I wrote to your publisher. I understand this isn't exactly comfortable for you, you're not enjoying yourself at the moment, but you have to acknowledge we have a common purpose here."

She acknowledged no such thing, but she didn't have to wait long for him to elucidate.

"Your bestseller husband was a plagiarist. You don't want people finding that out, just like you don't want them finding out you were the inspiration for his book. I'm also betting you don't want them looking too closely at your background or your family, because no telling what they'll find out. Rose, not only do I sympathize with you, I feel exactly the same: privacy is such an old-fashioned concept today, and so precious, isn't it? But even if none of that was true, there's something else, something we both want. We want Jacob Bonner's book to keep selling. Don't we want that?"

"Because of that 'private arrangement' you mentioned," she said, through gritted teeth.

"Exactly so. I'll be setting up a trust, or that's how you can describe it, if you want to describe it at all. We'll give it a good name, something dignified. Something in keeping with your *brand* as the lachrymose widow. The Jacob Finch Bonner Foundation. You can say it's devoted to something close to your heart. Suicide prevention. Or something close to his, like grants for writers who don't have any ideas of their own and have to steal from other writers. Now *there's* a field that needs targeted research. I don't care what we call it, but I'll be administering it for you. If you're good, I'll let you keep your own royalties. From your own little book, that is."

Kind of you, she thought, but she was undeniably distracted now. First, there was a definite impression of something hard and flat beneath her feet, something with edges, something horrifying. She palpated it with both feet as she listened, as she pretended to dig, still, lifting out the dirt from Dianna Parker's grave and setting it down, then surreptitiously returning some of that same dirt to the hole in the ground. But something even stranger than that, even more goading, supplicatory, bothersome, had joined the battle for her concentration, pushing back against the ordinary dread of her dead daughter's body, just beneath her feet. And that was the thing she couldn't quite grasp. Not yet.

"Why didn't you just email me?" she heard herself say. "Obviously, you knew where I was. Who I was. You could have sent me an email through my website. People do it all the time. You didn't have to involve anyone else. It seems like a lot of unnecessary trouble."

"No trouble. I may not be a *writer* like you and your husband, but I think I can handle an effective letter with minimal effort. Convey the information I wish to convey. Withhold the information I wish to withhold. Make sure the right events are set in motion to produce the right outcome."

Which was? Anna thought. But again, he couldn't resist explaining it all.

"In my many years as an attorney," said Pickens, "I have learned that there are conversations you only want to have when you can look a person in the eye. See into their soul, in other words. If they have one."

She resisted the urge to react, to give in to her now surging outrage, mainly because of that other thing, that troubling thing, still undefined, that was working on her still. It was something he'd said, or more accurately hadn't said, something that refused to punch through. It was taking far too long. It was taking precious time, and she didn't have much time to spare.

"I let your editor know there was a serious situation involving Jake's book. I knew she'd pass that along to you, and I knew you'd want to resolve the situation as quickly as possible. I've been waiting for you to come to Georgia and see me, and that's what you did. Very efficient, I'd say."

It had been, she supposed. Efficient. One well-written and well-planned letter had brought her here: the very model of efficiency.

And then, at last, she understood what that thing—that other thing, that hounding thing—was.

He had admitted, without any hesitation whatsoever, to sending the excerpt of Evan's manuscript to Wendy, two months earlier. But he had said nothing about the excerpts sent to her own address, nor the one sent to her in-laws. Not to mention that cryptic warning so many months earlier, in

Denver. He seemed . . . incredible as this was to admit, he seemed not to know about them. If he'd known, if he'd been responsible for those things as well, he'd have been as proud of sending them as he clearly was of sending the final one. There was no reason for him not to own them now. Besides, he'd all but boasted that he preferred to deal with "professionals" like himself, a designation that would not apply to genuinely bereaved parents like Jake's. What could that mean for the other excerpts and the messages she and Jake's parents had received? That Martin Purcell, after all, had been the one to send them? (The thought of it came with a jolt of relief, that her trip to Ripley might not have been a waste of her time, her effort, and not incidentally the risk to herself. But wanting that to be true—and she did want very, very much for it to be true—did not, alas, make it true. And if it wasn't true, and if it hadn't been Purcell, and if it also hadn't been Pickens, then she was still in a very bad place. A place even worse, in fact, than waist-deep in her daughter's grave in backwoods Georgia.)

These were pressing questions, well worth asking, but she never got the chance, because at that precise moment the blade of Pickens's shovel unmistakably met the cheap pine cover of Rose Parker's coffin, and their time together came to an end.

She looked up to see if he had heard. He did not appear to have heard.

"Tell me more," said Pickens, "about . . . Jacob *Finch* Bonner." There was a certain snideness in his tone, and she had a moment to wonder whether his obvious distaste for her late husband had stemmed entirely from their sole encounter, or whether that appropriated "Finch" in the middle of his name was some knee-jerk affront of its own.

She stopped digging. She seemed to lean on her shovel in exhaustion. In fact, she was wrapping her blistered hands around the handle, tightly enough to shred the remaining skin.

"You better make sure you have enough battery left," said Anna, "because what I'm going to tell you, you won't want to run out in the middle."

"I'm good—" he started to say, but he just had to check, because that's what anyone would do when they fear (as everyone does) their phone might betray them—lose signal, lose power, delete some crucial file, or even self-destruct at the errant swipe or random jostle in a back pocket—even if we are indeed *better at the tech than you might imagine*, and so Arthur Pickens, Esq., leaned over toward it and looked down at the ground, where the record button of his phone (which did indeed have more than enough battery to preserve every one of her many confessions, the ones she had made and the ones she never would) was still glowing red, and in that slim instant Anna swung the blade around, up and out of the hole, and hit him with its sharp edge behind his right ear. He fell, cursing, but almost immediately he was scrambling to get up, and this time she brought the shovel up over her own head, rotated it flat, bringing it down with all her strength. It hit him midway between the temple and his high forehead, and she didn't wait to see the result.

Anna placed the shovel up at the edge of the hole farthest from him, and scrambled up after it, then she picked it up again and stepped behind the headstone. He still had the gun in his right hand, and that hand was still moving, so she hit his head again and he let the gun go. She picked it up and put it on the ground a safe distance away. Then she reached beneath him for the phone, guided by its helpful light, and he grabbed her hand as it went past his own. She kicked him in the nearest useful place, the place most likely to still register pain. Instantly he let go of her wrist and pawed at his own crotch.

"Sorry," she said. It was automatic, but meaningless. She wasn't sure which part of this she was apologizing for—taking away his phone? Kicking him hard? Spoiling his elaborate plan to blackmail her? Or taking him out with his own shovel?—but it didn't really matter. She wasn't actually sorry about any of it.

She hit him one more time, and this time the back of the shovel made a wet, hard sound and left a wet, dark place behind. He was dead or on the way there, and again, she couldn't get herself to care too deeply about the distinction. She took his car keys from a jacket pocket, but that was all she took. If anyone ever found a reason to dig up this grave—again!—it would probably be because they already knew he was here, and in the absence of that extreme situation his belongings were probably safer here than anywhere else, where they might be found and reported. The phone, though, had technology she didn't fully understand, and she wanted to make sure that anyone tracking it would be able to follow it far from this place. First, she deleted that recording, then she powered it down and put it on the ground beside his gun.

She sat down on the ground beside him, braced herself as best she could, and shoved him with her feet. He rolled into the grave, landing with a satisfying smack against the wood of her daughter's coffin. She got painfully to her feet, feeling every moment of the ride and the dig and the ambient distress he'd subjected her to. The tarp kept the next part simple. She dragged it and the pile of dirt down over him, so that the blue plastic weave covered the body, and the dirt covered that, then she spent a few minutes brushing any remaining dislocated soil back into the hole before doing her best to level it off. Finally, she reassembled those squares of moss in their original pattern, placing them like ceramic tiles grouted by earth.

There were no last words, but at least Arthur Pickens, Esq., would never suffer the indignity of being made to cross the Mason-Dixon Line.

Anna picked up the gun and the phone and moved quickly through the graves. The shovel had been too dangerous to leave behind, but it felt only a little less dangerous to take with her. Reaching Pickens's car, she opened the back and pushed it inside, covering it with one of the blankets Pickens had thrown over her. The sight of that half-full gallon of water brought her own thirst raging back. She clawed off the plastic cap and gulped frantically, then she poured water into her palm and started to clean herself, but she was afraid of wasting it, afraid of being thirsty again. She brought it with her to the front seat and set it down on the passenger-side floor. There, to her relief, she found her nylon belt bag, and beneath it, crumpled into something that looked like a dead rodent, her wig. She put it on with her filthy fingers and stared at her altered self in the rearview mirror: eyes bloodshot, face dirt-streaked, all of it framed by that still alien wig.

The car keys, the water, the wig, the cell phone, the money. And the gun. All she had left, and fortunately all she needed. Anna sat for a long moment, fighting the urge to rush and forcing herself to think through everything that had happened in the graveyard, tracing Pickens's movements and her own to be sure there wasn't something either of them had left or lost, something she'd forgotten to do, but there was nothing. Carefully, she started the car and made herself learn the dashboard before executing a tight three-point turn and easing her way slowly down the lane. There were, as she remembered from the last time she'd driven here (or at least, the last time she'd driven here in a proper, seated position) no houses at all until the dirt road ended at the edge of Clayton. She forced herself to drive slowly through the dark town until she reached Highway 441.

She still wasn't sure which direction she was going to go. A few hours to the south, that Kroger bag containing the manuscript of her brother's novel still sat right out in the open, and yet, forcing herself to think like the investigator who might one day arrive to inspect the home of a missing lawyer, she doubted that three hundred pages of unpublished fiction by an entirely unknown author would attract more attention than, say, the aggrieved parties attached to *O'Reilly v. Phi Kappa Tau National Council,* or any of the divorces, custody battles, or bankruptcies Pickens had been overseeing with his trademark attentive and compassionate care. For that matter, Pickens had his very own paper trail of Bar Association run-ins and questionable personal behavior, more than enough for an outwardly upstanding southern lawyer to want to hide his assets and disappear. Of course it was a risk, letting that book remain on Pickens's dining table, but driving a dead man's car back to Athens and past the guard station of Club Harmonie, perhaps to track north Georgia mud onto the floors or be seen by a neighbor or a landscaper or a FedEx driver, let alone the cameras that were surely ubiquitous in his SOUTHERN LIVING INSPIRED COMMUNITY . . . well, those seemed like much greater risks.

When she reached the junction of East Savannah Street and Highway 441 in Clayton, she still hadn't made up her mind, and she sat for the full sixty seconds of the red light, looking at the 20 Penny gas station across the street, trying to choose.

When the light changed, she turned left and drove. Direction: north.

She could only hope that whoever finally came to dispose of Arthur Pickens's things cared as little for literature as Pickens himself had.

By the time the sun was up, she was well past Charlotte, North Carolina (where she had added Pickens's shovel to a bin of tools at a community garden center west of town), and well on her way to DC. On the Beltway she turned Pickens's phone back on, detoured to Dulles Airport, and drove around to the back of one of the chain hotels on its periphery. There, she wiped the phone off and hid it in some tall grass beside a dumpster. If anyone looking for Pickens in the days ahead made an effort to locate his phone, they would end up here: next to a dumpster, behind a hotel, on the doorstep of an international airport. And good luck following him from there.

After that she headed north again.

She had never known how much of her obvious success at hiding derived from the fact that no one had been looking for her, but she preferred not to test herself against advanced and constantly changing technologies. Major highways had cameras—this was generally known—so avoiding them was an easy call. On the other hand, she wanted to spend as little time as possible driving the car of a Georgia attorney who was bound to be reported missing at some point, and probably sooner rather than later, and declining the most direct route to her destination would obviously add many hours, even days, to the trip. The route she improvised as she drove took her northwest through Maryland, central Pennsylvania, and the Finger Lakes of New York. Then again, she had given herself some extra and much-needed time to think.

The last time she'd paid any thought to those women was back in 2013. She'd been unenrolled from UGA for a couple of months by then, and the only reason she was still in Athens was because she wanted that money safely in her bank account before she left town. Unfortunately, it was at this very point that her attorney's behavior had become concerning, not to say downright obstructionist. She'd been forced to visit his office again and again as he claimed various bullshit bank delays or protocols unique to the state of Georgia. *What was her hurry, anyway?* he actually asked her at one point.

That was when she'd given up on the version of Rose Parker that had served her so well in Georgia: the polite and self-reliant girl from the north who preferred not to share too much of her information or anything resembling an emotion. That day in his office, with his ill-advised lunch unfurled on the coffee table, she wondered aloud if it might speed things up to have the Bar Association review his work on her uncle's estate, and in a matter of days—like magic!—the money materialized in her account. More magical still: it was the correct amount. A week later she took her leave of Athens, Georgia.

Now Pickens was home, safe in the embrace of his native terroir, and the only remaining ties to the person she had once been, and the things that person had done, were two ladies of a certain age whose names she couldn't recall, at the end of a transactional chain with not one but two attorneys between them. A pair of women Jake had forced himself upon, awakening their curiosity about things that had nothing to do with them, and promising them gifts he'd never deliver—though to be fair he could hardly have known that to be the case. Still! He might have put those stupid books in the mail before he went flying off to Athens and the rest of his pointless crusade, and he hadn't, so all this truly was his fault, because you don't dangle a free anything in the face of a Vermonter and not follow through. Everybody knew that.

The women had been good buyers, she remembered that much. The house was in terrible shape at the time of the sale, and they didn't nickel-and-dime her after the inspection report came in, with all the expected issues and problems. The house was also full of Evan's things, not to mention 150 years of Parker belongings and detritus, and being sold that way, because she was hardly going back there to supervise a clean-out. Now she recalled that there had been queries, forwarded from the Rutland attorney, and then by Pickens, about removing items from the basement and the attic, and the furniture in many of the rooms, but she had declined the opportunity. There was nothing she wanted from that place, and also, in those hours after Evan's death she'd made sure to remove every single object that mattered. She'd been done with all of it, that house and everything in it, not to mention everyone who'd ever lived there.

Not so done, apparently.

By evening she was in Albany, and completely exhausted. She pulled into an unbranded motel and paid for a night with cash, and once inside her shabby little room she stood in the rust-stained shower for nearly forty-five minutes, letting hot water roll over her. She ate the food she'd bought at a drive-through in Rensselaer and looked at the gun for the first time since she'd tossed it onto the floor of Pickens's SUV. In his right hand, in the dark of that graveyard, she had only been able to discern the fact that it was a handgun, but now she saw that it was a .38. A Ruger. It seemed to work in two different ways, both with and without having to cock the hammer first. More options, she supposed. At any rate, it saved her the ordeal and personal risk of having to buy a gun, something she sus-pected she was going to need. This time, she wouldn't have the luxury of days to sit watching from the woods, or the gentle arms of Morpheus to receive these self-appointed guardians of her late brother's literary legacy. Not with a pillar of the Georgia bar who might be reported missing at any moment. Not while she was driving his car.

Anna climbed under the not-immaculately-clean bedspread, and slept for many hours, her blistered hands and throbbing ankle and wrist, the strain of hunching over the wheel of an unfamiliar car, putting those miles between herself and its dead owner, all succumbing to the great and heavy darkness. Almost as if nothing terrible still lay ahead.

29

The Story of a New Name

The woman who came to Anna's former front door was rail thin with a long, fiery red braid down her back. She was of some indeterminate age between forty and seventy, and for a moment Anna couldn't help but remember Arthur Pickens's comment about how women in the north might choose to age. He might have been right about this particular woman.

"Hello?" she said, good manners and plain suspicion fighting for the upper hand.

"Oh, hi?" Anna said. She was no longer wearing her wig. She looked like Anna Williams-Bonner again, or at least Anna Williams-Bonner with a significant new haircut. Somewhere between the Finger Lakes and home, she had decided that this version of herself was best suited to the circumstances, because the women who had purchased this house did not know what Arthur Pickens had known. They had no reason to connect Jacob Finch Bonner's widow with any member of the Parker family. "My name is Anna? You don't know me, but—"

"I know you," said the woman. Briefly, she smiled, showing distinctly gray teeth. "You're that writer."

"Yes!" Anna said, surprised. "I mean, yes, I wrote a book. But my husband was a writer. I think, you met him? I understand . . . he came here to your house?"

The woman knew the answer, obviously, but she didn't nod, at least not right away.

"Couple years back."

"Right. Right. You know, he died."

The woman nodded again. She was holding a cardigan sweater together over her chest. But it wasn't that cold out.

"I know this is going to sound so strange, but my husband had some books he was going to send you? They were on his desk? After he died?"

The upspeak, that lamentable habit of women everywhere who preferred to sound as if they had no idea what they were talking about, did not come naturally to her, but it suited the situation at hand. She was here as the pathetic and needy survivor, grasping at any tendril of her late husband. That was how she intended to cross this threshold. What happened next would be determined by who was home and how easy it proved to locate the manuscript. In an ideal world, she would have taken a few days or even longer to watch the house and wait for it to be empty, but she had no idea how long it would take for Pickens to be reported missing, for word of that to reach West Rutland, Vermont, and for the women to decide that sharing Evan Parker's novel with the world was the best way of protecting themselves. Actually, in an ideal world, she would never have been forced to come back here at all. But they had already left ideal far behind.

"I'm sure you can understand, I wasn't in the best of shape after he passed, and there were so many decisions I needed to make, dealing with his publisher, and the will. There were things I just never got to. It was only a couple of months ago that I finally tackled the stuff on his desk. Correspondence, people's manuscripts they'd sent him for his opinion, or advice. Or blurbs . . ." She stopped. "You know what a blurb is?"

"I do," the woman said, warily.

"And there were these copies of his books he'd signed, and he was going to send them out, I guess, next time he went to the post office. He'd addressed the envelope already, or I wouldn't have known who they were for. And I'm here on my way to Middlebury to do something up at the college there, so I thought I'd stop and drop them off." She paused to laugh in girlish self-deprecation. "I'm sure you probably forgot all about this. Such a little thing."

The woman's eyes narrowed. She had not forgotten. Even if Pickens hadn't told her as much, Anna would have seen that for herself.

"But . . . better late than never, right?"

"So you've got some books for me?" The woman held out her hand for them, and Anna placed the big manila envelope in that hand. She'd acquired the two paperbacks of *Crib* that morning at the RPI bookstore in Troy, and the envelope at a dollar store nearby. Back in Pickens's car, she'd signed and addressed her purchases in a pretty good approximation of her late husband's handwriting. She'd also bought herself a parka with deep pockets. It had enough padding to hide the gun.

"And he signed them?"

"I believe so. Yes."

"Well . . ." The woman seemed, finally, to falter. "I suppose I appreciate you bringing them by. Hope it didn't take you too far out of your way."

"No, not at all. I'm just driving from New York up to Middlebury. I think I get on Route 7 in Rutland next. That's not too far from here, is it?"

"Not too far," the woman said. And she looked as if she were thinking things over. "I guess . . . would you want a cup of coffee before you get on the road again?"

"Oh!" Anna said, with outsize surprise and gratitude. "That would be so nice! If it's no trouble, I mean."

"No trouble." But the woman looked as if she weren't sure that was true. Then, as an afterthought, she said: "I'm Betty."

"Hi, Betty. I'm Anna."

"You said," said Betty. "Sylvia's here somewhere."

Anna nodded, following her inside.

Only a step or two inside and she had to stop and gape. The place was appallingly transformed, the hall painted a vile shade of pink and every inch of wall covered by some syrupy sweet landscape, à la Thomas Kinkade, or folksy signs like the one that said: ALL YOU NEED IS LOVE . . . AND A CAT! There were plenty of cat figurines, too, one on each step of the staircase she had hauled her brother up, shortly before his death, and an actual, living, enormous gray cat, looking down at her from the second floor.

It made her think of their own cat, Whidbey, another silent witness to a crime in progress.

"Sylvia?"

The other woman emerged from the kitchen. "Who's this?" the woman said, sounding every bit as unenthusiastic as her partner.

"This," Betty said, "is Anna. She's the wife of that writer who came to see us, couple years back."

"Widow," Anna corrected.

"You remember him?"

"Sure," said Sylvia, who was Jack Sprat's wife beside her partner: plump and soft to Betty's teetering and narrow frame. "He never sent us those books."

"He was going to," Anna said, her voice full of pain. "But he *died.*"

Sylvia looked as if that was a less-than-adequate excuse.

"Yuh," said Betty, and when she said it, Anna experienced a deeply uncomfortable pulse of alarm. Something about this most unremarkable of utterances actually felt familiar to her. With a jolt of dismay, she understood that she had seen Betty before. Before today, and somewhere else. But where? And when?

Then, like a personal dark cloud in a high wind, it passed.

"Anyway, I was going to be driving north, and I realized it was right on the way. So I brought them to you."

"We're giving her some coffee," said Betty.

"Yes! Thank you!" But there was no winning over Sylvia, who turned and walked straight back into the kitchen. Anna followed.

"You know this area?" Betty said, indicating the kitchen table. It was not the Parker kitchen table. It was not the Parker anything in here, except for the stove, their faithful avocado specimen, circa 1974. It was apparently indestructible. Above it, another sign read: SYLVIA'S KITCHEN (SEASONED WITH LOVE).

"Hazelnut okay?" Sylvia said. "All we drink."

"Sure," Anna said. "With milk?"

"We got milk," said Betty, as if Anna had accused her of being uncivilized.

"How long have you lived here?" Anna asked, anxious to get the three of them on track.

"In Rutland? All my life. Sylvia's from up near Vergennes."

"I meant . . . here in this house."

"We bought it in '13 when the last owner died," Sylvia said. She had gone over to the counter and was filling up the coffeemaker with grounds, an action that naturally, and unpleasantly, reminded her of the last pot of coffee she herself had prepared here. Even across the room, the hazelnut odor was stomach churning. "Nobody else wanted it."

True enough, Anna thought.

"I used to drive past it when I was a kid," Betty said. "Thought it was haunted."

That was a bit extreme. Anna's parents had not been very house-proud, it was true. They'd let the old formal gardens behind the house go to seed, and they weren't big believers in upgrades or modernization—if something had been good enough for her father's forebears, it was good enough for them. The bathroom, with its marble from the family quarry, had never been updated, and the two of them slept in that same terrible bed her paternal ancestor had hauled up from New Bedford on a cart. Still, central Vermont was full of authentically falling-down houses. This one wasn't all that special.

"Only because of the folks who lived here," Sylvia said, as if Anna had spoken out loud. "They had a habit of dying suddenly. Usually here in the house."

"Oh." Anna wrinkled her nose. "I don't like to think about that kind of thing. So, what do you two do?"

It was a very New York and a very un-Vermont thing to ask. Betty, it turned out, ran the office of a chiropractor in downtown Rutland. Sylvia stayed home. Also, she did some quilting, just for fun.

The coffee was predictably vile. She pretended to drink it with both hands around the mug, as if she had never tasted anything so wonderful. She asked them more questions about their lives and learned that Sylvia and Betty had met through a quilting group in Brandon. (*Could you get any more Vermont than that?* Anna thought.) Betty came from a big family, and nearly all of them were still in Rutland County. Sylvia's family didn't speak to her.

"What about you?" said Betty. "Out west, right?"

"Right. But I live in New York now. I might leave soon. It's not the same without my husband."

"No, it wouldn't be," said Sylvia with a certain lack of compassion. "Then again, you two weren't married that long."

"No, not that long. I think, maybe, if we'd known each other longer I might have seen how much trouble he was in. How depressed he was. But I didn't."

Betty was stirring some sugar into her coffee. "He seemed just fine when he was here, sitting right here at this table."

At the very least, a profoundly insensitive thing to say. But typical, Anna already understood, for this person, and also not her present concern.

"Well, it's a mystery." Anna shrugged. Then she said: "How did you know I grew up out west?"

The two women glanced at each other. "Well, we saw that story about you in the *New York Times*," Betty said.

Anna looked at her.

"What, you think we don't read the *Times* up here?"

Frankly, yes, she wanted to say. "Oh no! Only, I'm surprised you remembered that."

"We read the book, too," Sylvia said. "Went right out and got it when it came out. Because we'd known your husband, you see."

"Oh. Yes, I see."

But she didn't, not completely. She felt the elusiveness of her own understanding, but it was something she didn't want to look too closely at. She needed to figure out where they kept their copy of Evan's manuscript, and then she wanted to take care of them both and get out of here. It wasn't going to be pleasant, but it was still the plan. Her only plan.

"How's the coffee?" Betty said.

"It's good. Could I have another cup? And you know what, I'd love to see more of this house. I mean, if that's okay."

"Why?" said Sylvia, taking Anna's cup over to the coffee-maker.

"Sylvia," Betty said, "it's fine. We understand. She wants to see the place her husband came, just before he died."

"I think that's right," Anna said helpfully. "You know, I think that's exactly it. I'm not really myself these days. Still."

"Totally understandable," said Betty, with finality.

They took her down the hall to what had been Rose's room, now outfitted for quilting with two sewing machines and a wall of shelves stuffed with stacks and bundles of fabric, then across the hall to what had been her own bedroom before being co-opted by Evan to write his fatal novel. Now it had only a lonely exercise bike and a little TV. The long living room was jammed with fussy items and fake flowers, and there were two matching leather sofas facing each other, each festooned with far too many pillows. The old chain of pineapple stencils still lined the inside of the front door. It had been spared from the awful pink paint but only by a few inches; around that, the stomach-churning shade of Pepto-Bismol. They looked absurd, those pineapples. Why on earth were they still here? She had never felt anything like affection for them, but if you were going to take the house this far from itself, why not go all the way?

There wasn't a sign of a manuscript anywhere. In fact, in spite of Betty's assertion that they were literary-minded readers of the *New York Times,* there didn't seem to be any books in the house at all. And these women had gone off to buy her novel after reading a story about her in the Arts section of the *New York Times*?

"Like to see the upstairs? You probably want to be on your way."

She did. She did, very much, want to be on her way, but not without what she'd come for.

"I'd love that."

She went up ahead of them. The cat was still there, on the top step. It ran from her as she approached.

"I love your furniture," Anna said. As her hand reached up the banister it brushed Pickens's gun in her coat pocket. "Are they family pieces?"

"Some," said Sylvia. "One of the rocking chairs in the bedroom came from my mother's side. We inherited the bed."

She pointed to the left. Then they were at the door of her parents' bedroom.

"That bed?" she managed to say.

"Yes. Inherited with the house, I mean." It was Sylvia speaking. "Too big to get rid of it, even if we wanted to! Had to spend our own money clearing this place out. You should have seen the basement. And the attic—wall-to-wall up there. But we saw this and we said: leave that bed, we'll keep that."

She had never thought she'd need to see it again. But then, she had never thought she would have to come back after the last time, not to this house and certainly not to this room. And yet here she was and here it was, right where she'd left it: the indestructible bed of her ancestors. It had outlived them, and her parents who had died in it, and the brother who had died in it, and the daughter who had been conceived in it. *It will outlive me, too*, Anna thought. *Whatever happens to me, this bed will last forever, as all evil things are wont to do.*

"Seem familiar?" Betty said.

And Anna thought, *I'm sorry, what?* because the thing Betty had just said, itself, seemed familiar, and for a moment there she got lost between the question and whatever it was the question might have been about, but then somebody pushed her so hard between the shoulder blades that she fell forward, stumbling against one of the bedposts where the hard shape of Pickens's gun inside her pocket caught her right thigh in a breathtaking jolt of pain. She had time to register relief that the gun hadn't accidentally fired, but that passed in an instant, because Betty, she saw, had a gun of her own, and she was holding it in a way that definitely implied she knew how to use it. A mystifying turn of events, though not for long.

"Welcome home, Dianna Parker," one of them said. She wasn't sure which.

30

Death of a She Devil

"You just want to sit tight," Betty said. "I know what a sneaky bitch you are. I have a pretty good idea what you've done since you left town. And everything you did before that."

Anna was trying to grab onto any one of the spinning ideas in her head. No one of them seemed any better than the others.

"I'm sorry," she finally said, "but what—"

"Oh, you're not sorry," said Betty. "One thing I know for sure, you've never once in your life been sorry. Not for any of it."

"I'm calling the cops," Sylvia said. "You stay here."

"No, don't leave," said Betty. "I don't trust myself not to shoot her."

There was a certain amount of useful information here, Anna thought vaguely. Of the two of them, Betty was the more angry, the more determined, but in spite of that she was restraining herself. Sylvia, by contrast, wanted to handle this matter, whatever this matter was, in a less heated way.

"Why would you shoot me?" Anna asked. "I just came to bring you some books! You were showing me around your house."

"*Your* house, Dianna Parker. Where you grew up. Where you killed your mother and father, somehow, when you weren't more than a teenager. A problem with the carbon monoxide, they ruled it, but I know it was something you did. They died, but you were here, too, and you were just fine? Sure. You *hated* them."

"I don't know what you're talking about," Anna insisted, but even to her own ears she sounded uncertain. "I'm not . . . this person."

"And your little girl. You certainly made her disappear. You take her off to college a year early, she's that smart, and neither one of you ever comes home? All we hear is there's been a tragic accident and Dianna is gone. Sad story, right? Only now I know you did something to that girl. I read it in a book."

"Two books," said Sylvia, but not very loudly.

"What girl?" Anna managed.

"*What girl?* Your daughter. Rose. Remember her? Last seen on the green in West Rutland with a few of her high school friends, the night before she left for college. Never heard from again except for a signature when we bought the house from her. But that wasn't her down there in Georgia signing our contract, was it? Or wherever you went next, and whatever you did, whatever name you had. It wasn't her. It was always you."

Anna shook her head. She was coming around to the idea that there was no viable argument here. At least, none she could immediately access.

"And there's Patrick. You remember Patrick, I take it."

A cold hand, rising up out of the bedsheets, clamping her mouth shut, stopping her breath. Just as it had, years ago, right here in this room.

"My brother never rode without a seat belt. What did you do, unlock it before you drove into that tree?"

My brother.

She was, for the first time in recent memory, dumbstruck, the word itself and even the words that made up that word—"dumb" and "struck"—rattling around her head, unrestrained and unstoppable, with *dumb as in stupid* and *dumb as in silent* doing their own private shuffle around the lethal weapon of *struck*. She kept trying to grab onto one of them, to make them hold still, but they were like massive wriggling fish, all muscle and teeth. Over and over again until she had to let it go.

In the end, all she could manage was an inelegant: "What did you say?"

"You heard me. *My brother. Never. Rode in a car. Without his seat belt.* None of us did. It's how our uncle died. Our mother's brother."

But that did not help at all, because there were suddenly too many brothers. Which one was she talking about? Betty was gripping her gun with both hands, as if one of them might try to take it from the other.

This time, the only word she could produce was: "No."

"Yes. You drove him off the road. You drove him into a tree. You were trying to kill him. Maybe you were trying to kill the both of you. Not that it's an excuse."

No. And it wasn't strictly true, either. She'd been trying to kill all three of them—that unwished for baby included—in one, final, and decisive obliteration. But he was the only one who'd died. Well, he'd been the most deserving, she supposed.

Now, at least, her words returned to her, the right words in the right order.

"Your brother was a rapist."

Betty lunged at her, and Anna felt the blunt end of something impossibly hard crash against her temple: one of the cannonball posts of the old bed. It felt as solid as an actual cannonball, and it took her breath and her balance away. She ended up down on the floor, eyeing a crack in a maple floorboard. Probably, it had been there for a century.

"How dare you!" Betty was screaming. "I know what happened between you two. You went after him at some party of Evan's, Miss Teenage Seduction. His best friend's little sister, and not exactly pretty, were you? But you just had to get the popular boy. I read all about it in Evan's book."

Anna put her blistered hand against her head where it had hit the bedpost, pressing it hard against the skin, trying to get to the information on the other side. It didn't seem like the right moment to try to elucidate the differences between fiction and fact, not to this one. This one wasn't all that invested, she was pretty sure, in the mysterious process of synthesizing art from language, imagination, and experience. This one had already made her mind up. *She was. Patrick's sister.* Patrick had had a couple of sisters, one of whom, she was pretty sure, was dead. That one, she had a vague idea, had dated Evan, which made her a member of an absurdly large group. But it was also possible, entirely possible, that Evan had actually fathered a kid with that sister. She seemed to recall knowing this, or having once known it, which was more than Evan himself had ever acknowledged or taken any responsibility for. But that was Evan, wasn't it? Just a super-well-liked high school athlete, doing what super-well-liked high school athletes have always done.

"And not just Patrick. Not just your parents, and your daughter," Betty said. "I know you killed Evan. You managed that, somehow. My sister Sally was in a meeting with him, for years. Neither of them was rock-solid sober, okay, but no way was he shooting drugs and writing a novel and running a business, all at the same time. I mean, I don't think so."

"Addiction is a progressive disease," Anna suggested. She had read that somewhere. "A shame, but very common."

"Not the sentimental type, are you?"

That much was true. She was not.

"You killed all of them, Dianna. And not only your own family. I'd put money on you for that husband of yours. And just look at you now, rich widow and literary martyr." She stopped for a moment and took a breath. "You might as well add my mother to that list. She never got over Patrick."

"Hon," said Sylvia, from the door, "I really think I'm going to call the cops."

"Don't move," Betty told her, without taking her eyes off Anna.

She needed more time: that was the only valuable thought Anna had, and it was on repeat in her head, circling again and again, blasting more relevant and practical thoughts out of its way every time it came back. All she really understood was that she had made a mistake, and that it was the same mistake Jake had made. Each had assumed the campaign against them had something to do with writers, but it had never been about writers, not in Jake's case, not in her own. The months she had spent on Martin Purcell and his Ripley cohorts, sifting through their terrible writing, looking for someone who'd known Evan Parker well enough to be in possession of his book? A waste, and that had to include Purcell's unnecessary death, not to speak of her own unnecessary proximity to that death: more waste. When it had always been so much more personal, so much closer to home. She couldn't get any closer to home than she was right this minute, crouched at the foot of her parents' ancient bed with her head in her hands.

"How did you find all this out?" she finally said, turning on the floor to lean against the bedpost. "I mean, at least tell me that much."

"Can we call the police," Sylvia said again. She was sounding desperate, now. This time Betty didn't even respond.

"Your brother sent a copy of his book to an agent in New York. It came back, but years after he sent it, when obviously there was no Evan at this address, not anymore. We didn't read it. We figured it was private. We thought it was right that it should go to his niece, to Rose, but we didn't know where she was. So we wrote to her lawyer in Georgia, but he said they weren't in touch. Okay, fine. We tried to do the right thing. But we're also curious, and now we're not so worried about anyone's privacy. Evan is dead. His sister Dianna is dead. His niece Rose, we can't reach her. So we read Evan Parker's manuscript. And guess what?"

But Anna didn't need to guess. She knew already.

"It's a story about a mom who not only kills her own kid, but she also takes that kid's scholarship, identity, everything. Buries that kid in the ground and then just goes on with her dead daughter's life. And we're thinking, you know, *Where have I read that story before?* In the book called *Crib*, by the guy who was once Evan Parker's teacher, up at Ripley College. I wrote to that lawyer again, in Georgia, and I sent the book to him. I told him, you know, there's something you need to know about this manuscript, and maybe could you try again to find Rose Parker? Because somebody stole her uncle's story and published it as his own. She really needs to know! But we never heard from him again."

The literary concerns of two Vermont women. She had been told very clearly what a low priority they'd been to Arthur Pickens.

"Then one day I open up my *New York Times* and here's a story about Jacob Finch Bonner's widow, and this beautiful, powerful book she's written about a husband who killed himself. Autobiographical, like a lot of first novels, I guess. We didn't even know Bonner was dead, let alone how he died. We just thought he was too famous and stuck-up to remember he promised to send us a signed copy."

"Two signed copies," Sylvia said, from the doorway.

"But we also noticed something else in there. Nobody else would have noticed, I don't think. You know what it was? Wait!" said Betty in triumph. "Let me show you. It's right here."

And she took a single step to her right and reached out a weathered hand. Then she plucked one of the pegs from the round rail of the ancient bed, revealing an empty compartment behind it. "Amazing, right? Who would ever think up such a thing, if they hadn't grown up with an old rope bed somebody turned into a bank vault? Why would the widow of that writer know this weirdo factoid about the bed we sleep in every night, the only piece of Parker family furniture we kept when we bought the house from Rose Parker? Most people today don't even know what a rope bed is, even if they tell their kids 'sleep tight.' And here you were: married to the guy who maybe stole Evan Parker's story, a woman of mystery who grew up with a rope bed of her own? That happened to have special holes where her own dad stashed his money? I kept going around and around, from Evan to Bonner to Bonner's widow, but even when I saw the connection, I couldn't believe it. Not even you, Dianna. Not even the girl I always believed drove my little brother into a tree on purpose and ruined our family. Not even after reading this story about a mother who kills her own daughter. Twice. In two different books! I still couldn't believe a real person, a real mother, would do that to her own child."

You're not a mother, Anna nearly said. It seemed a minor victory that she managed to restrain herself. Sylvia had retreated into the doorway. Betty was still holding the gun with both hands; her long red braid looked a little bit absurd, under the circumstances.

"That's when I said to Sylvia 'I think I might know where Rose Parker is.' I didn't tell her the rest of it, that I had a suspicion she might not be Rose, at all. All I wanted to do was get a look at you, close up. So I drove down to Brooklyn."

Brooklyn. She might as well have said Outer Mongolia. The notion of this creature of the hardscrabble north at the epicenter of literary life in the hippest of boroughs was just . . . bizarrely familiar. That sound of a sharp metallic click, currently ricocheting around her skull—that might have come from the hammer of Betty's gun, but it might also have come from a dead bolt, snapping open at last inside her brain.

Yes. That was *where.*

The Brooklyn Book Festival, in the signing line. One person of so many, one signing line of so many, one event of so many; it was no wonder she hadn't recalled this one face. Though she really should have. No other person had kicked off a conversation by saying, of Anna's late husband: "He was supposed to send me a copy of his book."

Never had a simple favor, so thoughtlessly promised, had such destroying consequences.

"From the picture in the paper, or the one on your book, I wouldn't have known. You had your daughter young, obviously, and people today dye their hair all kinds of things, including gray, not that that makes any sense to me. Also, I didn't remember you that well. I was the oldest in my family, and by the time you and Patrick were in high school I'd been gone for a while, up in Burlington. And I never laid eyes on Rose, even if she was my brother's kid. Too painful for my folks, the whole thing. They just wanted nothing to do with the Parkers after Patrick died."

That was a shame, Anna thought. If Patrick's bereaved parents had so much as hinted they'd like to know their grandchild, she would have handed them full custody and walked away. Rose could have grown up a Bessette, on the family farm, and they could have had the pleasure of dealing with her. How much better for everyone that would have been!

"Even up on that stage, in Brooklyn, I wasn't sure. Not until I got up close to you, at that table where you were signing your book. And then I could see it, finally. It wasn't the daughter I was looking at. It was the mother. In the flesh. Dianna Parker, the one who kept walking away from accidents where other people died. That meant Rose Parker was the one who was dead. Just like in Evan's book. And Jake's."

Now she was on a first-name basis with Jake, Anna observed.

"What is it you want?" she said, with considerable exasperation. She herself wanted desperately to take hold of the gun in her pocket. On the other hand, she was afraid to make a move for it until she was ready. She didn't think she was completely ready. And which of the two actions—with the hammer? Without the hammer?—was she supposed to use? She seemed to be spending more time than necessary on that question. "You want to go to the police, yelling about supposed crimes from years ago, some of them very far from Rutland? Go right ahead. They'll laugh you out of the station. Arthur Pickens wanted money. Is that what you want?"

This stopped Betty short.

"You've been to see Pickens? Why?"

She didn't know what the lawyer had been up to, Anna saw. It was obvious.

"You weren't the only one sending out bits of my brother's book. His went to my agent."

With a certain undeniable pleasure, she watched this, and then its implications, wash across Betty's pale face.

"You misjudged him, apparently. And he returned the favor. He said you were kindly, moral ladies who only cared about justice for Evan Parker."

Under other circumstances, it might have been a connection: they were both women the late Arthur Pickens, Esq., had seriously underestimated. But right now, one of those women had a gun pointed at the other's head. It wasn't a situation conducive to bonding.

"Never met the man," Betty said. "Don't give a rat's ass about his opinion. But you, Dianna. I doubt I gave you so much as a sleepless night, but if I did, you deserved every minute. That so-called harassment your husband went through? Supposedly that was the reason he killed himself? You talked about it all the time, in interviews, even that *New York Times* story. It's part of your mythology, the anonymous troll who accused him of plagiarism. But if anyone was hounding your husband, it was you. Because he was telling your private business, even if he had no idea he was doing it. I just thought you deserved a little taste of that yourself. So we were out in Denver at a quilt convention, and we saw in the bookstore that you were coming to read from your book. I thought, why not? And I paid for a copy and arranged for you to sign it and have it sent to Vermont. And when they asked, is there some personal message I want the author to inscribe, I just thought I'd leave you with a little fear of exposure. That's all it ever was for me. I didn't want your money. I don't even disagree with you about the police. But I'll tell you what else I didn't want: you on my doorstep. I'm not like you. I wish you hadn't come. But here you are."

"Betty," Sylvia hissed from the doorway.

"They're expecting me in Middlebury."

"Oh, I doubt that," Betty said. "But whatever, it's not my problem. This was your decision, and don't think for a minute I don't know what you came here to do. Just so we're clear on who's responsible for what's going to happen. I'm not letting you leave here."

For a flash of a moment, she didn't care. Then she realized where they were—not just in this hated house but in this specific room, beside her own private nightmare of a bed—and something inside her went white with rage. That was so not fair. That was so not acceptable. She categorically refused to die here.

"Anywhere else, but not next to this bed. Your brother raped me on this bed."

And then, as Anna had hoped, Betty lost control of herself again. The woman seemed to melt forward—human wraith, human wrath, but still human—and Anna grasped Pickens's gun from her jacket pocket and brought it up at an angle, aiming for the underside of the chin looming above her, and though she could not, in the undeniable stress of the moment, be entirely sure by which of the gun's two ways she fired it, she most definitely did fire it, the instant it met the loose white skin beneath Betty's lower jaw. There was a sound like a bone cracking, but not a single bone—all the bones—and even hearing it carried a kind of awful, imagined pain. Somebody was screaming, and Anna honestly didn't know whether it was Sylvia or herself, but when she aimed the gun at the woman in the doorway and shot again, the screaming stopped, and then all three of them were on the floor, two of them bleeding, one very still, and then the second just as still. Only Anna found that she was still alive and intact, though covered with the blood of at least one of the others. It was, for not a brief moment, disorienting. Holding her breath, she used the sheet on that terrible bed to wipe the lawyer's gun, then she took Betty's gun out of her right hand and put it into her own deep pocket. She put Pickens's gun into the dead woman's hand, making sure Betty's index finger was on the trigger, her other three fingers curled around the grip. The gist of the scenario would be very clear—a murder, and then, almost immediately, a suicide—so long as Vermont medical examiners shared that habit of listening for horses, not zebras, with their counterparts in Clayton, Georgia. As for the fired gun, she certainly hoped it would prove as untraceable as the lawyer had promised.

She was not happy about Sylvia, who was from up around Vergennes, who made garish quilts and had terrible taste in décor, and whose family did not speak to her. Sylvia had wanted to call the police, making her—between herself and her partner, at least—the voice of relative reason. Then again, Anna was not particularly happy about Betty, either. She herself was no one's idea of a good person; that she knew, and she hadn't needed Arthur Pickens to tell her. But it did not follow that she considered herself a bad person, either. As annoying and tenacious as Betty in particular had shown herself to be, Anna had not acted out of personal grievance, malice, or greed, or at least not only those things. Never once had she imposed her will on a person who hadn't first chosen to constrain her, assault her, thwart her, or malign her. The world, she knew, was full of people who seemed to enjoy doing harm for its own sake, and she had no hope of ever understanding those people, even if she wanted to understand them (which, to be honest, she did not). But she wasn't one of them. People like that, she also knew, could not be fixed, nor even persuaded to behave differently. Why exhaust oneself trying to revise a person's essential nature? It was impossible. It made more sense to accept the things one could not change.

Driving north in her long arc to the west of Washington, Philadelphia, Baltimore, and New York, she'd thought through so many possible scenarios, but this one, the one that had unfolded upstairs in her parents' bedroom, had somehow eluded her. She'd certainly begun by hoping to find an empty house, locate and remove the manuscript, and get as far away as she could before the women materialized, but she'd gradually come to accept that leaving even one of them behind would only defer the very real danger to herself. They might be the sweetest ladies alive, two principled souls who sincerely wanted justice for the wronged novelists of the world, but the cryptic message in Denver, sent suggestively from Ripley, and the excerpts of her brother's novel mailed from Vermont to herself and to Jake's parents were already far too serious to earn a reprieve. She didn't relish the prospect. Not at all. But at the end of the day, this would have to be a terminal visit for both of them.

The best resolution to her problem had always been the one that posed the least danger to herself, and merely repossessing the manuscript was not that resolution. Entering an empty house, searching the rooms to find those offensive pages (for the second time in her life!) would only have alerted the women to the fact that someone had been here, conjuring further theories and igniting ever more aggressive waves of harassment. This time there would be police reports, journalists, letters from attorneys far more capable than Arthur Pickens, Esq.: a significant escalation, the very opposite of a resolution. Until these final moments on the hard floor of her parents' bedroom, with her back against the wall of that reviled bed and a gun unexpectedly pointed at her head for the second time in as many days, she'd had no idea how much they actually knew of her circumstances and history. It only served to clarify things. It only served to justify what was necessary.

Now the two women were yards apart on the same floor, blood from Sylvia's head wound drenching the floral hooked rug in the hallway, blood from Betty's imploded jaw filling up the gap between two of the wide maple boards. She'd been lucky with her aim; she'd never spent much time firing guns, though she'd grown up around them, like most rural Vermonters. But they'd both been so close, and of the three of them, only Anna had known that she also had a gun, and exactly when she was going to reach for it. Clearly, calling Patrick Bessette a rapist was a quick and effective way to make his sister drop her guard. The first time Anna had done it, Betty's reaction came as a surprise. The second time, it was no surprise at all. She had both planned for it and taken the opportunity it offered.

Whoever came to find them here, whenever they came, would discover the two women in a moment of sad and grotesque violence. So brutal! So unexpected! But then, as she herself had learned from, literally, hundreds of survivors on her book tour, and from so many more in letters to the author of *The Afterword,* suicidal violence was always a shock. Even when people knew or feared it might come, even with ideation, even with a plan, even with stated intentions, even with previous attempts. That was an extra layer to its horror.

Anna took one final look back at that room. She registered the bizarre truth that—despite the bodies of the two dead women on the floor—the rope bed was still the most horrific thing in it, and always would be. Then she moved quickly through the upstairs rooms, looking—again—for Evan's novel, as if she were in a personal and perpetually looping horror sequence. In the room across the hall, the one that had belonged to her brother, the enormous cat from the head of the stairs was lounging on the bed, atop one of Sylvia's garish quilts. There was a modern desk at the room's only window, and through it she had an enviable view of the woods behind the house. She could make out the spot where she had camped, years earlier, to watch her brother in his nightly routine, and in the virtuous toil of an aspiring author. He had never seen her coming. He ought to have seen her coming. He ought to have feared her, just as these women ought to have feared her. It was a mistake too many people had made. Never once had she allowed an injustice against herself to stand, and that was a policy that continued to serve her.

The manuscript was in one of the desk drawers, and underneath it there was a disassembled photocopy, missing those excerpts that had been mailed to Jake's parents' home, and to her own apartment. That was all. Unlike the last time she had performed this errand, in this house, there were no other notes, files, legal pads, thumb drives, or drafts marked working or anything else to signify the creation of art, the everyday slog of putting words on a page. Those dead people across the hall, soon to star in a flash fiction of their own, were not writers. They were characters.

She was a writer.

She took the manuscript and the photocopy and went downstairs.

She was nearly at the foot of the staircase when her eye fell, inevitably, on those pineapples stenciled around the front door, and as it did she had a sudden idea, for the first time, of the impact the stencil might possibly have had on Jake. The stencil had been a feature of the Parker home, probably from the time of the first Parker, the one who'd hauled that bed up from New Bedford. It was also a feature of Diandra and Ruby's home in her brother's novel. She had never had a chance to ask Jake what he'd learned during that visit—how he had made the connection between Evan Parker's book and Evan Parker's life—but looking at the doorway now, she saw the visceral answer to that question. Those pineapples, in their bizarre, pink-free zone around the old door, would have been more than just a surprising coincidence; they would have taught Jake that Evan's story derived from something close to him, something familiar, meaning that the characters in that story had been similarly close and familiar. It would also have taught Jake that his most pressing question was not whether he had stolen from Evan, but whether Evan himself had stolen from *someone else*.

He had. He had stolen from her.

Now, immobilized by those pineapples, she had to think of the times she had stood where she was standing now, simply trying to possess, or repossess, what ought to have been hers without question. The time with Evan, dead in the room upstairs, hauling that trash bag down the hallway. And well before that, when all she had ever wanted was to extract her story, *her own story*, from this place. From the parents who had not believed her, not valued her, not registered her sovereignty over herself. From the child she had never wanted. From the brother who thought nothing of appropriating her character, exposing her most devastating secrets and distorting her gravest injuries. And now from those two upstairs, who had considered it their right to threaten and harangue her. So many times before. But not again. This time would be the final time. This time she would leave no possibility of return.

Anna turned and walked to the back of the house.

Sylvia was a cook, or at least enough of one to have an array of cooking oils in the larder, far more of a range than the usual canola or olive. Anna opened a glass bottle of peanut oil and poured all of it into a frying pan on the avocado-colored stove. The pan still had some bacon from that morning's breakfast. As she lit the burner, and that bacon began to emit its bacon smell, the gray cat entered the kitchen and looked up, optimistically.

Anna picked it up and set it outside the back door. Then she waited, impatiently, for the oil to heat, then smoke, writing the fictional version of this house's ultimate tragedy: a distracted cook, called upstairs by an angry voice.

An escalating argument.

An act of destruction, then, perhaps very quickly, an act of self-destruction.

Meanwhile, forgotten by all parties, who were now—in any case—past the ability to remember: the pan of ruinous oil downstairs, catching fire. Anna fought the urge to help things along with a match, but she did move a long pink dishcloth close to the pan, draping it over the edge of a stockpot on the next burner. The first flames began soon after that, and the last thing Anna saw before she left was the billow of fire, reaching up to engulf that pathetic hand-painted sign: SYLVIA'S KITCHEN (SEASONED WITH LOVE).

31

Anything Is Possible

Nine days after Anna Williams-Bonner left home, she got into a cab at Newark Liberty Airport and took it to the West Village. It would have been nice to have a credit card for this final leg, but she paid cash, and all the way home she told the driver about her trip to Seattle, and her week on Vashon Island trying to write a novel in an old inn near the ferry. She also took a receipt.

Upstairs in the apartment, she powered on her phone and listened to a series of increasingly manic voicemails from the Realtors, Laurie and Lori, describing the four offers they'd received on the day after the open house, and the ensuing bidding war. The high bidder wanted an accelerated closing: Was that okay?

It was very much okay.

After leaving Vermont she had meandered her way back to Dulles, taking some of the same back roads she'd driven on her northward journey. She left Pickens's car behind the same airport Marriott where she'd hidden his phone. The phone was right where she'd placed it, though the battery had long since run out. She left it on the passenger-side floor of the car, then she locked up and walked to the Metrorail stop at the airport, taking the Silver Line into Washington and found her way to the bus station on Massachusetts Avenue. There, she tossed Pickens's keys and bought a ticket to Trenton. At Trenton she got on a New Jersey Transit train to the airport. She left her wig in the trash bin of the train's bathroom.

Already the apartment felt utterly alien. Freshly painted, decorated with unfamiliar art. She welcomed the weirdness of that as she washed off the dangerous, wrenching, and brutal days on the road. She ordered food, answered her most crucial messages, and put herself to bed, letting the terror of what had happened and what had nearly happened find its way out of her, and some version of calm began to return, though it took nearly a week to feel like herself again. She was safe, or as safe as she could imagine being. She was free to live whatever life she wanted to live now, wherever she wanted to live it. It was as near to joy as anything she was capable of feeling.

One evening, a couple of weeks after she'd come back, she left the apartment and walked out into a glorious spring evening, on her way to meet Wendy at Odeon. Over a good bottle of chardonnay and the first asparagus of the year, the two of them covered various topics: Anna's stay with friends in Seattle, her days on Vashon thinking through a new book project, and the daring haircut she had received at her old salon. Wendy wanted to discuss some of the ideas Macmillan's team were developing for *The Afterword*'s paperback tour, which would begin in a few months.

"I want to make sure the booksellers at each of the stops are going to have Jake's books, too," said Wendy. She also had a new haircut, though Anna could not trust herself to say anything nice about it. "His books and your books, they belong together. I think there's a real cross-pollination, if you know what I mean."

Cross-contamination, you mean, Anna thought.

"I'm not sure I do."

"Well, you know. We've talked about this before. Writer couples aren't rare, but it's rare that both are gifted *and* successful. When they are, there's a whole layer of . . . let's see if we can follow an idea from this book by one of them to an idea from that book by the other. It's sort of fun. People write dissertations!"

She wanted no dissertations written about her.

"I don't know. I don't feel right about standing in his reflected glory. Last time I was out doing events, people actually asked me to sign copies of *Crib*."

"So sign them! Why not?"

"Why not? It isn't right. Jake was the real writer. *Crib* isn't mine to sign."

"Anna, please! I'm the editor for both books, and I absolve you. How long are you going to be hung up about this? Okay, Jake had the fancy MFA from Iowa, but it took you one book to get where you are. And the Read With Jenna, and the TV sale, and all the end-of-year lists we were on! *The Afterword* has done beautifully. It's already being taught, did you know that? I'm hearing from friends who are seeing it on syllabi! Not to mention sales. Ten months after publication, to be where we are, it's a fantastic result. We're thrilled with it. Be proud of yourself. I cannot deal with the way women undervalue themselves."

Well, she couldn't disagree with that.

"I'm sorry."

"And stop apologizing!"

They smiled at each other.

Wendy was right, Anna thought. She would go forth across America for a second time, talking to people about her novel and keeping her eyes open for a place where she might want to live next. New York had, by this time, too many memories, and too few of them pleasant. Maybe she should go west again (though not back to Seattle). Maybe she would go south again (though not back to Georgia). It didn't really matter where she lived, because her work was portable; that was one of the best things about being a writer. She could have a house that overlooked some shoreline, or a mountain range. She could live in a city with good coffee shops and an arts district. Maybe she would go to that town in Indiana with all the modern architecture and buy herself a house of glass and stone. Maybe she would move to Austin. Everybody seemed to be moving to Austin. There must be a reason.

Her editor had seemed to understand that she was on the cusp of a change. It wasn't just that she was selling her apartment, it was also her emergence from the tumult of her sudden widowhood. But Wendy had also made a not-so-idle comment that evening, to the effect that second novels were harder. Or so she had heard from so many of her authors.

"Oh, I don't know," Anna had said. "*The Afterword,* it just came pouring out on a raft of pain, you know? And now I kind of feel like the slate is clean. I can write about anything, now. It's kind of amazing."

"I totally get that!" her editor said. "Everyone understands that the writer's personal experience often becomes the catalyst for that first novel. And that's fine. Autobiographical . . . there's nothing wrong with it. But people don't always realize they're not actually limited by their lived experience. Sometimes I'm the one who has to remind my writers: Hey! It's fiction! *You get to make things up!* I mean, how many of us get to do that in our lives, let alone for work?"

Anna nodded. This was an excellent point.

"I think you're right," she told her editor. And they moved on to other things.

Later, as she crossed Houston Street and began the final stretch of her walk back to the apartment she and Jake had shared, she kept coming back to this idea. How fortunate she was, really, to have chosen this particular profession. Writing novels was a great fit for her. It had no horizon, it had no geographical constraints, it would rise or fall solely on her own ability to do good work, which was nothing more nor less than she had ever asked of herself. And she was good at it, obviously; you didn't produce a bestseller like *The Afterword* if you weren't good at it, whatever anyone said, or whatever assumptions the "real writers" at places like that artists' colony might make. So why not? She would write another novel, and another one after that. She would, as a rule, avoid autobiography in her fiction, but look how much that left to explore! Other people, living other lives—she had always been fascinated by that, even before becoming, herself, a successful writer. And also: she was absolutely going to make peace with the notion of herself as Jake's widow. She *was* Jake's widow. And if Wendy was correct about such things, and Wendy was usually correct about such things, being Jake's widow was an excellent thing to be, financially, at least. Why shouldn't she be one-half of a literary couple, with all the rights and privileges pertaining thereto, just because the other half of that literary couple happened to be dead? She'd never need to worry that Jake would outshine her with another book, or abandon her for another wife. She'd never have to defer to him in public or pretend to take his advice on matters of craft. He was the perfect literary helpmeet: gifted, successful, and deceased.

Another thing Wendy was right about: Anna would have to get over this squeamishness when it came to signing her late husband's books, or at least the only one of his books anyone had ever asked her to sign. There was a good reason people loved *Crib,* and it had not so much to do with her late husband's deathless prose. The mania over Jake's novel derived from the outsize human emotions at its core, a scale of resentment and drama and retribution that seemed, even to herself, more closely attuned to Greek mythology or classical opera than to contemporary lives, where such storylines had been shrunk to the proportions of a season's arc on a *Real Housewives* show. But *Crib* had come from her own true life, her own true actions, which belonged to her in a way neither her late brother nor her late husband could ever have hoped to understand—if, indeed, they had ever tried. And so, at the end of the day, both of those novels belonged to her as much as her own novel, *The Afterword,* did. Without her decisiveness and fortitude, without her courage to reach for her own happiness, to take possession (repossession) of her own life from those appropriators (whose only talent was to have recognized a good story when they'd heard it), neither of those books would have been written. Left to their own dubious devices, Evan and Jake would have remained mired in milquetoast stories about disappointed artists and former athletes entering middle age. Who wanted to read about that?

Exactly.

The Afterword was hers, and Anna was proud of it, but wasn't she entitled to take a certain pride in *Crib* as well? That wasn't something she'd be explaining to anyone, for obvious reasons! But sure: if somebody came up at a reading or a talk extending a copy of Jacob Finch Bonner's celebrated novel for her signature . . . she would sign it, and happily. Why wouldn't she? Most people slid through life. They allowed others to take from them, steal from them, repurpose their labor and creativity, and they capitulated without so much as a peep of objection. That was pathetic. That was not in her nature. Writing fiction, though—it called for a certain audacity, an autonomy, and a stubborn insistence on ownership, qualities she had always been blessed with. In abundance.

The more she considered it, the more she understood that she'd been making fiction far longer than she'd been writing it, and fiction had taken her far from where she'd begun. Fiction had filled her life with people who knew her worth as fully—though perhaps not as intimately—as she did, herself. She would hardly stop making it now.

Acknowledgments

Thank you to Lisa Goldfarb, MD, and Brent Forester, MD, MSc, for speaking to me about matters pharmacological, and to Harold Schechter, maven of mayhem, for help with what I might otherwise have referred to as "gun stuff." I am grateful to Debbie Michel and Christina Baker Kline for their exceptionally close readings, not to speak of their treasured friendship.

I would be remiss if I did not acknowledge the influence of Thomas Perry's work, particularly his Jane Whitefield series of novels. No one writes more effectively about evasion or pursuit: "She never used her own name, never started off in the direction of her final destination, never missed a chance to mislead, but never bet her life on any plan she had made in advance" (*Shadow Woman*, 1997).

No fictional counterparts can ever convey my admiration for and gratitude to my agent, Suzanne Gluck, and my editor, Deb Futter, without whom this being-a-writer journey (and yes, it pains me to use the term "journey," but no other word suffices here) would have been very different. They are loyal, committed, incisive, wicked smart, and—let me be clear—admirably quick to turn a manuscript around, even an unsolicited one. At WME, I also thank Tracy Fisher, Fiona Baird, Anna DeRoy, Andrea Blatt, and Lane Kizziah. I'm so grateful to the amazing team at Celadon, including Anna Belle Hindenlang, Jamie Noven, Jamie Raab, Randi Kramer, Faith Tomlin, Rachel Chou, Christine Mykityshyn, and Shelly

Perron. Elsewhere, immense thanks to Kristen Campo, Louisa Joyner, and Julia Whelan.

Thank you, Ragdale, for the gift of two weeks in your beautiful Prairie House, where parts of *The Devil and Webster*, *The Latecomer*, and *The Sequel* were written.

Thanks and love, as ever, to family and friends. This novel was written in the shadow of my father's death. He was a lifelong reader and especially enjoyed a thriller. That's why this one's dedicated to him.